FROM THE INTRODUCTION
BY PIERS ANTHONY

I wanted to do something original and worthwhile. I realize that this makes me an oddity among writers, um, editors, but that's the way I am. I have delusions of significance.

How about assembling a volume of those stories that are worthy of special recognition, but have never received it? The ones that other anthologists passed by?

Now that appealed to me. I have always rooted for the underdog and cheered when the worm turned. I know from my own thorough experience in receiving rejection slips that the average editor is an idiot, and of course the average anthologist is a bird of a similar feather: very few of *my* stories have been anthologized. A volume like this could do two notable favors for the genre: first, it would demonstrate in a concrete way just how stupid editors are, and second, it could give deserved recognition to long-neglected stories and authors.

Thus was UNCOLLECTED STARS conceived.

UNCOLLECTED STARS

EDITED &
WITH AN INTRODUCTION BY
PIERS ANTHONY
WITH BARRY MALZBERG,
MARTIN H. GREENBERG & CHARLES G. WAUGH

AVON
PUBLISHERS OF BARD, CAMELOT, DISCUS AND FLARE BOOKS

UNCOLLECTED STARS is an original publication of Avon Books. This work has never before appeared in book form. This is a work of fiction. Any similarity to actual persons or events is purely coincidental.

AVON BOOKS
A division of
The Hearst Corporation
1790 Broadway
New York, New York, 10019

First Avon Printing, February 1986

AVON TRADEMARK REG. U. S. PAT. OFF. AND IN OTHER COUNTRIES, MARCA REGISTRADA, HECHO EN U. S. A.

Printed in the U. S. A.

WFH 10 9 8 7 6 5 4 3 2 1

Acknowledgments

"Time Enough," by Lewis Padgett, copyright 1946 by Henry Kuttner & C. L. Moore. Reprinted by permission of Don Congdon Associates, Inc.

"The Soul-Empty Ones," by Walter M. Miller, Jr., copyright 1951 by Walter M. Miller, Jr.; copyright renewed 1979. Reprinted by permission of Don Congdon Associates, Inc.

"Defender of the Faith," by Alfred Coppel, copyright 1952 by Columbia Publications. Reprinted from *Science Fiction Quarterly* by permission of the author.

"All of You," by James V. McConnell, copyright 1953 by the Galaxy Publishing Corporation. Reprinted by permission of the author.

"The Holes," by Michael Shaara, copyright 1954 by the Ziff-Davis Publishing Company. Reprinted by permission of the author and the author's agents, Scott Meredith Literary Agency, Inc., 845 Third Avenue, New York, New York 10022.

"Beast in the House," by Michael Sharra, copyright 1954 by Hanro Corporation. Reprinted by permission of the author and the author's agents, Scott Meredith Literary Agency, 845 Third Avenue, New York, New York 10022.

"Little Boy," by Jerome Bixby, copyright 1954 by the Galaxy Publishing Corporation. Reprinted by permission of Forrest J Ackerman, 2495 Glendower Avenue, Hollywood, California 90027.

"Unwillingly to School," by Pauline Ashwell, copyright © 1958 by Pauline Ashwell. Reprinted from *Astounding Science Fiction* by permission of the author.

"Brother Robot," by Henry Slesar, copyright © 1958 by the Ziff-Davis Publishing Company. Reprinted by permission of the author.

Contents

Introduction	*Piers Anthony*	1
Time Enough	*Lewis Padgett*	6
The Soul-Empty Ones	*Walter M. Miller, Jr.*	26
Defender of the Faith	*Alfred Coppel*	62
All of You	*James V. McConnell*	76
The Holes	*Michael Shaara*	82
Beast in the House	*Michael Shaara*	91
Little Boy	*Jerome Bixby*	102
Unwillingly to School	*Pauline Ashwell*	116
Brother Robot	*Henry Slesar*	163
The Risk Profession	*Donald E. Westlake*	178
The Stuff	*Henry Slesar*	205
Arcturus Times Three	*Jack Sharkey*	211
They Are Not Robbed	*Richard McKenna*	244
The Creatures of Man	*Verge Foray*	275
Only Yesterday	*Ted White*	291
An Agent in Place	*Laurence M. Janifer*	301
Afterword	*Barry N. Malzberg*	311

INTRODUCTION

Piers Anthony

Welcome to my maiden effort at editing. Of the all-time best science fiction stories published, my personal favorites, not one is represented here. Let me explain.

As I see it, an editor's life is easy. He just relaxes, reads, picks what he likes, appends some smart and halfway irrelevant remark, and turns it over to his secretary for the dull details, such as scheduling the artwork and paying the authors. This doesn't require any real talent. I recall one editor saying to hopeful writers: "Your manuscript can be replaced by the next one on the pile." Of course that meant that the janitor could have done the job—a point that editor seemed to have overlooked. His magazine is now defunct; I can't think why.

An anthologist's job is even easier. He just glances through his collection of magazines, picks out the stories by the biggest names, and puts them into a separate volume for some grateful book publisher to publish. He doesn't have to mess with the dread Slush Pile—that festering stack of unsolicited manuscripts that overflows the desk, spills across the floor, and causes regular editors to run out of rejection slips before making a dent in it. Editors really don't like slush piles; they are fire hazards, and termites nest in their nether reaches, and the faint odor of rotting cabbage wafts out. There is only one solution: periodically the editors vacate the premises, moving to new offices, leaving the ever-growing slush pile behind, its bug eyes casting about for new prey to slime. That's why editorial addresses change so often. At least, that is my view of it. But as I said, the anthologist is spared that hazard of the trade, and makes good money for doing what any reader could do better. True, true; ask any reader.

Naturally I decided to try my hand as an anthologist.

Now, I don't like to admit error, partly because I don't make errors. But in the course of this job I did experience a certain, um, clarification of the nature of editing. For one thing, I don't know anything about the details of making payments to authors; I'm used to struggling to extract money *from* publishers, and my switches are corroded on GET. For another, I don't know how to assemble a volume from pieces of other volumes. Does one simply cut out stories with scissors and paste them into a new book? In any event, I gave away my two-thousand-magazine science-fiction collection a decade or so ago, so have nothing to snip.

Enter Marty Greenberg, an experienced anthologist. "Fear not," he assured me. "I will do all the scutwork." He arranged to fax copies of the stories from the magazines, and to pay the authors, and all that. All I would have to do was make the selections. That of course was no problem; I have known for twenty years which stories are the finest ever published in the genre.

But—who would want to read yet another anthology of old favorites? Arthur Clarke's "The Star," Robert A. Heinlein's "By His Bootstraps," Isaac Asimov's "Little Lost Robot," William Tenn's "Child's Play," Theodore Sturgeon's "The Girl Had Guts," Tom Godwin's "The Cold Equations"—great stories, all, but what service to the field would yet another presentation represent? I wanted to do something original and worthwhile. I realized that this makes me an oddity among writers, um, editors, but that's the way I am. I had delusions of significance.

Marty sighed. Well, he said diplomatically, how about assembling a volume of those stories that are worthy of special recognition but have never received it? The ones that other anthologists passed by?

Now, that appealed to me. I have always rooted for the underdog, and cheered when the worm turned. I know from my own thorough experience in receiving rejection slips that the average editor is an idiot, and of course the average anthologist is a bird of similar feather: very few of *my* stories have been anthologized. A volume like this could do two notable favors for the genre: first, it would demonstrate in a concrete way just how stupid editors are; and second, it could give deserved recognition to long-neglected stories and authors.

Thus was *Uncollected Stars* conceived.

But I had yet another problem. I wanted to select the best from the whole genre, from its origin to the present. But there was a fifteen-year gap in my reading, because when I vacated the story market myself (because three out of four stories I wrote were rejected, and I couldn't earn my living that way) I stopped reading the magazines. Naturally, after I left, the magazines declined, and some expired—but some did hang on, and some new ones appeared, so fairness required that they be checked. I always try to be fair to the idiots I deal with, much as it galls me.

But Marty Greenberg had the answer for that, too. He rounded up competent folk who had covered the missing segment. Thus this volume came to have four whole editors. That's an unusual bargain, four for the price of one.

The others surveyed the genre, searching out the best stories that had never before been anthologized, faxed them, and sent them along to me. Now at last I could play Editor in style, picking and choosing with lordly impunity, lifting up one and casting down another. What power! Ah, this was the editorial life! And I got paid for it, too.

Sigh. There were about five hundred pages of stories, all told, and I am a slow reader, and my time is pressed. I discovered that our rule for selection had eliminated all my favorites. The eligible stories I liked that the other editors didn't like were also excluded, not because of any perversity on their part, but because they simply weren't aware of them. Why didn't I just tell them what I liked? Because I have a memory for names and titles that somewhat resembles a sieve. Sometimes I have trouble remembering the titles of my own novels. Of course I remembered the basic plots, but—well, let me give you an example.

About ten to twenty years ago, give or take five, I read a brilliant story in *The Magazine of Fantasy and Science Fiction*, or maybe it was *Fantasy*. I don't remember the author or the editor, but I do remember the editor's introductory blurb: "This is a horrible story." And it was—an absolutely delightfully horrible story. Now of course that makes its identity quite clear to you . . . oh, it doesn't? Fancy that! Very well. I'll give another hint: it was about a woman on a farm, who had a visit from a female friend. She inadvertently offended this friend, who had magical powers, and the chain of horrors commenced, concluding with the farm's mare giving birth to what must have been a centaur. It was evident that the visitor had bewitched the woman's husband into mating with the mare, and . . .

And I don't even know whether it has been anthologized elsewhere; it might be ineligible for this volume anyway. But that's just one example.

There is also the problem of the borderlines: whether to choose a story with a weakness or to reject one with a strength? Whether to eliminate a good one because a similar one is already represented, while running a lesser one because it is the only decent example of its particular type available? I want a volume that speaks to the diversity of the genre I have known and loved for nigh forty years. As a reader, and a writer, I believe that there should be a single overriding qualification for representation here: merit. But as editor, I find that there are assorted types of merit, and many shades of interpretation, and I am conscious of the overall balance of the volume. Also, do I run one by a Name author, in the hope that this will increase the sales and bring more favorable reviews, regardless of the quality of the piece, or do I go for an unknown author, who really needs the exposure? I find myself hemmed in by considerations and qualifications that the unwashed noneditor is not equipped to fathom. And so I also find myself compromising, doing some of this and some of that, never quite satisfied, constantly second-guessing myself, and skirting around the great mottled lump of dissatisfaction that grows like a cancer on my project. And I find myself beginning to get a glimmer why the average editor seems both arbitrary and wishy-washy, and why he constantly makes mistakes that any reader could have avoided. *Any* compromise seems like a mistake, if you care to look at it that way, and your own material is not at stake. Pronouncements are easy to make when you have no responsibility.

Now the critics, who are the least responsible of creatures, will take off on *this* volume, faintly praising this story, roundly condemning that one, and completely ignoring the editors. They will apply standards incomprehensible to ordinary folk, and will rate this anthology a C−, for larger collections only. But do we see any critics trying to assemble their own anthologies? . . .

However, we do have good stories here, and I believe that

readers who enjoy the science fiction of Anthony (and maybe a few of my fantasy readers too) should like them. In fact, to give you somewhat more than you may deserve, we have Barry Malzberg as a coeditor. Now, this is significant, because not only is Barry an established novelist in his own right, and a former editor, he is also one of the more significant critics of the genre. He authored *Engines of the Night,* a highly respected critique of the genre. In short, he Has Credits. I feel that critics, as a class, are two and a half steps beneath editors, which places them five steps beneath the janitor, but there are exceptions, and Barry Malzberg is one of them. A writer, as Vardis Fisher explained, must often choose between God and Caesar. That is, between what is meaningful and what is commercial. Unfortunately, though the spirit may be willing to seek God, the flesh is weak, especially when starving—and only Caesar pays in gold. Barry Malzberg elected, generally, to pursue God, while Piers Anthony washed out of God early and so went for Caesar. Consequently, the typical chain bookstore carries from five to twenty-five Anthony titles, give or take six, and half a Malzberg title, give or take a quarter. This volume happens to be the quarter-Malzberg title, this time around. But this is one critic who has taken up the gauntlet, and is helping to assemble an anthology of stories.

So, you see, Anthony and Malzberg represent different approaches to writing. This does not mean that one or the other is superior (indeed, success often seems to be inversely proportional to merit), but that if these two agree that a given story is good, it probably *is* good. In fact, if the two of us agree, and you readers disagree, you readers are probably wrong. Feel free to test your mettle: the very first story in this volume is one that we agree on. Dare you differ?

TIME ENOUGH

Lewis Padgett

There are a number of standard science-fiction themes, and we
have a fair sampling of them in this volume. One major one is
immortality. Death is not a thing many people like to contem-
plate, and it is an awareness that afflicts me in particular; in
fact, I have done a novel in which Death is the protagonist.
Obviously, when dealing with the stuff of dreams, it is tempt-
ing to conjecture the absence of death—life that does not end.
Immortality. We fancy that this would be a happy state. But
some of us have thought about this enough to realize that immortality, rather than being a blessing, could be a curse. Death
may be viewed not as the termination of an otherwise satisfy-
ing life, but as the release from a horrendous struggle. This
applies not only to those who believe in an exalted life after
death, but to those, like me, who believe that there is no such
thing. Evidently the author of this story has pondered the matter also, and he presents another aspect that I think is accurate.
Science fiction is for thinking people; here is one to think about.
                                                                    —PA

This is my little coup de theatre; a brilliant Henry Kuttner/C. L.
Moore story from their vintage period and under their vintage
joint pseudonym which has never been anthologized; which
in fact is utterly unknown to even those who have the greatest
familiarity with and admiration for their work. Why is this so?
My theory is that the vile illustrator (uncredited in Astounding
as no illustrator before or since was uncredited), by giving
away the devastating climax of the story at the outset, drained
it for the reader of force and made it appear, retrospectively,
minor. Another theory is that the theme of this story is black
even by the stands of this pair of writers and by the standards of
this postapocalyptic period in Astounding. In any case, here it

is, brought back alive for the first time in forty years and never, hopefully, to be underground again (although, granted the point of the story, this is not necessarily a good idea).

Much has been written of Henry Kuttner (1914–1958) and his wife C. L. Moore; under various pseudonyms (notably Padgett, Lawrence O'Donnell) they dominated the science fiction of the forties; as far as can be deduced, everything they published after their marriage in 1940 was collaborative to one degree or the next. Catherine Moore remarried after Henry Kuttner's tragic early death, has published no fiction since then, was guest of honor at the 1981 Denver World Science Fiction Convention, and remains one of the reverenced names of the field.

—bnm

Sam Dyson found the secret of immortality five hundred years after the Blowup. Since research along such lines was strictly forbidden, he felt a panicky shock when the man from Administration walked into his office and almost casually told Dyson that immortality was nothing new.

"This is top secret," the Administrator said, slapping a parcel of manifold sheets on Dyson's desk. "Not these papers, of course,—but what I'm telling you and what you're going to see. We hardly ever let anybody in on the secret. In your case we're making an exception, because you're probably the only guy who can correlate the necessary fieldwork and know what the answers to the questions mean. There are plenty of intangibles in your work, and that's why you've got to handle it personally."

Dyson's current assignment, which had originally interested him in the problem of immortality, dealt with artificial intellectual mutation. He sat back, trying not to show any particular emotion, and blinked at the Administrator.

"I thought the Archives—"

"The Archives are a legend, fostered by propaganda. There ain't no Archives. A few scattered artifacts, that's all. Hardly anything survived the Blowup except the human race."

And yet the government-controlled Archives were supposed to be the source of all modern knowledge!

"This is all secret, Dyson. You won't talk. Sometimes we have to use mnemonic-erasure on blabbermouths, but blabbermouths aren't often let in on such private affairs. You know how to keep your mouth shut. The truth is, we get our scraps of pre-Blowup science from human brains—certain people who were alive when the radiations began to run wild. We keep the Old 'Uns segregated; it'd be dangerous if the world knew immortals existed. There'd be a lot of dissatisfaction.''

Sweat chilled Dyson's flanks. He said, "Of course I've heard the rumors of immortals—''

"All sorts of legends came out of the Blowup and the Lost Years. We've issued counterpropaganda to neutralize the original legend. A straight denial would have had no effect at all. We started a whispering campaign that sure, there were immortals, but they lived only a few hundred years, and they were such screwy mutants they were all insane. That part of the public that believes rumors won't envy the immortals. As for legends, ever heard of the Invisible Snake that was supposed to punish carnal sin? It wasn't till after we rediscovered the microscope that we identified the Snake with the spirochete. You'll often find truth in myths, but sometimes it isn't wise to reveal the truth.''

Dyson wondered if Administration could possibly have found out about his forbidden research. He hadn't *known* there were immortals; he'd investigated the legends, and his own work in controlled radiation and mental mutation had pointed the way.

The Administrator talked some more. Then he advised Dyson to televise his uncle, Roger Peaslee. "Peaslee's been to a Home and seen the Old 'Uns. Don't look surprised; of course he was sworn to silence. But he'll talk about it to you now; he knows you're going to the—Archives!''

But Dyson felt uneasy until his visitor had left. Then he called his uncle, who held a high post with Radioactives, and asked questions.

"It'll surprise you, I think," Peaslee said, with a sympathetic grin. "You may need psych conditioning when you get back, too. It's rather depressing. Still, until we get time travel, there's no other way of reaching back to Blowup days.''

"I never knew—''

"Naturally. Well, you'll see what a Home's like. There'll be an interpreter assigned to give you the dope. And, as a matter of fact, it's good conditioning. You're going to Cozy Nook, aren't you?''

"I think . . . yes, that's it. There are several?''

Peaslee nodded.

"You may run into some of your ancestors there. I know one of your great-greats is in Cozy Nook. It's a funny feeling, to look at and talk to somebody who five hundred years ago was responsible for your birth. But you mustn't let her know who you are."

"Why not?"

"It's a special setup. The interpreter will give you the angles. All sorts of precautions have to be taken. There's a corps of psychologists who work on nothing but the Homes. You'll find out. And I'm busy, Sam. See you when you get back. I hear you're getting married."

"That's right," Dyson said. "We're both government-certified, too." His smile was slightly crooked.

"Rebel," Peaslee said, and broke the circuit. The image slowly faded, leaving only a play of pastel colors driving softly across the screen's surface. Dyson sat back and considered.

Presumably neoradar had not discovered his hidden laboratory, or there would have been trouble. Not serious trouble, in this paternalistic administration. Discussions; the semantics of logicians, and, in the end, Dyson knew that he would be argued around to the other side. They could twist logic damnably. And, very likely, they were right. If research in certain radiogenetic fields had been forbidden, the reasons for that step would hold even heavy water.

Immortality.

Within limits, of course. There were principles of half-life—of entropy—nothing lasts forever. But there were different yardsticks. It would be immortality by normal standards.

So, it had been achieved once before, quite by accident. That particular accident had left the planet in insane chaos for hundreds of years, providing a peculiarly unstable foundation for the new culture that had arisen since. It was rather like a building constructed, without plans, from the alloys and masonry of an earlier one. There were gaps and missing peristyles.

Dyson thumbed through the manifold sheets on his desk. They contained guides, problems in his current research—not the secret research in the hidden laboratory, but the government-approved work on intellectual mutation. To a layman some of the terms wouldn't have meant anything, but Dyson was a capable technician. *Item 24: Check psychopathology of genius-types in pre-Blowup era, continuing line of investigation toward current times.* . . .

He left a transference call for the interpreter, pulled on a cloak, and took a glider to Marta Hallam's apartment. She was drinking maté on the terrace, a small, fragile, attractive girl who efficiently put a silver tube in another maté gourd as soon as she had kissed Dyson. He sat beside her and rubbed his forehead with thumb and forefinger.

"We'll furlough in a few weeks," Marta said. "You work too hard. I'll see that you don't."

He looked at her and saw her against a misty background of a thousand years in the future—older, of course, but superficial attractiveness wasn't imported. He'd grow older, too. But neither of them would die. And the treatment did not cause sterility. Overcrowding of the planet could be handled by migration to other worlds; the old rocket fuels had already been rediscovered. Through research in a Home, perhaps, Dyson guessed.

Marta said, "What are you so glum about? Do you want to marry somebody else?"

There was only one way to answer that. After a brief while, Dyson grumbled that he hated to be certified like a bottle of milk.

"You'll be glad of it after we have children," Marta said. "If our genes had been haywire, we might have had a string of freaks."

"I know. I just don't like—"

"Look," she said, staring at him. "At worst, we'd have been treated, to compensate for negative Rh or anything like that. Or our kids would have had to be put in an incubation clinic. A year or two of separation from them at most. And worth it, when you figure that they'd have come out healthy specimens."

Dyson said cryptically, "Things would have been a lot easier if we'd never had the Blowup."

"Things would have been a lot easier if we'd stayed unicellular blobs," Marta amplified. "You can't eat your cake and keep the soda bicarb on the shelf."

"A philosopher, eh? Never mind. I've got something up my sleeve—"

But he didn't finish that, and stayed where he was for a while, drinking maté and noticing how lovely Marta's profile was against the skyline and the immense, darkening blue above. After a while the interpreter announced himself, having got Dyson's transference notice, and the two men went out together into the chilly night.

Five hundred years before, an atom was split and the balance of power blew up. Prior to that time, a number of people had been playing tug-of-war with a number of ropes. Nuclear fission, in effect, handed those people knives. They learned how to cut the ropes, and, too late, discovered that the little game had been played on the summit of a crag whose precipitous sides dropped away to abysmal depths beneath.

The knife was a key as well. It opened fantastic new doors. Thus the Blowup. Had the Blowup been due only to the atomic blast, man might have rebuilt more easily, granting that the planet remained habitable. However, one of the doors the key opened led into a curious, perilous place where physical laws were unstable. Truth is a variable. But no one knew how to vary it until after unlimited atomic power had been thrown on the market.

Within limits, anything could happen, and plenty of things did. Call it a war. Call it chaos. Call it the Blowup. Call it a shifting of a kaleidoscope in which the patterns rearranged themselves constantly. In the end, the status quo reestablished itself. Man chewed rat bones, but he was an intelligent animal. When the ground became solid under his feet again, he began to rebuild.

Not easily. Hundreds of years had passed. And *very little of the earlier culture had survived.*

When you consider how much of human knowledge is due to pyramiding, that's easier to understand. Penicillin was discovered because somebody invented a microscope because somebody learned how to grind lenses because somebody found out how to make glass because somebody could make fire. There were gaps in the chain. An atomic war would have blown up the planet or ravaged it, but the catastrophe would have been quick—or complete—and if the planet survived, there would have been artifacts and records and the memories of mankind. But the Blowup lasted for a long time—time itself was used as a variable once during the homicidal, suicidal, fratricidal struggle—and *there were no records.*

Not many, at least. And they weren't selective. Eventually cities rose again, but there were odd gaps in the science of the new civilization. Some of those holes filled themselves in automatically, and a few useful records were dug up from time to time, but not many, and the only real clue men had to the scientific culture of pre-Blowup days was something that had remained stable through the variable-truth-atomic cataclysm.

The colloid of the human brain.

Eyewitnesses.

The Old 'Uns in the secret, segregated Homes, who had lived for five centuries and longer.

Will Mackenzie, the interpreter, was a thin, rangy, freckled man of forty, with the slow, easy motions one automatically associated with a sturdier, plumper physique. His blue eyes were lazy, his voice was soothing, and when Dyson fumbled at the unaccustomed uniform, his helpful motions were lazily efficient.

"A necktie?" Dyson said. "A which?"

"Necktie," Mackenzie explained. "That's right. Don't ask me why. Some of the Old 'Uns don't bother with it, but they're inclined to be fussy. They get conservative after the first hundred years, you know."

Dyson had submerged that mild uneasiness and was determined to play this role at its face value. Administration might suspect his sub rosa research, but, at worst, there would be no punishment. Merely terribly convincing argument. And probably they did not suspect. Anyway, Dyson realized suddenly, there were two sides to an argument, and it was possible that he might convince the logicians—though that had never been done before. His current job was to dig out the information he needed from the Old 'Uns and—that ended it. He stared into the enormous closet with its rows of unlikely costumes.

"You mean they go around in those clothes all the time?" he asked Mackenzie.

"Yeah," Mackenzie said. He peeled off his functionally aesthetic garments and donned a duplicate of Dyson's apparel. "You get used to these things. Well, there are a few things I've got to tell you. We've plenty of time. The Old 'Uns go to bed early, so you can't do anything till tomorrow, and probably not much then. They're suspicious at first."

"Then why do I have to wear this now?"

"So you can get used to it. Sit down. Hike up your pants at the knee, like this—see? Now sit."

He pawed at the rough, unfamiliar cloth, settled himself, and picked up a smoke from the table. Mackenzie sat with an accomplished ease Dyson envied, and pressed buttons that resulted in drinks sliding slowly out from an aperture in the wall.

"We're not *in* Cozy Nook yet," the interpreter said. "This is the conditioning and control station. None of the Old 'Uns know what goes on outside. They think there's still a war."

"But—"

Mackenzie said, "You've never been in a Home before. Well, remember that the Old 'Uns are abnormal. A little—" He shrugged. "You'll see. I've got to give you a lecture. O.K. At the time of the Blowup, the radioactivity caused a cycle of mutations. One type was a group of immortals. They won't live forever—"

Dyson had already done his own research on that point. Radium eventually turns to lead. After a long, long time the energy quotients of the immortals would sink below the level necessary to sustain life. A short time as the life of a solar system goes—a long time measured against the normal human span. A hundred thousand years, perhaps. There was no certain way to ascertain, except the empirical one.

Mackenzie said, "A lot of the Old 'Uns were killed during the Blowup. They're vulnerable to accidents, though they've a tremendously high resistance to disease. It wasn't till after the Blowup, after reconstruction had started, that anybody knew the Old 'Uns were—what they were. There'd been tribal legends—the local shaman had lived forever, you know the typical stuff. We correlated those legends, found a grain of truth in them, and investigated. The Old 'Uns were tested in the labs. I don't know the technical part. But I do know they were exposed to certain radiations, and their body structures were altered."

Dyson said, "How old do they average?"

"Roughly, five hundred years. During the radioactive days. It isn't hereditary, immortality, and there haven't been any such radioactives since, except in a few delayed-reaction areas." Mackenzie had been thrown off his routine speech by the interruption. He took a drink.

He said, "You'll have to see the Old 'Uns before you'll understand the entire picture. We have to keep them segregated here. They have information we need. It's like an unclassified, huge library. The only link we have with pre-Blowup times. And, of course, we have to keep the Old 'Uns happy. That isn't easy. Supersenility—" He took another drink and pushed a button.

Dyson said, "They're human, aren't they?"

"Physically, sure. Ugly as sin, though. Mentally, they've gone off at some queer tangents."

"One of my ancestors is here."

Mackenzie looked at him queerly. "Don't meet her. There's a guy named Fell who was a technician during the Blowup, and a woman named Hobson who was a witness of some of the incidents you're investigating. Maybe you can get enough out of those two. Don't let curiosity get the better of you."

"Why not?" Dyson asked. "I'm interested."

Mackenzie's glass had suddenly emptied.

"It takes special training to be an interpreter here. As for being a caretaker . . . one of the group that keeps the Old 'Uns happy . . . they're handpicked."

He told Dyson more.

The next morning Mackenzie showed his guest a compact gadget that fitted into the ear. It was a sonor, arranged so that the two men could talk, unheard by others, simply by forming words inaudibly. The natural body noises provided the volume, and it was efficient, once Dyson had got used to the rhythmic rise and fall of his heartbeat.

"They hate people to use 'Speranto in front of them," Mackenzie said. "Stick to English. If you've got something private to say, use the sonor, or they'll think you're talking about them. Ready?"

"Sure." Dyson readjusted his necktie uncomfortably. He followed the interpreter through a valve, down a ramp, and through another barrier. Filtered, warm sunlight hit him. He was standing at the top of an escalator that flowed smoothly down to the village below—Cozy Nook.

A high wall rimmed the Home. Camouflage nets were spread above, irregularly colored brown and green. Dyson remembered that the Old 'Uns had been told this was still wartime. A pattern of winding streets, parks, and houses was below.

Dyson said, "That many? There must be a hundred houses here, Mackenzie."

"Some of 'em are for interpreters, psychologists, nurses, and guests. Only forty or fifty Old 'Uns, but they're a handful."

"They seem pretty active," Dyson said, watching figures move about the streets. "I don't see any surface cars."

"Or air-floaters, either," Mackenzie said. "We depend on sliding ways and pneumo tubes for transportation here. There's not much territory to cover. The idea is to keep the Old 'Uns happy, and a lot of them would want to drive cars if there were any around. Their reactions are too slow. Even with safeties, there'd be accidents. Let's go down. Do you want to see Fell first, or Hobson?"

"Well . . . Fell's the technician? Let's try him."

"Over." Mackenzie nodded, and they went down the escalator. As they descended, Dyson noticed that among the modern houses were some that seemed anachronistic: a wooden cottage, a red-brick monstrosity, an ugly glass-and-concrete structure with distorted planes and bulges. But he was more interested in the inhabitants of the Home.

Trees rose up, blocking their vision, as they descended. They were ejected gently on a paved square, lined with padded benches. A man was standing there, staring at them, and Dyson looked at him curiously.

In his ear a voice said, "He's one of the Old 'Uns." Mackenzie was using the inaudible sonor.

The man was old. Five hundred years old, Dyson thought, and suddenly was staggered by the concept. Five centuries had passed since this man was born, and he would go on without change while time flowed in flux without touching him.

What effect had immortality had upon this man?

For one thing, he had not been granted eternal youth. The half-time basic precluded that. Each year he grew older, but not quite as old as he had grown the preceding year. He was stooped—Dyson was to learn to recognize that particular stigma of the Old 'Uns—and his body seemed to hang loosely from the rigid crossbars of his clavicle. His head, totally bald, thrust forward, and small eyes squinted inquisitively at Dyson. Nose and ears were grotesquely enlarged. Yet the man was merely old—not monstrous.

He said something Dyson could not understand. The sound held inquiry, and, at random, he said, "How do you do. My name is Dyson—"

"Shut up!" the sonor said urgently in his ear, and Mackenzie moved forward to intercept the old man, who was edging toward the escalator. Gibberish spewed from the interpreter's lips, and answering gibberish came from the Old 'Un. Occasionally Dyson could trace a familiar word, but the conversation made no sense to him.

The old man suddenly turned and scuttled off. Mackenzie shrugged.

"Hope he didn't catch your name. He probably didn't. There's a woman here with the same name—you said you had an ancestor in Cozy Nook, didn't you? We don't like the Old 'Uns to get any real concept of time. It unsettles them. If Mander should tell her—" He shook his head. "I guess he won't. Their memories aren't good at all. Let's find Fell."

He guided Dyson along one of the shaded walks. From porches bright eyes stared inquisitively at the pair. They passed workers, easily distinguishable from the Old 'Uns, and once or twice they passed one of the immortals. There could be no difficulty in recognizing them.

"What did Mander want?" Dyson asked.

"He wanted out," Mackenzie said briefly. "He's only a couple of hundred years old. Result of one of the freak radiation areas blowing off two centuries ago."

"Was he speaking English?"

"His form of it. You see—they lack empathy. They forget to notice how their words sound to the listener. They slur and mispronounce and in the end it takes a trained interpreter to understand them. Here's Fell's place." They mounted a porch, touched a sensitive plate, and the door opened. A young man appeared on the threshold.

"Oh, hello," he said, nodding to Mackenzie. "What's up?"

"Research business. How's Fell?"

The male nurse grimaced expressively. "Come in and find out. He's had breakfast, but—"

They went in. Fell was sitting by a fire, a hunched, huddled figure so bent over that only the top of his bald, white head was visible. The nurse retired, and Mackenzie, motioning Dyson to a chair, approached the Old 'Un.

"Professor Fell," he said softly. "Professor Fell. Professor Fell—"

It went on like that for a long time. Dyson's nerves tightened. He stared around the room, noticing the musty, choking atmosphere that not even a precipitron could eliminate. Here was none of the dignity of age. This foul-smelling, crouching old man huddled in his chair—

Fell lifted his head wearily and let it fall again. He spoke. The words were unintelligible.

"Professor Fell," Mackenzie said. "We've come for a talk. Professor—"

The figure roused again. It spoke.

Mackenzie used the sonor. "They understand English—some of 'em, anyway. Fell isn't like Mander. I'll have him talking soon."

But it took a long time, and Dyson had a throbbing headache before a grain of information was elicited from Fell. The Old 'Un had entirely lost the sense of selectivity. Or, rather, he had acquired his own arbitrary one. It was impossible to keep him from straying from the subject. Mackenzie did his best to act as a filter, but it was difficult.

And yet this old man had been alive five hundred years ago.

Dyson thought of a maté tube, pierced with a number of tiny holes at the end to admit the liquid. Fell was such a tube, stretching back into the unrecorded past—and he, too, was pierced with a thousand such holes through which the irrelevant came in painful, spasmic gushes. Someone had cooked an egg too long once—the price of wool was monstrous—some unknown politician was crooked—it must be arthritis, or else—that boy, what was his name? Tim, Tom, something like that—he'd been a genius-type, yes, but the poor boy—it isn't as warm now as it used to be—

Who? Don't bother me. I don't remember. I mean I don't want to be bothered. I'll tell you something, that reagent I made once—

It was all very dull; every schoolboy today knew about that reagent. But Mackenzie had to sit and listen to the interminable tale, though he mercifully spared Dyson most of it. Then, gradually, he edged Fell back to the subject.

Oh, the genius boy—he developed migraine. The specific didn't work long. Medicine's got a lot to learn. I remember once—

Dyson made a few notes.

What he most wanted were factors in the physiomental off-norm variations of the genius-types that had been produced at random by the Blowup. Fell had been a technician at that time, and an excellent research man. But all his notes, naturally, had vanished in the aftermath, when painfully rebuilt units of civilization kept tumbling down again, and the man's memory was leaky. Once Dyson made careful notes before he realized that Fell was giving him the formula for a martini in chemical terminology.

Then Fell got irritable. He hammered weakly on the arm of his chair and demanded an eggnog, and Mackenzie, with a shrug, got up and let the male nurse take over. The interpreter went out into the filtered sunlight with Dyson.

"Any luck?"

"Some," Dyson said, referring to his notes. "It's a very spotty picture, though."

"You've got to allow for exaggerations. It's necessary to double-check their memories before you can believe 'em. Luckily, Fell isn't a pathological liar like some of the Old 'Uns. Want to look up the Hobson woman?"

Dyson nodded, and they strolled through the village. Dyson saw eyes watching him suspiciously, but most of the Old 'Uns were engrossed in their own affairs.

"Just what's the angle on your research?" Mackenzie asked. "Or is it confidential?"

"We're trying to increase mental capacity," Dyson explained. "You remember the IQ boys born after the Blowup. Or, rather, you've heard stories about them."

"Geniuses. Uh-huh. Some were crazy as bedbugs, weren't they?"

"Specialized. You've heard of Ahmed. He had a genius for military organization, but after he'd conquered, he didn't know how to reconstruct. He ended up very happy, in a private room playing with tin soldiers. Trouble is, Mackenzie, there's a natural check-and-balance. You can't increase intelligence artificially without loading the seesaw, at the wrong end. There are all kinds of angles. We want to build up mental capacity without weakening the brain colloid in other directions. The brainier you are, the less stable you are, usually. You're too apt to get off on one particular hobby and ride it exclusively. I've heard stories about a man named Ferguson, born about three hundred years ago, who was pretty nearly a superman. But he got interested in chess, and pretty soon that was all he cared about."

"The Old 'Uns won't play games, especially competitive ones. But they're certainly not geniuses."

"None of them?"

Mackenzie said, "At the climacteric, their minds freeze into complete inelasticity. You can date them by that. Their coiffures, their clothes, their vocabularies—that's the label. I suppose senility is just the stopping point."

Dyson thought of half-time, and then stopped short as a musical note thrummed through the village. Almost instantly there was a crowd in the street. The Old 'Uns gathered, thronging closely and moving toward the sound. Mackenzie said, "It's a fire."

"You're not fireproofed?"

"Not against arson. Some fool probably decided he was being persecuted or ignored and started a fire to get even. Let's—" He was thrust away from Dyson by the mob. The musty odor became actively unpleasant. Dyson, pressed in on all sides by the grotesque, deformed Old 'Uns, told himself desperately that physical aspects were unimportant. But if only he were more *used* to deformity—

He pushed his way free and felt a hand on his arm. He looked down into the face of Mander, the Old 'Un he had met at the foot of the escalator that had brought him down to Cozy Nook. Mander was grimacing and beckoning furiously. Gibberish, urgent and unintelligible, poured from his lips. He tugged at Dyson's arm.

Dyson looked around for Mackenzie, but the interpreter was gone. He tried vainly to interrupt the Old 'Un; it was impossible. So he let himself be pulled a few yards away, and then stopped.

"Mackenzie," he said slowly. "Where is Mackenzie?"

Mander's face twisted as he strained to understand. Then his bald head bobbed in assent. He pointed, gripped Dyson's arm again, and started off. With some misgivings, Dyson let himself accompany the Old 'Un. Did the man really understand?

It wasn't far to their destination. Dyson didn't really expect Mackenzie to be in the antique wooden house he entered, but by this time he was curious. There was a darkened room, a sickening sweet odor that was patchouli, though Dyson did not identify it, and he was looking at a shapeless huddle in an armchair, a thing that stirred and lifted a face that had all run to fat, white violet-veined, with sacks of fat hanging loosely and bobbing when the tiny mouth opened and it spoke.

It was very dim in the room. The furniture, replicas of old things made to the Old 'Uns' description, loomed disturbingly. Through the patchouli came other odors, indescribable and entirely out of place in this clean, aseptic, modern age.

"Im'n-s'n," the fat woman said thinly.

Dyson said, "I beg your pardon. I'm looking for Mackenzie—"

Mander clutching painfully at his biceps, a bickering argument broke out between the two Old 'Uns. The woman shrilled Mander down. She beckoned to Dyson, and he came closer. Her mouth moved painfully. She said, with slow effort:

"I'm Jane Dyson. Mander said you were here."

His own ancestor. Dyson stared. It was impossible to trace any resemblance, and certainly there was no feeling of kinship, but it was as though the past had stopped and touched him tangibly. This woman had been alive five hundred years ago, and her flesh was his own. From her had come the seed that became, in time, Sam Dyson.

He couldn't speak, for there was no precedent to guide him. Mander chattered again, and Jane Dyson heaved her huge body forward and wheezed, "They're not fooling me . . . no war . . . I know there's no war! Keeping me locked up here— You get me out of here!"

"But—wait a minute! I'd better get Mackenzie—"

Again Mander squealed. Jane Dyson made feeble motions. She seemed to smile.

"No hurry. I'm your aunt—anyway. We'll have a cup of tea—"

Mander rolled a table forward. The tea service was already laid out, the tea poured in thermocups that kept it at a stable temperature.

"Cup of tea. Talk about it. *Sit—down!*"

All he wanted to do was escape. He had never realized the sheer, sweating embarrassment of meeting an ancestor, especially such a one as this. But he sat down, took a cup, and said, "I'm very busy. I can't stay long. If I could come back later—"

"You can get us out of here. Special exits—we know where, but we can't open them. Funny metal plates on them—"

Emergency exits were no novelty, but why couldn't the locks be activated by the Old 'Uns? Perhaps the locks had been keyed so that they would not respond to the altered physiochemistry of the immortals. Wondering how to escape, Dyson took a gulp of scalding, bitter tea—

Atrophied taste buds made delicacy of taste impossible. Among the Old 'Uns there were no gourmets. Strong curries, chiles—

Then the drug hit him, and his mind drowned in slow, oily surges of lethargic tides.

Some sort of hypnotic, of course. Under the surface he could still think, a little, but he was fettered. He was a robot. He was an automaton. He remembered being put in a dark place and hidden until nightfall. Then he remembered being led furtively through the avenues to an exit. His trained hands automatically opened the lock. Those escape doors were only for emergency use, but his will was passive. He went out into the moonlight with Jane Dyson and Mander.

It was unreclaimed country around the Home. The Old 'Uns didn't know that highways were no longer used. They wanted to hit a highway and follow it to a city. They bickered endlessly and led Dyson deeper and deeper into the wilderness.

They had a motive. Jane Dyson, the stronger character, overrode Mander's weak objections. She was going home, to her husband and family. But often her mind failed to grasp that concept, and she asked Dyson questions he could not answer.

It wasn't shadowy to him; it was not dreamlike. It had a pellucid, merciless clarity, the old man and the old woman hobbling and gasping along beside him, guiding him, talking sometimes in their strange, incomprehensible tongue, while he could not warn them, could not speak except in answer to direct orders. The drug, he learned, was a variant of pentothal.

"I seen them use it," Jane Dyson wheezed. "I got in and took a bottle of it. Lucky I did, too. But I knew what I was doing. They think I'm a fool—"

Mander he could not understand at all. But Jane Dyson could communicate with him, though she found it painful to articulate the words in sufficient clarity.

"Can't fool us . . . keeping us locked up! We'll fix 'em. Get to my folks . . . uh! Got to rest—"

She was inordinately fat, and Mander was cramped and crippled and bent into a bow. Under the clear moonlight it was utterly grotesque. It could not happen. They went on and on, dragging themselves painfully down gullies, up slopes, heading northward for some mysterious reason, and more and more the hands that had originally been merely guiding became a drag. The Old 'Uns clung to Dyson as their strength failed. They ordered him to keep on. They hung their weight on his aching arms and forced their brittle legs to keep moving.

There was a cleared field, and a house, with lights in the windows. Jane Dyson knocked impatiently on the door. When it opened, a taffy-haired girl who might have been seven stood looking up inquiringly. Dyson, paralyzed with the drug, saw shocked fear come into the clear blue eyes.

But it passed as Jane Dyson, thrusting forward, mumbled, "Is your mother home? Run get your mother, little girl. That's it."

The girl said, "Nobody's home but me. They won't be back till eleven."

The old woman had pushed her way in, and Mander urged Dyson across the threshold. The girl had retreated, still staring. Jane plopped herself into a relaxer and panted.

"Got to rest . . . where's your mother? Run get her. That's it. I want a nice cup of tea."

The girl was watching Dyson, fascinated by his paralysis. She sensed something amiss, but her standards of comparison were few. She fell back on polite habit.

"I can get you some maté, ma'am."

"Tea? Yes, yes. Hurry, Betty."

The girl went out. Mander crouched by a heating plate, mumbling. Dyson stood stiffly, his insides crawling coldly.

Jane Dyson muttered, "Glad to be home. Betty's my fourth, you know. They said the radiations would cause trouble . . . that fool scientist said I was susceptible, but the children were all normal. Somebody's been changing the house around. Where's Tom?" She eyed Dyson. "You're not Tom. I'm . . . what's this?" The girl came back with three maté gourds. Jane seized hers greedily.

"You mustn't boil the water too long, Betty," she said.

"I know. It takes out the air—"

"Now you be still. Sit down and be quiet."

Jane drank her maté noisily, but without comment. Dyson had a queer thought, but she and the child were at a contact point, passing each other, in a temporal dimension. They had much in common. The child had little experience, and the old woman had had much, but could no longer use hers. Yet real contact was impossible, for the only superiority the Old 'Un had over the child was the factor of age, and she could not let herself respect the child's mentality or even communicate, save with condescension.

Jane Dyson dozed. The child sat silent, watching and waiting, with occasional puzzled glances at Mander and Dyson. Once Jane ordered the girl to move to another chair so she wouldn't catch cold by the window—which wasn't open. Dyson thought of immortality and knew himself to be a fool.

For man has natural three-dimensional limits, and he also has four-dimensional ones, considering time as an extension. When he reaches those limits, he ceases to grow and mature, and forms rigidly within the mold of those limiting walls. It is stasis, which is retrogression unless all else stands still as well. A man who reaches his limits is tending toward subhumanity. Only when he becomes superhuman in time and space can immortality become practical.

Standing there, with only his mind free, Dyson had other ideas. The real answer might be entirely subjective. Immortality might be achieved without extending the superficial life span at all. If you could reason sufficiently fast, you could squeeze a year's reasoning into a day or a minute—

For example, each minute now lasted a hundred years.

Jane Dyson woke up with a start. She staggered to her feet. "We can't stay," she said. "I've got to get on home for dinner. Tell your mother—" She mumbled and hobbled toward the door. Mander, apathetically silent, followed. Only Jane remembered Dyson, and she called to him from the threshold. The little girl, standing wide-eyed, watched Dyson stiffly follow the others out.

They went on, but they found no more houses. At last weariness stopped the Old 'Uns. They sheltered in a gully. Mander crawled under a bush and tried to sleep. It was too cold. He got up, hobbled back, and pulled off the old woman's cloak. She fought him feebly. He got the cloak, went back, and slept, snoring. Dyson could do nothing but stand motionless.

Jane Dyson dozed and woke and talked and dozed again. She brought up scattered, irrelevant memories of the past and spread them out for Dyson's approval. The situation was almost ideal. She had a listener who couldn't interrupt or get away.

"Thought they could fool an old woman like me. . . . I'm not old. Making me chew bones. Was that it? There was a bad time for a while. Where's Tom? Just leave me alone—"

And—"Telling me I was going to live forever! Scientists! He was right, though. I found that out. I *was* susceptible. It scared me. Everything going to pot, and Tom dying and me going on. . . . I got some pills. I'd got hold of them. More'n once I nearly swallowed them, too. You don't live forever if you take poison, that's certain. But I was smart. I waited awhile. Time enough, I said. It's cold."

Her mottled, suety cheeks quivered. Dyson waited. He was beginning to feel sensation again. The hypnotic was wearing off.

Rattling, painful snores came from the invisible Mander, hidden in the gloom. A cold wind sighed down the gully. Jane Dyson's fat white face was pale in the faint light of distant, uninterested stars. She stirred and laughed a high, nickering laugh.

"I just had the funniest dream," she said. "I dreamed Tom was dead and I was old."

* * *

A copter picked up Dyson and the Old 'Uns half an hour later. But no explanations were made until he was back in the city, and even then they waited till Dyson had time to visit his secret laboratory and return. Then his uncle, Roger Peaslee, came into Dyson's apartment and sat down without invitation, looking sympathetic.

Dyson was white and sweating. He put down his glass, heavily loaded with whiskey, and stared at Peaslee.

"It was a frame, wasn't it?" he asked.

Peaslee nodded. He said, "Logic will convince a man he's wrong, *provided* the right argument is used. Sometimes it's impossible to find the right argument."

"When Administration sent me to the Home, I thought they'd found out I was doing immortality research."

"Yes. As soon as they found out, they sent you to Cozy Nook. That was the argument."

"Well, it was convincing. A whole night in the company of those—" Dyson drank. He didn't seem to feel it. He was still very pale.

Peaslee said, "We framed that escape, too, as you've guessed. But we kept an eye on you all along, to make sure you and the Old 'Uns would be safe."

"It was hard on them."

"No. They'll forget. They'll think it was another dream. Most of the time they don't know they're old, you see. A simple defense mechanism of senility. As for that little girl, I'll admit that wasn't planned. But no harm was done. The Old 'Uns didn't shock or horrify her. And nobody will believe her—which is fine, because the Archive myth has to stand for a while."

Dyson didn't answer. Peaslee looked at him more intently.

"Don't take it so hard, Sam. You lost an argument, that's all. You know now that age without increasing maturity doesn't mean anything. You've got to keep going ahead. Stasis is fatal. When we can find out how to overcome that, it'll be safe to make people immortal. Right?"

"Right."

"We want to study that laboratory of yours, before we dismantle it. Where's it hidden?"

Dyson told him. Then he poured himself another drink, downed it, and stood up. He picked up a sheet of paper from the table and tossed it at his uncle.

"Maybe you can use that, too," he said. "I was just down at the lab making some tests. I got scared."

"Eh?"

"Jane Dyson was especially susceptible to the particular radiations that cause immortality. Like cancer, you know. You can't inherit it, but you can inherit the susceptibility. Well, I remembered that I'd been working a lot with those radiations, in secret. So I tested myself just now."

Peaslee opened his mouth, but he didn't say anything.

Dyson said, "It wouldn't have bothered most people—those radiations. But Jane Dyson passed on her susceptibility to me. It was accidental. But—I was exposed. *Why didn't Administration get on to me sooner!*"

Peaslee said slowly: "You don't mean—"

Dyson turned away from the look beginning to dawn in his uncle's eyes.

An hour later he stood in his bathroom alone, a sharp blade in his hand. The mirror watched him questioningly. He was drunk, but not very; it wouldn't be so easy to get drunk from now on. *From now on—*

He laid the cold edge of the knife against one wrist. A stroke would let out the blood from his immortal body, stop his immortal heart in midbeat, turn him from an immortal into a very mortal corpse. His face felt stiff. The whiskey taste in his mouth couldn't rinse out the musty smell of senility.

The thought: *Of course there's Marta. Fourscore and ten is the normal span. If I cut it off now, I'll be losing a good many years. When I'm ninety, it would be time enough. Suppose I went on for a little while longer, married Marta—*

He looked at the knife and then into the glass. He said aloud: "When I'm ninety I'll commit suicide."

Young, firm-fleshed, ruddy with health, his face looked enigmatically back at him from the mirror. Age would come of course. As for death—

There would be time enough, sixty years from now, when he faced a mirror and knew that he had gone beyond maturity and into the darkening, twilight years. He would know, when the time came—of course he would know!

And in Cozy Nook, Jane Dyson stirred and moaned in her sleep, dreaming that she was old.

THE SOUL-EMPTY ONES

Walter M. Miller, Jr.

Miller, to my mind, is a writer of exceptional power. He is the author of what may be my all-time favorite story, "Vengeance for Nikolai," and the novel A Canticle for Leibowitz. Whenever I see his name on fiction, I know it will stir me. The present entry is not his best, for reasons explained in the introduction to this volume, but I remember it across three decades as a good, solid adventure. What distinguishes man from animal, apart from intelligence? Is it his soul? If so, what is the status of an android—that is, a creature crafted in the laboratory—who is made in the complete image of man, feelings and all? Fast action plus a good thematic question—this, to me, is the essence of conventional science fiction.

—PA

Miller had a sensational career beginning in 1951, published stunning novellas and short stories in the magazines ("The Darfstellar," Astounding 1/55, won a Hugo), topped it off with the 1959 A Canticle for Leibowitz, considered by many to be the single finest science-fiction novel ever published (it is in everyone's top ten), and then utterly ceased to publish. No one knows why. A mysterious, emblematic figure of science fiction's most ambitious (and emblematic) decade, Miller lives in a southern state in virtual isolation from the genre to which he gave so much; there are vague rumors of a novel in progress. "The Soul-Empty Ones," a characteristic story and apparently Miller's only unreprinted shorter work, appeared in Astounding in 1952, incited praise from James Blish (collected in his volume of criticism, The Issue At Hand), and has not been read by other than collectors and specialists in the last quarter of a century. Until now.

—bnm

They heard the mournful bleat of his ramshorn in the night, warning them that he was friend, asking the sentries not to unleash the avalanches upon the mountain trail where he rode. They returned to their stools and huddled about the lamplight, waiting—two warriors and a woman. The woman was watching the window; and toward the valley, bright bonfires yellowed the darkness.

"He should never have gone," the girl said tonelessly.

The warriors, father and son, made no answer. They were valley men, from the sea, and guests in the house of Daner. The younger one looked at his sire and shook his head slowly. The father clenched his jaw stubbornly. "I could not let you go to blaspheme," he growled defensively. "The invaders are the sons of men. If Daner wishes to attack them, he is our host, and we cannot prevent it. But we shall not violate that which is written of the invaders. They have come to save us."

"Even if they kill us, and take our meat?" muttered the blond youth.

"Even so. We are their servants, for the sons of men created our fathers out of the flesh of beasts, and gave them the appearance of men." The old one's eyes glowed with the passionate light of conviction.

The young one inclined his head gravely and submissively, for such was the way of the valley people toward their parents.

The girl spoke coldly. "At first, I thought you were cowardly, old man. Now I think your whole tribe is cowardly."

Without a change of expression, the gray-haired one lifted his arms into the lamplight. His battles were written upon them in a crisscross of white knife scars. He lowered them silently without speaking.

"It's in the mind that you are cowardly," said the girl. "We of the Natani fight our enemies. If our enemies be gods, then we shall fight gods."

"Men are not gods," said the young one, whose name was Falon.

His father slapped him sharply across the back of the neck. "That is sacrilege," he warned. "When you speak of the invaders. They are men and gods."

The girl watched them with contempt. "Among the Natani, when a man loses his manhood by age, he goes into the forest with his war knife and does not return. And if he neglects to go willingly, his sons escort him and see that he uses the knife. When a man is so old that his mind is dull, it is better for him to die."

The old warrior glowered at his hostess, but remained polite. "Your people have strange ways," he said acidly.

Suddenly a man came in out of the blackness and stood swaying in the doorway. He clutched his dogskin jacket against his bleeding chest as a sponge. He was panting softly. The three occupants of the small stone hut came slowly to their feet, and the woman said one word:

"Daner!"

The man mopped his forehead and staggered a step forward. He kicked the door closed with his heel. His skin had gone bloodless gray, and his eyes wandered wildly about the room for a moment. Then he sagged to his knees. Falon came to his aid, but Daner shook him off.

"They're really the sons of men," he gasped.

"Did you doubt it?" asked the old valley man.

Daner nodded. His mouth leaked a trickle of red, and he spat irritably. "I saw their skyboats. I fought with a guard. They are the sons of men . . . but they . . . are no longer men." He sank to a sitting position and leaned back against the door, staring at the woman. "Ea-Daner," he breathed softly.

"Come care for your man, you wench!" growled the old one. "Can't you see he's dying?"

The girl stood back a few feet, watching her husband with sadness and longing, but not with pity. He was staring at her with deep black eyes, abnormally brightened by pain. His breath was a wet hiss. Both of them ignored their valley guests.

"Sing me 'The Song of the Empty of Soul,' Ea, my wife, " he choked, then began struggling to his feet. Falon, who knew a little of the Natani ways, helped him pull erect.

Daner pawed at the door, opened it, and stood looking out into the night for a moment. A dark line of trees hovered to the west. Daner drew his war knife and stood listening to the yapping of the wild dogs in the forest. "Sing, woman."

She sang. In a low, rich voice, she began the chant of the Soul-Empty Ones. The chant was weary, slowly repeating its five monotonous notes, speaking of men who had gone away, and of their Soul-Empty servants they had left behind.

Daner stepped from the doorsill, and became a wavering shadow, receding slowly toward the trees.

The song said that if a man be truly the son of men, the wild dogs would not devour him in the time of death. But if he be Empty of Soul, if he be only the mocking image of Man, then the wild dogs would feed—for his flesh was of the beast, and his ancestor's seed had been warped by Man to grow in human shape.

The two valley warriors stood clumsily; their ways were not of the Natani mountain folk. Their etiquette forbade them interfere in their host's action. Daner had disappeared into the shadows. Ea-Daner, his wife, sang softly into the night, but her face was rivered with moisture from her eyes, large dark eyes, full of anger and sadness.

The song choked off. From the distance came a savage man-snarl. It was answered by a yelp; then a chorus of wild-dog barks and growls raged in the forest, drowning the cries of the man. The girl stopped singing and closed the door. She returned to her stool and gazed out toward the bonfires. Her face was empty, and she was no longer crying.

Father and son exchanged glances. Nothing could be done. They sat together, across the room from the girl.

After a long time, the elder spoke. "Among our people, it is customary for a widow to return to her father's house. You have no father. Will you join my house as a daughter?"

She shook her head. "My people would call me an outcast. And your people would remember that I am a Natani."

"What will you do?" asked Falon.

"We have a custom," she replied vaguely.

Falon growled disgustedly. "I have fought your tribe. I have fought many tribes. They all have different ways, but are of the same flesh. Custom! Bah! One way is as good as another, and no-way-at-all is the best. I have given myself to the devil, because the devil is the only god in whom all the tribes believe. But he never answers my prayers, and I think I'll spit on his name."

He was rewarded by another slap from his father. "You are the devil's indeed!" raged the old man.

Falon accepted it calmly, and shrugged toward the girl. "What will you do, Ea-Daner?"

She gazed at him through dull grief. "I will follow the way. I will mourn for seven days. Then I will take a war knife and go to kill one of my husband's enemies. When it is done, I will follow his path to the forest. It is the way of the Natani widow.''

Falon stared at her in unbelief. His shaggy blond eyebrows gloomed into a frown. ''No!'' he growled. ''I am ashamed that the ways of my father's house have made me sit here like a woman while Daner went to fight against the sons of men! Daner said nothing. He respected our ways. He has opened his home to us. I shan't let his woman be ripped apart by the wild dogs!''

''Quiet!'' shouted his father. ''You are a guest! If our hosts are barbarians, then you must tolerate them!''

The girl caught her breath angrily, then subsided. ''Your father is right, Falon,'' she said coldly. ''I don't admire the way you grovel before him, but he is right.''

Falon squirmed and worked his jaw in anger. He was angry with both of them. His father had been a good man and a strong warrior; but Falon wondered if the way of obedience was any holier than the other ways. The Natani had no high regard for it. Ea-Daner had no father, because the old man had gone away with his war knife when he became a burden on the tribe. But Falon had always obeyed, not out of respect for the law, but out of admiration for the man. He sighed and shrugged.

''Very well, then, Ea-Daner, you shall observe your custom. And I will go with you to the places of the invader.''

''You will not fight with the sons of men!'' his father grumbled sullenly. ''You will not speak of it again.''

Falon's eyes flared heatedly. ''You would let a woman go to be killed and perhaps devoured by the invaders?''

''She is a Natani. And it is the right of the sons of men to do as they will with her, or with us. I even dislike hiding from them. They created our fathers, and they made them so that their children would also be in the image of man—in spite of the glow-curse that lived in the ground and made the sons of animals unlike their fathers.''

''Nevertheless, I—''

''You will not speak of it again!''

Falon stared at the angry oldster, whose steely eyes barked commands at him. Falon shivered. Respect for the aged was engrained in the fibers of his being. But Daner's death was fresh in his mind. And he was no longer in the valleys of his people, where the invaders had landed their skyboats. Was the way of the tribe more important than the life of the tribe? If one believed in the gods—then, yes.

Taking a deep breath, Falon stood up. He glanced down at the old man. The steel-blue eyes were biting into his face. Falon turned his back on them and walked slowly across the room. He sat beside the girl and faced his father calmly. It was open rebellion.

"I am no longer a man of the valley," he said quietly. "Nor am I to be a Natani," he added for the benefit of the girl. "I shall have no ways but the ways of embracing the friend and killing the enemy."

"Then it is my duty to kill my son," said the scarred warrior. He came to his feet and drew his war knife calmly.

Falon sat frozen in horror, remembering how the old man had wept when the invaders took Falon's mother to their food pens. The old one advanced, crouching slightly, waiting briefly for his son to draw. But Falon remained motionless.

"You may have an instant in which to draw," purred the oldster. "Then I shall kill you unarmed."

Falon did nothing. His father lunged with a snarl, and the knife's steel sang a hissing arc. Its point dug into the stool where the youth had been sitting. Falon stood crouched across the room, still weaponless. The girl watched with a slight frown.

"So, you choose to flee, but not fight," the father growled.

Falon said nothing. His chest rose and fell slowly, and his eyes flickered over the old one's tough and wiry body, watching for muscular hints of another lunge. But the warrior was crafty. He relaxed suddenly, and straightened. Reflexively, Falon mirrored the sudden unwinding of tension. The elder was upon him like a cat, twining his legs about Falon's, and encircling his throat with a brawny arm.

Falon caught the knife-thrust with his forearm, then managed to catch his father's wrist. Locked together, they crashed to the floor. Falon felt hot hate panting in his face. His only desire was to free himself and flee, even to the forest.

They struggled in silence. With a strength born of the faith that a man must be stronger than his sons, the elder pressed the knife deeper toward Falon's throat. With a weakness born of despair, Falon found himself unable to hold it away. Their embrace was slippery with wetness from the wound in his forearm. And the arm was failing.

"I . . . offer you . . . as a holy . . . sacrifice," panted the oldster, as the knife began scratching skin.

"Father . . . don't—" Then he saw Ea-Daner standing over the old man's shoulder. She was lifting a war club. He closed his eyes.

The sharp crack frightened and sickened him. The knife clattered away from his throat, and his father's body went limp.

Slowly, he extricated himself from the tangle, and surveyed the oldster's head. The scalp was split, and the gray hair sogging with slow blood.

"You killed him!" he accused.

The girl snorted. "He's not dead. I didn't hit him hard. Feel his skull. It's not broken. And he's breathing."

Falon satisfied himself that she spoke the truth. Then he climbed to his feet, grumbling unhappily. He looked down at the old man and deeply regretted his rebelliousness. The father's love of the law was greater than his love for a son. But there was no undoing it now. The elder was committed to kill him, even if he retracted. He turned to the girl.

"I must go before he comes to his senses," he murmured sadly. "You'll tend his head wound?"

She was thoughtful for a moment, then a speculative gleam came into her eyes. "I understood you meant to help me avenge my husband?"

Falon frowned. "I now regret it."

"Do the valley folk treat their own word with contempt?"

Falon shrugged guiltily. "I'm no longer of the valley. But I'll keep my word, if you wish." He turned away and moved to the window to watch the bonfires. "I owe you a life," he murmured. "Perhaps Daner would have returned alive, if I had accompanied him. I turned against my father too late."

"No, Soul-Falon, I knew when Daner left that he meant to fight until he was no longer able—then drag himself back for the forests. If you had gone too, it would have been the same. I no longer weep, because I *knew.*"

Falon was staring at her peculiarly. "You called me Soul-Falon," he said wonderingly; for it was a title given only to those who had won high respect, and it suggested the impossible—that the Soul-Empty One was really a man. Was she mocking him? "Why do you call me that?" he asked suspiciously.

The girl's slender body inclined in a slight bow. "You exchanged your honor for a new god. What greater thing can a man offer than honor among his people?''

He frowned for a moment, then realized she meant it. Did the Natani hold anything above honor? ''I have no new gods,'' he growled. ''When I find the right god, I shall serve him. But until then, I serve myself—and those who please me.''

The old man's breathing became a low moan. He was beginning to come awake. Falon moved toward the door.

''When he awakes, he may be so angry that he forgets he's your guest,'' warned the young warrior. ''You'd better come with me.''

She hesitated. ''The law of mourning states that a widow must remain—''

''Shall I call you Soul-Ea?''

She suffered an uncomfortable moment, then shrugged, and slipped a war knife in her belt thong. Her sandals padded softly after him as he moved out into the darkness and untethered the horses. The steeds' legs were still wrapped in heavy leather strips to protect them against the slashing fangs of the wild dogs.

''Leave Daner's horse for your father,'' said the girl with unsentimental practicality. ''The mare's tired, and she'll be slow if he tries to follow us.''

They swung into the small rawhide saddles and trotted across the clearing. Dim moonlight from a thin silver crescent illuminated their way. Two trails led from the hut that overlooked the cliff. Falon knew that one of them wound along the clifftops to a low place, then turned back beneath the cliff and found its way eventually to the valley. The other penetrated deeper into the mountains. He had given his word, and he let the girl choose the path.

She took the valley road. Falon sighed and spurred after her. It was sure death, to approach the invader's camp. They had the old god-weapons, which would greet all hostile attacks from the Soul-Empty Ones. And if the Empties came in peace, the sons of men would have another occupant for their stock pens. He shivered slightly. According to the old writings, men had been kindly toward their artificial creatures. They created them so that the glow-curse that once lived in the earth would not cause their children to be born as freaks. And they had left Earth to the Empties, promising that they would come again, when the glow-curse passed away.

He remembered Daner's words. And Daner was right, for Falon had also caught glimpses of the invaders before he fled the valley. They were no longer men, although they looked as if they had once been human. They were covered with a thick coat of curly brown hair, but their bodies were spindly and weak, as if they had been a long time in a place where there was no need for walking. Their eyes were huge, with great black pupils; and they blinked irritably in the bright sunlight. Their mouths were small and delicate, but set with four sharp teeth in front, and the jaws were strong—for ripping dainty mouthfuls of flesh.

They had landed in the valley more than a month earlier—while a red star was the morning star. Perhaps it was an omen, he thought—and perhaps they had *been* to the red star, for the old writings said that they had gone to a star to await the curse's lifting. But in the valley, they were building a city. And Falon knew that more of them were yet to come—for the city was large, while the invaders were few.

"Do you think, Ea-Daner," he asked as they rode, "that the invaders really own the world? That they have a right to the land—and to us?"

She considered it briefly, then snorted over her shoulder. "They owned it once, Falon. My grandfather believed that they cursed it themselves with the glow-curse, and that it drove them away. How do they still own it? But that is not a worry for me. If they were gods of the gods, I should still seek the blood that will pay for Daner's."

He noticed that the grief in her voice had changed to a cool and deadly anger. And he wondered. Did the alchemy of Natani custom so quickly change grief into rage?

"How long were you Daner's woman?" he asked.

"Only a few months," she replied. "He stole me from my father in the spring."

Falon reflected briefly that the Natani marriage customs were different than those of the valley peoples, who formally purchased a wife from her parents. The Natani pretended to be more forceful, but the "wife stealing" could be anything from a simple elopement, agreeable even to the parents, to a real kidnaping, involving a reluctant bride. He decided not to press the question.

"Among my people," he said, "I would ask you to be my wife—so that you would not be disgraced by returning to your father's house.'' He hesitated, watching the girl's trim back swaying in the half-light of the moon. ''How would you answer me?''

She shook her head, making her dark hair dance. ''Doesn't a valley widow mourn?''

''To mourn is to pity oneself. The dead feel nothing. The mourner does not pity the dead. He pities himself for having lost the living.''

She glanced back at him over her shoulder. ''You speak as if you believe these things. I thought you were renouncing your people?''

''There is some wisdom, and some foolishness, in every people's way. But you haven't answered my question.''

She shrugged. ''We are not among your people, Falon.'' Then her voice softened, ''I watched you fight the old one. You are quick and strong, and your mind is good. You would be a good man. Daner was a gloomy one. He treated me well, except when I tried to run away at first. But he never laughed. Do you ever laugh, Falon?''

Embarrassed, he said nothing.

''But this is pointless,'' she said, ''for I am a daughter of my people.''

''Do you still intend,'' he asked nervously, ''to follow your husband to the wild dogs?''

She nodded silently, then, after a thoughtful moment, asked, ''Do you believe it's foolishness—to try to kill some of the invader?''

Falon weighed it carefully. His defiance of his own law might weaken her resolve, if he persisted in trying to convince her against the suicidal attempts. But he spoke sadly.

''We are the Soul-Empty Ones. There are many of us in the world. If one invader could be killed for every dozen they kill of us, we would win. No, Ea, I don't think it's foolishness to fight for lives. But I think it's foolishness to fight for tribes, or to give yourself to the wild dogs.''

She reined her horse around a bend in the trail, then halted to stare out at the distant bonfires. ''I'll tell you why we do that, Falon. There's a legend among my people that the wild dogs were once the pets of Man, of Soul-Man, I mean. And it is said that the dogs scent the soul, and will not devour true Soul-Flesh. And the legend is also a prophecy. It says that someday, children will be born to the Natani who are Soul-Children—and that the wild dogs will again know their masters, and come to lick their hands. The Natani drag themselves to the forest when they die, in the hope that the dogs will not molest them. Then they will know that the prophecy has come, and the dead will go to the Place of Watching, as the Soul-Men who made us did go.''

She spurred her horse gently and moved on. But Falon was still staring at the bonfires. Why did the invader keep them burning nightly? Of what were they afraid in the darkness?

''I wonder if the dogs could scent the souls of the sons of men—of the invaders,'' he mused aloud.

''Certainly!'' she said flatly.

Falon wondered about the source of her certainty—from legend or from fact. But he felt that he had questioned her enough. They rode for several miles in silence, moving slowly along the down-going trail. The forests to their flanks were as usual, wailing with the cries of the dog packs.

Falon reined up suddenly. He hissed at Ea-Daner to halt, then rode up beside her. The dim shadow of her face questioned him.

''Listen! Up ahead!''

They paused in immobility, trying to sort out the sounds—the dog packs, a nightbird's cry, the horses' wet breathing, and—

''Dogs,'' murmured Ea-Daner. ''Feeding on a carcass in the pathway. Their growls—'' Suddenly she stiffened and made a small sound of terror in her throat. ''Do you suppose it could be—''

''No, no!'' he assured her quickly. ''A wounded man couldn't come this far on foot. And you heard—''

She was sobbing again. ''Follow me,'' grunted Falon, and trotted on ahead. He found the sharp dog-spikes in his saddlebag and fitted them onto the toes of his sandals. They were six inches of gleaming steel, and sharpened to needlelike points. He called to the girl to do the same. The dogs usually weighed the odds carefully before they attacked a horseman. But if interrupted at mealtime, they were apt to be irritable. He unwound a short coil of rawhide to use as a whip.

He passed a turn in the trail. A dozen of the gaunt, white animals were snarling in a cluster about something that lay on the ground. Their dim writhing shadows made a ghostly spectacle as Falon spurred his mount to a gallop, and howled a shrill cry to startle them.

"Hi-yeee! Yee yee!"

Massive canine heads lifted in the wind. Then the pack burst apart. These were not the dogs left by Man, but only their changed descendants. They scurried toward the shadows, then formed a loose ring that closed about the horsemen as they burst into the midst. A dog leaped for Falon's thigh, then fell back yelping as the toe-spike stabbed his throat. The horse reared as another leaped at his neck, and the hoofs beat at the savage hound.

"Try to ride them down!" Falon shouted to the girl. "Ride in a tight circle!"

Ea-Daner began galloping her stallion at a ten-foot radius from the bleeding figure on the ground. She was shrieking unfeminine curses at the brutes as she lashed out with her whip and her spike. Falon reined to a halt within the circle and dismounted. He was inviting a torn throat if a dog dared to slip past Ea. But he knelt beside the body, and started to lift it in his arms. Then he paused.

At first, he thought that the creature was an invader. It was scrawny and small-boned, but its body was not covered with the black fur. Neither was it a Soul-Empty One—for in designing the Empties, Man had seen no reason to give them separate toes. But Falon paused to long.

"Dog! Look out!" screamed the girl.

Falon reflexively hunched his chin against his chest and guarded his abdomen with his arms as he drew his war knife. A hurtling body knocked him off balance, and long fangs tore savagely at his face. He howled with fear and rage as he fell on his back. The dog was straddling him, and roaring fiercely as he mauled Falon's face and tried to get at his throat.

Falon locked his legs about the beast's belly, arched his body, and stretched away. The great forepaws tore at his chest as he rolled onto his side and began stabbing blindly at the massive head, aiming for a point just below the ear, and trying to avoid the snapping jaws. As the knife bit home, the fangs sank in his arm— then relaxed slightly. With his other hand, Falon forced the weakening jaws apart, pressed the knife deeper, and crunched it through thin bone to the base of the brain. The animal fell aside.

Panting, he climbed to his feet and seized the animal by the hind legs. The girl was still riding her shrieking circuit, too fast for the dogs to attack. Falon swung the dead carcass about him, then heaved it toward the pack. Two others leaped upon it. The rest paused in their snarling pursuit of the horse. They trotted toward their limp comrade. Falon mounted his stallion quickly.

"Draw up beside me here!" he shouted to the girl.

She obeyed, and they stood flank to flank with the man-thing on the ground between them. The pack swarmed about the dead one.

"Look, they're dragging it away!" said Ea.

"They see they can have a feast without a fight," Falon muttered.

A few seconds later, the pack had dragged the carcass back into the forest, leaving the horsemen in peace. Ea glanced down at the man-thing.

"What is it?" she asked.

"I don't know. But I think it's still alive." Dismounting, he knelt again beside the frail body, and felt for a heartbeat. It was faintly perceptible, but blood leaked from a thousand gashes. A moan came from its throat. Falon saw that it was hopelessly mutilated.

"What are you?" he asked gently.

The man-thing's eyes were open. They wandered toward the crescent moon, then found Falon's hulking shadow.

"You . . . you look— Are you a man?" the thing murmured in a tongue that Falon had studied for tribal ritual.

"He speaks the ancient holy language," Falon gasped. Then he answered in kind. "Are you an invader?"

Dim comprehension came into the eyes. "You . . . are an . . . android."

Falon shook his head. "I am a Soul-Empty One."

The eyes wandered toward the moon again. "I . . . escaped them. I was looking for . . . your camps. The dogs—" His speech trailed off and the eyes grew dull.

Falon felt for the heartbeat, then shook his head. Gently, he lifted the body, and tied it securely behind his saddle. "Whoever he is, we'll bury him, after the sun rises." He noticed that Ea made no comment about the relative merits of tribal death-customs, despite the fact that she must feel repugnance toward burial.

Falon felt his face as they rode away. It dripped steadily from the numerous gashes, and his left cheek felt like soggy lace.

"We'll stop at the creek just ahead," said the girl. "I'll clean you up."

The dog-sounds had faded behind them. They dismounted, and

tied their horses in the brush. Falon stretched out on a flat rock while Ea removed her homespun blouse and soaked it in the creek. She cleaned his wounds carefully and tenderly, while he tried to recover his breath and fight off the nausea of shock.

"Rest awhile," she murmured, "and sleep if you can. You've lost much blood. It's nearly dawn, and the dogs will soon go to their thickets."

Falon allowed himself the vanity of only one protest before he agreed to relax for a time. He felt something less than half alive. Ea stretched her blouse across a bush to dry, then came to sit beside him, with her back to the moon so that her face was in blackness.

"Keep your hands away from your wounds," she warned. "They'll bleed again."

He grinned weakly. "I'll have some nice scars," he said. "The valley women think a man is handsome if he has enough war scars. I think my popularity will increase. Do you like warriors with mauled faces, Ea?"

"The white scars are becoming, but not the red, not the fresh ones," she replied calmly.

"Mine will be red and ugly," he sighed, "but the valley women like them."

The girl said nothing, but shifted uneasily. He gazed at the moon's gleam on her soft shoulders.

"Will you still give yourself to the wild dogs if we return from the valley?"

She shivered and shook her head. "The Natani have scattered. A scattered people perhaps begins to lose its gods. And you've shown me a bad example, Soul-Falon. I have no longing for the dogs. But if the Natani found me alive—after Daner's death—they would kill me."

"Did you love him greatly?"

"I was beginning to love him—yes. He stole me without my consent, but he was kind—and a good warrior."

"Since you're breaking your custom, will you marry again?"

She was thoughtful for a moment. "Soul-Falon, if your cow died, would you cease to drink milk—because of bereavement?"

He chuckled. "I don't know. I don't have a cow. Do you compare Daner to a cow?"

"The Natani *love* animals," she said in a defensive tone.

"I am no longer a valley man and you are no longer a Natani. Do you still insist we go down against the invaders—alone?"

"Yes! Blood must buy blood, and Daner is dead."

"I was only thinking—perhaps it would be better to pause and plan. The most we can hope to do alone is ambush a guard or two before they kill us. It is foolish to talk of life when we approach death so blindly. I don't mind dying, if we can kill some invaders. But perhaps we can live, if we stop to think."

"We have today to think," she murmured, glancing toward the eastern sky. "We'll have to wait for nightfall again—before we go out into the open places of the valley."

"I am wondering," Falon said sleepily, "about the man-thing we took from the dogs. He said he escaped. Did he escape from the sons of men? If so, they might send guards to search for him."

She glanced nervously toward the trail.

"No, Ea—they wouldn't come at night. Not those puny bodies. They have god-weapons, but darkness spoils their value. But when the sun rises, we must proceed with caution."

She nodded, then yawned. "Do you think it's safe to sleep a little now? The sky is getting lighter, and the dogs are silent."

He breathed wearily. "Sleep, Ea. We may not sleep again."

She stretched out on her side, with her back toward him. "Soul-Falon?"

"Hm-m-m?"

"What did the man-thing mean—'android'?"

"Who knows? Go to sleep—Soul-Ea."

"It is a foolish title—'Soul,' " she said drowsily.

A feverish sun burned Falon to dazed wakefulness. His face was stiff as stretched rawhide, and the pain clogged his senses. He sat up weakly, and glanced at Ea. She was still asleep, her dark head cushioned on her arms; and her shapely back was glistening with moisture. Falon had hinted that he was interested in her—but only out of politeness—for it was valley etiquette to treat a new widow as if she were a maiden newly come of age, and to court her with cautious flirtation. And a valley man always hoped that if he died, his wife would remarry quickly—lest others say, "Who but the dead one would want her?"

But as Falon glanced at the dozing Ea in the morning sunlight, her bronzed and healthy loveliness struck him. The dark hair spread breeze-tossed across the rock, and it gleamed in the sun.

She would make me a good wife indeed, thought Falon. But then he thought of the Natani ways that were bred into her soul—the little ways that she would regard as proper, despite her larger rebellion—and he felt helpless. He knew almost nothing about Natani ritual for stealing brides. But it was certainly not simply a matter of tossing a girl over one's shoulder and riding away. And if he courted her by valley-custom, she might respond with disgust or mockery. He shrugged and decided that it was hopeless. They had small chance of surviving their fool's errand.

He thought of capture—and shuddered. Ea, being herded into the invaders' food pens—it was not a pleasant thought. There must be no capture.

A gust of wind brought a faint purring sound to his ears. He listened for a moment, stiffening anxiously. Then he stood up. It was one of the invaders' small skycarts. He had seen them hovering about the valley—with great rotary blades spinning above them. They could hang motionless in the air, or speed ahead like a frightened bird.

The brush obscured his view, and he could not see the skycart, but it seemed to be coming closer. He hurried to untether the horses; then he led them under a scrubby tree and tied them to the trunk. Ea was rubbing her eyes and sitting up when he returned to the rock.

"Is my blouse dry, Soul-Falon?"

He fetched it for her, then caught her arm and led her under the tree with the horses. She heard the purr of the skycart, and her eyes swept the morning sky.

"Put your blouse on," he grumbled.

"Am I ugly, Soul-Falon?" she asked in a hurt tone, but obeyed him.

He faced her angrily. "Woman! You cause me to think of breaking my word. You cause me to think of forgetting the invader, and of stealing you away to the mountains. I wish that you were ugly indeed. But you trouble me with your carelessness."

"I am sorry," she said coldly, "but your dogskin jacket was no good for bathing wounds."

He noticed the dark stains on the blouse, and turned away in shame. He knew too little of Natani women, and he realized he was being foolish.

The skycart was still out of sight, but the horses were becoming restless at the sound. As Falon patted his stallion's flanks, he glanced at the body of the man-thing—still tied across the steed's back. His mouth tightened grimly. The creature had evidently been desperate to have braved the forest alone, unarmed, and afoot. Desperate or ignorant. Had he escaped from the invader, and was the skycart perhaps searching for him? It was moving very slowly indeed—as he had seen them move when searching the hills for the villages of the Empties.

An idea struck him suddenly. He turned to the girl. "You know these paths. Is there a clearing near here—large enough for the skycar to sit upon?"

Ea nodded. "A hundred paces from here, the creekbed widens, and floods have washed the bedrock clean. Duck beneath the brush and you can see it."

"Is it the *only* clearing?"

She nodded again. "Why do you ask? Are you afraid the cart will land in it?"

Falon said nothing, but hastily untied the body from his horse. He carried it quickly to the flat rock where they had slept, and he placed the man-thing gently upon it—where he would be in full view from the sky. The skycart crept into distant view as Falon hurried back into the brush. Ea was watching him with an anxious and bewildered stare.

"They'll see him!" she gasped.

"I hope they do! Hurry! Let's go to the clearing!"

He caught her arm, and the began racing along the shallow creekbed, their sandals splashing in the narrow trickle of shallow water. For a few seconds they ducked beneath overhanging brush, but soon the brush receded, and the bed broadened out into a flat expanse of dry rock, broken only by the wear marks of high waters. Then they were in the open, running along the brushline.

"In here!" he barked, and plunged over a root-tangled embankment and into a dense thicket. She followed, and they crouched quietly in the thick foliage, as the purr of the skycart became a nearby drone.

"What are we going to do?" Ea asked tensely.

"Wait, and hope. Perhaps you'll get your knife wet."

Falon peered up through the leaves, and saw the skycart briefly as it moved past. But the sound of its engine took on a new note, and soon he knew that it was hovering over the rock where the body lay. Ea made a small sound of fright in her throat.

After a moment, the skycart moved over the clearing and hung growling fifty feet above them. As it began to settle, Falon saw a fur-coated face peering out from its cabin. He hissed at Ea to remain silent.

The skycart dropped slowly into the clearing, rolled a short distance, and stopped, a pebble's toss from the hidden tribesmen. Its occupants remained inside for a moment, peering about the perimeter of brush. Then a hatch opened, and one of the feeble creatures climbed painfully out. There were three of them, and Falon shuddered as he saw the evil snouts of their flamethrowers.

One of them remained to guard the ship, while the others began moving slowly up the creekbed, their weapons at the ready, and their eyes searching the brush with suspicion. They spoke in low voices, but Falon noticed that they did not use the ancient sacred tongue of Man. He frowned in puzzlement. The valley folk who had been close enough to hear their speech swore that they used the holy language.

"Now?" whispered the girl.

Falon shook his head. "Wait until they find the horses," he hissed in her ear.

The spider-legged creatures moved feebly, as if they were carrying heavy weights; and they were a long time covering the distance to the flat rock. The guard was sitting in the hatchway with his flame gun across his lap. His huge eyes blinked painfully in the harsh morning sunlight as he watched the thickets about the clearing. But he soon became incautious, and directed his stare in the direction his companions had gone.

Falon heard a whinny from the horses, then a shrill shout from the invaders. The guard stood up. Startled, he moved a few steps up the creekbed, absorbed in the shouts of his companions. Falon drew his war knife, and weighed the distance carefully. A miss would mean death. Ea saw what he meant to do, and she slipped her own knife to him.

Falon stood up, his shoulders bursting through the foliage. He aimed calmly, riveting his attention on an accurate throw, and ignoring the fact that the guard had seen him and was lifting his weapon to fire. The knife left Falon's hand as casually as if he had been tossing it at a bit of fur tacked to a door.

The flame gun belched, but the blast washed across the creekbed, and splashed upward to set the brush afire. The guard screamed and toppled. The intense reflected heat singed Falon's hair, and made his stiff face shriek with pain. He burst from the flaming brush, tugging the girl after him.

The guard was sitting on the rocks and bending over his abdomen. The gun had clattered to the ground. The creature had tugged the knife from his belly, and he clutched it foolishly as he shrieked gibberish at it. The others had heard him and were hurrying back from the horses.

Falon seized the gun and kicked the guard in the head. The creature crumpled with a crushed skull. *The gods die easily,* he thought, as he raced along the brushline, keeping out of view.

He fumbled with the gun, trying to discover its firing principle. He touched a stud, then howled as a jet of flame flared the brush on his left. He retreated from the flames, then aimed at the growth that overhung the narrowing creek toward the horses. A stream of incendiary set an inferno among the branches, sealing off the invaders from their ship.

"Into the skycart!" he barked at Ea.

She sprinted toward it, then stopped at the hatch, peering inside. "How will you make the god-machine fly?" she asked.

He came to stare over her shoulder, then cursed softly. Evidently the skycart had no mind of its own, for the cabin was full of things to push and things to pull. The complexity bewildered him. He stood thoughtfully staring at them.

"They'll creep around the fire in a few moments," warned Ea.

Falon pushed her into the ship, then turned to shout toward the spreading blaze. "We have your skycart! If we destroy it, you will be left to the wild dogs!"

"The wild dogs won't attack the sons of men!" Ea hissed.

He glanced at her coolly. If she were right, they were lost. But no sound came from beyond the fire. But the invaders had had time to move around it through the brush, while the man and the girl presented perfect targets in the center of the clearing.

"Fire your god-weapons," Falon jeered. "And destroy your skycart." He spoke the ancient holy tongue, but now he wondered if the invaders could really understand it.

They seemed to be holding a conference somewhere in the brush. Suddenly Falon heard the horses neighing shrilly above the crackling of the fire. There came a sound of trampling in the dry tangles, then a scream. A flame gun belched, and the horses shrieked briefly.

"One of them was trampled," Falon gasped. "Man's pets no longer know his odor."

He listened for more sounds from the horses, but none came. "They've killed our mounts," he growled, then shouted again.

"Don't the pets know their masters? Hurry back, you gods, or perhaps the skycart will also forget."

A shrill and frightened voice answered him. "You can't escape, android! You can't fly the copter."

"And neither can you, if we destroy it!"

There was a short silence, then: "What do you want, android?"

"You will come into the clearing unarmed."

The invader responded with a defiant curse. Falon turned the flame gun diagonally upward and fired a hissing streak to the leeward. It arced high, then spat into the brush two hundred paces from the clearing. Flames burst upward. He set seven similar fires at even intervals about them.

"Soon they will burn together in a ring," he shouted. "Then they will burn inward and drive you to us. You have four choices: flee to the forest; or wait for the fire to drive you to us; or destroy your ship by killing us; or surrender now. If you surrender, we'll let you live. If you choose otherwise, you die."

"And you also, android!"

Falon said nothing. He stayed in the hatchway, keeping an eye on the brush for signs of movement. The fires were spreading rapidly. After a few minutes, the clearing would become a roasting oven.

"Don't fire, android!" called the invader at last.

"Then stand up! Hold your weapon above your head."

The creature appeared fifty paces up the slope and moved slowly toward them. Falon kept his flame gun ready.

"Where's the other?" he called.

"Your beasts crushed him with their hoofs."

Falon covered him silently until he tore his way into the clearing. "Take his weapon, Ea," he murmured. The girl obeyed, but her hand twitched longingly toward her knife as she approached. The creature's eyes widened and he backed away from her.

"Let him live, Ea!"

She snatched the invader's weapon, spat at him contemptuously, then marched back to the ship. Her face was white with hate, and she was trembling.

"Sit in the skycart," he told her, then barked at the captive. "You'll fly us away, before the fire sweeps in."

The prisoner obeyed silently. They climbed into the aircraft as the clearing became choked with smoke and hot ashes. The engine coughed to life, and the ship arose quickly from the clearing. The girl murmured with frightened awe as the ground receded beneath them. Falon was uneasy, but he kept his eyes and his gun on the back of the pilot's furry neck. The creature chuckled with gloating triumph.

"Shoot the flame rifle, android," he hissed. "And we shall all burn together."

Falon frowned uncomfortably for a moment. "Quiet!" he barked. "Do you think we prefer your food pens to quick and easy death? If you do not obey, then we shall all die as you suggest."

The pilot glanced back mockingly, but said nothing.

"You tempt me to kill you," Falon hissed. "Why do you gloat?"

"The fires you set, android. The forests are dry. Many of your people will be driven down into the valleys. It is a strategy we intended to use—as soon as our city had grown enough to accommodate the large numbers of prisoners we will take. But you have made it necessary to destroy, rather than capture."

Ea glanced back at the fires. "He speaks truth," she whispered to Falon, who already felt a gnawing despair.

"Bah, hairy one! How will you kill thousands? There are only a few of you! Your god-weapons aren't omnipotent. Numbers will crush you."

The pilot laughed scornfully. "Will your tribesmen attack their gods? They are afraid, android. You two are only rebels. The tribes will flee, not fight. And even if some of them fought, we have the advantage. We could retreat to our ships while enemies broke their knives on the hull."

The ship was rising high over the forest, higher than any mountain Falon had ever climbed. He stared out across the valley toward the seacoast where the fishing boats of his people lay idle by their docks. The owners were in captivity or in flight. The city of the invaders was taking form—a great rectangle, thousands of paces from end to end. A dozen metallic gleams were scattered about the area—the skyboats in which the invader had descended from the heavens.

He noticed the food pens. There were two of them—high stockades, overlooked by watchtowers with armed guards. He could see the enclosures' occupants as antlike figures in the distance. Neither pen seemed crowded. He frowned suddenly, wondering if the man-thing had been confined to one of the pens. The creature had been neither invader nor Empty. Falon felt a vague suspicion. He glanced at the pilot again.

"The dead one told us many things before he died," he said cautiously.

The creature stiffened, then shot him a suspicious glance. "The escaped android? What could *he* have told you?"

"Android?" Falon's hunch was coming clearer. "Do you call *yourself* an android?" he jeered.

"Of course not! I am a man! 'Android' is our word for 'Soul-Empty One.' "

"Then the dead one is not of your race, eh?"

"You have eyes, don't you?"

"But neither is he of our race!" Falon snapped. "For we have no toes. He is a soul-man!"

The pilot was trembling slightly. "If the dead one told you this, then we shall all die—lest you escape and speak of this to others!" He wrenched at the controls, and the ship darted valleyward—toward the city. "Fire, android! Fire, and destroy us! Or be taken to the food pens!"

"Kill him!" snarled Ea. "Perhaps we can fly the ship. Kill him with your knife, Soul-Falon!"

The pilot, hearing this, shut off the engines. The ship began hurtling earthward, and Falon clutched at his seat to keep balance.

"Fly to your city!" he shouted above the rush of air. "We will submit!"

Ea growled at him contemptuously, drew her knife, and lunged toward the pilot. Falon wrestled with her, trying to wrench the knife from her grasp. "I know what I'm doing," he hissed in her ear.

Still she fought, cursing him for a coward, and trying to get to the pilot. Falon howled as her teeth sank into his arm, then he clubbed his fist against her head. She moaned and sagged limply.

"Start the engine!" he shouted. "We'll submit."

"Give me your weapons, then," growled the pilot.

Falon surrendered them quickly. The ship's engine coughed to life as they fell into the smoke of the forest fire. The blazes were licking up at them as the rotors milled at the air and bore them up once more.

"Death is not to your liking, eh, android?" sneered the invader. "You'll find our food pens are very comfortable."

Falon said nothing for a time as he stared remorsefully at the unconscious girl. Then he spoke calmly to the pilot.

"Of course, there were others with us when we found the dead one. They will spread the word that you are not the sons of men."

"You lie!" gasped the pilot.

"Very well," murmured Falon. "Wait and see for yourselves. The news will spread, and then our tribes will fight instead of flee."

The pilot considered this anxiously for a moment. Then he snorted. "I shall take you to Kepol. *He* will decide whether or not you speak the truth."

Falon smiled inwardly and glanced back at the fires beneath them. They were creeping faster now, and soon the blaze would be sweeping down the gentle slopes to drive the inhabitants of the forest into the valley. Thousands of Natani and valley warriors would swarm out onto the flatlands. Most would not attack, but only try to flee from the creatures whom they thought were demigods.

Falon watched the invaders' installations as the ship drew nearer. Workmen were swarming busily about the growing city. First he noticed that the workmen were hairless. Then he saw that they were not Empties, but the scrawny soul-men. Furry figures stood guard over them as they worked. He saw that the soul-men were being used as slaves.

Soon they were hovering over the city, and, glancing down, he noticed that the occupants of one pen were soul-men, while the other was for Empties. Evidently the soul-men were considered too valuable as workers to use as food. The two pens were at opposite ends of the city, as if the invaders didn't care to have the two groups contacting one another. Falon wondered if the *captive* Empties knew that their overlords weren't soul-men, as they had once believed.

The girl came half awake as they landed. She immediately tore into Falon with teeth and nails. Guards were congregating about the ship as the pilot climbed out. He held off the furious Ea while a dozen three-fingered hands tugged at them, and dragged them from the plane. The pilot spoke to the guards in a language Falon could not understand.

Suddenly the butt of a weapon crashed against his head, and he felt himself go weak. He was dimly aware of being tossed on a cart and rolled away. Then the sunlight faded into gloom, and he knew he was inside a building. Bright self-lights exploded in his skull with each jog of the cart, and his senses were clogged with pain.

At last the jouncing ceased, and he lay quietly for a time, listening to the chatter of the invaders' voices. They spoke in the strange tongue, but one voice seemed to dominate the others.

A torrent of icy water brought him to full consciousness. He sat up on the cart and found himself in a small but resplendent throne room. A small wizened creature occupied a raised dais. Over his head hung a great golden globe with two smaller globes revolving slowly about it. The walls were giant landscape murals, depicting a gaunt red earth the likes of which Falon had never seen.

"On your feet before Lord Kepol, android!" growled a guard, prodding him with a small weapon.

Falon came weakly erect, but a sharp blow behind his knees sent him sprawling. The creature called Kepol cackled.

"This one is too muscular to eat," he said to the guards. "Place him in restraints so that he can have no exercise, and force-feed him. His liver will grow large and tender."

A guard bowed. "It shall be done, Lordship. Do you wish to hear him speak?"

The king-creature croaked impatiently. "This pilot is a fool. If a few of the androids believe we are not men, what harm can be done? Most of them would not believe such rumors. They have no concept of our world. But let him speak."

"Speak, android!" A booted foot pushed at Falon's ribs.

"I've got nothing to say."

The boot crashed against his mouth, and a brief flash of blackness struck him again. He spat a broken tooth.

"Speak!"

"Very well. What the pilot says is true. Others know that you are not men. They will come soon to kill all of you."

The boot drew back again angrily, but hesitated. For the king-creature was cackling with senile laughter. The guards joined in politely.

"When will they come, android?" jeered the king.

"The forest fires will cause them to come at once. They will sweep over your city and drive you into the sea."

"With knives—against machine guns and flamethrowers?" The king glanced at a guard. "This one bores me. Flog him, then bring me the girl. That will be more amusing."

Falon felt loops of wire being slipped over his wrists. Then he was jerked erect, suspended from the ceiling so that his toes scarcely touched the floor.

"Shall we do nothing about the forest fires, Your Lordship?" a guard asked.

The king sighed. "Oh . . . I suppose it would be wise to send a platoon to meet the savages when they emerge. Our fattening pens need replenishing. And we can see if there is any truth in what the captive says. I doubt that they suspect us, but if they do, there is small harm done."

Falon smiled to himself as the first lash cut across his back. He had accomplished the first step in his mission. A platoon was being sent.

The whip master was an expert. He began at the shoulders and worked stroke by stroke toward the waist, pausing occasionally to rub his fingers roughly over the wounds. Falon wailed and tried to faint, but the torture was calculated to leave him conscious. From his dais, the king-creature was chortling with dreamy sensuality as he watched.

"Take him to the man pen," ordered the king when they were finished. "And keep him away from other androids. He knows things that could prove troublesome."

As Falon was led away, he saw Ea just outside the throne room. She was bound and naked to the waist. Her eyes hated him silently. He shuddered and looked away. For she was the sacrifice which he had no right to make.

The man pen was nearly deserted, for the soul-men were busy with the building of the city. Falon was led across a sandy courtyard and into a small cell, where he was chained to a cot. A guard pressed a hypodermic into his arm.

"This will make you eat, android," he said with a leer, "and grow weak and fat."

Falon set his jaw and said nothing. The guard went away, leaving him alone in his cell.

An old man came to stare through the bars. His eyes were wide with the dull glow of fatalistic acceptance. He was thin and brown, his hands gnarled by the wear of slave work. He saw Falon's toe-less feet and frowned. "Android!" he murmured in soft puzzlement. "Why did they put you in here?"

Falon's throat worked with emotion. Here was a descendant of his creators. Man—who had gone away as a conqueror and returned as a slave. Nervously Falon met the calm blue-eyed gaze for a moment. But his childhood training was too strong. Here was Man! Quietly he slipped to his knees and bowed his head. The man breathed slow surprise.

"Why do you kneel, android? I am but a slave, such as yourself. We are brothers."

Falon shivered. "You are of the immortal ones!"

"Immortal?" The man shrugged. "We have forgotten our ancient legends." He chuckled. "Have your people kept them alive for us?"

Falon nodded humbly. "We have kept for you what we were told to keep, soul-man. We have waited many centuries."

The man stared toward one of the watchtowers. "If only we had trusted you! If only we had told you where the weapons were hidden. But some of the ancients said that if we gave you too much knowledge, you would destroy us when we tried to return. Now you have nothing with which to defend yourselves against our new masters."

Falon lifted his head slightly. "Weapons, you say? God-weapons?"

"Yes, they're hidden in vaults beneath the ancient cities. We sent a man to tell you where to find them. But he probably failed in his mission. Do you know anything of him? Come, man! Get off your knees!"

Self-consciously, Falon sat on the edge of his cot. "We found this man dead in the trail—last night." He paused and lowered his eyes. It had been easy to lie to the invaders, but it would be harder lying to the gods. He steeled himself for a rebuke. "The emissary failed to tell us of the god-weapons, but he told us that the invaders were not men. The tribes now know this fact. In a few hours, they will attack. Will you help us, soul-man?"

The man gasped and wrinkled his face in unbelief. "*Attack!* With only knives and spears? Android, this is insanity!"

Falon nodded. "But notice how smoke is dimming the sun,

soul-man. The forest fires are driving the people forth. They have no choice but to attack."

"It's suicide!"

Falon nodded. "But it is to save you that they do it. And to save the earth for both of us. Will you help?"

The man leaned thoughtfully against the bars. "Our people are slaves. They have learned to obey their masters. It is hard to say, android. They would rally to a hopeful cause—but this seems a hopeless one."

"So it seems. I have planted a seed in the mind of the one known as Kepol. He also thinks it is hopeless, but when he sees a certain thing, the seed may bloom into panic. He underestimates us now. If later he comes to overestimate us, we may have a chance."

"What do you propose to do?"

Falon was loath to take the initiative and tell a soul-man what to do. It seemed somehow improper to him. "Tell me," he asked cautiously, "can you fly the skyboats in which the invaders brought you?"

The man chuckled grimly. "Why not? It was our civilization that built them. The invaders were but savages on Mars, before we came to teach them our ways. They learned from us, then enslaved us. Yes, we can fly the rockets. But why do you ask?"

"I am uncertain as yet. Tell me another thing. How did the one man escape?"

The man frowned, then shook his head. "This, I shall not tell you. We were months in preparing his escape. And the way is still open. Others might follow him. I cannot trust you yet, android."

Falon made no protest. "You've told me what I want to know—that others can escape. Can many go at once?"

The man was thoughtful for a moment. "It would take a little time—to evacuate the entire man pen. But the others are already outside, working on the city."

"They will be brought back soon," Falon said dogmatically. "Wait and see."

The man smiled faintly. "You're sure of yourself, android. You tempt me to trust you."

"It would be best."

"Very well. The escape route is only a tunnel from beneath your cot to the center of the city." The man glanced around at the towers, then tossed Falon a key. "This will unlock your door. We filed it from a spoon. Let your unlocking of it be a signal. I'll speak to the others if they return, as you say."

Man and android eyed each other for a moment through the bars.

"Can you get word to the ones who are working on the city?" Falon asked.

The man nodded. "That is possible. What would you have them know?"

"Tell them to watch the forests. Tell them to set up a cry that the tribes are coming to save us."

"You think this will frighten our captors, android?"

"No, they will laugh. But when the time comes, the thought will be in their minds—and perhaps we can change it to fear."

The man nodded thoughtfully. "I suppose it can do no harm. We'll keep you informed about the fire's progress. If the wind doesn't change, it should burn quickly toward the valley."

The man departed, and Falon lay back upon the cot to think of Ea in the throne room. He had no doubt of her fate. When the king was finished with her, she would be assigned to the android pen for fattening. He had given her over into the sensual hands of the invader, and he resolved to atone for it by sheer recklessness when the time came for action. If the gods watched, then perhaps his own blood would pay for whatever she was suffering.

But another thought occupied his mind. The soul-man had called him "brother"—and the memory of the word lingered. It blended with the death-chant which Ea had sung for Daner when he went to die in the manner of his tribe—"The Song of the Soul-Empty Ones." "Brother," the man had said. Did one call an animal "brother"? Yet the man knew he was an android.

Several old men moved about in the stockade. Apparently their duties were to "keep house" for the younger laborers. Falon wondered about the women. None were visible. Perhaps they had been left upon the invaders' world. Or perhaps the invaders had other plans for women.

Soon he heard the sound of distant shouting from the direction of the city, but could make no sense of it. Apparently, however, the workmen were setting up a cry that rescue was imminent. If only they would come to believe it themselves!

The hypodermic injection was taking effect. He felt a ravenous hunger that made his stomach tighten into a knot of pain. A horrifying thought struck him suddenly, and he shouted to the men in the yard at the stockade. One of them approached him slowly.

"Tell me, soul-man," Falon breathed. "What sort of food do the invaders bring you? Is there any—meat?"

The man stiffened and turned away. "Once they brought us meat, android. Three men ate of it. We saw that the three met with . . . uh, fatal accidents. Since then, the Mars-Lords have brought us only fish and greens."

He moved away, his back rigid with insult. Falon tried to call an apology after him, but could find no words.

The sunlight was growing gloomy with the smoke of the forest fires, but the wind had died. Falon prayed that it would not reverse itself and come out of the east.

He examined his chains and found the sleeve which fastened them to the cot was loose. The soul-men had evidently pried it slightly open. Then he found that the bolts which fastened the cot legs to the concrete floor had been worked free, then returned to their places. They could be extracted with a slight tug, the plate unscrewed, and the sleeve slipped off the leg. But he left them in place, lest a guard come. Beneath the cot was a dusty sheet of steel which evidently covered the tunnel's mouth.

When a guard brought food, Falon devoured it before the creature left his cell and begged for more.

"You will be fat indeed, android," chuckled the Martian.

Toward sunset, a clamor in the courtyard told him that the soul-men were being returned to the stockade. The light had grown forge-red, and the air was acrid with faint-smoke smell. The man, who was called Penult, came again to Falon's cell.

"The smoke obscures our vision, android," he said. "The Mars-Lords have sent a patrol to police the edge of the hills, but we can longer see them." He frowned. "The lords seem worried about something. They scuttle about chattering among themselves, and they listen secretly to their radios."

"Radios?"

"The voices with which they speak to the patrol. I think they are preparing to send others. Helicopters are taking off, but the smoke must choke their visibility. What can be happening?"

"The tribes are attacking, of course," lied Falon. He noticed that the wind had arisen again. It was sweeping the smoke along in the downdrafts from the foothills.

"What are your plans, android?" asked Penult. Several others had gathered behind him, but he hissed them away lest they attract the suspicion of the watchtowers.

"Wait until the invaders become desperate and send too many on their patrols. Then we shall rise up against the ones that remain."

"Be we have no weapons."

"We have surprise. We have fear. We have your tunnel. And we must have lightning swiftness. If you can gain access to their skyboats, can you destroy them or fly them?"

Penult shook his head doubtfully. "We will discuss it among ourselves. I will see what the others wish to do." He moved away.

Dusk fell. Lights flickered on from the watchtowers, bathing the stockade in smoky brilliance. The courtyard was thronging with soul-men who wandered freely about their common barracks. Beyond the wall of the man pen, the evening was filled with angry and anxious sounds as the Mars-Lords readied more patrols for battle.

Falon knew that if they remained about the city, they would be safe. But the first patrol had undoubtedly been engulfed in the tide of wild dogs that swept from the forests. Their weapons would be ineffective in the blanket of smoke that settled about them. And the gaunt dog packs would be crazed by fear of the fire. Thousands of the brutes had rolled out across the plain, and the small patrol had been taken by surprise. The horsemen would come last. They would wait until the dogs had gone before they fled the fires. Perhaps they would arrive in time to see the dogs devouring the bodies of their gods. Perhaps then they would attack.

Penult stopped at Falon's cell. "We have managed to contact the android pen," he said. "In a few moments they will start a riot within their stockade, to distract the watchtower guards. Be ready to unlock the door."

"Good, Soul-Penult! Pick us a dozen good men to rush the towers when we come from the tunnel. Let them go first, and I will be with them."

Penult shrugged. "It is as good a way to die as any."

Falon tugged the bolts from the floor, and slipped the chain's sleeve from the leg of his cot. The manacles were still fastened to his ankles and wrists, but he decided that they might make good weapons.

One of the searchlights winked away from the courtyard. Falon watched its hazy beam stab toward the opposite end of the city. Then he heard dim sounds of distant shouting. The riot had begun. Other lights followed the first, leaving the man pen illuminated only by the floods about the walls.

Quickly he slipped from his cot and moved to the door. A soul-man sidled in front of his cell to block the view from the towers while Falon twisted the key in the lock. Then he pushed the cot aside. A man came to help him move the steel plate. They pushed it away noiselessly, and the tunnel's mouth yawned beneath them. The cell was filling with men while the guard's eyes were distracted toward the android pen.

"We are all here, android," a voice whispered.

Falon glanced doubtfully toward the courtyard. The men were thronging near the cell, kicking up dust to obscure the tower's vision. Evidently they had not seen; for Falon was certain that the invaders would not hesitate to blister the entire group with their flamethrowers if they suspected escape. Already there were sounds of explosions from the other end of the city. Perhaps they were massacring the inhabitants of the other pen. He thought grimly of Ea.

A man had lowered himself into the tunnel. Falon followed him quickly, to be swallowed by damp and cramped blackness. They proceeded on their hands and knees.

Falon called back over his shoulder. "Tell the others to wait for us to emerge before they enter."

"They're setting the barracks and the stockade walls on fire, android," hissed the man behind him. "It will provide another distraction."

It was a long crawl from the stockade to the center of the city. He thought grimly of the possibility that the tunnel would be discovered by guards coming to quench the barracks fire. The small party might emerge into the very arms of the waiting Mars-Lords.

The tunnel was not made for comfort, and Falon's chains hindered his progress. He became entangled frequently, and bruised his kneecaps as he tripped over them. There was no room to turn around. If guards met them at the exit there could be no retreat.

The lead man stopped suddenly. "We're here!" he hissed. "Help me hoist the slab of rock, android."

Falon lay upon his back and pressed his feet against the ceiling.

It moved upward. A slit of dim light appeared. The soul-man peered outside, then fell back with a whimper of fright.

"A guard!" he gasped. "Not a dozen feet away! He's watching the man pen."

Falon cursed softly and lowered the lid of the exit. "Did he see the stone move?" he asked.

"No! But he seemed to hear it."

Suddenly there was a dull thumping sound from overhead. The guard was stomping on the stone slab, listening to its hollowness.

With an angry growl, Falon tensed his legs, then heaved. The stone opened upward, carrying the guard off balance. He fell with the slab across his leg, and his shriek was but another sound in the general melee as Falon burst upon him and kicked his weapon aside. The Martian, still shrieking, fumbled at something in his belt. Falon kicked him to death before he brought it into play.

The dozen soul-men climbed out into the gloom and raced for the black shadows of a half-completed masonry wall in the heart of the growing city. One of them seized the small weapon in the guard's belt, while Falon caught up the flamethrower.

The city was lighted only by the dim smoky aura of searchlights aimed at the man pens. The riot had diminished in the android pen, but an occasional burst of sharp explosions belched toward it from one of the watchtowers. Falon's people were sacrificing themselves to draw attention away from the soul-men.

"Split in two groups!" Falon hissed. "Tackle the two nearest towers."

They separated and diverged, following the shadows of the walls. Leadership was impossible, for the operation was too hastily planned. Falon trusted in the hope that each man's mind had been long occupied with thoughts of escape, and that each knew the weakest spots in the invaders' defenses.

A few of the searchlights were stabbing out toward the west, where sounds of the dog packs were becoming faintly perceptible. Somewhere out upon the plains, the invaders' patrols were tiny island-fortresses in the infiltrating wave of dogs and horsemen. They could easily form into tight groups and defend themselves against the hordes with their explosives and flamethrowers, but they would be unable to stem the tide of flesh whose only real desire was to escape the fires. But some of the Natani might be attacking, when they saw that the dogs did not regard the Mars-Lords as their masters.

* * *

At the corner of the city, Falon's group found itself within stone's throw of a tower. They crouched in the darkness for a moment, watching the lights sweep westward. For now that the futile android riot was put down, the guards saw no threat save the unreal one on the plains. The threat's grimness was increased by the shroud of smoke that hid it and gave it mystery in the Martian eyes.

The man who had seized the belt weapon nudged Falon and whispered, "I'll stay here and cover your dash, android."

Falon nodded and glanced around quickly. They would be within the floodlights' glow, once they bounded across the wall-scurrying targets for all the towers. Suddenly he gasped. A man was running up the ladder of the tower to which the other group had gone. A searchlight caught him in its pencil. Then a blast of machine-gun fire plucked him off and sent him pitching earthward.

"Hurry!" Falon barked, and leaped across the wall.

They sprinted single file toward the base of the tower. A light winked down to splash them with brilliance. The man fired from the shadows behind them, and the light winked out. Dust sprayed up about Falon's feet as the guards shot from overhead. A streak of flame lanced downward, and two of the men screamed as it burst upward in a small inferno. The covering fire brought a guard hurtling from the tower. Falon leaped over his body and began scaling the steel ladder toward the cage.

A roar of voices came from the man pens. The barracks were blazing while a handful of guards played hoses over the walls.

Falon climbed steadily, expecting at an moment to feel a searing burst of flame spray over him. But the guards above him were firing blindly toward the shadows whence came the covering fire. And the other towers were playing their lights about their own skirts, watching for similar attacks.

A slug ricocheted off the hatchway as he burst through it into the cage. Another tore through his thigh as he whipped the chain in a great arc, lashing it about the legs of one of the guards. He jerked the creature off his feet, then dived at the other, who was trying to bring a machine gun into play. The android's attack swept him off balance, and Falon heaved him bodily from the tower.

Another man burst through the hatch and disposed of the guard who was being dragged about by Falon's chain.

Falon threw himself to the floor as a burst of bullets sprayed the open space above the waist-high steel walls of the cage. The nearest tower had opened fire upon them. Falon leaped for the permanently mounted flamethrower and sent a white-hot jet arcing toward the other cage. It fell short. He tried another burst, arcing it higher. It splashed home and the incendiary made a small furnace of the other tower, from which the guards hastily descended. The other towers were beyond flame-gun range, but they sprayed Falon's newly won outpost with machine-gun fire.

"Lie flat!" shouted the man. "The armor will turn back the bullets."

Falon flung himself headlong while the rain of small-arms fire pelted the steel walls. He ripped a sleeve from his rawhide jacket and made a tourniquet for his flesh wound. "Where are the other four?" he gasped.

"Dead," shouted his companion above the din.

A crashing roar came from the direction of the man pen. The barrage suddenly ceased. Falon chanced a glance over the low rim of the cage. One wall of the flaming stockade had collapsed, and men were pouring through the broken gap to overwhelm the firemen. The towers were turning their weapons upon the torrent of escapees. Falon's companion manned the machine gun and turned it on the invaders. "We'll draw their fire!" he called.

The second group had taken their objective, and another tower had fallen into the rebels' hands. Men poured through the stockade gap while the towers exchanged fire among themselves.

"They're trying to make it to the ships!" the gunner called. Then he fell back with half his face torn away.

Falon crawled to the gun and tried to operate it, but being unfamiliar with the god-weapons, he was only exposing himself to death. He dropped it in favor of the flamethrower, lay beside the hatch, and shot down at the occasional unfortunate Martian that scurried within his range.

Several of the towers were silent now, including the other captive one. Falon slipped through the hatch and climbed down the steel ladder. His descent went unnoticed as the battle raged about the city and among the ships. He noticed that fire was spurting from several rockets, but they were still in the hands of the invader; for the man pen's escapees were still fighting for possession of the nearest ship.

* * *

Falon sprinted for the city's wall as a pair of wild dogs attacked him from the shadows. He fried them with a blast from the flame gun, then hurdled the wall and climbed atop a heap of masonry. Most of the lights were out now, and the darkness was illuminated only by the flaming stockade. The wild-dog packs were trotting in from the west, mingling in the battle to attack man, android, and Martian alike.

One of the ships blasted off into the night, but Falon felt certain that it was not commanded by men. It was the throne ship, in which the king resided. Another followed it; but the second seemed to be piloted by the escapees.

The battle had become chaos. Falon stumbled through the masonry, stepping over an occasional body, and looking for a fight. But most of the Martians had taken up positions about the ships. He noticed that few of them were among the dead, who were mostly men and androids. But the rebels could afford to lose more than the Martians.

A few horsemen were joining the fray as the battle on the plains moved eastward. They rode into the tides of flesh that rolled about the ships. Falon saw a rider spit a Martian on his dog-spike and lift him to the saddle. The Martian shot him, then fell back to be trampled by the horse.

The two ships were returning. Falon flung himself down behind a wall as the throne ship shrieked past, splashing a wide swath of blinding brightness down the length of the city. The second ship, which had been in hot pursuit, nosed upward and spiraled off over the ocean to make a wide circle in the opposite direction. Falon, sensing a sky battle, ducked quickly out of the city's walls, caught the bridle of a runaway horse, and swung into the saddle.

The throne ship was coming back for another run, while the other was streaking back from the south. Falon realized vaguely what the man-pilot meant to do. He glanced toward the ground battle. It had subsided, and the warriors were scurrying for cover. Shrieks of "Collision!" and "Explosion!" arose from the mobs.

Hardly knowing what to expect, Falon decided quickly to follow their example. He reined the mare to a standstill, then swung out of the saddle and clung to her flank, hiding himself from the approaching ships. He saw them come together as he ducked his head behind the mare's neck.

The ground beneath him became bathed in pale violet. Then a dazzling and unearthly brilliance made him close his eyes. For several seconds there was no sound, save the snarls of the dog packs. Then the force of a thousand avalanches struck him. He fell beneath the mare, still guarding his face behind her neck. The breath went out of him in a surge of blackness. He struggled for a moment, then lay quietly in ever-deepening night.

Daylight awakened him, gloomy gray dawnlight. The mare had tried to stagger to her feet, but had fallen again a few feet away. The valley was silent, save for the whisper of ocean breakers in the distance. He sat up weakly and knew that some of his ribs were broken. He looked around.

The plain was littered with bodies of dogs, men, and Martians. A spiral of smoke arose lazily from the wreckage. Then he saw figures moving about in the ruins. He managed a feeble shout, and two of them approached him. One was man, the other android. He knew neither of them, but the man seemed to recognize him as the prisoner who had occupied the cell in the man pen. Falon lowered his head and moaned with pain. The man knelt beside him.

"We've been looking for you, android," he murmured.

Falon glanced at the destruction again, and murmured guiltily. The man chuckled, and helped him to his feet. "We've got a chance now," he said. "We can go to the ancient cities for the hidden weapons before the Martians can send a fleet. Mars won't even find out about it for a while. The ships were all damaged in that blast."

"Were many killed?"

"Half of us perhaps. You androids are lucky. Our ancestors gave you a resistance against radiation burns—so you wouldn't mutate from the residual radioactivity left by the last war."

Falon failed to understand. "Not so lucky," he muttered. "*Our* dead do not go to the Place of Watching."

The man eyed him peculiarly, then laughed gently. Falon flushed slightly; for the laughter had seemed to call him a child.

"Come, android," the man said. "People are waiting for you."

"Who?"

"A surly old codger who says he's your father, and a girl who says she's your woman."

Falon moved a few steps between them, then sagged heavily.

"He's unconscious," said the android, "or dead."

They lifted him gently in their arms. "Hell!" grunted the human. "Did you ever see a dead man *grin?*"

DEFENDER OF THE FAITH

Alfred Coppel

Science fiction does not have to be conventional or gentle, as this story shows, so long as it is interesting and has a point to make. This author was reasonably prolific during the period I consider to be the Golden Age of science fiction (but this period differs for each reader), the late 1940s to early 1950s. When I looked up the name in my references, I discovered to my surprise that he is Hispanic: his proper name is Alfredo José de Marini y Coppel, Jr. (But that's not the only handsome Hispanic name in the genre: Lester del Rey's full name is a small paragraph long.) Anyway, I like this savage short story. I have been called a sexist, apparently because I poke fun at women as well as at men, and I wonder whether this story shows the type of world my accusers would prefer.

—PA

Coppel, like John D. MacDonald, published a good quantity of science fiction in the 1940s and early 1950s at the outset of his career, showed himself to have an excellent command of the genre, and then departed for other fields; in his case the documentary novel and the juvenile. Unlike MacDonald, he did not achieve best-selling status in his later field of endeavor, and his science fiction has languished, being neither collected nor often reprinted. "Genemaster" was one of the very few stories he did for the field after 1952.

—bnm

Mention should be made of two excellent novels by Coppel, Dark December (1960), a riveting account of one man's search for his family across an America decimated by nuclear war, and The Burning Mountain (1983). This latter work is a wonderful alternate history in which the test of the first nuclear weapon at Los Alamos ends in failure, and the Allies actually invade the Japanese home islands. The book, which was almost totally ignored by the science-fiction community (I know of no reviews in SF media), stands comparison with the best works of its type, although it is basically a war story. Several other books by Coppel, especially Thirty-four East *(1974), while essentially "thrillers," can also be considered SF.*

MHG

The teacher's voice droned on and on in the stuffy room. Jere, weary from a six-hour patrol, could scarcely stay awake. Her head bobbed, and Ella jabbed an elbow into her ribs. "Keep your eyes open," she whispered.

Jere straightened with an effort, squaring her shoulders. A world of fatigue seemed to be pressing down on her, and she had the rebellious thought that patrolling wasn't fit work for a woman. Ella was looking disapprovingly at her, lips compressed. Jere squirmed uncomfortably, more conscious of the hard stool and the glaring fluorotubes than of the teacher's endless repetitions.

—*at least,* Jere thought, *she might try and make it interesting.*

The teacher, wearing major's leaves on her blouse, was grinding out the same line, the one that never changed. If Jere had heard it once, she had heard it a million times.

—*all right,* she thought sulkily, *I believe it. It's all true. So what?*

The major was saying that San Francisco was entitled to free access to natural resources: oil, fissionables, men—and that was the reason for the war. It seemed to Jere that the Three-Cornered War had been going on ever since she could remember. When it wasn't against Los Angeles and Denver, it was Phoenix or Reno. Always someone. There simply wasn't enough of anything to go around— particularly men.

At 2100 hours, the class ended and the Scouts filed out of the classroom stiffly, aching from the two-hour ordeal on the uncommonly uncomfortable stools.

From the window of the small room she shared with Ella and two other girls of her section, Jere could see the bomb-shattered city spread out below. To the north were twisted towers that the older women claimed once supported a bridge across the narrow mouth of the bay; in the west, the ruins of what had once been

Oakland glowed with an eerie radioactive light. A full moon rode high in the sky.

"Bomber's moon," Ella said uneasily.

"Denver has no planes," Jere replied, slipping off her uniform blouse.

"They have missiles," Ella declared; "while you were out a dud landed in the bay." She sniffed scornfully. "Interception was terrible."

"Interception generally is."

Jere lay gratefully on her hard pallet and closed her eyes. But Ella stood at the window, contemplating the moonlight. "Jere," she said. "Did you hear about the men?"

Jere opened her eyes. "Which men?"

"The ones Captain Belle's section captured yesterday."

"How many?"

"Twenty, I think."

Jere whistled softly. "Denvers?"

"No. Angelenos."

"That should bring reprisals, all right; those L.A. witches won't take it lying down." She pursed her lips, staring at the roof. "Where are they now?"

Ella shrugged. "In the breeder pens." She gave a short, bitter laugh. "We won't get any."

"Men aren't for the Fighting Sections, Ella," Jere said gently.

"Why aren't they?" Ella demanded. "We do all the work, take all the risks."

"The men are for the Mother Sections, Ella," Jere said. "It's always been that way." And then, because she could see that Ella was unsatisfied with her answer, she added: "Pen-men are no good anyway. You've seen them. Fat and white. Ugly, I'd say."

Ella sat down on the bed and kicked off her flight boots. "What would you know about it?"

"Nothing," Jere admitted. "But I know some Mother Section people who've seen wild ones; they say they're much handsomer."

"Savages," Ella said.

"Maybe." Jere stretched and closed her eyes again. Once, she had had a series of dreams about a world where there was a man for each woman. A strange sort of place without ruins or missiles or Three-Cornered War. It had been pleasant to dream like that, but she'd told someone and Psycho Section had taken her in hand and explained the dreams away. It was always dangerous, they told her, to dream like that; such ideas, even in sleep, endangered the Matriarchy itself. For three months she had gone to sleep with a somnoteacher whispering in her ears. The dreams never came back, though she thought of them often.

The undulating wail of the attack alarm interrupted her reverie. A harsh voice crackled from the wall speaker.

"Radarplot has picked up jetcraft fifty miles south of the city. All Interception Section pilots man their craft. All Scout Section pilots stand by to assist. Mother Sections to shelter."

"So Denver has no planes," Ella said breathlessly, pulling on her boots.

"Angelenas, dear," Jere said, getting to her feet. "Probably Beesixfours. Damn them anyway."

In the far distance, flakguns had begun their usual futile hacking at the sky. The whine of jets warming and milling about on the flight decks filled the city.

Ella and Jere ran down the corridors, crowded with women, toward the hangar deck. From the Mother Section areas, a great squalling and shrieking filled the building with noise; far under the ground, the men were being herded into steel and concrete vaults for safekeeping.

On the hangar deck, there was some measure of order; interceptors were being trundled out onto the flight deck, and a few missiles were being loaded into the catapult launchers. The two-place scoutcraft were being refueled and their guns armed.

Jere found her own ship near the end of the line. Her radar operator, a thin-faced girl with stringy hair leaking out from under her helmet, was standing by.

"Are we fueled, May?" Jere asked, struggling into her flight gear.

"They haven't fixed the tail gun," May said unhappily. "Is it Angelenas, Miss Jere? Oh, Mother! I was afraid it would be them ever since I heard about the men: those Angelenas really fight, they do."

"We'll do all right, May," Jere said, with an assurance she didn't feel, thinking of multiple pompom guns on the Beesixfours. "Those jetcraft are old as the hills."

May cast a doubting eye at the scarred flank of their own machine. "So's ours," she said sourly.

The steady crumping noise of the flakguns ceased as the first flight of interceptors took the air. The silence was thick; then the thin, whistling noise of Beesixfours filtered down onto the waiting city. Jere estimated there were at least ten of them.

"Why're we always fighting, Miss Jere?" May demanded suddenly. "Bombing and stealing and fighting all the time—"

"May!"

"I'm sorry, Miss Jere," May said. "I didn't mean to talk like that. I'm nervous, I guess—"

"All right," Jere said. "We both know better than to ask questions like that. Thank God, there wasn't anybody from Guard Section to hear you or I'd be riding without radar tonight. Let's forget it."

"Thanks, miss," May said.

"Scout Section craft stand by to support interception!" The words of the Fighter Controller came through the wall speakers, cutting through the clangor of the hangar deck.

"Interception flubbed it again," May said bitterly.

As though to accent her words, there was a thunderous roar in the distance.

"Hit in the bay," Jere said. In her mind she could see the mounting column of glowing water. "I wonder how many got it along the waterfront." Tomorrow, and for weeks, there would be radioactive mist in the air; people would die slowly, retching, with their hair falling out in clumps. "Damn them, damn them!"

"Blue Scout Section scramble!" the speaker shrieked.

—*this is a bad one,* Jere thought. *A maximum effort.* The Angelenas were really seething tonight.

"We'll be next, May," Jere said. "We can't wait for the gun. Get aboard."

Sitting in the vibrating jet, Jere could see Ella's blue-winged craft moving into takeoff position. There was a flicker of blue fire from the nozzle and the flutter of a white scarf as Ella waved. Then she was gone, streaking up into the night.

High overhead a fission bomb flared, white-hot. From seventy thousand feet, it etched the city in light, blotting out the moon.

Jere wondered how many plutonium bombs the attackers were carrying. There had been a great deal of talk about a new thorium reactor in Los Angeles, and a growing stockpile of bombs. She had taken pictures of the supposed installation herself, not less than a month before, from a hundred thousand feet.

Her practiced eyes flicked over the battered dials on the panel. The turbine was vibrating terribly, but there wasn't a machine shop in San Francisco capable of repairing it to original specifications, and the motor itself was nearly a hundred years old. It dated from the era before the Three-Cornered War—a time when there were still men who could fly and work and fight. Though they did not fight other cities then, Jere wondered briefly if such a time had ever really been at all. History said that the Matriarchy had always existed; but legend claimed that once there were as many men as women and that they had been the rulers. The thought was incomprehensible.

—those fat, white breeders?

Yet the old women claimed it was so, and they said that wars had decimated the male population—until now there were so few that women had to fight for them.

—breed or die. The slogan. The cause.

—we fight, all right, Jere thought bitterly, *we fight for a handful of men, of whom perhaps seventy percent are sterile and have to be destroyed. We fight for a puddle of uncontaminated water. A pile of hard coal. A half-ruined factory or a barren field.*

"Red Flight scramble!"

The command drove the rebellious thoughts from her mind and she rolled the jet forward, toward the gaping dark mouth of the hangar. Her lips moved very silently as she repeated to herself the short prayer she had used before battle since girlhood.

Great Mother God protect your servant Jere, a Fighter for the Right and a Defender of the Faith. Give me victory and give my city fertility and safety and unmarked young—

As she emerged onto the flight deck, Jere could see a large section of the wooden structures along the waterfront burning, ignited by the flash of the bomb in the bay. She cursed the Angelenas through set lips, and lined her jetcraft up with the runway, throttling that uneven engine with a practiced hand.

"Ready, May?" she asked into the intercom.

The girl's reply came back muffled. "Ready, miss. I wish we had the gun, though; I really do."

"Don't worry about it now," Jere snapped. "Does the radar work?"

"I got a blip, miss," May said.

The Red Flight leader was vanishing down the deck, spitting sparks from her half-tuned engine. Jere saw her ship vanish below the level of the runway and dip into the deep canyon between buildings; she held her breath until she saw the glowing nozzle of the jetcraft clear and climbing steeply.

Jere ran the throttle forward, and the scout picked up speed with a sickening rush. The dim blue lights at the end of the runway hurtled under the sharply swept-back wings and they were airborne, banking low over the burning waterfront, and swinging out over the still-churning waters of the bay.

The geig began to chatter as they skirted the radioactive cloud and cut back, spiraling upward in an ever-tightening, ever-steepening climb.

"Clear contact," May reported. "They're at seventy thousand feet course two hundred and forty-five degrees. Probably making another bomb run."

—*exactly what they're doing,* Jere thought. And they wouldn't waste another fission bomb on the bay. Target would be the breeding pens and the vaults. What they couldn't keep, they'd destroy if they could.

A streak of fire raced down from the sky, falling like a stone. An interceptor shot down. Jere felt the old familiar stirring of the blood, the thrill of battle. She had the feeling of wishing her fingers had claws and that they might be tearing into the flesh of the women in the night-riding bombers.

—*this world,* she thought, *this bleak world. It's a way of life. MY way of life. Maybe things were better once, maybe life was like those erotic dreams, but this is the way it is NOW and that's what counts. Women should FIGHT. . . .*

"Change course to oh-one-nine," May said.

Jere swung the jet around, still climbing. The moonlight was taking on the peculiar crystal brilliance of high flight. The altimeter needle touched fifty-thousand feet. Outside, on the frames of the pressurized Plexiglas rime ice was forming.

"Change to oh-two-four," May said through the intercom. "Four bogies."

Jere banked the jet until the gyro held steady on the new course. "Anything from IFF?"

"Nothing, Miss Jere," said May's metallic voice in her helmetphones. "We might just as well be all alone up here."

From the moonlit darkness beneath them, a trio of rocket trails came streaking up and past. Five thousand feet above them, there was a fiery blast as one missile found a bomber and disintegrated it.

"Oh, Mother," May said; "they actually hit something."

"That'll shake them up," Jere said with satisfaction.

Pieces of the burning bomber rained down around them, and Jere zigzagged the jet skillfully to avoid them.

"We're up with them, miss," May reported. "You can pick them up on your screen now—if you can get it working."

The tiny radar screen in Jere's panel flicked on and the bombers were there, three of them now, etched in a greenish light. Jere centered them on the grid and armed the wing rockets.

"Closing," Jere reported.

"It'll be on the guns," May said.

The altimeter needle hovered near seventy-thousand feet. The night sky was black as pitch, and the stars and moon glittered like bits of jewel. Ahead, Jere could catch the glint of metal flanks and the soft bluish glow of the Beesixfours' jets.

Far below, there was a sudden fireball and a rising mushroom of flame; the bombers swung about sharply to the south.

"That was a bad one, miss," May whispered in a choked voice. "Oh, that was really a bad one."

—damn them, damn them, Jere *thought. We try to live and they come up with their bombers and their raiding—*

She forgot entirely about the breeders in the vaults that had caused the raid. She thought only of her city, shuddering under the impact of bombs, and the heavy, cowering women of the Mother Sections huddling in the dark shelters. Under her face mask, her lips pulled back in a savage grimace of hate. She triggered the first flight of rockets and they swept out of the wing tubes in a shower of reddish fire.

"Missed! Damn!"

She closed further on the fleeing bombers, arming the next flight of missiles. There were flashes of fire up ahead, and the arching trail of incendiary bullets streaking past at unbelievable speeds. The pompom guns on the bombers were blazing at the pursuing jet.

May had swung the turret around, forgetting about the useless tail guns, and was firing over Jere's head at the dark shapes ahead. The jet was filled with the stench of cordite. It vibrated to the heavy thudding of the twin twenty-millimeter guns.

Jere caught the last bomber in the line ahead and centered it in the radarscope. The rockets flashed out and the Beesixfour erupted in a gout of oily flame. Jere's scout flashed through the fire and on toward the next raider.

"Parasite fighter, miss!" May shouted.

A tiny jet had left the parent bomber and was somewhere behind them. Jere's mouth went dry; she pulled the scout around in a tight turn. The wingtips stalled and she lost speed and altitude correcting. Streaks of red whipped past the Plexiglas of her cockpit. The parasite was closing in from behind and she couldn't shake free.

She felt suddenly very tired; her movements of the controls were leaden, fatigued. She heard the crash of metal tearing and a high-pitched whine of pressure escaping from the cockpit.

"Miss! Help me, Jere—I'm hit!"

"May!"

No reply. Jere shoved the nose down into a streaking dive. The parasite followed. A stream of explosive shells found the wingtips, moved in. The scout buffeted erratically, and its agony whipped over into a bone-wrenching spin. Jere heard herself praying—

—great Mother God protect your servant Jere a Fighter for the Right and a Defender of the Faith—

The cockpit was full of smoke and flame, and still the parasite followed, blazing away.

"May, jump!"

There was no reply. Jere twisted around to look back; there was dark blood on the transparent canopy.

She pulled back the shell and stood up. A million wind devils snatched at her and then she was falling free, through star-shot darkness and freezing cold. With the last of her strength, she pulled the ripcord and the ribbonchute streamed out of its pack. There was a jarring impact as it opened, and then nothing. . . .

Jere opened her eyes in bright sunlight. There was deep grass under her. For a time, she didn't know what it was—for she had never been outside the city except by air, and there was almost no vegetation at all in the irradiated ground of San Francisco.

A man squatted by her side. A man unlike any Jere had ever seen.

She thought—*a wild one.*

He was burned dark from the sun, and he was dressed in a shirt of animal skins and little else. His face was bearded and across his bare shoulders hung a rifle of archaic design.

"We heard the fight last night," he said.

Jere said nothing. Her hands grasped her own weapons, and found them untouched.

"You women are really making a mess of things, you know," he said.

"Where am I?" Jere said, ignoring his insolence.

"Near Saratoga?"

"What's Saratoga?"

"It used to be a town." He shifted easily on his haunches, with an animal's lithe movements.

"How far from the city?"

He grinned, showing sharp white teeth through the dark bush of his beard. "What city?"

"San Francisco, of course," Jere said indignantly. "Did you take me for an Angelena?"

"You all look alike," he said; "you all look alike to me."

Jere ignored the insult and said: "How far from San Francisco."

"Sixty miles, maybe; depends on how you go."

"I must get back."

"Yes? Why?"

Jere sat up, and unhooked her chute harness. What would this stupid savage know about the need for fighters to protect the Matriarchy? It would be useless to explain.

"You can't get back," he said finally. "The guard-robots wouldn't let you through; they never let anyone through."

Jere thought about that. It was true that she had never been out of the city on the ground. And it was also true the guards never let anyone approach any city. How else could a city be protected? No Fighting Section woman lost outside the city had ever returned.

"You wise girls have fixed things good," the man said, grinning. "You've cut the cities off from any possible contact with the people who live in between the cities. And with all the fighting you do, no one ever gets a chance to change things. You fight mostly over men, don't you?" There was a peculiarly suggestive and irritating inflection in his voice.

Jere felt an impulse to put him in his place. "Men," she said stiffly. "Not wild animals."

The man picked a straw of green grass and thrust it between his lips. "You may have something there," he said. "But it seems to me you're missing a bet. There are men about, even if they are a bit on the wild side. They'd sort of like to get things started again—" He looked at her appraisingly.

Jere quite suddenly remembered all the lectures, the reiterated statements, the history she had learned—

—*after male domination had almost wrecked the world, the women established the Matriarchy for the survival of the race. Men are wicked, quarrelsome, dirty, untrustworthy, and savage. Only a few picked specimens can be tolerated, and those only by the self-sacrificing women of the Mother Sections who subject themselves to them as an act of Faith so that the race might survive—*

"Like the old days," Jere said scornfully.

"The old days weren't so bad, I hear tell," the man said. "I know men didn't do such a good job of running the world, but you women haven't even done as well."

"We're surviving," Jere said positively. "And that's what counts."

"So are we," the man said. "And our women aren't filled up with all those goofball things they teach you city women; they tell you that men are no good—mainly because there aren't enough of them to go around."

Jere got to her feet. "I don't have to listen to this," she said.

The man stood beside her. "Oh, but you do."

Jere stared at him.

"Because, you see, you belong to me now. I found you."

"Are you mad?"

"I must be," he said showing those white teeth, "even to think of taking on another city woman. You fighters are all devils to get along with, but I've done it before and I guess I can do it again."

"*Another city woman?*" Jere was too stunned to say more.

"Sure. I got three wives; you'll be the fourth. Two of them are from Phoenix; they were shot down in a raid on Frisco—I found them and patched them up. They were hard to get on with for a while, but they learned. Life isn't so bad out here, you know; we get along. And someday, there will be enough of us men to go back to the cities and make all you crazy females quit bombing each other all to hell."

"Great Mother!" Jere backed away from him and reached for her pistol. He moved so swiftly she hardly knew what struck her. There was a stinging pain across her face and the pistol was flying through the air. He stopped, picked it up, and shoved it into his waistband.

"Now come along, like a good girl," he said.

* * *

His camp was two days' hike from where he found her; since she was unused to making her way on foot through the woods, he made a concession to her and they stopped for the night by a small stream.

The water, to her surprise, was uncontaminated. She watched while he stripped and bathed—always with his weapons near at hand.

He shot a brace of small birds—of a kind unknown to Jere, who knew only the ugly mutated sea gulls that infested the city—and they made a meal of them as the sun sank below the western hills.

"You're being a good girl," he said approvingly, watching her. "There's no use fighting the inevitable. You'll like it once you get used to living away from the city. No crazy dames in bombers trying to atomize you; no uniforms and saluting and acting like a bunch of tin soldiers. Plenty to eat out here."

"Why don't the men come back to the cities?" Jere asked, thinking of the strength it would give San Francisco to have a real surplus of males.

"Why, first off, there's the guard-robots. But I suppose they could be gotten around someway. Mainly it's because there aren't enough of us yet; we wouldn't take kindly to being a natural resource. And a lot of us here are sterile from the radiation, too. You know they'd never keep a sterile man alive in the city. Breed or die; isn't that what they teach you in the towns?"

"Yes, it is."

"Now look." He bent over and drew a map in the dirt. The lines were clear and etched in the firelight. "Here's where we're going. See?" He named the confluence of two streams that Jere knew well from the air. "That's our camp. There are maybe a hundred and fifty men there, with their wives. About three hundred and sixty people in all; well hidden. We're going to make that into a town one day, and then we won't have to hide from city raiders. When that's done, we'll make other towns; together, all of us will fix it so's we can get back into the cities and stop all this foolishness about women blowing themselves up over a few males. Oh, things'll be fine then; they really will. Maybe you'll live to see it. Your children will, and that's sure."

—a hundred and fifty men! A wealth of males. If San Francisco had those for itself—

Jere said: "It's a fine dream."

"You bet it is. Oh, people have buggered up the world—but time will come when things are good again."

—a hundred and fifty men!

Jere looked at the lines etched in the dirt. So many times she had flown over that spot, never knowing.

The night grew dark in the forest, and the fire died to a bed of embers. The man slipped an arm over Jere's shoulders. "You see? Isn't this better?"

"Of course."

—a hundred and fifty!

"You'll be all right."

"I'll be all right."

For the first time in her life, Jere was kissed.

The fire died.

Jere lay open-eyed beside the man, listening to his heavy, regular breathing. The stars, through the intertwining branches of the trees, seemed closer then they ever had through the thick plastic of a jetcraft.

She twisted on her side to look at him. His bare chest, black in the darkness, rose and fell evenly. He slept heavily, confidently.

Jere remembered the bombers in the night and May dying trapped in a metal shell nine miles in the sky. The red blossoming of a bomb gutting a city and the lingering radiance of the deep craters where nothing lived. The bare rooms of the Fighting Sections where unsexed women lived out barren, hungry lives with nothing to assuage their pangs but the cold fury of battle with their sisters.

The fat, white men in the pens, weak and soft to the touch, and the heavy-footed women in the Mother Sections praying for undeformed infants, while the night outside wailed and shrieked with attack alarms.

—great Mother God protect Jere a Defender of the Faith—
—things could be different.

Jere rolled away from the sleeping man and sat up, thinking.

—a hundred and fifty men. If San Francisco had those men—
—breed or die.

She covered herself against the cold and got to her knees, reaching. It was there, glinting in the early-morning moonlight. Her hand touched cold metal, squeezed it.

She remembered the map scratched into the dirt with a stick. One hundred and fifty men, all healthy; a wealth of men.

She stood up, a small, taut figure in the darkness. The man stirred, opened his eyes. They were wide, looking up at her out of a face in shadows.

"Jere—" he said.

She squeezed the trigger and a flat crack died into silence through the glades. The man stiffened—

"Jere—"

She fired again.

Dawn was breaking as she gathered her gear and began walking north, toward the city. The man had told her that the guard-robots could be passed—someway. She'd find the way. And in her mind she carried a map—a map that could lead a raiding party to a spot where a camp lay hidden near the confluence of two streams. A camp with one hundred and fifty healthy males for the breeding pens of San Francisco.

She walked swiftly, head high, trying not to remember the long night. For after all, men were such fools—and she was a Defender of the Faith.

ALL OF YOU

James V. McConnell

I understand the author was the editor of Worm Runner's Digest, one of the great nefarious scientific publications. (I love it when the worm turns, though this is not precisely what that digest is about. As I recall, they cut up educated flatworms and fed them to other flatworms, and the others became educated. Interesting implications for education.) Here, as promised, is the romance—perhaps not quite the kind you expected. But what truer love can there be than this?

—PA

Kornbluth's "The Mindworm" takes seriously what the famous iconoclast McConnell uses for offhand, surrealistic attack reminiscent of Ionesco or the latter-day Jules Feiffer. I find the story, for that reason, even more disturbing than Kornbluth's creditable but probably overanthologized work.

—bnm

Ann Arbor–based James McConnell is the author of at least two wonderful stories ineligible for inclusion in this book, both published in IF in the mid-fifties—the short novel "Avoidance Situation," and "Learning Theory," one of the great stories about psychology and psychologists. McConnell is on my list of writers who I wish would either have written more or (only if alive) resume their careers; this list is considerably shorter than my list of writers who I wish had never written science fiction, but then quantity isn't everything.

—MHG

How well I remember you, my darling. I see you even now as I saw you then, that strange orange evening when your silver steed

76

plunged down to find a haven upon my world of Frth. Even these months hence I can picture in exact detail the full male warmth of your glorious body as it was that hallowed night. I can recall in minuteness the wavy black and silver of your hair, the soothing ruddiness of your complexion, and the enticing brownness of your eyes.

Run, run, oh, my darling!

I had been with the other women that first night and was returning to my dwelling by myself when I saw the tongue of flame lash across the sky. For a moment I thought the gods were spitting fire at me. But then the flame melted to earth a short distance away, its amber heat searing the foliage to a charred blue. And through the flame I made out the silver sheen of your carriage.

You will never understand the emotions that caught at me when I realized who and what you might be! When I was young, the Matriarch had mentioned the coming of gods who rode in fiery chariots, but in the intervening years I had lapsed into disbelief. And suddenly, as if to prove the error of my lagging faith, you appeared. Will you ever comprehend the overwhelming sensations I felt that night?

I ran to you then with the speed of a thousand, as you must run tonight.

Faster, my love, faster! Tonight your fear must give you wings!

The fire had burned a path to your chariot when I reached it, and I ran through the hot ashes heedless of the pain to my naked feet. For I knew that you must be inside, waiting for me to come to you. The door was open, and so I entered.

And you were there, crouched behind some monstrous piece of metal, hoping, perhaps, to shield your glorious body from my sight. But I looked and saw your wonderful stature and knew at once that my heart was lost to you forever. The empathetic organs of my body began to pulsate with devotion. My mind reached out and touched at yours, offering to you the utter devotion of an eternal slave.

What a delicious thing it is to recall the delicate trembling of your beautiful jowls as you looked at me, determining, I am sure, my worth and worthiness. But I had faith. Remember that, my darling. I knew that you would not deny me the companionship I so avidly sought.

For a long time—what a horribly delightful time it was for me!—you stayed huddled in your corner, immobile save for the scarcely perceptible quivering of your tantalizing body. Until I could stand it no longer and moved forward to caress you. And you opened your eyes widely as if to see me better and raised your hands in the universal sign of acceptance and resignation. And I knew that you were mine!

I reached my long and hopelessly slender arms around the glory of your soft and yielding torso and felt the rapid and elated beating of your heart. And I led you gently from your heavenly steed to the quiet coolness of my love-dwelling.

I awoke before you did that bright morning after the night you came to me. For a long time I lay beside you, thrilled by the warmth of your flesh, my eyes closed to the delicious experience. And then, you too awoke and my mind made contact with yours.

"Where am I?"

As you spoke these words your eyes traveled up and down the length of my reeling body. I entered your mind half hesitantly, fearful of what I would find there. For I am still young and ill formed, running to slenderness instead of to the corpulence that is the universal mark of beauty.

But, oh, my darling, what a great and overwhelming pleasure it was to find that you seemed to approve of what you saw, and in your mind I beheld visions of pleasures which I had before then only dreamed of. Somehow, to you, I seemed beautiful, and was glad.

And then I felt the tenor of your thinking shift and you repeated, "Where am I?"

I told you with my mind, and then again with my voice. But still you did not understand. And so I drew on the ground a picture of the sun and the other five planets and wrote FRTH in large letters by ours, the sixth planet, and made you realize that this was where you were. Then I pointed to the fifth planet and again at you.

In your supreme cleverness you caught on at once.

"No," you said softly, "I am not from there." You drew on the ground some distance away another sun, surrounded by nine planets, and pointed out the third. "Here's my home."

You smiled then and lay back on the couch. Your mind clouded a bit, and although I could follow all your thoughts, many of them seemed strange and incomprehensible.

"Good ole Mother Earth. Home, sweet home. I don't even know where it is from here. Lost, that's what I am, lost. Maybe I'll never see New York again, never again eat clam chowder, never watch another baseball game, never again see her.''

You began to cry. I reached out to you, taking you into my arms, running my fingers slowly through your hair, sending you comforting and sympathetic thoughts.

''I hated it. I despised Earth—loathed it. And everybody on it,'' you wept. ''Most of all I hated her. Oh, I loved her, but I came to hate her. Can you understand?''

But now, my heart's desire, you must not wail, you must not tarry. Oh, there! . . . You've stumbled! Get up, my love! Stand up and run! For death is close behind you!

That first night away from you, how my body ached with loneliness, how I longed for the enveloping warmness of your soft and pliable flesh! But I held myself firm to my purpose, for by then my plan was complete.

The next day I visited you at the man-compound. How proud and attractive you looked, how you stood out in beauty from the so poorly formed male specimens of Frth's impoverished race.

I brought to you that day the richest, most pungently flavored foods to be found in Frth. Day by day I tempted you to eat, adding pound after pound of handsomeness to your already perfect body. The Matriarch watched my every move jealously, but with a secret smile. For she planned to have you for herself. That, I and all my sisters understood.

And so I let her watch and smile, for she knew nothing of my plan. And I, alone, knew that she would be forced to accept one of the shabby, overmuscular Frthian males in your place. How I hated her!

For three long months I fed you. Then, one morning, the Matriarch stopped me as I came away from the man-compound.

''Why do you waste so much of your time and company on the foreign man-god?'' she asked me tauntingly, a twisted grin on her face. ''Do you not realize that in just two more nights the mating season will begin and the man-compound will be opened to all the eligible women in Frth?''

''I do this because I love him, Most Venerable One, and because I cannot do otherwise, no matter what the outcome.''

''Ah, it is well. You are young and fleet of foot. Perhaps you will outdistance the others after all,'' she said.

But I knew it to be a lie. She would never have allowed you in

the open competition. However, I did not care. For I alone knew
that you would be mine long before then.

Late that evening I slipped away from my dwelling and hid beside the man-compound where you were an unwilling prisoner.
The guards were few, for all but one or two were resting well for
the festivities that would begin the following night. All that night
they would spend in sacred dancing and celebration, and with the
first rays of the sun the next morning, the doors to the man-
compound would be opened to them. This year's pitiful crop of
just-maturing males would be up for competition, going to the
fleetest of the eligible women.

I waited for hours, hesitantly, frightened, wondering if my plan
would work.

And then, I felt creep over me the wonderful sensation of wom-
anhood, and I knew I had won!

I had outguessed the Matriarch! She had forgotten that when a
woman of our race first comes to maturity, the mating cycle is
often out of harmony with the rest of our group. Usually it begins a
full two days early! I was mature, ready for you a full two days before the Old One had thought I would be!

With all the stealth at my command I overcame the two of my
sisters guarding the compound. I threw open the wooden gate and
walked boldly into your pen.

You looked at me in surprise, but when you saw it was I, your
look changed to horror. Oh, that I could make you understand how
this thrilled and delighted me! I reached out to your mind, and,
sharing your thoughts, I understood and was happy.

For the other males in the compound had told you something of
the finale of our fertility rites! You had not comprehended all of
what they had said, your mind was in confusion, but you had gathered enough to be terribly frightened.

"Josephine," you cried out, "you can't! Not me! You don't
want me, Josephine, you—you—cannibal!"

I opened my arms to embrace you, but you ducked and
squirmed away from me and fled screaming from the compound,
the layers of fat bouncing as you waddled rapidly into the night.

Thankful beyond words I set out slowly to follow you. For this
was as it had to be. Frthian males must always run from the females, or the mating cycle cannot come to fullness.

The secretions that my body carries are poisonous under normal
circumstances. But, when administered to a male who is com-

pletely fatigued, to a male who has run for so many hours that he cannot move another step, the poisons do not kill. Instead, they create a suspended animation.

If you had not discovered just enough to flee when you saw me, you would have been dead by now. For I could not have long controlled my passions. Then I, too, would have died from the premature use of the poisons.

But it is hours now since you have fled from me through the blue darkness of the forests. How carefully, how devotedly I have followed you, pacing your every step, anticipating your every movement, listening to your fat screams with infinite delight.

Soon it will be time and I will catch up with you. The sheaths of my fangs will retract and I will give to you the searing kiss of a fully matured woman. And slowly, softly, you will collapse in my arms.

Gently I will pick you up and carry you back to our dwelling. I will rest your body well on the bier of honor, making you as comfortable as possible.

And then, after the mating cycle is completed, we will wait.

As I go about my daily tasks, moving around your resting place, my mind will be with yours constantly, sharing your every thought. For your mind will be unaffected by the paralysis of your body.

Linked together mentally we will come to know the intimate secrets of the beginning of new life. Thus united we will experience the glorious day when the eggs that I have laid break open and your children emerge to feed upon your rich flesh.

We will feel, as if we were one, our offspring as they burrow through your tissues, drawing sustenance from your ampleness.

How proud, how happy you will be to feel them growing larger, growing stronger, within you every day! And over the long, long months I will share with you these exquisite sensations.

Oh, you will father so many strong children!

Now it is time. You are lying on the ground beside me, panting. I feel the great weariness of you. I see the great shiningness in your eyes—and I am ready.

Do not fight me—this part is so swift! Just one deep kiss, one gentle nip you will not even feel, a long caress of love . . .

Oh, my darling, I love you so!

THE HOLES

Michael Shaara

I don't know the author personally, but I feel I've had a kind of interaction with him. He wrote one of my favorite stories, "All the Way Back," which I believe was his first to be published, relating to a superior sapient species called the Antha. There was something about that name that appealed to me. A decade later, in 1962, when I was a state social worker in Florida, my supervisor mentioned knowing a science-fiction writer—and lo, it was Shaara. (I wonder whether she mentions me now.) I understand he became a professor at a Florida university, and published a Civil War novel, The Killer Angels, that won a Pulitzer prize. More recently a collection of his stories, Soldier Boy, was published. Here are two of his, not his best, but entertaining in two rather different ways. Both are mysteries, and horror stories, but the one is obvious nonsense, while the other just might be true.

—PA

Shaara is one of the great unknown talents of science fiction. Publishing in Galaxy in the early fifties in the great, fertile period of that magazine, appearing side by side with Pohl, Kornbluth, Sheckley, Klass, Knight, Bester, and the others, he was not inferior to any of them and superior to most. Why he never wrote a novel in science fiction, why in fact he quit the field, is explained in the introductory/biographical material in Soldier Boy, a splendid 1982 collection brought out by Timescape Books.

—bnm

Barry is mistaken here, and it's evidence of how science fiction has merged into the mainstream or vice versa, but Shaara's 1981 novel The Herald is conventional (in theme, not execution) science fiction. I don't think it's as good as his excellent short fiction, but it is a solid analysis of an obsessed scientist who ends up (apparently—there is some ambiguity) destroying all life on Earth.

—MHG

The sand in the morning was soft and white. The sun was still low and the land was laced with shadows—long lean streaks of shadows—and in among the dark laces the hole stood out like a coal-black eye. It was perfectly round. The small gray ship that flew in from the west passed directly over it and came round in a wide circle. It fluttered back and forth nervously in the cool morning air. In the emptiness of the desert there was no motion, no sound. It settled down silently on a small white hill.

After a while two men came out of the ship, walked down cautiously through the sand to the rim of the hole. The first man, McCabe, was dark and beefy and bullheaded. The second, Royal, was very slim, with stiff scrubby hair like a desert tree. Royal was much more cautious than McCabe; he reached out to the big man and pulled him back from the edge.

McCabe grunted with annoyance.

"It's only a *hole*, Frank," he grumbled. "Don't be so damn jumpy."

"A hole with what in the bottom?" Royal said. "You hang your head over the edge you're liable to lose it. Get back."

McCabe backed off glumly. A slight, lean smile edged Royal's face. He bent down in the sand, picked up a large rock. With one hand at his holster, he tossed the rock carefully into the hole. He crouched tensely, waiting.

There was no sound.

Royal relaxed slowly. McCabe grinned at him. "You got nerves in your pants," McCabe said.

Royal nodded, not listening.

"When the rock fell," he said, "did you hear anything?"

McCabe looked blank.

"I don't recall," he said. "Why?"

"I didn't," Royal said. "Not a thing. Must be pretty deep."

McCabe nodded, grinned again.

"Can I look down *now*, Papa?"

Royal said nothing. Although to McCabe his great caution was often ridiculous, Royal did not allow himself to become bothered.

He had been in the Mapping Command for eight years, and he was still alive. McCabe was new. In a little while, if he lived, he would begin to walk just as nervously as Royal, and perhaps with greater caution; and he would learn to expect the impossible. Alien worlds have alien rules, you either learn quickly or not at all. But McCabe was still green and fearless, and although Royal did not like being saddled with a man like this, he did not dwell on it. He walked with McCabe to the rim of the hole.

McCabe whistled.

The hole fell straight down into blackness. It was perfectly round, perhaps fifteen feet across, and the sides were smooth. Remarkably smooth. The opening was sharp, even with the sleek black roundness of a giant pipe.

"Deep son of a gun," McCabe said. "What do you think it is?"

Royal shrugged. "If there was any life on this planet—which there isn't—I'd say it looked like the hole of a giant worm."

McCabe jumped, and it was Royal's turn to smile.

"No," he went on thoughtfully, "it's not animal. But not natural either. Too round. Do you happen to remember if perfect circles ever occur in nature?"

McCabe thought for a moment, then shook his head.

"Neither do I," Royal said, "but we will proceed on the assumption that they don't. And now we will find out how deep this one is."

The half-smile returned to Royal's face. He found another rock.

"Listen carefully," he said, "and check your watch. Count off the time until you hear the rock hit bottom."

Royal reached out and held the rock as far as he could out over the center of the hole, then let it drop. It fell quickly out of sight.

McCabe counted.

There was no sound.

After five seconds they looked at each other.

After another few seconds McCabe stopped counting. There had been no sound at all.

"Soft bottom," Royal said. "I'll ricochet one off the walls."

He dropped another rock. They stood together and heard it fall, crashing back and forth from wall to wall, fading slowly beyond hearing. They did not hear it land.

"Son of a *gun!*" McCabe grinned. "It's a couple of hundred feet, at least."

"At least," Royal said, "possibly more. And straight down."

It was very odd. There was nothing really weird or exciting about it, just a deep round hole in the ground, but still, it was very odd.

"Listen," Royal said suddenly, "I just want to check. There's a small single-beam radar unit in the scout sled. It's too big for me but you can handle it. Let's go."

He turned and ran up toward the ship. McCabe grunted after him, protesting. "What the hell for? What good is radar at a couple of hundred feet?"

"Suppose it's more than a couple of hundred feet?" Royal said. McCabe didn't follow

"Straight down?"

"Not likely. All the same it's worth a check." Royal reached the sled and began very quickly to unbolt the radar.

McCabe knelt down by him and argued. "Oh hell, Frank, why don't we go home? We're through here, all we got to do is take samples and go home. By golly, we've been out now for close to—"

Royal interrupted him abruptly, a thin hard line of tenseness in his voice.

"The sides are smooth," he said quietly. "Didn't you see that? Use your eyes, man, use your eyes. The sides are perfectly smooth. Haven't you ever heard of *erosion?*"

McCabe's mouth opened slightly, but he said nothing.

"It should rain on this planet pretty often," Royal said, working carefully at the radar, "in this place it should rain at least every few months. When do you figure it rained last?"

Now McCabe got it. He looked up quickly into the blue-gray morning sky.

"A few months maybe," Royal said, heaving at the radar, "just a few months. Either the hole was dug just *days* ago or—" he paused, looked at McCabe with a wide, white smile—"or somebody's been keeping it clean."

"Holy smoke!" McCabe murmured, stunned.

"We'll have to make a report," Royal said, "but first we'll find out how deep this thing is. When we find the depth, we may be able to figure the purpose. Why would somebody dig a hole, then keep it clean?"

He pushed the radar toward McCabe. The beefy man heaved it

silently to his shoulder, carried it down the hill, and set it up above the rim of the hole.

Royal turned it on and waited, watching the screen, playing one more round of the dark, lethal game which had been his life for eight years. He was expecting the hole to be deep, very deep, but even though he had lived with the impossible for many years, he could never have expected how really deep it was.

The radar screen stayed blank.

According to radar, the hole had no bottom.

When your life has depended for a long while upon machines— upon tubes and wires and gadgets of all kinds—you must come to trust these things as a part of yourself. Radar is a spaceman's eyes, his only infallible eyes. He does not consider the possibility of his instruments failing because he has seldom heard of them doing so. When defects occur they come at speeds beyond light, and a report on why you died can never be made.

But even though Royal took the radar apart and put it back together again and found nothing wrong, anywhere, he could not believe what the radar said. There could not possibly be a hole all the way through the planet. Temperature, pressure at the planet's core, would be so tremendous that no open space could exist. But there was nothing wrong with the radar. A beam had gone down, it had not bounced back, and there was no conclusion that Royal could draw but that there was nothing in the hole to bounce back from.

"A *bead!*" McCabe wheezed. "Whole damn planet's one great big bead!" His huge, merry voice roared in the empty morning air.

Royal, watching, did not laugh. Already a solution, and a fear, was forming within him. There was a thing in the hole which baffled radar, and which, from time to time, came out in the sun.

Royal stood up in the sand. He backed away from the hole, turned, and walked quickly to the ship. In a few moments McCabe came chortling in, lugging the radar. The ship lifted.

"Home, James!" McCabe shouted happily. "I got to tell the boys—"

Royal paid no attention. He bent down over some maps. The ship turned in orbit—swung off toward the dark side of the planet.

McCabe objected at first, then understood.

"You sure are a thorough son of a gun," McCabe said.

* * *

Ten hours later, as morning dawned on the opposite side of the planet, they stood upon rocks in a long low valley, gazing down at the second hole.

This one had no bottom either.

"Well, that's it," McCabe muttered in amazement. "It really by God *does* go all the way through!"

"Impossible," Royal said curtly. He had no intention of letting himself be thrown by this. "There's no material in the universe strong enough to open up a hole through the core of a planet."

McCabe pointed wordlessly at the hole.

"Absorption," Royal said. He knelt down carefully over the hole. "There's something down there that absorbs. When the radar beam goes down, something attracts it, *absorbs* it. That would account for no signal returning."

McCabe thought for a moment.

"All right. Yeah. Sure. But there's two holes."

"There are probably a *lot* of holes," Royal said insistently, "all over the planet. There might be a hole in every open space, for all we know. We still don't know what causes the things. Maybe they're mining shafts. Maybe some aliens dropped by here a little while ago and sent down shafts looking for some kind of deep ore."

He was convincing neither McCabe nor himself, and he knew it. But he went on. "And how do we know this hole is directly opposite the other one? We didn't calculate, did we? All we did was approximate the right area, and then we came over and looked around—"

"And we found another hole!" McCabe shouted. "Damn it, Frank, this is ridiculous!"

"There are other holes. There have to be other holes. We'll look."

"Where? The things are only a few feet across. We could look for ten years—"

Royal had begun to pace back and forth. "There must be a pattern. If it was mining, they probably dug at regular intervals. We'll look at the points halfway between the holes, then a third, then a quarter. All right?"

McCabe threw up his hands. "We could be here until winter."

Royal had stopped. He was looking now at the second hole. "Funny," he said.

"What?"

"The size of this hole. Wouldn't you say it was bigger than the other?"

McCabe looked.

"It is, by God! It's about twenty feet wide. The other was only fifteen."

"Let's measure to make sure."

They did. The second hole was bigger. Like everything else, that did not make any sense either.

They searched at regular intervals. They found no holes.

Royal was mystified.

A bead?

But there was no sense in searching any further. Millions upon millions of square miles of rock and sand and low bushy trees lay before them; in all that area there might be thousands of holes, but there was not much purpose in searching for them.

And then Royal had a brainstorm.

They flew up to the northern icecap. In the flat white ice of the north they looked, where holes would stand out like great blots. Altogether, before they stopped looking, they found seven holes.

None of them had a bottom. They lay in the snow with no pattern, some of them very close together, and if the number here was any clue then the rest of the planet was probably riddled with them. The biggest was almost forty feet across. There were others no larger than a foot. All bottomless.

Royal did not bother to check the other cap. He had no idea what to do now, but he could not leave. They flew back to the desert—to the first hole.

"It's animal," Royal said.

Night was coming on and the air of the desert was moist and cold. McCabe was standing near the rim of the hole, flapping his arms and grumbling. Royal waited quietly near him, watching the hole, thinking. He had waited long enough and all the while his instinct had been working, and now the pieces were falling in together. Royal smiled thinly.

"It's alive," he said.

McCabe jumped.

"What's alive?"

"The thing in the hole," Royal said. "Add it up. One: a signal goes down, no signal comes out. Therefore, the signal must have been absorbed. It *couldn't* have gone all the way through. Two:

none of the holes show sign of erosion. All were dug recently, or are being kept clean.''

He paused. In his mind it was very clear.

"Now,'' he went on softly, talking almost to himself, "suppose there is a thing down there that absorbs. That would account for the radar not coming back, and also for the lack of dirt if the things were dug recently. The thing ate its way down. From time to time—for air maybe—the thing comes back up. When it comes it widens the hole, smoothes it out.''

McCabe shuddered.

"Man, you've got the biggest imagination in fourteen galaxies.''

"Could it be?''

McCabe turned away. "Sure. But it looks to me like you need an explanation real bad, so you're just putting one together. What could live down there?''

"It would have to be very warm,'' Royal said.

After a moment McCabe whirled impatiently. "Look, Frank, for crying out loud, why don't we go home and let the techs figure this out. We been here long enough to—''

He broke off suddenly. He was staring at the hole.

"Frank.''

Royal saw it too.

"It's bigger.''

Royal stared at the hole.

"The damn thing is wider,'' McCabe said, awed. "It's *grown.*''

Royal knelt quickly to the ground, ran his fingers through the sand.

"Look at the ground. It's—it's turning to dust.''

McCabe was too big a man. When he turned suddenly to run his heels dug deep in the sand near the rim. The sand gave way. Suddenly, beneath his feet, the sand began crumbling and sliding down into the hole.

McCabe screamed.

Royal leaped back. In one huge agonized reach he caught McCabe's flailing hand. The sand, the dust, slid quickly away. McCabe lay on his stomach with his feet falling down into the hole.

Royal set himself, heaved.

Desperately, his face flat and yellow and his eyes bulging white, McCabe clutched and clawed and inched back out of the hole. He pulled out the last few feet himself. Behind him the dust was still sliding softly, in a gray liquid sea.

They did not wait at the rim. They dashed headlong for the ship.

It ended in space, in the ship, with the black night velvet around them. It ended suddenly, and with the utmost horror, because they thought they were through and they lay back and rested.

McCabe sat numbly in the astrogation room, smoking a long white line of cigarettes. In his mind was a picture of himself falling, falling down the long dark tunnel to the core of the planet. And then he fell a little way further, fell *up*, pushed by his own momentum, until gravity caught into him and sucked him back down, down again to the core and past, and then up and down, back and forth, falling forever in the black tunnel, a pendulum, human, screaming. McCabe sat smoking numbly.

Royal got ready to make out his report. Animal in origin. He sat at his desk now. He had survived one more alien place, had come away with its secret. He chuckled aloud.

A few moments later he poured a cup of hot coffee. The steam scorched him and he put his numbed fingers to his mouth. Then he looked at his hand.

For a long, long terrible while, he looked at his hand.

Not an animal, he thought. Not an animal at all.

A disease.

He sat down to wait. He thought of writing a letter, or explaining in the log, but in a little while there would be no letter, no log, and there was nothing he could do. Nothing but sit and wait, and stare at the center of his palm—

—where the flesh turned to dust around a small black hole.

BEAST IN THE HOUSE

Michael Shaara

You know how the ears of a dog move? Nothing scary in that . . .

—PA

The dog walked out of the trees on the far side of the mountain and paused for a moment in the sun. Betty was on the porch, knitting. Her head was down and she did not see it. The dog's head swiveled slowly, gunlike, came to rest with the black nose pointed up the hill. The morning was clear and cool, the grass was freshly wet. After a moment the dog began to move.

It came on across the meadow and up the long hill, moving in a steady, unvarying line toward Betty and the house. It broke through the bushes down by the garage, came up the gravel path with stiff even strides, until the shadow of it blotted the corner of her eye. Startled, she looked up.

At the front steps it stopped and waited, watching. Betty dropped her knitting in her lap.

"Well, hel-*lo*," said Betty, smiling. She leaned forward and held out a hand toward the dog, making coaxing, clucking noises. But the dog did not move. It stood motionless on the gravel before her, watching her silently with round brassy eyes.

"Whose dog are you?" said Betty, clucking again cheerfully. These silent mountain mornings were often very lonely; with the baby asleep they were lonelier still. She rose up from the rocker and walked down the porch steps, her hand outstretched. It backed stiffly away.

"Oh, come on." She smiled. "I won't hurt you."

The dog continued to back away, stopped when she stopped, but did not turn its eyes. After a while she gave up trying to say hello and went back up onto the porch. The dog kept watching her gravely and she was forced to laugh.

"Coward," she said coaxingly, "fraidy cat."

The dog did not move.

It was not a neighbor's dog. Even though she knew very little about dogs she was certain she had never seen this one before. It was a big dog, larger than most; she hazarded a guess that it was what they called a police dog. It was long and trim, sleek, with high, stiff pointed ears. Deciding that perhaps if she fed the dog it might begin to cotton up to her, she went inside to the icebox for some cold scraps of chicken. While she was inside she heard the dog come onto the porch. But when she returned it ran quickly back down the steps. It resumed its position on the lawn, watching.

She set down the chicken on the lawn, but the dog wouldn't touch it. It seemed preoccupied with her. For several moments she smiled and asked it questions, but it never even sat down, and it never moved its eyes from her face.

Presently she felt a slight annoyance. There was something odd in the dog's stare, something nerveless and chill and unvarying, almost *clinical,* as if the thing were examining her. She shrugged and bent to her knitting, forgetful and relaxed for a moment.

But she couldn't help looking up. The dog's eyes, like balls of cold metal, were still on her. It was a peculiar, ridiculous thing, to be stared at like this by a dog. She began to grow irritated.

"All right," she said at last, peevishly, "if you won't be friends, then shoo!"

The dog did not move. She went down off the porch and tried to chase it. But it only retreated as before, silently, watching. When she tired and sat down, it took up its place on the lawn again and waited.

Well, I never, she said to herself. She had no idea what the dog wanted. Gradually, under the pressure of the cold metal eyes, she felt the beginnings of a slight fear. The thing was certainly strange. She knew very little about the behavior of dogs, but she had never known a dog—or any animal, for that matter—to sit so long in one place just to watch.

Unless it was about to pounce, the thought came to her.

Momentarily she felt unnerved. But it was silly, she chided herself, dogs didn't do that sort of thing. And there was nothing hostile about the dog. It was just standing there, stiff-legged and gray, observing.

Now for the first time she began to examine the dog in detail. She sensed immediately that something was wrong—*physically* wrong. It was a short while before she could place it—those blank, staring eyes distracted her—but then she remembered.

The ears of the dog did not move.

All around her in the air there were light, sudden sounds, far-off grindings of trucks on the highway, quick calls of birds; yet the ears of the dog did not move at all. *But the ears should move*, Betty thought confusedly. She had noticed even as a little girl that the ears of most animals were never still, that they swiveled automatically to follow sudden sounds even when the animal was preoccupied. The ears of this dog were high and free, and . . . why didn't they move?

It was very odd. She had begun to retreat unconsciously toward the screen door behind her when she heard the baby begin to cry. Suddenly she felt released from thinking of the dog, and she went inside almost gratefully to prepare the bottle. A few moments later she came back quickly and locked the door.

Shortly after noon she looked out again and the dog was gone. She was relieved for a moment, and at the same time she felt angry with herself for being upset over such a little thing. Then she saw the dog again. The door of the garage was open, and she saw the dog come out and look immediately toward the house, toward the window, as if it knew she was there. She watched with a new, growing terror as the dog walked stiffly across the grass and disappeared behind the barn.

This morning, when her husband left, she had locked the garage door!

Of that she was certain, yet the door now faced her—dark and open. She continued to tell herself that she was being perfectly silly, but she went around immediately and checked all the locks on all the doors and windows of the house. For the rest of the afternoon she sat stiffly in the parlor trying to read, halting occasionally with real fright as the dark form of the dog padded by her window. Toward the end of the afternoon there was a crash from the cellar. Somehow the dog had gotten in. Immediately, and for some unknown reason, she feared for the baby. She ran to bolt the door and listen, terrified. But there was no sound. Finally she thought of her husband's gun. She found it in a drawer and locked herself in the nursery with the baby. In the evening when her husband returned she was hysterical.

The next day was Saturday and Harry stayed home. He knew his wife well enough not to be amused at what she had told him; he took the gun and searched for the dog carefully, but it was gone. How it had gotten into the cellar or the garage he had no idea. Like most country men he had a respect for dogs, but he supposed that the doors had not been locked. Anyway, by morning Betty seemed to be pretty well recovered and calm. He saw no reason to talk about the dog anymore and went out to the barn to putter with the homemade three-inch telescope which was his hobby. Later on he came back to the house for a while to play with the baby. The day passed and the dog did not return.

In the evening, as was their custom, they went out under the stars. They lay down in the cool grass of the lawn. Harry began to talk about a great many things, about the office and about taking up painting as a hobby, and about the way the baby called everything "didi." Betty lay back and said nothing.

She was a tiny girl, moody, new to the wide mountain loneliness and in many ways unsure. She was given to long silent periods which she could not explain and which Harry had learned not to try to question. As she lay now restlessly in the silent dark, a small-edged wheel of uneasiness whirling inside her, Harry did not ask what was wrong. Instead he became consciously boyish and cheerful, began to talk happily about nothing in particular.

It did not occur to him that she might still be thinking of the dog—by this time he had forgotten the dog completely. What he was doing was ritual. In a little while she would reach over and pat his hand and begin to smile, and whatever had bothered her would die away. He was fully aware of the childlike, deceptively naive and charming quality which he seemed to be able to turn on at will, and he saw no reason not to use it. And she knew that too, but it did not bother her.

On this evening, as always, she began to respond. She was just beginning to return to herself when she saw the dog.

She put one hand to the throat of her blouse. With the other she clutched Harry's arm. The dog was not moving and Harry had to search before he saw it.

It was a sharp-pointed shadow, black and lean, by the corner of the garage. The moon shone down with a pale, glowing flow; in the softness and the radiance the dog stood out with an odd unmoving heaviness. Its legs drove sharply into the ground below it, like black roots. It had been standing there, perhaps, for quite some time.

Harry started to rise. At his movement the dog turned and walked silently into the bushes, vanished. Harry was about to walk down toward the spot when Betty pulled at his arm.

"No!" she said earnestly, and he was astonished at the strong edge of fear in her voice. "No, please, let it go!"

"But, honey—" He looked at her, then back toward the bushes where the dog had disappeared. He was about to say that it was only a *dog,* when he recalled quite clearly that it was, after all, a fairly large animal.

"Well," he said, "all right." He patted her arm soothingly. He was thinking that the thing might just possibly be wild. And there was no sense in dashing off into the woods to look for it. Not in the dark, at any rate, although if it kept coming back like this, frightening Betty—

"Was that the same dog?" He led her toward the house. She nodded, looking back over her shoulder. She was trembling.

"I think so. I . . . couldn't really see, but I think so."

He folded his arm protectively on her shoulder, squeezed warmly.

"Poor old hound's probably just looking for a home. Probably lost. Let's go put out a plate of—"

"It was watching, just like the other time."

He grinned.

"Unfortunately, it didn't see much. Remind me to draw the blinds tonight."

"Harry, it was watching us."

She was insistent; her hands were balled at her sides and she continued to look back.

"What does it want?" she said, still trembling.

"Now, honey—"

"It was looking for something." She stopped on the porch and stared out into the blackness. "It was looking for something in the house and the garage. What does it want?"

He marched her firmly inside and put her to bed. He promised to go out looking for the thing in the morning. Joking was of no value now, and so he turned on the radio and played soft music. He chatted brightly about baby-sitting problems. The light was out and he was almost alseep when he heard the soft pads come up on the porch.

Suddenly and thoroughly angry, he dashed to the door. When he reached it the dog was gone.

The same thing happened again three times during the night.

In the morning Ed Benson drove down from his farm on the hill, pulled up with a sliding crunch on the gravel in front of the porch. Normally, he was a glum and unexcited man. But right now he was very much annoyed, and his face was bright red against the gray of his hair as he slammed the car door and stalked up onto the porch.

"Some louse," he roared huskily, flinging out a red-plaid arm to point at the mountain, "some slimy miserable, cotton-pickin' louse done killed a dog!"

Harry grinned instantly, without thinking of the effect on Benson. It had been a long night, mostly sleepless. So the doggone thing had pestered one porch too many. He wiped the grin off as Benson glared at him. "What in hell are you laughin' at? Dog killin' all right by you? Why, for two cents I'd whomp—"

"No, no, Ed, no," Harry said quickly, soberly. "I wasn't thinkin' about that at all, really. Now—what's the trouble? Somebody kill a dog? Who? What dog?"

"I don't know who killed it and I don't know what dog!" Benson roared again, impotently. "All I know is they's a poor mangled carcass lyin' up there on the mountain. Skinned. *Skinned,* by God, can you tie that?"

Harry's eyes widened. He did not have Benson's great love for dogs—which in most cases surpassed his love for people—but Harry had never heard of anyone skinning a dog. The thought was revolting.

"—and if I ever find the mangy louse that done it, I'll strangle him, I swear!"

He went on to ask if Harry had seen any strangers around lately. No mountain man would have done such a thing. Harry was shaking his head when Betty came out onto the porch.

She had heard the word "dog." She stood wiping her hands nervously on a dishtowel, the sleeplessness of last night thick in her eyes.

In the presence of a woman Benson calmed a little and told them what had happened.

"I found the carcass out back in the woods this morning. The skin was gone. Can you figure that? They skinned the dog neat like a rabbit, then took the skin. Why in hell would they want the skin?"

He lifted his bony hands helplessly. Harry was still shocked.

"Are you sure it was a dog's body?" Betty said.

"Sure I'm sure. Couldn't be nothin' else. Too big. Looked like a German police dog. Only dog I know like that is Bill Kuhn's, over at Huntsville, but I called him right away and he said his dog was right there."

He stopped to look with surprise at Betty. She was relaxing now, lifting a hand to smooth back her hair as the tenseness went out of her. She spoke to Harry.

"I'll bet it was the same one."

Harry nodded.

"The same what?" Benson asked, looking from one to the other. They told him about the dog on the porch, and he agreed that it was mighty queer for a dog to act like that. But he ended up shaking his head.

"Couldn't have been the same dog."

"Why?" Betty's head lifted quickly.

"Your dog was here last night. The one I found had been dead for a couple of days."

Harry frowned his disappointment. "You're sure?"

"Doggone it," Benson exploded, irked, " 'course I'm sure. I seen a lot o' dead animals in my time . . . say," he suddenly added, thrusting his nose belligerently up at Harry, "you act like you *want* that dog to be dead!"

Betty turned away. Harry smiled with embarrassment.

"Well, no, not really. But it sure was a pain in the neck. Scared heck out of Betty. It—uh—broke into the house."

"That so?" said Benson with raised eyebrows. And then he added: "Well, hell, ma'am, ain't no dog'll hurt you, not if you treat it right. Couldn't of been mad, you'd've seen that right off."

Betty spun suddenly, remembering. She spoke to Benson with a tight, now obviously worried voice.

"Ed, shouldn't a dog's ears move?"

Benson looked at her blankly.

"I mean," she said hesitantly, "a big dog like that with pointed ears—not ears that hung down, but high, pointed like a cat's. Shouldn't ears like that move? When the dog is looking at you and there's a sound somewhere, the ears should turn toward the sound, shouldn't they?''

''Well, hell,'' Benson said, his face screwed up in a baffled frown, ''sure they move. The dog can't keep 'em still. Why?''

The waited for her to explain, but she looked at their faces and could say nothing. They had not seen the dog, nor the ears . . . nor the brassy eyes. She sensed a horror in all this which she could not impart to anyone, and she knew it. And maybe she was after all just a green helpless girl from the city. For her pride's sake now she did not say anything. Just then the baby began to cry and she turned and went into the house.

That the dog Benson had found and the dog they had seen were the same was a thing which would not have occurred to Harry in a thousand years. He thought no further than the fact that Benson had said the animal had been dead for two days. That ended it. It also, for a time, ended it for Betty. But not for long. The dog had come after her into the house. It had opened a locked door. In the horrifying visits of the night before was all the proof she needed that the dog was evil; the dog was danger. But because there was nothing she could say to Harry, to anyone, she went off by herself to think. It occurred to her at last that the two dogs were the same.

Harry, in the meanwhile, passed a miserable day. Little Hal was cutting teeth and wouldn't stop crying. Betty was no help, and when Harry went out into the garage he couldn't find half his tools. He had to put the baby to sleep himself and it was only at the end of the day, as he stood gazing down at the slight woolly mound of his boy, that he was able to regain his smile. *Poor little codger,* he thought. He turned out the light and tiptoed into the bedroom. His smile faded. Betty was awake.

He sat down and pulled off a shoe.

''If that damn thing comes again tonight,'' he announced dramatically but with honest feeling, ''I will skin it myself.''

Betty spoke suddenly from the other bed.

''Harry,'' she said in a very small voice—the same voice she always used when she had something to say which she knew he would not like—''Harry, will you listen to something?''

He heaved the other shoe. ''Sure,'' he said cheerfully. ''Dogs?''

She sat up in bed and nodded earnestly.

"Don't think I'm silly, please, just listen. Don't you think it's funny about the *two* big dogs? I mean, two big dogs, both the same size, both maybe the same kind, both of them new around here, the one skinned and the other a—a prowler?"

He shrugged. Of course it was strange.

"And the way it came into the house and into the garage, and just . . . stood there, watching." She paused, not wanting to get to the point. He waited patiently.

"Well . . ."

He turned to look at her.

"Come on, pet, get it out. What's your idea?"

Her words came out in a sudden rush.

"The skin! What happened to the skin?" She said it with some violence, lifting her eyes to meet his with mingled doubt and defiance. "Why would anyone skin a dog and take the skin. *Why?* What possible reason could there be? And why should a dog the same size, two days later—a dog that breaks into houses and has ears that don't move—why should *another* dog come out of nowhere?"

He stared at her blankly.

"Honey—"

"You didn't *see*," she insisted, "you didn't see the eyes. They weren't a dog's eyes. They were—" She broke off as he stared in amazement. "I don't know," she moaned. "I don't know."

He knelt down on the bed and took her in his arms. She pushed him away.

"It was the same dog!" she cried, almost shouting. "But the thing we saw was only the skin!"

"Ssh! The baby!" Harry said.

"But it wasn't a dog at all. There was something *inside*."

He sat on the bed not knowing what to say. He had never seen her like this, and the business about the dog was so completely ridiculous that he could not understand her at all. He wished mightily that he had seen the damn thing.

He waited until she quieted—she kept asking him why didn't the ears move—and then reached over to the end table for a cigarette. He handed her one. She pushed it away.

"You won't even think about it," she said with despair.

He made the mistake of trying to be funny.

"But, pet," he grinned cheerfully, "you tell me. What in the sweet holy Hannah would want to crawl inside a dog?"

He did not expect any answer. He could not possibly have expected the answer he got. But she had been thinking, and once she had believed that the two dogs were the same the rest of it followed.

"Someone . . . something . . . is watching."

He drew a blank, an absolute blank.

Her face was set. "Suppose, just suppose that there really were . . . beings . . . from somewhere else. From another world. It's possible, isn't it? Isn't it?"

After a moment he nodded dumbly.

"Would they be like people, necessarily? No. Maybe they couldn't even live on Earth. Maybe that's why the saucers have never landed."

At that he jumped.

"Oh, now, honey—"

She refused to be interrupted.

"Listen, please. Hear me out. It's all possible. If there are people from someplace else and they're different from us, they can't come down, can they? They can learn all about our science, maybe, that we have radios and airplanes. But what can they learn about us, about people? They don't know our language, our customs. From way up there they can't really learn anything. They have to come down. They have to come down if they want samples of the real thing."

His grin died slowly. She had obviously thought a great deal about this and had worked it all out. And even if he could not possibly believe all she was saying, he was by nature an objective man and at least he had to admit the possibility.

She waited, watching him. He sat and tried to think it through, to show her where she was wrong.

All she had said so far was possible. Granted. In the morning, of course, in the broad plain dullness of daylight, it would be a lot less possible. But now in the night he could think about it. There was a warm bed near him and a darkness over the land outside, and a legion of dark thoughts became almost overwhelmingly real.

Aliens. He had a brief, digusting picture of slimy things with tentacles. But whatever they were—if they were—they would most likely not be able to pass unnoticed among men and women. And there were, so people said, the flying saucers.

Thus the skinned dog.

He followed the logic with an increasing chill.

From above, the telescopes, it could be observed that dogs and cats and a few other small animals seem to pass freely among men without undue notice. How simple then, thought Harry incredulously, to land in some out-of-the-way place—like the mountain—and trap a stray dog. It would be simple to skin it carefully without damaging the pelt, and to insert an . . . observer.

His mind did not waver, it dragged him on.

The observer could be an actual alien—if they were that small—or a robotic device. When the dog had stood so long observing Betty, had it been, perhaps, taking pictures?

Well, this was silly, this was absolutely ridiculous. He was about to say so to Betty when he remembered the tools he had searched for in the garage—tools he had not been able to find.

In the garage.

He rose up suddenly.

"Where are you going?"

"I'll be back in a minute. By gum, this is the craziest thing I ever heard." He shook his head quickly, unable to suppress a bewildered grin. What if the tools were really gone from the garage? Along with its observing, wouldn't the thing take samples?

He was dressing quickly, laughing aloud at the weirdness of it all, when he heard the sound. It was a faint sliding noise as of a window falling and being stopped. It was coming from the nursery. Betty screamed.

No time for the gun. He leaped past the door and crashed into a chair, wrecking it to get to the door beyond. He tore at the knob, the greatest fear he had ever known boiling and screaming in his mind. He stared agonizingly into the black. Even before he turned on the light he felt the fresh cool breeze from the open window, and a part of him died. Because the thing had been watching to take one more sample—the one sample it would obviously have to take—and he stared with utter horror at the crib.

The crib was empty.

They searched all night and into the morning, but they never found the baby. Not ever. What they did find at last, hung from a bush like an old worn rag, was the empty skin of a large gray-and-black dog.

LITTLE BOY

Jerome Bixby

And when the adults, in their infinite wisdom, play with their toys and destroy cities, what of the children? Science fiction has cried warning again and again; I have written novels with a similar setting, as have many others. So, though this is a familiar theme, it is worth presenting again. When will we ever learn?*

—PA

Jerome Bixby is the author of one of those ever-anthologized (5,271,000 times) stories, the 1953 "It's a Good Life," from Fred Pohl's first Star Science Fiction, which is simply one of the scariest science-fiction stories ever written, far more terrifying than "Who Goes There?" or "Black Destroyer," to give you an idea. He did a lot of other competent science-fiction stories ("The Holes Around Mars," Galaxy, 1954) through the 1950s, played an important, quiet role as assistant editor at several science-fiction magazines, went on to Hollywood in the 1960s and was the author of the original screen treatment of Fantastic Voyage (novelization by Isaac Asimov, film by Raquel Welch). A sequel to Fantastic Voyage, also based upon a Bixby treatment, by Philip José Farmer will appear at about the same time as this anthology.

—BNM

He dropped over the stone wall and flattened to the ground. He looked warily about him like a young wolf, head down, eyes up. His name was Steven—but he'd forgotten that. His face was a sun-

* Never, Piers. Never.—bnm

burned, bitter, filthy eleven-year-old face—tight lips, lean cheeks, sharp blue eyes with startlingly clear whites. His clothes were rags—a pair of corduroy trousers without any knees; a man's white shirt, far too big for him, full of holes, stained, reeking with sweat; a pair of dirty brown sneakers.

He lay, knife in hand, and waited to see if anyone had seen him coming over the wall or heard his almost soundless landing on the weedgrown dirt.

Above and behind him was the gray stone wall that ran along Central Park West all the way from Columbus Circle to the edge of Harlem. He had jumped over just north of Seventy-second Street. Here the park was considerably below street level—the wall was about three feet high on the sidewalk side and about nine feet high on the park side. From where he lay at the foot of the wall only the jagged leaning tops of the shattered apartment buildings across the street were visible. Like the teeth of a skull's smile they caught the late-afternoon sunlight that drifted across the park.

For five minutes Steven had knelt motionless on one of the cement benches on the other side of the wall, just the top of his head and his eyes protruding over the top. He had seen no one moving in the park. Every few seconds he had looked up and down the street behind him to make sure that no one was sneaking up on him that way. Once he had seen a man dart out halfway across the street, then wheel and vanish back into the rubble where one whole side of an apartment house had collapsed into Sixty-eighth Street.

Steven knew the reason for that. A dozen blocks down the street, from around Columbus Circle, had come the distant hollow racket of a pack of dogs.

Then he had jumped over the wall—partly because the dogs might head this way, partly because the best time to move was when you couldn't see anyone else. After all, you could never be *sure* that no one was seeing *you*. You just moved, and then you waited to see if anything happened. If someone came at you, you fought. Or ran, if the other looked too dangerous.

No one came at him this time. Only a few days ago he'd come into the park and two men had been hidden in the bushes a few yards from the wall. They'd been lying very still, and had covered themselves with leaves, so he hadn't seen them; and they'd been looking the other way, waiting for someone to come along one of the paths or through the trees, so they hadn't seen him looking over the wall.

The instant he'd landed, they were up and chasing him, yelling that if he'd drop his knife and any food he had they'd let him go. He dropped the knife, because he had others at home—and when they stopped to paw for it in the leaves, he got away.

Now he got into a crouching position, very slowly. His nostrils dilated as he sniffed the breeze. Sometimes you knew men were near by their smell—the ones who didn't stand outside when it rained and scrub the smell off them.

He smelled nothing. He looked and listened some more, his blue eyes hard and bright. He saw nothing except trees, rocks, bushes, all crowded by thick weeds. He heard nothing except the movement of greenery in the afternoon breeze, the far-off baying of the dog pack, the flutter of birds, the scamper of a squirrel.

He whirled at the scamper. When he saw that it was a squirrel, he locked his lips, almost tasting it. But it was too far away to kill with the knife, and he didn't want to risk stoning it, because that made noise. You stoned squirrels only after you'd scouted all around, and even then it was dangerous—someone might hear you anyway and sneak up and kill you for the squirrel, or for anything else you had, or just kill you—there were some men who did that. Not for guns or knives or food or anything else that Steven could see . . . they just killed, and howled like dogs when they did it. He'd watched them. They were the men with the funny looks in their eyes—the ones who tried to get you to come close to them by pretending to offer you food or something.

In a half-crouch Steven started moving deeper into the park, pausing each time he reached any cover to look around. He came to a long green slope and went down it soundlessly, stepping on rocks whenever he could. He crossed the weedgrown bridle path, darting from the shelter of a bush on one side to press against the trunk of a tree on the other.

He moved so silently that he surprised another squirrel on the tree trunk. In one furious motion Steven had his knife out of his belt, and sliced it at the squirrel so fast the blade went *whuh* in the air—but the squirrel was faster. It scurried up out of reach, and the knife just clipped off the end of its tail. It went higher, and out onto a branch, and chittered at him. It was funny about squirrels—they didn't seem to feel anything in their tails. Once he'd caught one that way, and it had twisted and run off, leaving the snapped-off tail in his hand.

Dogs weren't that way—once he'd fought a crippled stray from a pack, and he'd got it by the tail and swung it around and brained it on a lamppost.

Dogs . . . squirrels . . .

Steven had some dim, almost dreamlike memory of dogs that acted friendly, dogs that didn't roam the streets in packs and pull you down and tear you apart and eat you alive; and he had a memory of the squirrels in the park being so tame that they'd eat right out of your hand . . .

But that had been a long, long time ago—before men had started hunting squirrels, and sometimes dogs, for food, and dogs had started hunting men.

Steven turned south and paralleled the bridle path, going always wherever the cover was thickest, moving as silently as the breeze. He was going no place in particular—his purpose was simply to see someone before that someone saw him, to see if the other had anything worth taking, and, if so, take it if possible. Also, he'd try to get a squirrel.

Far ahead of him, across the bridle path and the half-mile or so of tree-clumped park that lay beyond, was Central Park South—a sawtoothed ridge of gray-white rubble. And beyond that lay the ruin of midtown Manhattan. The bomb had exploded low over Thirty-fourth Street and Seventh Avenue that night six years ago, and everything for a mile in every direction had been leveled in ten seconds. The crater started at around Twenty-sixth and sloped down to where Thirty-fourth had been and then up again to Fortieth, and it glowed at night. It wasn't safe to go down around the crater, Steven knew. He'd heard some men talking about it—they'd said that anyone who went there got sick; something would go wrong with their skin and their blood, and they'd start glowing too, and die.

Steven had understood only part of that. The men had seen him and chased him. He'd gotten away, and since then had never ventured below Central Park South.

It was a "war," they'd said. He didn't know much about that either . . . who was winning, or had won, or even if it was still being fought. He had only the vaguest notion of what a war was—it was some kind of fight, but he didn't think it was over food. Someone had "bombed" the city—once he had heard a man call the city a "country"—and that was about as early as he could remember anything. In his memory was the flash and roar of that night and, hours before that, cars with loud voices driving up and down the streets warning everybody to get out of the city because of the "war." But Steven's father had been drunk that night, lying on the couch in the living room of their apartment on the upper West Side, and even the bomb hadn't waked him up. The cars with the voices had waked Steven up; he'd gone back to sleep after a while, and then the bomb had waked him up again. He'd gone to the window and climbed out onto the fire escape, and seen the people running in the street, and listened to all the screaming and the steady rumble of still-falling masonry, and watched the people on foot trample each other and people in cars drive across the bodies and knock other people down and out of the way, and still other people jump on the cars and pull out the drivers and try to drive away themselves until someone pulled *them* out. . . . Steven had watched, fascinated, because it was more exciting than anything he'd ever seen, like a movie. Then a man had stood under the fire escape, holding up his arms, and shouted up at Steven to jump for God's sake, little boy, and that had frightened Steven and he went back inside. His father had always told him never to play with strangers.

Next afternoon Steven's father had gotten up and gone downstairs to get a drink, and when he saw what had happened, he'd come back making choked noises in his throat and saying over and over again, "Everybody worth a damn got out . . . now it's a jungle . . . all the scum left, like me—and the ones they hurt, like you, Stevie . . ." He'd put some cans of food in a bag and started to take Steven out of the city, but a madman with a shotgun had blown the side of his head off before they'd gone five blocks. Not to get the food or anything . . . looting was going on all over, but there wasn't any food problem yet . . . the man was just one of the ones who killed for no reason at all. There'd been a lot like that the first few weeks after the bomb, but most of them hadn't lasted long—they wanted to die, it looked like, about as much as they wanted to kill.

Steven had gotten away. He was five years old and small and fast on his feet, and the madman missed with the other barrel.

Steven had fled like an animal, and since then had lived like one. He'd stayed away from the men, remembering how his father had looked with half a head—and because the few times men had seen him, they'd chased him; either they were afraid he'd steal from them, or they wanted his knife or belt or something. Once or

twice men had shouted that they wouldn't hurt him, they only
wanted to help him—but he didn't believe them. Not after seeing
his father that way, and after the times they had tried to kill him.

He watched the men, though, sneaking around their fires at
night—sometimes because he was lonely and, later on, hoping to
find scraps of food. He saw how they lived, and that was the way
he lived too. He saw them raid grocery stores—he raided the stores
after they left. He saw them carrying knives and guns—he found a
knife and carried it; he hadn't yet found a gun. They ran from the
dogs; he learned to run from them, after seeing them catch a man
once. The men raided other stores, taking clothes and lots of things
whose use Steven didn't understand. Steven took some clothes at
first, but he didn't care much about what he wore—both his shirt
and his heavy winter coat had come from dead men. He found toy
stores, and had a lot of toys. The men collected and hoarded wads
of green paper, and sometimes fought and killed each other over it.
Steven vaguely remembered that it was called "money," and that
it was very important. He found it too, here and there, in dead
men's pockets, in boxes with sliding drawers in stores—but he
couldn't find any use for it, so his hoard of it lay hidden in the hole
in the floor under the pile of blankets that was his bed.

Eventually he saw the men begin to kill for food, when food became scarce. When that happened—the food scarcity, and the
killing—many of the men left the city, going across the bridges and
through the tunnels under the rivers, heading for the "country."

He didn't follow them. The city was all he'd ever known.

He stayed. Along with the men who said they'd rather stay in
the city where there was still plenty of food for those who were
willing to hunt hard and sometimes kill for it, and, in addition,
beds to sleep in, rooms for protection from the weather and dogs
and other men, all the clothes you could wear, and lots of other
stuff just lying around for the taking.

He stayed, and so he learned to kill, when necessary, for his
food. He had six knives, and with them he'd killed men higher
than he could count. He was good at hiding—in trees, in hallways,
behind bushes, under cars—and he was small enough to do a good
job of trailing when he saw somebody who looked as though they
were carrying food in their pockets or in the bags almost everyone
carried. And he knew where to strike with the knife.

His home was the rubble of an apartment building just north of
Columbus Circle, on Broadway. No one else lived there; only he

knew the way through the broken corridors and fallen walls and piles of stone to his room on the seventh floor. Every day or so he went out into the park—to get food or anything at all he could get that he wanted. He was still looking for a gun. Food was the main thing, though; he had lots of cans up in his room, but he'd heard enough of the men's talk to know that it was wise to use them only when you didn't have anything else, and get what you could day by day.

And, of course, there was water—when it didn't rain or snow for a while, he had to get water from the lakes in the park.

That was hard sometimes. You could go two or three days without water, even if you went to one of the lakes and stayed hidden there all day, because it might be that long before a moment came when no one was near enough to kill you when you made your dash from the bushes and filled your pail and dashed back. There were more skeletons around the lakes than anyplace.

The dogs were coming up Central Park West. Their racket bounced off the broken buildings lining the street, and came down into the park, and even the squirrels and birds were quieter, as if not wanting to attract attention.

Steven froze by the bole of a tree, ready to climb if the dogs came over the wall at him. He'd done that once before. You climbed up and waited while the dogs danced red-eyed beneath you, until they heard or smelled someone else, and then they were off, bounding hungrily after the new quarry. They'd learned that men in trees just didn't come down.

The dogs passed the point in the park where Steven waited. He knew from the sound that they weren't after anybody—just prowling. The howls and snarls and scratchy sounds of nails on concrete faded slowly.

Steven didn't move until they were almost inaudible in the distance.

Then, when he did move, he took only one step—and froze again.

Someone was coming toward him.

Just a shadow of a motion, a whisper of sound, a breath—someone was coming along the path on the other side of the bushes.

Steven's lips curled back to reveal decayed teeth. He brought out his knife from his belt and stood utterly still, waiting for the steps to go on so he could trail along behind his quarry, off to one side, judging the other's stature from glimpses through the bushes, and ascertaining whether he was carrying anything worth killing him for.

But the footsteps didn't pass. They stopped on the other side of the bushes. Then leaves rustled as whoever it was bent to come through the bushes. Steven hugged his tree trunk, and saw a short thin figure coming toward him through the green leaves, a bent-over figure. He raised the knife, started to bring its point down in the short arc that would end in the back of the other's neck . . .

He dropped the knife.

Wide-eyed, not breathing, he stared at her.

Knife in hand, its point aimed at his belly, she stared back.

She was dressed in a man's trousers, torn off at the ankles, and a yellow blouse that might have belonged to her mother, and new-looking shoes she must have found, or killed for, only a week or so ago. Her face was as sunburned and dirty as his.

A squirrel chittered over their heads as they stared at each other.

Steven noted expertly that she seemed to be carrying no food and had no gun. No one with a gun would carry a drawn knife.

She still held the knife ready, though the point had drooped. She moistened her lips.

He wondered if she would attack. He obviously didn't have any food either, so maybe she wouldn't. But if she did—well, she was only a little larger than he was; he could probably kill her with her own knife, though he might even get his own knife from the ground before she got to him.

But it was a *woman,* he knew . . . without knowing exactly what a woman was, or how he knew. The hair was long—but then, some of the men's hair was long too. It was something different— something about the face and body. He hadn't seen many women, and certainly never one as little as this, but he knew that's what it was. A *woman.*

Once he'd seen some men kill another man who'd killed a woman for her food. By their angry shouts he knew that killing a woman was different somehow.

And he remembered a woman. And a word: mother. A face and a word, a voice and a warmth and a not-sour body smell . . . she was dead. He didn't remember who had killed her. Somehow he thought she had been killed *before* everything changed, *before* the ''bomb'' fell; but he couldn't remember very well, and didn't know how she'd been killed or even why people had killed each other in those days. . . . Not for food, he thought; he could remember having plenty to eat. Another word: cancer. His father had said it about his mother. Maybe somebody had killed her to get that, instead of food. Anyway, somebody had killed her, because she was dead, and people didn't just *die*.

Seeing a *woman*, and such a little one . . . it had startled him so much he had dropped his knife.

But he could still kill her if he had to.

She stirred, her eyes wide on his. She moved just an inch or so.

Steven crouched, almost too fast to see, and his knife was in his hand, ready from this position to get in under her stab and cut her belly open.

She made a strangled sound and shook her head.

Steven pulled his swing, without quite knowing why. He struck her knife out of her hand with his blade, and it went spinning into the leaves.

He took a step toward her, lips curled back.

She retreated two steps, and her back was against a tree trunk.

He came up to her and stood with his knifepoint pressing into her belly just above where the blouse entered the man's pants.

She whimpered and shook her head and whimpered again.

He scowled at her. Looked her up and down. She was wearing a tarnished ring on her right hand, with a stone that sparkled. He liked it. He decided to kill her. He pressed the knifepoint harder, and twisted.

She said, "Little boy—" and started to cry.

Memories assailed Steven:

Jump for God's sake, little boy . . .

Distrust. Kill her.

My little boy . . . my son . . .

His knifepoint wavered. He scowled.

Don't run away, little boy—we won't hurt you. . . .

Kill.

Tears were rolling down her cheeks.

My son, my baby . . . I'm crying because I have to go away for a long time . . .

Steven stepped back. She was weaponless, and a woman—whatever that was.

Leaves rustled. Steven and the girl froze motionless.

It was only a squirrel in the bushes.

He bent silently, looked around under the leafy green bushes that surrounded them, almost at ground level. If there had been men nearby, he could have seen their legs. He saw nothing. He kept one eye on the girl as he bent. She wasn't crying, now that he'd taken the knife away. She was watching him and rubbing her belly where he'd pressed it.

When he straightened, she took a step away from the tree, moving as silently as he ever had. Suddenly she stooped to pick up her knife, made a slashing motion at the ground with it, looked up at him.

He was in midair. On her. She flattened beneath him with a squeal. She was stronger than he was, and experienced. She brought her knife back over her shoulder, and if he hadn't ducked his head it would have laid his face open. When she brought it down for another try, he clubbed the back of her hand with the hilt of his knife, and she gasped and dropped it.

Astride her, he raised his knife to kill her. She was pointing with her left hand, frantically, at something that lay on the ground beside them, and saying, "No, no, little boy, no, no—" Then she just whimpered, knowing that his knife was poised, and kept stabbing her finger at the ground. Because she was helpless, he paused, looked, and saw a squirrel lying there, head bleeding.

He understood. She hadn't been trying to kill him. She had seen the squirrel, and gotten it.

He decided to kill her anyway. For the squirrel.

"No, little boy—"

He hesitated.

"Friends, little boy . . ."

After a moment he rolled off her.

She sat up, cheeks tear-streaked. She pointed at the squirrel, then at Steven, and shook her head violently.

Knife threatening her, he reached out to pick up the squirrel.

Mine, the knife said.

At that point the squirrel, which had been only momentarily stunned by her blow, shook itself and scrambled for the bushes. His hand missed it by inches. He lunged for it, flat on his belly, and caught its tail with one hand.

As another squirrel's tail had done long ago, this one broke off.

He lay there for a moment, snarling, the tail in his hand; and when he turned over, the girl had her knife in her hand and her teeth were bared at him.

Blue eyes blazing, he got to his feet, expecting her to attack any second. He dropped the tail. He crouched to fight.

She didn't attack.

Nor, for some reason, did he.

The way her chapped lips were stretched back over her teeth disturbed him . . . or rather it unsettled him, because it *didn't* disturb him. At least not the way a snarl did. It didn't put him on guard, every muscle tense; it didn't make him feel that he had to fight. She didn't look angry or eager to have anything he had or ready to kill . . . he didn't know the word for how she looked.

She weighed her knife in her hand. Then she stuck it in her belt, and said again, *"Friends, little boy."*

He stared. At her strange snarl that wasn't a snarl. At the knife she had put away. He had never seen anyone do that before.

Slowly he felt his own lips curl back into an expression he could hardly remember. He felt the way he felt sometimes late at night when, safe and alone in his room, he would play a little with his toys. He didn't feel like killing her anymore. He felt like . . . like *friends.*

He looked at the squirrel tail lying on the ground. He worried it with a foot, then kicked it away. It wasn't good to eat—and he thought of how the squirrel had looked scrambling off, and felt his lips stretch tighter.

He tried to think of the word. Finally it came.

"Funny squirrel," he said, through his tight lips.

He stuck his knife in his belt.

They stared at each other, feeling each other's pleasure at the peacemaking.

She bent, picked up a small stone, and flipped it at him. He made no attempt to catch it, and it struck him on the hip. He half crouched, instantly wary, hand on knife. A thrown stone had only one meaning.

But she was still smiling, and she shook her head. "No, little boy," she said. *"Play."* She tossed another stone, high in the air.

He reached out and caught it as it descended.

He started to toss it back to her, and remembered only at the last moment not to hurl it at her head.

He tossed it, and she missed it.

He grinned at her.

She tossed another one back at him, and he missed, and they both grinned.

Then he grunted, remembering something from the dim past. He picked up a small fallen branch from the ground.

When he looked up, she was poised to run.

This time he shook his head, waving the stick gently. "Play," he said.

She threw another stone, eyes warily on the stick. He swung, missed.

He hit the next one, and the sharp crack, and the noise the stone made rattling off into the bushes, flattened him to the ground, eyes searching for sign of men.

She was beside him. He smelled her body and her breath.

They saw no one.

He looked at her lying beside him. She was grinning again.

Then she laughed; and, without knowing what he was doing or why—he could hardly remember ever doing it before—he laughed too.

It felt good. Like the snarl that wasn't a snarl, only better. It seemed to come from way inside. He laughed again, sitting up. He laughed a third time, tight hesitant sounds that came out of his throat and stretched his lips until they wouldn't stretch anymore.

Tears were on his cheeks, and he was laughing very tightly, very steadily, and she was laughing the same way, and they lay that way for a few minutes until they were trembling and their stomachs ached, and the laughter was almost crying.

He saw her face, so close by, and felt an impulse. He rolled over and started to scuffle with her. When she realized that he wasn't trying to kill her, that he was playing, she scuffled back, rubbing his face in the dirt harder than he had hers, because she was stronger.

He spat dirt and grass and grinned at her, and they fell apart.

Footsteps.

His knife was out and ready, and so was hers.

Legs moved on the other side of the bushes, stopped.

Silently, almost stepping between the leaves on the ground, Steven and the girl crawled out the other side of the bushes and took up positions against tree trunks, just enough of their heads protruding to see around.

A man came probing into the head-high bushes from the path side . . . stood there a moment looking around, only a vague brown shape through the leaves.

He grunted, went out to the path again, walked on.

Steven and the girl followed him by his sounds, trailing about twenty feet behind, until Steven got a good look at him when he passed an open space between the bushes.

He was a big man in brownish green clothes—new-looking clothes, not full of holes. He walked almost carelessly, as if he didn't care who heard him.

And Steven saw the reason for that.

Men with guns always walked louder. This man wore a holstered gun at his belt, and carried another one—a long gun something like a rifle, only bulkier.

Steven's lips curled. He darted a look at the girl. Across his mind flashed the vague idea of sharing whatever the man had with her, but he didn't know how to let her know.

She was looking at the guns, eyes wide. Afraid. She shook her head.

Steven snarled silently at her, put a hand on her chest, shoved gently.

She stayed there as he moved on.

Silently he drifted from tree to tree, bush to bush, getting ahead of his quarry. The big man's shoes clumped noisily along. Steven had no trouble telling where he was.

At last Steven spotted a good tree, a thick-foliaged one, about forty feet up the path, where the sun would be in the man's eyes.

If the man kept following the path—

He did.

And when he passed below the tree, Steven was waiting on the low branch that overhung the path—waiting with his face taut and his eyes staring and his knife ready. One stab at the base of the skull, and the guns would be his.

He jumped.

They brought them into the camp. By this time Steven and the girl had found that their captors were far too strong and too many to escape from, and quite adept at protecting themselves from the foulest of blows. But still the two of them struggled now and then, panting like animals.

Everything at the camp, which was over on Long Island, near Flushing Bay, was neat and trim and olive-drab, and it was almost evening now, and as the jeep rolled up the avenue between the rows of tents Steven and the girl stopped struggling to blink at the first artificial lights they'd seen in a very long time.

In the lieutenant's tent, the big man Steven had tried to kill said to the man behind the desk, "Like a jaguar, sir. Right out of the tree he came. I had him spotted, of course, but he did a peach of a job of trailing me. If I *hadn't* been ready for him, I'd be a dogtag."

The lieutenant looked at Steven and the girl, standing before him, and the four soldiers who stood behind them, one to each strong dirty young arm.

"The others got the girl, eh?" he said.

"Yessir. When we first heard 'em, I started making enough noise to cover the rest of the boys." The sergeant grinned. "I swear, he came at me as neat as any commando ever did."

"God," said the lieutenant, and closed his eyes for a moment. "What a thing. Let this war be the last one, Sipich. So *this* is what happened to New York in six years. Maniacs. Murderers. Worst of all, wolf-children. And the rest of the country . . ."

"Well, we're back now, sir. We can start putting it all back together—"

"God," said the lieutenant again. "Do you think the pieces will fit?" He looked at Steven. "What is your name, son?"

Steven snarled.

"Take them away," said the lieutenant wearily. "Feed them. Delouse them. Send them to the Georgia camp."

"They'll be O.K., sir. In a year or so they'll be smiling all over the place, taking an interest in things. Kids are kids, sir."

"*Are* they? *These* kids, Sipich? . . . I don't know. I just don't know."

The sergeant gave an order, and the four soldiers urged Steven and the girl out of the tent. There was a bleat of pain as one of the children placed a kick.

The sergeant started to follow his men out. At the tent flaps he paused. "Sir . . . maybe you'd like to know: we found these two because they were playing and laughing. We were scouting the park, and heard them laughing."

"They were?" said the lieutenant, looking up from the forms he was filling out. *"Playing?"*

"It's still there, sir. Deep down. It has to be."

"I see," said the lieutenant slowly. "Yes, I suppose it is. And now we've got to dig it up."

"Well . . . we buried it, sir."

UNWILLINGLY TO SCHOOL

Pauline Ashwell

I like little girls, having raised a couple myself, and I am sympathetic to the problems of reading. It took me three years to pass first grade, because I couldn't learn to read, and I still read very slowly, and one of my daughters had a problem with dyslexia. So I relate well to this story. But apart from that, it represents the qualities we have sought for this volume: it's a good, original, space-setting adventure with a completely human cast of characters and some nice points to make. I suspect that it was passed over by other anthologists mainly because the author was unknown; very little was ever published under this byline. That's too bad; this is some writer!

—PA

Ashwell's sequel to this story, "The Lost Kafoozalum," was reprinted, many years later, by Richard Lupoff in his What If? *Volume II; he felt that the sequel should have won the short-fiction Hugo that year. Better than most sequels, it was, nonetheless, clearly inferior to its predecessor, which is magnificently a story ahead of its time, perfect pre-Friedan feminism written in the center of the darkest fifties. Pauline Ashwell (who Tiptree-like also published a few stories as Paul Ash) is a British writer of whom almost nothing is known; she has not been prolific but bestirred herself to do yet another Lizzie Lee story in* Analog *a couple of years ago.*

—bnm

This may look like a moviegram of Brownian Movement but no such luck; it is Russett Interplanetary College of Humanities Opening Day, four thousand three hundred twenty-seven other freshers milling around and me in the middle with a little ticket on

116

my chest says Lee, L. because my given name is something not to mention; they say these kids came from one hundred twenty-four planets just to study at Russett but personally of all points in the known continuum this is the one I would rather be any place But.

Freshers come all sizes, all colors but a fair number are girls so there is one thing we will be finding in common anyway.

This may come as a surprise, that I am a girl, I mean. My tutor at Prelim School says my speech is feminine as spoken but written down looks like the kind of male character who spits sideways.

I reply that I talk like my Dad he is a character all right, male too but does not spit, if you spent your formative years with a filter in your kisser neither would you.

He says my flair for seeing the functional significance of the minutiae of behavior is obviously what got me chosen for the Cultural Engineering course.

Huh.

I know what got me into that all right I am not so dumb as I look.

You think I flatter myself? Brother, by what goes on I look dumb indeed. Maybe this is because of my hair, curly and pale colored—all right, blond. My eyes are blue as they come which is by no means sky color whatever books say, my skin is pink some places white others when washed and a visitor we had once said I had a rosebud mouth.

I am seven then, I do not hold it against her right away there are no roses where I grew up, when I landed here on Earth I hunt one up to see was it a compliment.

Brother.

I find later they come other colors but this one is frostbite mauve, and the shape!

I wish to state here my mouth has two lips like anyone else.

Where I grew up is Excenus 23, how I got hauled off it is due to a string of catastrophes but the name of the biggest is D. J. M'Clare.

Excenus sun is what they call a swarmer, ninety-seven small planets in close orbits plus odd chunks too many to count, Twenty-three is the biggest, gravitation one point oh seven Earth diameter a fraction less, if you ever heard of the place it was because they mine areopagite there. Ninety-four percent production for sale in the known volume of space comes from mines on Twenty-three; but for that, no reason to live there at all.

My Dad started as a miner and made his pile, then he took up farming and spent the lot, he has it all back again now.

Areopagite forms only in drydust conditions meaning humidity at ground level never above two and one half percent rainfall. None, hence from this farming on Excenus is something special, but miners are like other people they have to eat too.

When Dad started there was him and Uncle Charlie and their first year they fed two thousand men, nowadays the planetary population is eleven thousand three hundred twenty and there are seven other farmers, most of them started working for Dad and graduated to farms of their own. Nobody on Excenus eats trucked concentrates now.

Uncle Charlie is Hon as in secretary meaning no real relation. He is an engineer, when Dad met him down on his luck but able and willing to build diggers, harvesters, weathermaker for ten thousand acres out of any junk to hand. Had to be done like that because Excenus Haulage Company, the big company did all the shipping in and out of the planet, sold food concentrates. No competition welcome therefore no shipments seeds, agricultural, machinery, all that, would have been allowed through.

It takes Charlie two years to do his job, meanwhile Dad bones up the agricultural side. Nowadays there are a lot of books on drydust farming, they cover soilmaking, microbiology, economical use of weather, seed selection, plenty more; at that time there were fewer and Dad read them all.

If he had sent for the usual texts E. H. C. might have caught on and had a little accident in transit, so Dad gets them in as *books,* I mean antique style, chopped in pieces and hinged together down the side. They are labeled Curio Facsimiles and disguised with antique picture covers mostly show the damnedest females you ever saw, dressed in bits and pieces mostly crooked; some of them dead. People collect these things for some reason. Dad has one or two put on top with texts to match the outside, rest are textbooks on agriculture like I said.

Charlie offers to make reader-reels from them but Dad turns it down. He still has all those books packed in a row, when I was little he used to tell me how he learned all his farming studying that way, without using machines, it just showed you could still do it if you had to. Dad never had any education and it bothers him; I used to think that was why he kept on telling me this.

* * *

Well there are plenty of troubles not least with E. H. C. but Dad is not the type to give up; reason he started farming in the first place was he caught on E. H. C. were making it impossible for anyone to do just that; Dad does not like people who try and stop him even if it was not what he wanted in the first place.

I am born soon after the farm is really set, my mother walked out when I was three. She was fresh out of college with an agricultural degree when he met her, maybe the trouble was Dad caught on she knew less about drydust farming than he did, maybe other things. Excenus 23 is no place for a woman they say.

It is O.K. by me but I was born in the place.

Dad and Charlie raised me between them like the crops, this is to say carefully.

There are plenty more people now in Green Valley where the farms are, thirty or so and they change all the time. People who come out farm for a bit make their pile then go. We even get women some times. Peoples' wives from Town come out to board sometimes, Dad lets them because he thinks they will Mother me.

Well mostly I manage to steer them off and no hard feelings, it is my home after all they got to be reasonable about it if they want to stay. Seems they do as a rule, Town is kind of tough to live in. Several stayed a year or more. So it is not true to say I grew up in a wholly masculine environment, I knew up to seven women for quite a while.

Green Valley is outside the mining area and about six hundred miles from Town. This has to be, Town gets most of its water combing the air and so do the weathermakers for the farms; anyway mining and farming do not mix so good. The Valley is twenty miles each way hedged by hill ridges up to seventy feet high. Outside is stone flats, dust bowl and tangle-mats of *Gordianus* scrub. Forty miles round about I know it pretty well but the rest of the planet is about the same, except for Town.

This is where I was born, I was all set to stay there till Dad had his accident, first catastrophe on the way to this place.

I am up one day in a helivan watching the harvest on a thousand-acre strip at the edge of the farm, there is a moderate wind blowing from over the hill, so we are keeping the weather-lid over each row until just before the harvester gets there so as to keep the dust out of the grain. I am directing this.

Here at the edge the weather-lid is just above the corn, it runs from the weathermaker in the middle of the farm in a big cone like

a very flat tent, fifty feet high in the middle and four miles across.
You cannot see it of course unless the wind blows dust across, or
there is rain inside; the lid is just a layer of air polarized to keep
dust one side, water vapor the other; just now you can see plainly
where puffs of dust go skittering across.

The harvester gets to the end of a row on the far side from the
road. I signal Biff Plater at Control and he draws the weather-lid in
twenty yards. The harvester lifts its scanner at the end of the strip,
wheels, and comes through the next swathe, with the big cutter
pushing six inches above ground, stalks sliding back into the
thrasher bagged corn following on the trailer behind.

Then I see Dad come along the road riding the biggest kor on the
farm. Kors are *Pseudocamelopus birsutinaris* part of the indige-
nous fauna we started taming to ride on about a year ago. Dad does
not really enjoy it, he cannot get used to having no brakes but he
will not give up. I see right away he is having trouble, the kor
slipped its bridle and navigating on its own, long neck straight out
and Dad slipping to and fro in the saddle; his mouth filter is
bumped out and waving behind.

The harvester is half up the field. I do not want the kor to be
scared I yell to Biff, Turn it off quick! but the controls are the other
side of the shack from the weather ones.

Then the kor sees the scanner rearing on its stalk, it is not frightened at all thinks this is the great great grandfather of the species
and charges straight across to say hello.

I am yelling to Biff and got my eyes shut, then he is yelling right
back, I have to open them and look down.

The kor has gone straight into the cutter the second before it
stopped. Dad has been thrown and the harvester stopped with one
tread a foot from his head and a corner gone over his arm.

I bring the heli down yelling for help on all frequencies.

Dad is breathing but flat out; fractured skull, ulna and radius
like a jigsaw puzzle, multiple injuries to the chest; the kor is in
three pieces mixed up with the machine.

We call the hospital in Town and they direct first aid over two-
way visiphone while the ambulance comes. It takes seventy minutes and I am swearing to myself we will hire a permanent doctor if
we have to shanghai him, after this.

The ambulance arrives and the doctor says we have done as well
as can be expected, fortunately Dad is tough but it will be a two-
month hospital job at the least.

They crate him up in splint plastic and load him into the ambulance. Buffalo Cole has packed me a bag, I get in too.

I am out again first thing, passengers not allowed.

I get out the long-distance heli and go straight to Town, I am waiting in the hospital when they arrive. I wait till they have Dad unpacked before I start to inquire.

These hospitals! It is all they will do to let me look at him, when I do he is lying in a kind of tank; his chest is the wrong shape, there is a mass of tubes round his head running to a pump, this is for resorption of blood clots in the brain; more too the other end for external aeration of the blood, he is not going to use his lungs for a bit.

I think this does not look real, Dad in all this plumbing; then I hear my breathing goes odd, next thing you know the doctors steer me outside.

They say it will be a week before the blood clots go and Dad wakes up but they will report by visiphone every day.

I say No need they can tell me when I visit each day.

They are deaf or something, they repeat they will call Green Valley each morning at thirteen o'clock.

I say Is that when they would prefer me to call in?

At last they have got it, they say Surely I will not fly six hundred miles every day?

I say No I shall be stopping right here in Town.

Then they want to know what friends I am stopping with, I say at a hotel of course.

Consternation all round No place for young girls to stop in this town, they make it out the toughest hellhole in the known volume.

I say Nuts there are hotels for transients and their wives too.

They flap wildly in all directions and offer me a bed in the nurses' hostel which is men only ordinarily but they will make an exception.

I say thanks very much, No.

In the end they tell me to go to the Royal Hotel it is the most respectable of the local dumps, do not on any account make a mistake and go to the Royal Arms which is a pub in the toughest quarter of the town; they tell me how to go.

I put my luggage bag in my pocket, for some reason I have clutched it throughout; and I go.

Way I feel I do not go to the hotel straight off, I walk around a bit. I have been into Town of course shopping with Dad, maybe twice a year, but I do not seem to know it so well as I thought.

Then I find I have got to the Royal Arms or just near it anyway.

It is now late evening the sky is black except for stars, planets, and meteors crashing through every minute or two. The town is lit up but there are few in the streets, quiet folk are home in another quarter the rest still fueling up indoors. Way I feel is some toughery would suit me fine to take my mind off, because taming kors was my idea in the first place. Maybe I will get a chance to try out that judo trick I learned from Buffalo Cole.

So I slip through the noise-valve doors one after another and go into the pub.

Brother.

The noise trap is efficient all right, outdoors no more than a mutter so there is a real wallop inside. Every idea in my head is knocked clean out of it, even the thought I might go away. Among other things are three juke boxes in three corners going full blast and I cannot hear them at all.

Part of the decibels come from just conversation, part is encouragement to a three-way fight in the middle of the floor. I am still gaping when two of the parties gang up on the third and toss him all the way to the door. I dodge just in time, he rebounds off the inner valve and falls right at my feet.

Everyone turns and sees me, and the juke boxes all become audible at once.

I go down on my knees to see if the character I have just missed meeting is still breathing or not. His pulse is going all right but his face is a poor color wherever blood lets me see, I yell for water but competing with the juke boxes get nowhere. I am taking breath to try again when someone turns them off at the main, silence comes down like cotton-wool.

I ask for water in a whisper, someone brings it and tries to take me away.

I find I am clinging to the guy yelling He is hurt he is hurt! There is blood balling in little drops on my evercleans and smeared over my hands, I am trying to wipe it off with a disposable; not suited to this of course it crushes and goes away to dust and then the cotton-wool feeling in my ears spreads elsewhere.

Then I am lying on my back with water running down my chin and a sensation of hush all round.

I try to sit up and something stops me. Someone murmurs soft nothings that fail to make sense.

I keep quiet till I have it sorted and then I figure I have fainted clean away.

Me, Lizzie Lee.

I sit up and find I am on a couch in a sort of backroom and there are faces all round. Half of them seem knocked out of shape or with knobs on, bashed recently or previous.

The faces all jostle and I hear they are telling those behind She is sitting up! and the glad news getting passed along.

Someone pushes through the faces carrying a tray with food for six, I deduce they think I fainted from hunger or something.

I would put them right on this when I realize the feeling in my middle is because I last ate ten hours ago.

I weigh in and they appear pleased by this.

So I feel an explanation is owed and I tell them my Dad is in hospital with an accident, you would not think they could get so upset about a perfect stranger, sure this will not last but it is genuine feeling just now for all that.

There is more buzzing and a kind of rustle and I find they are taking up a collection.

I am horrified, I cry No, no, they are very kind but I truly cannot accept.

And they think this is proper pride or something, they start to mutter again and someone says Well then no need to worry, Knotty will give me a job as long as I need it, won't he? Knotty is in the crowd somewhere, seems he is keeper of this pub. His seems to agree and I figure out he'd better.

I do not see why they are so sure I am indigent until I happen to glance down. I am still in my work evercleans I was wearing when Dad got hurt; also it breaks on me suddenly this is the worst quarter of the town no girl would come here if she could afford to be elsewhere, even then not into the Royal Arms unless full of sweet innocence or something.

And I cannot speak.

When a bunch of strangers are mooning over your problems because you are a poor young thing you cannot tell them you walked in to look for a fight.

Truly, I could swear out loud.

In two shakes of a vibrator they have it fixed, Knotty will give me a job as long as I need one and I can have a room above the pub and at least fifty husky miners have sworn a personal guarantee no one within miles will lift a finger in any way I could not wish.

So what can I do?'

I thank them and I walk out into the bar and when I get there I find the laws of human nature are not wholly suspended, there is a fight going on.

My bodyguard behind me gives a concerted roar and the fight stops and they look sheepish at me.

It is so clear they expect me to look shocked and sorrowful that I cannot help it, this is just what I do.

I ask the cause of the fight and they shuffle and the bigger one says he is very sorry and would like to apologize Miss.

It turns out he has come in since I arrived and wishes to get drunk with the minimum delay, the assembled party tell him Damsel in distress back of the bar and he says to hell with that, she is probably faking it anyway; he sees this was error and regrets it very much.

And I have to make a production over forgiveness, he will never believe me unless I do.

So I am stuck.

You think all this will wear off in a day or two? Brother, so do I. At first, that is. But it does not. I have reformed the place overnight.

I begin to think getting drunk each night and working it off by fighting are not really their personal choice, all they need is a little stimulus to snap them out of it; such as the influence of a good woman maybe and looks like I am elected.

I get so busy listening to assorted troubles and soothing fights before they come to the boil, apart from any job Knotty can give me such as putting glasses in the washer and dishing the drinks, I hardly have time to think about Dad except at the hospital each day.

He is dead out for seven days just like they said, while the blood clots get loose from his brain; also they set his ribs and arm and tack up things inside. My miner friends all cheer me up they say This is a good hospital and tell me all the times they have been put together again themselves, I say Oh and Ah so often I am quite tired it seems to please them anyway.

Then Dad comes awake.

He does not do it while I am there of course, but I am allowed to sit with him two hours the day after, they have shifted him out of the tank into a proper bed, and taken the plumbing away. Towards the end while I am there he comes round and says Hello Liz how have you been?

And I want to cry but I am damned if I will, I say I am fine. And he is already asleep again.

I ring home like I do every day. Charlie is out so I leave a message, then I go back to the pub. I feel truly I could sing all the way, I do not notice until Knotty says so that I am singing anyway. Knotty is in a sour mood but when I tell him about Dad he fetches out half a smile and says will I be leaving then?

I say No Dad has another one month and twenty-one days in hospital to go.

At this his face falls under three gravities and he says All very well for me. I say why? can he not afford to pay me?

He says what troubles him is the pub. Since I came liquor drinking is down two-fifths, if anybody starts to get drunk the rest stop him in case something occurs to sully my pure girlish mind, it becomes clear that to Knotty this sobriety is not pleasing at all.

Well it is far from being my wish either, at least I think that at first then I think again Do I really want my pals back to the old routine drunk every night dead drunk Friday to Monday? This do-gooding is insidious stuff.

I go on thinking about it when I have time, this is not often because the boys are so pleased to hear Dad is better they allow each other to get quite lit, I have to head off one row after another.

I begin to think anyway this situation cannot last long, the pressure is building up visibly something is going to blow they need outlets for aggression and getting none just now. Also I must do something for Knotty. I could tell him Dad will pay back his losses but Knotty's head is solid bone; if I once got into it I am not a dear little down-and-out, he would let it out again at the diagrammatic wrong time.

Things have got to end but they have got to end tidy with no hard feelings, I shall need help for this.

I got out that night as soon as Knotty is in bed and get to a public visiphone. I dial home, never mind it is one in the morning I want Uncle Charlie.

What I get is Buffalo Cole looking sleepy, he lets out the yip he learned from an old stereo and asks where I am and where I have been so long and so loud I cannot tell him for quite a while.

Then he tells me Charlie is here in Town.

He has assumed I am staying at the hospital. They phoned today as usual, he asked for me and found I was somewhere on my own; he busted into Town straight off like a kor calf into a cornfield and been hunting for me all over tearing out hair in bunches.

He is staying with a friend the far side of Town, I ring.

Brother.

Now he has found me he has no wish to talk to me I am to stay in the visiphone booth and not move till called for well I suppose I can wiggle my ears if I like.

Charlie arrives in a heli four minutes later and mad enough to burn helium, he gives me the kind of character my pals sketch for each other when I am not supposed to be by.

He is not interested in excuses, he will get me out of whatever mess I am in for my father's sake; I will come to a bad end someday but I can have the grace to keep it till the old man is on his feet again.

I have learned something these last few days, I do not yell back. I say I have been very foolish and I need advice.

Do not think this fools him but he is taken aback slightly. I get something said before he recovers and in the end I tell the whole thing hardly interrupted at all.

At the end he gives me a peculiar look like when one of his hatcharia gave birth to a parrot and says nothing at all.

I say Look Charlie my idea is this; he says Liz your ideas are the start of this trouble in the first place, you have been getting ideas ever since I knew them and every one worse than the one before, just let me think about this.

Then he says Well if you leave without explanations I suppose we will have these desperate characters hunting for you all over Town and if the truth gets out there will be a rumpus because of that, I guess you better go back there for tonight anyway, how are you going to get back in?

I say I have a key, does he think I crawled out of the window? From his look I rather gather he does. Men are children at heart.

All the same I go back quietly and sleep like a tombstone.

In the morning I see Charlie at the hospital and he says he has an idea but seems he prefers to sit on it and see how will it hatch, I do not tell him what I think of this.

Then Dad wakes and says a few words and things look brighter and afterwards Charlie swears he has a real idea how I can get out of this without any hurt feelings, it just needs a bit more work on it.

I go back to the Arms thinking my troubles are half over, Brother what error, this is where they begin.

That evening I am chinning to some types who cut up yesterday, I tell them how shocked I am how surprised how sad because they have backslid, they are always sure I feel like this. If I do not say it they get upset because they suppose my feelings too deep for words; I can do this sort of thing no hands now.

Just the same it takes some concentration, when the stranger comes in I hardly notice him at all.

He is a tall chap in the usual evercleans with filter mask over his shoulder, all that is strange is I have not seen him before, men stick to their own pubs as a rule.

He slides into a corner and swaps words with the regulators and I forget him altogether.

The clock strikes twelve, two hours to midnight closing, enter a tall dark stranger.

Short hair and big shoulders and the face that launched the campaign for Great Outdoors Shampoo, maybe twenty-two years old, he takes a quick look round and I guess he does not think much of the place.

Well he should have seen it a week ago, now there is only one single jukebox going and people are just chatting over drinks, not a fight in the place.

He comes up to the bar and taps someone on the shoulder to make way; try touching anyone a fortnight back and stand well clear! This time the fellow stops his fist before it goes six inches and then moves over an inch or two and I am face to face with the stranger over the gap.

He looks at me and registers more surprise than I thought his face could hold, I say What are you drinking sir?

He swallows hard and says Beer please; something is displeasing him like mad but I cannot see how it is me.

I give him his beer and he gives me an unloving look and moves away, he horns in on one of the gatherings and starts to chat.

I am busy but I keep an eye on him and it seems to me the chat is getting too emphatic for health, I beckon over a miner called Dogface and ask what goes on.

He says That character been annoying you Liz? I say No is he annoying anyone else? Dogface says he asks too damn many questions someone will paste him any minute now.

I sign for another miner called Swede, these two are the steadiest around; I say Ride herd on this character and keep him out of trouble.

They say How? I say get into conversation and stop him talking to anyone who is prone to get mad.

They look doubtful so I tell them to talk to him, he is asking questions well tell him answers, tell him about life on Excenus you can see he is a fresh-out Terrie, tell him about mining; that will be instructive for him.

Next time I look Dogface and Swede are one on each side of him talking away, the other types have all drifted off.

The stranger stays for an hour and they stick by him all the while, when he leaves no one has laid a finger on him, I have done a good deed this day. Dogface and Swede say they never knew they had so much to talk about, just the same the stranger did not look grateful to me.

Next day I go to the hospital as usual wondering if Charlie has hatched his idea.

Halfway there I feel eyes on the back of my neck. I look round and there he is again, the tall dark stranger I mean.

He strides up and says he wants to speak to me.

His tone is such that I think of Buffalo's judo trick but he looks the type to brush it off with a careless reflex, I could wish there were more people around.

I say What about?

He says I know damned well what about, this is poaching and he will not stand for it, he will complain to something I do not catch.

I say he must be thinking of somebody else.

He sizzles behind his teeth and says I need not think I can get out of it by playing innocent because he will be able to trace me perfectly well. I obviously come from that establishment for muddy minded morons Pananthropic Institute of Social Research; everybody knows Excenus is Russett's fieldwork place and no other school would crash it, let alone horning in on a practical that way.

Furthermore the dodge I am using was corny in the Ark or earlier.

I am much perplexed but more angry and ask what he is proposing to do.

He says Don't worry I will find out later, I guess he does not know either; but before I can say so he goes striding away.

I walk on getting madder as I go, this mystery on top of everything else is enough to drive me round the fourth dimension, and he will catch on to his mistake and I shall never hear it explained; however when I arrive I forget him because Dad is awake and fit for talking to.

Several times I wonder Shall I tell him the whole thing? but he is still sick, this is no time to tell him I am serving in a bar in the toughest part of the town.

We talk quietly about the farm and plans for next year and things we did when I was little, all of a sudden I want to cry.

Then Charlie comes. One visitor at a time I have to go, Charlie needs some instructions about the farm.

I think I will go out and walk around, I do not like waiting in the hospital they think women belong some other place. I am halfway down the outside steps when there is a shadow over me and a voice says Excuse me, Miss Lee?

I turn and stare.

Brother what is this, are they making a stereo on Excenus, this is the handsomest man I ever came across. He makes the one this morning look like a credit for twenty all from one mold, I am certain I never saw him before.

He says We met last night though that was hardly an introduction, he is glad of an excuse to make my acquaintance now.

I think No this cannot be, yes it is, this is the gink I hardly noticed last night; same face same voice same hands and I never looked at him twice, how in Space is it done?

Brother, he called me Miss Lee!

I say there must be some mistake and turn towards the hospital again.

He says the hospital clerk told him my name and he saw me come out of the Royal Arms this morning.

Sing Hey for the life of a hunted fawn, now I am good and mad, just crazy. He says he thinks a talk would be mutually profitable, what I think is something quite different and I say it out loud. He has a way of doing things with his eyebrows to look amused, men have been killed for less.

He says What would the clientele of the Royal Arms think of that?

I say what the hell is that to him? He says he will be delighted to explain if I will give him the opportunity but this is hardly a suitable place to talk.

There are no places suitable and I tell him so.

He says he has a helicar there, if I would care to drive it anywhere I like he will give me the key.

I begin to see what will happen if this specimen opens his face to Knotty and Co; I must know what his game is; I say O.K.

We are just getting into the heli when the air is sundered, Liz! here is Uncle Charlie and my reputation in pieces again.

He charges across and my companion says Mr. Blair? which is Charlie's name though I hardly remember, and he hands over a card with a name and some words on it.

Charlie reads it and looks baffled but not mad any longer.

I sneak a look at it, it says D. J. M'Clare and a string of initials, Russett Interplanetary College of Humanities, Earth, it has Department of Cultural Engineering in little letters lower down.

Charlie says Liz what in Space are you doing now?

M'Clare says he has to make Miss Lee a rather complicated apology, this being no place to do which he has suggested a ride, it will be much better if Mr. Blair will come along too.

I do not know how it is done but ten seconds later Charlie is inviting him for a drink to the house where he is staying and I am tagging along behind.

The house is close to the hospital and well to do all right the air is humidified right through. I choose lemonade to drink, I never cared for alcohol much and I am more tired of the smell; when Charlie has done bustling with drinks M'Clare begins.

He says he understands Miss Lee had an encounter this morning with his pupil Douglas Laydon.

I say Great whirling nebulae not the lunatic who called me a poacher? He says Very likely, Laydon came here to do a practical test and finding I had anticipated him was somewhat upset.

He explains that students in Cultural Engineering have a fieldwork test after two years, this one had to make a survey of the principal factors leading to violence and try out short-term methods for abating same in a selected portion of the community on Excenus 23 namely the Royal Arms pub.

M'Clare says Excenus 23 is a very suitable spot for this kind of fieldwork, the social problems stay constant but the population turns over so fast they are not likely to catch on.

Charlie nods to show he gets this, I get it too and start to be angry; not just mad but real angry inside, I say You mean that dumb-bell came out here to push people around just for the exercise?

He says fieldwork is an essential part of the course for a Cultural Engineering degree, I say Hell and hokum nobody has any right to interfere with people just for practice, he says Not everybody possesses your natural technique Miss Lee.

I say Look that is different, I was not trying to find out what makes people tick then fiddle with the springs and think I done something clever.

Charlie says Shut up Liz.

This man does not believe me, well I did not start this on purpose but now I remember all the times I listened to someone tell me his troubles and thought What a good girl am I to listen to this poor sucker, how wise how clever how well I understand; I do not like thinking of this.

Then I find Charlie has started to tell M'Clare the whole thing.

I will say for Charlie he tells it pretty fair, he does understand why I cannot just let my pals find out I have fooled them, whatever he may have said; but why does he want to tell it to this character, who will not see it at all?

Then he says Well, Professor, if I understand what Cultural Engineering stands for this is a problem right in your line, I would very much welcome advice.

M'Clare says nothing and Charlie says it is a very minor matter of course, M'Clare says There he does not agree.

He says if these tough types caught on that their dear little down-and-out was really rich it would not stop at personal unpleasantness, the whole relation between the mining and farming communities might well be upset.

I would like to sneer but cannot because it is perfectly true, Dad is pretty rich and has a big effect on local affairs; if the miners think his daughter been slumming around making fools of them no knowing what comes after.

M'Clare says However it should be easy enough to fix things so no one can catch on.

Charlie says it is not so simple, Liz has to be got away where no one will chase after her; fortunately very few people in Town are in a position to recognize her, but where can she go now.

I say Look that is easy give me a job on the farm.

Charlie says Suppose they take a fancy to visit you, you think Buffalo Cole is going to remember you are the hired help came there last Tuesday? That is the one place you can be certain sure someone will give you away.

Besides just at present they know your name but have not connected it with Farmer Lee. No, Liz we have to get you a job as companion or something to someone here in Town, a respectable woman the miners will keep right away from.

I say Charlie there are maybe three respectable women in Town; if you park me on one all my pals will come round to make sure I have not hired into a brothel by mistake. How will your lady friend care for that? Charlie says What worries him is where to find a woman anyone could believe had voluntarily saddled herself with a hellcat like me.

M'Clare makes a little cough and Charlie says What does he think?

M'Clare says our solutions are too prosaic and too partial, this is a classic example of the fauntleroy situation and should be worked out as such.

I say What the hell is a fauntleroy?

He says this means a situation in which one younger and apparently weaker person exerts influence over a group of adults by appealing to their protective instincts.

Appeal hell! he says. Unintentionally, no doubt. He says the situation can only be properly resolved if the subject appears to be in no further need of protection against the trouble, whatever it may be; in this case financial.

Charlie says You mean we should tell them Liz has come into money and moved to a hotel?

M'Clare says that again would be only a partial solution, he thinks it would be better if Little Orphan Liz and her sick father were rescued by a Rich Uncle arriving next Wednesday from Earth.

Charlie says Why is Liz short of money if she has a rich uncle ready to assist? M'Clare says he is also a long-lost uncle only recently made his pile and just managed to trace the one remaining relative he has looked for ever since.

I say Why is this better than he died and left me the cash? He says Money for nothing morally unsatisfactory and a bad ending, this way you give something in return; also your lonely uncle can take you and your father straight off to Earth and leave nothing for anyone to ask questions about.

I do not believe anyone will swallow this hunk of cereal, too convenient all round.

According to M'Clare that does not matter, it is the right kind of improbable event for this situation. My pals will think it quite right and proper for their little ray of sunshine to be snatched up into un-earned affluence and cheer the declining years of her rich relative and bring him together with his estranged brother-in-law; right ending to the situation. Statistical probability irrelevant to the workings of Destiny.

Charlie says Where will we find an uncle? He himself is too well known, to hire an actor means going off the planet. M'Clare says as it happens he has to leave the planet this afternoon and will be returning next Wednesday himself.

Charlie says You mean you'd do it? That's really wonderful what do you say Liz? What I want to say is, I will not have this cultural corkscrew add himself to my family, but the lemonade tangles in my epiglottis; people have died that way but Do they care?

M'Clare says of course he must get Mr. Lee's permission for this masquerade; I just thought of that one now I am left with noth-ing to say except Hellanhokum I ought to be back at the bar.

I do not trust M'Clare one Angstrom I could see he was thinking of something else the whole time, probably What interesting op-portunities for fieldwork if the whole thing got given away; if Dad is really over his concussion he will put a stopper on the whole thing.

Does he hell!

Charlie takes M'Clare along, never mind visiting hours are over, they spill the whole thing to Dad before the professor catches his ship.

Well I will say they made a job of it. When I go along in the morning absolutely no bites in the furniture, Dad is still weakened of course.

He say Liz, girl, you are as crazy as a kor-calf, you got as much sense as a shorted servo, the moment I take my eye off you you stir up more trouble than a barrel of hooch on a dry planet. It is a long time since I was surprised at anything you do; here he goes off into ancient history not relevant to this affair.

This business, he says, has put the triple tungsten-plated tin top on it, even you must know what could have happened to you going into a place like that, Liz girl how could you do such a thing?

I say Dad I know it was crazy but you have it all wrong, miners may be tough but those types were real good to me.

He says Liz your capacity to fall on your feet is what scares me the worst of all, one of these days the probabilities will catch up with you all in one go. Look at this Professor M'Clare probably the one man in the Universe would know how to get you out of this with no one catching on, and he turns up here and now.

Well I was all set to get out myself with Charlie helping, but it seems to soothe Dad to think about M'Clare so I let him. That smoothy put himself over all right.

It develops where he has gone is Magnus 9 in the next system to let an examinee loose on some suckers there; he has left a list of instructions with Charlie, and Dad says I am to order myself according to these and not dare to breathe unless so directed.

They are all about what I am to do and say, Charlie stands over me while I learn them by heart, he does not seem to trust me but Hellanall does he think I want to fluff in the middle of a script like this?

Tuesday evening is when the scene starts, my pals ask What is on my mind they hope my old man is not worse is he?

I say I have had a message from a ship just coming within communicator distance and is landing tomorrow. I am to meet someone, whose name got scrambled, at the Space Gate at five-thirty A.M.; I cannot think who this can be it worries me a little Dad has so many troubles already.

At this my pals look grim and say If it is debts I can count on them and if it is anything else I can still count on them, I feel ashamed again.

Five-thirty is a horrible time to start. I am yawning and chilled through, the night breeze is still up and dust creeping in among the long pylon shadows in little puffed whirlwinds; the three ships on the field got their hatches down and goods stacked round and look broken and untidy.

First a little black dot in the sky then bigger and bigger covering more and more stars, it does not seem to come nearer but only to spread, then suddenly a great bulging thing with light modeling its under side and right over head, I want to duck.

It swings across a little to the nearest pylons. They jerk and the arms come up with a clang, reaching after the ship. There is a flash and bang as they make contact just under the gallery where it bulges, then a long slow glide as they fold and she comes down into place like a grasshopper folding its legs.

I find my breathing hitched up, I take a deep lungful of cold morning dust and start coughing.

My pals rally round and pat me on the back.

I thought there were only three present but there seem to be more, I cannot see the passengers get off until half are into the Gate, M'Clare is not in sight hell he did not see me perhaps he has ditched me.

The speaker system makes with a crack like splitting rocks and says Will Miss Lee believed to be somewhere around the Gate come to the manager's office at once please?

I take another deep breath more carefully.

My pals seem to think it is sinister, I now have seven on the premises and they wish to come too. In the end they elect Swede and Dogface bodyguards and the rest wait outside.

I cannot remember one single word I ought to say.

In the office is a man in uniform and another one not, I guess I look blank but not as blank as I feel the human face could hardly, how has he done it this time?

It was several seconds before I recognized him at all. He looks older and kind of worn you would guess he had a hardish life and certainly not cultured at all.

I say I was called for, my name is Lee.

He says slowly, Yes, he thinks he would have known me,

I am very like my mother, and he calls me Elizabeth.

Every word is clean out of my head, fortunately my pals take over and wish to know how come?

M'Clare looks at them with a frown and says neither of them is James Lee, surely?

I say No they are friends of mine, does he mean he is my mother's brother because I thought he was dead?

This is not the right place for that the script is gone to the Coalsack already.

M'Clare says Yes he really is John M'Clare, he brings out papers to prove it. My friends give them the once over several times and seem to be satisfied, then they want to know sternly Why had he not helped us before?

M'Clare brings out letters from a tracing firm that cover two years and a bit, I will say he is a worker he has vamped all this stuff in three days with other things to do, I suppose Cultural Engineering calls for forgery once in a while.

My pals seem satisfied.

I say Why was he looking for us seeing he and Dad never got along? This is the script as originally laid down.

M'Clare alters the next bit ad lib and I don't take it in but it goes over with my pals all right, they tell him all about Dad's accident which they think happened prospecting, and about me and the bar; just then in comes M'Clare's acquaintance well to do in business locally meaning Uncle Charlie, apologizing for being late though M'Clare told him how late to be.

My pals shuffle and say Well Miss Lee you will not want us now.

I say What is this Miss Lee stuff you have been calling me Lizzie for weeks. I had to tell them my name or they will call me Bubbles or something.

M'Clare says he has a great deal to discuss with his niece and Dad, not to mention Charlie, but he wants to hear all about my doings and I will want to tell all my friends; maybe if he calls round to the Royal Arms in the evening they will be there?

They shuffle but seem gratified, they go.

Charlie sits down and the manager goes and Charlie says *Whew!* I sit down and do not say anything at all.

Well Knotty will be pleased to get rid of me that is one life brightened anyway.

I do not want another day like that one, six hours doing nothing in a hotel. I see Dad about five minutes, he uses up the rest of visitor's time with M'Clare or Charlie in and me out, then Charlie flies back home to get something or other and I want to go too, I want to go home! I will never come to this town again, I can't anyway until my pals have all left the planet. I wish all this lying were over.

Evening M'Clare and I go out to the bar.

Knotty has had a letter from me all about it and of course everyone knows, minute we get inside the door I see everybody is worked up and ready to fight at the drop of a hint, fauntleroy situation or not if they think my rich uncle is trying to snoot them all the trouble missed during the last fortnight will occur at one go.

Then M'Clare spots Dogface and Swede at the back of the crowd and says Hello, five minutes later it is drinks all round and everything Jo-block smooth, I could not have done it better myself.

Then he is making a speech.

It is all about Kindness to dumb creatures meaning me, I do not listen but watch the faces, judging by them he is going good. I hear the last words, something about Now he has found his niece and her father he does not want to lose sight of them and his brother-in-law has consented the whole family goes back to Earth in two days' time.

It occurs to me suddenly How am I going to get off the ship? They have found some sick cuss wants to get to Earth and will play my Dad ten minutes to get a free passage, but my pals are bound to turn up to see me off how am I to slip away?

Then I stop thinking because Dogface says slowly So this is the end, hey Liz?

And someone else says Well it was good while it lasted.

And I cry, I put my head down on the table among the drinks and cry like hell, because I am deceitful and they are kind to me and I wish I could tell the truth for a change.

Someone pats me on the back and shoves a disposable into my hand, I think it is one of my pals till I smell it, nobody bought this on Excenus! I am so surprised I wad it up and it goes to dust so I have to stop crying right away.

I even manage to say Good-bye and I will never forget them. They say they will never forget me.

We say about ten thousand good-byes and go.

Next day the hospital say Dad overtired, they have sedated him, seems he was half the night talking to M'Clare and Charlie what the hell were they thinking of to let him? My uncle will call for me. I expect Charlie what I get is M'Clare.

We are to go shopping buying some clothes for me to wear on Earth, it seems to me this is carrying realism too far but I do not want any more time in the hotel with nothing to do.

Fortunately the tailoring clerk does not know me, we have a machine out at the farm; he takes a matrix and slaps up about ten suits and dresses; they will be no use here at all, no place for condensers or canteen I cannot even give them away.

However I am not bothered so much about that, M'Clare is all the time trying to get me to talk, he says for instance Have I ever thought about going to College? I say Sure, I count my blessings now and then.

We are somehow on the subject of education and what teaching have I had so far? I say Usual machines and reels, I want to get off this so I start to talk about Excenus he cannot compete there. I tell him about our manners, customs, morals, finance, farming, geography, geology, mining of areopagite, I am instructive right back to the hotel I hope now he has had enough of it.

In the evening they let me see Dad.

They say You really ought not to be allowed in he has had his quota of visitors today already, I say Who? but need I ask, it was Mr. M'Clare.

The nurse says I am allowed to see Dad because he refuses to go to sleep until he has told me something, but I must be careful not to argue it will retard his recovery if he gets excited again.

Dad is dead white and breathing noisy but full of spirit, the nurse says You may have five minutes and Dad says No one is rationing his time for him when he is ready he will ring. The nurse is a sturdy six footer and Dad is five foot four, they glare it out. Dad wins in the end.

Well I intend to keep it down to five minutes myself, I say Hello Dad what cooks?

He says Lizzie girl what do you think of this M'Clare?

I think quite a number of things but I say He is very clever, I think.

Dad says Sure he is clever, Professor at a big college on Earth gets students from all the planets in the known volume, I been talking to him and he says you have a flair.

I say Huh?

Dad says I have a flair for this cultural engineering business, Professor M'Clare told him so.

I say Well I promised you already I will keep it under control in future.

Dad starts to go red and I say Look two minutes gone already, what did you want to tell me? say it straight, and he says Going to send you to College, girl.

I say What!

Dad says Liz, Excenus is no place for a young girl all her life. Time you seen some other worlds and I cannot leave the farm and got no one have an eye to you, now M'Clare says he will get you into this College and that is just what I need.

I say But—!

Dad says They got schools on Earth for kids like you, been on an outback planet or education restricted other ways, they are called Prelim Schools; well you got the Rudiments already; M'Clare says after three months Prelim you should be fit to get into Russett College of Humanities, he will act as your official guardian while on Earth. Do not argue with me Liz!

The nurse comes back and says I must go in thirty seconds not more, Dad is gray in the face and looks fit to come to pieces, I say All right Dad of course you know best.

He says Kiss me Lizzie, and good-bye.

Then the nurse chases me Out.

This is M'Clare's doing playing on Dad when he is mixed in the head, he knows damned well this thing is impossible if he were only in his right mind. I go tearing back to the hotel to look for M'Clare.

I find he is out.

I sit there seething one hour twenty-seven minutes until he comes in. I say I have to speak to him right now.

I do not know if he is looking bored or amused but it is an expression should be wiped off with rag, he says Certainly, can it wait till we reach his room?

We get there and I say Look what is this nonsense you have talked Dad into about taking me to some College on Earth or something? Because it is straight out crazy and if Dad were right in the head he would know.

M'Clare sits down and says, "Really, Lysistrata, what a spoiled young woman you are."

Who the hell told him, that name is the one thing I really do hold against Dad.

M'Clare goes on that he did not understand at first why my father refused to have me told about the scheme until it was all fixed, but he evidently knew the best way to avoid a lot of fuss.

I say I am not going to leave Excenus.

M'Clare says I cannot possibly avoid leaving Excenus I have got to go on the ship tomorrow haven't I?

I say they can send me back by lifeship, he says it is far too late to arrange that now.

I say then I will come back from the first stop on the way.

He says he is officially my guardian from the moment we leave the planet and he cannot allow me to travel alone, reason for all this rush is so he can see me to College himself, What is the matter with me don't I want to see the World anyway?

Sure, some time, but I don't have to go to College for that.

M'Clare says that is my mistake, Earth had such a rush of sightseers from the Out Planets entrance not permitted anymore except on business, only way I can get there is as a student except I might marry an Earthman some day, I say Hell I would rather go to College than that.

Just the same when I have had enough of it I am coming straight back home.

M'Clare says I will do no such thing.

Great whirling nebulae he cannot keep me on Earth if I want to go! he says On the contrary he has no power to do anything else, my father appointed him my guardian on condition I was to do a four-year course at Russett. Of course if I am determined to return to Excenus home and Dad rather than make the effort to adjust myself to an environment where I have not got everyone securely under my thumb there is an easy way out, I have to take a Prelim test in three months and if I fail to make it no power on Earth could get me into Russett, and he would have to send me back home.

We have to start early in the morning so Good night.

I go to my room, if there was anything I could bite holes in that is what I would do.

I will pass that exam if it takes twenty-eight hours a day, no this is to be on Earth well all the time that they have; I will get into M'Clare's class and make him Sorry he interfered with me.

What does he think I am? Dad too, he would have sent me to school long ago except we both knew I would never make the grade.

I am next thing to illiterate, that's why.

Oh, I can read in a way, I can pick up one word after another as they come up in the machine, but I cannot use it right; Dad is the same.

Dad used to think it was because he learned to use it too late, then when I was old enough to learn he found I was the same, some kink in the genes I suppose. Both of us, we cannot read with the machine any faster than an old-style book.

I did not know this was wrong until I was eleven. Dad hid the booklet came with the machine then one day I found it, part of it says like this:

It has sometimes been suggested that the reading rate should be used as a measure of general intelligence. This is fallacious. The rate at which information can be absorbed, and therefore the rate at which words move across the viewer, is broadly correlated with some aspects of intelligence, but not with all. Mathematicians of genius tend to read slower than the average, and so do some creative artists. All that can safely be said is that people of normal intelligence have reading rates somewhere above five thousand and that it is exceptional for anyone to pass the ten thousand mark: the few who do so are usually people of genius in a narrowly specialized field.

My reading rate is so low the dial does not show, I work out with a stop watch it is eight hundred or thereabouts.

I go and ask Dad; it is the first time he let me see him feeling bad, it is all he can do to talk about it at all, he keeps telling me it is not so bad really he got on all right and he cannot read properly any more than me; he shows me those old books of his all over again.

After this we do not talk about it and I do not want to talk about it now. Not to anyone at all.

That is the longest night I remember in my life, nineteen years of it.

In the morning we got to the Gate. My pals are there seeing me off, I do not cry because I have just found something makes me so mad I am just waiting to get in the ship and say what I think to M'Clare.

Then we go into the ship.

I cannot say anything now we have to strap in for takeoff. The feeling is like being in a swing stopped at the top of its beat. I cannot help waiting for it to come down, but after a bit I grasp we are up to stay and get unhitched.

In the corridor is a crewman, he says Hello miss not sick? I say Ought I to be?

He asks am I an old traveler? when I say First time up he makes clicking noises to say I am clever or lucky or both.

We are getting acquainted when I feel eyes on my backbone and there is M'Clare.

M'Clare says Hello, Lizzie, not sick?

I say I do not have to pretend he is my uncle anymore and I prefer to be called Miss Lee, I will not have a person like him calling me Lizzie or in fact anything else, as of now we are not speaking anymore.

He raises an eyebrow and says Dear him. I start to go but he hooks a hand round my arm and says What is all this about?

I say I have been talking to that poor sucker come out of hospital and pretending to be my Dad. He is a heart case thinks he will be cured when he gets to Earth able to get around like anyone else, I know if he could be cured on Earth he could be cured on Excenus just as well, he will simply have to go on lying in bed and not even anyone he knows around, it is the dirtiest trick I ever knew.

Well he is not smiling now anyway.

He asks have I told the man he will not be cured, I say What does he take me for?

He says, I could answer that but I won't. You are quite right in thinking that it would do very little good to take a man with a diseased heart to Earth, but as it happens he will not be going there at all.

Close to Earth, M'Clare goes on, there is a body called the Moon with approximately one-eighth the gravitational pull, there is a big sanatorium on it for men like this one, the rare case not curable by operation or drugs; and if he cannot live a quiet normal life he will at least be able to get out of bed and probably do some sort of job, this has been explained to him and he seems to think it good enough.

Sweet spirits of sawdust I have heard of that sanatorium before, why does the deck not open and swallow me up.

I say I am sorry, M'Clare says Why?

I say I am sorry I spoke without making sure of the facts.

I do not beg his pardon because I would not have it on a plate.

M'Clare says my uncle gave him a letter to deliver to me when the ship was under way, he shoves it in my hand and goes away.

It is written with Dad's styler, he fell on it during the accident and the L went wobbly, what it says is this.

Dear Liz,

About this College, I know you said I know best but did not mean it at all, just the same I reckon I do. You got to look at it another way. When they got the readers out at my old school and found I could not use them they reckoned I was no good for learning, but they were wrong. There is more to being educated than just books or you could sit and read them at home.

You and I are handicapped same way so we have to use our heads to get over it. All that is in books came out of somebody's head, well you and I just got to use our own instead of other people's. Of course there is facts but a lot of books use the same facts over and over, I found that when I started to study.

There is another thing for you, they told me at school I would never be any good for studying but I reckon I did all right.

It is high time you saw some other worlds than this one but I would not send you to College if I did not think you could get through. M'Clare says you have this Flair. We will look forward to seeing you four years from now, don't forget to write. Your loving father, J. X. Lee. P.S. I got a list of books you will want for Prelim School and Charlie had Information Store copy them, they are in your cabin. J. X. Lee.

Poor old Dad.

Well I suppose I better give it a try, and what's more I better get on with it.

The reels are in my cabin, a whole box of them it will take me a year to get through, the sooner the quicker I suppose.

I jam one in sit down in the machine put on the blinkers and turn the switch.

There is the usual warmup, the words slide on slow at first then quicker then the thing goes *click* and settles down, the lines glide across just fast enough to keep pace with my eyes. I have picked myself something on Terrestrial Biology and Evolution, I realize suddenly I will be among it in a couple of weeks, lions and elephants and kangaroos; well I cannot stop to think now I have to beat that exam.

Most of those weeks I study like a drain.

They have cut day-length in the ship to twenty-four hours already. I have difficulty sleeping at first but I adjust in the end. Between readings I mooch round and talk to the crew, I am careful not to be the little ray of sunshine but we get on all right. I go and see the man with the sick heart a few times, he wants to know all about the Moon so I read up and relay as well as I can.

It sounds dull to me but compared to lying in bed I can see it is high-voltage thrill.

He thanks me every day for the whole voyage, I keep saying we only did it because we wanted someone to impersonate Dad. I think there ought to be ways for people like him to get enough money to go to the Moon how can you earn it lying in bed? He agrees with this but does not get ideas very much, I think I will write about it to Dad.

We stop at the Moon to put him down but no time to look round, M'Clare had to be back at Russett day before yesterday, I suppose he lost time picking me up; well I did not ask him to.

Dropping to Earth I am allowed maybe half a second in the control room to look at the screen, I say What is all that white stuff? they say It is raining down there.

More than half of what I see is water and more coming down!

When the Earthbound ask what interests me most on Earth I say All that water and nothing to pay; they do not know what it means getting water out of near-dry air, condensing breath out of doors, humidity suit to save sweat on a long haul: first time on Earth I go for a walk I get thirsty and nearly panic, on Excenus that would mean canteen given out rush fast for the nearest house.

They told me it was raining; all the same when we walk out of the ship I think at first they are washing the field from up above, I stand there with my mouth open to see; fortunately M'Clare is not looking and I come to quite soon.

Seems all this water has drawbacks too, round here they have to carry rainproofing instead of canteens.

I spend three days seeing sights and never turn on a book.

Prelim School.

Worst is, I do not have a reader of my own now, only reading rooms and I have to keep it private that I read more than two hours a day or someone will catch on and I will be Out before I have a chance to try if what Dad says will work out.

There is more to teaching than books for one thing Class Debates, these are new to me of course but so they are to the others and these I can take. Man to man with my tutor at least I can make him laugh, he says The rugged unpunctuated simplicity of my style of writing is not suited to academic topics even when leavened with polysyllables end of quote, but it is all these books are getting me down.

In the end I get a system, I read the longest reel on each topic and then the other one the author doesn't like, that way I get both sides to the question.

Three months and the exam; afterwards I keep remembering all the things I should have said till I take a twenty-four-hour pill and go to bed till the marking is over.

I wake up and comes a little blue ticket to say I am Through, please report to Russett College in three days for term to begin.

Well, what am I grinning about?

All this means is four years more of the same and M'Clare too added on.

I go for a walk in the rain to cool off but I keep on grinning just the same.

It comes to me as a notion I may not get through Russett term without telling M'Clare all about himself, so I get round and see as much of Earth as I can; more variety than at home.

So then three days are up and here I am in Russett entrance hall with more people than I ever saw in my life at one time.

There are these speaker mechs which are such a feature of Terrestrial life all round the room. One starts up in the usual muted roar like a spacer at a funeral, it says All students for Cultural Engineering Year One gather round please.

This means me.

Cultural Engineering is not a big department, only fifty of us coagulated round this mech but like I said they come all kinds, there is one I see projecting above the throng so brunet he is nearly purple, not just the hair but all over. What is the matter with him he looks like the longest streak of sorrow I ever did see.

Well there are other ways to get pushed into this place than through basic urges thalamic or otherwise, just look at me.

The mech starts again and we are all hanging on what drops from its diaphragm, it says we are to File along corridor G to Room 31 alpha and there take the desk allotted by the monitor and no other.

This we do; even by Terrie standards it is a long hike for indoors.

I wonder what is a monitor, one of these mechs without which the Earthbound cannot tell which way is tomorrow? Then we are stopped and sounds of argument float back from ahead.

That settles it, Terries do not argue with mechs and I am conditioned already, it is a way to get no place at all: there is someone human dealing with the line.

We go forward in little jerks till I can hear, it is one of those Terrie voices always sound like they are done on purpose to me.

We come round the corner to a door and I can see, this monitor is indeed human or at least so classified.

Here we go, it is only me this could happen to.

Each person says a name and the monitor repeats it to the kind of box he carries and this lights up with figures on it. I wonder why the box needs a human along and then I remember, one hundred twenty-four different planets and accents to match. I guess this is one point where Man can be a real help to Machine.

I am glad I saw him before he saw me: I tell him Lee, L. and he looks at me in a bored way and then does a double take and drops the thing.

I pick it up and say Lee, L. in cultivated tones, it lights up just the same, Q8 which means the desk where I have to sit.

The desks are in pairs. When I track Q8 to its lair Q7 is empty, I sit and wonder what the gremlins will send me by way of a partner.

I do not wait long. Here she comes, tall and dark and looks like she had brains right down her spinal column, she will have one of those done-on-purpose voices in which I will hear much good advice when the ice breaks in a month or so. Brother this is no place for me.

She looks straight past my shoulder and does not utter while she is sitting down.

I cannot see her badge which is on the other side. She has what looks to me like a genuine imitation korhide pouch and is taking styler and block out of it, then she looks at me sideways and suddenly lights up all over with a grin like Uncle Charlie's, saying as follows, "Why, are you Lizzie Lee?"

I do not switch reactions fast enough, I hear my voice say coldly that my name is Lee, certainly.

She looks like she stubbed her toe. I realize suddenly she is just a kid, maybe a year younger than I am, and feeling shy. I say quick that I make people call me Lizzie because my real name is too awful to mention.

She lights up again and says So is hers, let us found a Society for the Prevention of Parents or something.

Her brooch says B Laydon, she says her first name will not even abbreviate so people here got to call her just B.

I am just round to wondering where she heard my name when she says That stuffed singlet in the doorway is of course her big brother Douglas and she has been wanting to meet me ever since.

Here Big Brother Douglas puts the box under his arm and fades gently away, the big doors behind the rostrum slide open as the clock turns to fourteen hours and Drums and Trumpets here comes Mr. M'Clare.

B Laydon whispers I think Professor M'Clare is wonderful do not you?

Brother.

I know M'Clare is going to deliver the Opening Address of the Year to Cultural Engineering students, it is my guess all such come out of the same can so I take time off for some thought.

Mostly I am trying to decide what to do. Prelim School was tough enough, so this will be tough², is it worth going through just to show M'Clare I can do it?

Sure it is but can I?

I go on thinking on these lines, such as what Dad will say if I want to give it up; I just about decided all I can do is wait and see when suddenly it is Time up, clock shows 1500 hours exactly just as the last word is spoken and Exit M'Clare.

Some thing I will say.

I look round and all the faces suggest I should maybe have listened after all.

B Laydon is wrapt like a parcel or something, then she catches me looking at her and wriggles slightly.

She says We have been allotted rooms together, sharing a study, do I mind it?

I assume this is because we come together in the alphabet and say Why should I?

She says Well. On the form it said Put down anyone you would like to room with and she wrote Miss Lee.

I ask did she do this because mine was the only name she knew or does she always do the opposite of what Big Brother Douglas tells her, she answers Both.

O.K. by me anyway.

Our rooms are halfway up the center tower, when we find them first thing I see is a little ticket in the delivery slot says Miss Lee call on Professor M'Clare at fifteen-thirty please.

Guardian or no I have seen him not more than twice since landing which means not more than twice too often; still I go along ready to be polite.

He lets me sit opposite and looks thoughtful in a way I do not care for.

He says "Well, Miss Lee, you passed your qualifying exam."

I say Yes because this is true.

He says, it was a very economical performance exceeding the minimum level by two marks exactly.

Hells bells I did not know that, marks are not published, but I swallow hard and try to look as though I meant it that way.

M'Clare says the Admission Board are reluctant to take students who come so close to the borderline but they decided after some hesitation to accept me, as my Prelim Tutor considered that once I settled down as a student and made up my mind to do a little work I should get up to standard easily enough.

He says However from now on it is up to me, I will be examined on this term's work in twelve weeks' time and am expected to get at least ten percent above pass level which cannot be done by neglecting most of the work set, from now on there are no textbooks to rely on.

He presents these facts for my consideration, Good afternoon.

I swagger out feeling lower than sea level.

It is no use feeling sore, I took a lot of trouble to hide the fact that I did a lot of work for that exam, but I feel sore just the same.

The thing I want to do most is get one hundred percent marks in everything just to show him, I got a feeling this is just exactly how he meant me to react, because the more I think about it the more sure I am very few things happen by accident around M'Clare.

Take rooming, for instance.

I find very quickly that most people taking Cultural Engineering have not got the partners they put in for, this makes me wonder why B got what she wanted, meaning me.

Naturally the first thing I think of is she has been elected Good Influence, this makes me pretty cagey of course but after a day or two I see I must think again.

B always says she does not *look* for trouble. This may be true, she is very absentminded and at first I get the idea she just gets into a scrape through having her mind on something else at the time, but later I find she has Principles and these are at the back of it.

First time I hear about these is three nights after Opening, there is a knock at my bedroom window at maybe three hours. I am not properly awake and do not think to question how somebody can be there, seeing it is five hundred feet up the tower; I open the window and B falls inside.

I am just about ready to conclude I must be dreaming when B unstraps a small antigrav pack, mountaineering type, and says Somebody offered her the beastly thing as a secondhand bargain, she has been trying it out and it doesn't work.

Of course an antigrav cannot fail altogether. If the space-warp section could break down they would not be used for building the way they are. What has gone wrong is the phase-tuning arrangement and the thing can be either right on or right off but nothing in between.

B says she stepped off the top of the tower maybe an hour ago and got stuck straight away. She stepped a little too hard and got out of reach of the tower parapet. She only picked that night for it because there was no wind, so she had no chance of being blown back again. She just had to turn the antigrav off, a snatch at a time, and drop little by little until the slope of the tower caught up with her. Then she went on turning it snap on and snap off and kind of slithering down the stonework until she got to about the right floor, and then she had to claw halfway round the building.

B says she was just going to tap at the window above mine and then she saw that frightful Neo-Pueblo statue Old Groucho is so proud of, then she came one farther down and found me but I certainly take plenty of waking.

Well I am wide awake now and I speak to her severely.

I say it is her career, her neck, neither of them mine, but she knows as well as I do jumping off the tower is the one thing in this University is utterly forbidden and no Ifs.

B says That's just because some idiots tried to jump in a high wind and got blown into the stonework.

I say Be that as it may if she had waked up Old Groucho—Professor of Interpenetration Mechanics ninety last week—she would have been expelled straight away, I add further she knows best if it would be worth it.

B says she is a practicing Pragmatist.

This turns out to mean she belongs to a bunch who say Rules are made mostly for conditions that exist only a little bit of the time, e.g. this one about the tower, B is quite right that is not dangerous except in a high wind—not if you have an antigrav I mean.

B says Pragmatists lead a Full Life because they have to make up their own minds when rules really apply and act accordingly, she says you do not lead a Full Life if you obey a lot of regulations when they are not necessary and it is a Principle of Pragmatism not to do this.

B says further it is because Terries go on and on obeying regulations unnecessarily that Outsiders think they are Sissy.

I say Huh?

B says it is not her fault she never had any proper adventures.

I remark If her idea of an adventure is to get hauled in front of the Dean why did she not go ahead and wake up Old Groucho instead of me?

B says the adventure part is just taking the risk, everybody ought to take some risks now and then and breaking rules is the only one available just now.

This causes me to gawp quite a bit, because Earth seems to me maybe fifteen times as dangerous as any planet I heard of so far.

There are risks on all planets, but mostly life is organized to avoid them. Like back home, the big risk is to get caught without water; there is only about one chance in one thousand for that to happen, but everybody wears humidity suits just the same.

On Earth you got a sample of about all the risks there are, mountains and deserts and floods and the sea and wild animals and poisons, now it occurs to me Terries could get rid of most of them if they really cared to try, but their idea of a nice vacation is to take as many as possible just for fun.

Well later on it occurs to me I should never have understood this about Terries but for talking to B, and I look round and find a lot of the Terries got paired up with Outsiders for roommates and maybe this is why.

I say to B some of what I think about risks and it cheers her up for a moment, but she goes on getting into trouble on Pragmatic Principles just the same.

Me, I am in trouble too but not on principle.

The work at first turned out not so bad as I expected, which is not to say it was good.

Each week we have a different Director of Studies and we study a different Topic, with lectures and stereos and visits to museums and of course we read Books.

Further we have what are called Class Debates, kind of an argument with only one person speaking at a time and the Director to referee.

Terries say this last is kid stuff, the Outsiders met it mostly in Prelim School if then so they really study hard so as to do it good. Next thing you know the Terries are outclassed and trying hard to catch up, so a strenuous time is had by all, I begin to see there is a real thing between the two groups though no one likes to mention it out loud.

Class Debates I do not mind, I been used to arguing with Dad all my life, what gets me is Essays. We do one each week to sum up, and all my sums come wrong.

Reason for this is we get about fifteen books to read every week and are not allowed more than three hours a day with a reading machine, this is plenty for most people but I only get through a quarter of the stuff.

If you only know a quarter of the relevant facts you get things cockeyed and I can find no way round this.

My first essay comes back marked Some original ideas but more reference to actual examples needed, style wants polishing up.

The second has Original!! but what about the FACTS, style needs toning down.

More of the same.

After three weeks I am about ready to declare; then I find B gets assorted beefs written on her essays too and takes it for granted everybody does, she says Teachers always tell you what you do wrong not what you do right, this is Education.

I stick it some more.

I will say it is interesting all right. We are studying Influences on Cultural Trends, of which there are plenty some obvious some not.

Most of the class are looking forward to becoming Influences themselves, we have not been taught how to do this yet but everyone figures that comes next. It seems to me though that whatever you call it it comes down to pushing people around when they are not looking, and this is something I do not approve of more than halfway.

There is just one person in the class besides me does not seem to feel certain all is for the best. This is the dark fellow I noticed on Opening day, six foot six and built like a pencil. His name is Likofo Komom'baraze and he is a genuine African; they are rare at Russett because Africans look down on Applied studies, preferring everything Pure. Most of them study Mathematics and Literature and so on at their own universities or the Sorbonne or somewhere, seems he is the first ever to take Cultural Engineering and not so sure he likes it.

This is a bond between us and we become friendly in a kind of way, I find he is not so unhappy as he looks but Africans are proverbially melancholy according to B.

I say to Komo one time that I am worried about the exams, he looks astonished and says, But, Lizzie, you are so clever! turns out he thinks this because the things I say in class debates do not come out of any book he knows of, but it is encouraging just the same.

I need encouragement.

Seventh week of term the Director of Studies is M'Clare.

Maybe it makes not so much difference, but that week I do everything wrong. To start with I manage to put in twice the legitimate time reading for several days, I get through seven books and addle myself thoroughly. In Debates I cannot so much as open my mouth, I am thinking about that Essay all the time, I sit up nights writing it and then tear the stuff up. In the end I guess I just join up bits that I remember out of books and pass that in.

B thinks my behavior odd, but she has caught on now I do not regard M'Clare as the most wonderful thing that ever happened.

The last debate of the week comes after essays have been handed in, I try to pay attention but I am too tired. I notice Komo is trying to say something and stuttering quite a bit, but I do not take in what it is about.

Next day I run into Komo after breakfast and he says Lizzie why were you so silent all the week?

What we studied this time was various pieces of Terrie history where someone deliberately set out to shape things according to his own ideas, I begin to see why Komo is somewhat peeved with me.

Komo says, "Everybody concentrated on the practicability of the modus operandi employed, without considering the ethical aspects of the matter. I think it is at least debatable whether any individual has the right to try and determine the course of evolution of a society, most of the members of which are ignorant of his intentions. I hoped that the discussion would clear my mind, but nobody mentioned this side of it except me."

I know why Komo is worried about this, his old man who is a Tartar by all accounts has the idea he wants to reestablish a tribal society in Africa like they had five hundred years ago; this is why he sent Komo to study at Russett and Komo is only half sold on the idea.

I say "Listen, Komo, this is only the first term and as far as I can see M'Clare is only warming up, we have not got to the real stuff at all yet. I think we shall be able to judge it better when we know more about it, also maybe some of the stuff later in the course might be real helpful if you have to argue with your Dad."

Komo slowly brightens and says "Yes, you are a wise girl, Lizzie Lee."

Here we meet B and some others and conversation broadens, a minute later someone comes along with a little ticket saying Miss Lee see Professor M'Clare at 1130 hours please.

Wise girl, huh?

Komo is still brooding on Ethics and the conversation has got on to Free Will, I listen a bit and then say, "Listen, folks, where did you hatch? you do what you can and what you can't you don't, what is not set by your genes is limited by your environment let alone we were not the first to think of pushing people around, where does the freedom come in?"

They gape and B says Oh but Lizzie, don't you remember what M'Clare said on Opening Day?

This remark I am tired of, it seems M'Clare put the whole course into that one hour so Why we go on studying I do not know.

I say No I did not listen and I am tired of hearing that sentence, did nobody write the lecture down?

B gasps and says there is a recording in the library.

It was quite a speech, I will say.

There is quite a bit about free will. M'Clare says Anyone who feels they have a right to fiddle with other people's lives has no business at Russett. But there is no such thing as absolute freedom, it is a contradiction in terms. Even when you do what you want, your wants are determined by your mental makeup and previous experience. If you do nothing and want nothing, that is not freedom of will but freedom from will, no will at all.

But, he says, all the time we are making choices, some known and some not: the more you look the more you see this. Quote, "It has probably not occurred to you that there is an alternative to sitting here until the hour strikes, and yet the forces that prevent you from walking out are probably not insurmountable. I say 'Probably' because a cultural inhibition can be as absolute as a physical impossibility. Whatever we do means submitting to one set of forces and resisting others. Those of you who are listening are obeying the forces of courtesy, interest or the hope that I may say something useful in examinations, and resisting the forces that tend to draw your minds on to other things. Some of you may have made the opposite choice. The more we consider our doings the more choices we see, and the more we see the better hope we have of understanding human affairs.''

Here there are examples how people often do not make the choice they would really prefer, they are got at for being sissy or something. Or social institutions get in the way even when everyone knows what should be done, Hard cases make bad law and Bad law makes hard cases too. M'Clare says also You are always free to resist your environment, but to do so limits all your choices afterwards, this comes to Make environments so they do not have to be resisted.

There is lots more but this bit has something to do with me, though you may not think so yet.

If I have any choices now, well I can throw my hand in or try to work something out; all I can think of is telling M'Clare how I cannot use a reading machine.

I am not so sure that is a choice, when he said Inhibitions can be absolute, Brother no fooling that is perfectly true.

Right now I can choose to sit here and do nothing or go and get some work done, there is a Balance of forces over that but then I go along to a Reading Room.

I have a long list of books I ought to have read, I just take the first, dial for it and fit it in the machine.

I think, Now I can choose to concentrate or I can let my mind go off on this mess I got into it and What Dad is going to say, no one in their senses would choose that last one. I set my chronoscope for twenty past eleven and put the blinkers on.

I switch the machine on, it lights and starts to go.

Then it goes crazy.

What should have warned me, there is no click. There is the usual warmup, slow then faster, but instead of a little jump and then ordinary speed it gets faster and faster and before I realize it I am caught.

It is like being stuck in concrete except this is inside me, in my head, and growing, it spreads and pushes, it is too big for my skull it is going to *burst* and then I have let out a most almighty yell and torn out of the thing, I find later I left a bit of hair in the blinkers but I am out of it.

There is no one around, I run as though that machine had legs to come after me, I run right out in the campus and nearly crash with a tree, then I put my back to it and start breathing again.

Whatever I have done until now, judging by the feel of my ribs breathing was no part of it.

After a bit I sit down, I still have my back to the tree, I leave thinking till later and just sit.

Then I jump up and yell again.

I have left that crazy machine to itself, someone may sit in it this minute and get driven clean out of their head.

I run back not quite so fast as I came and burst in, someone just sitting down I yell out loud and yank him out of it.

It is a Third Year I do not know, from another class, he is much astonished by me.

I explain.

I guess I make it dramatic, he looks quite scared, meanwhile a small crowd has gathered around the door.

Along comes Doc Beschrievene expert at this kind of machine to see Why breach of the rule of silence in this block.

He trots straight in and starts inspecting the chair, then he says Exactly what happened, Miss Lee?

I say My God I have to see Mr. M'Clare!

I have been scratching my wrist for minutes, I now find the alarm of my chronoscope is trying to make itself felt, once again I am breaking records away from there.

I arrive one minute late but M'Clare has a visitor already so I can even get my breath, I also catch up on my apprehensions about this interview; seem to me the choice is get slung out as a slacker or get slung out as moron and I truly do not know which one I care for less.

Then the visitor goes and I stumble in.

M'Clare has a kind of unusual look, his eyes have gone flat and a little way back behind the lids, I do not get it at first then I suddenly see he is very tired.

However his voice is just as usual, not angry but maybe a little tired too, he says "Well, Miss Lee, they say actions speak louder than words and you certainly have given us a demonstration; you've made it quite clear that you could do the work but you aren't going to, and while it would be interesting to see if you could gauge the requirements of the examiners so exactly this time I don't think it would justify the time taken to mark your papers. What do you want to do? Go back to Excenus straight away or take a vacation first?''

I simply do not have anything to say, I feel I have been wrapped and sealed and stuck in the delivery hatch, he goes on, ''It's a pity, I think. I thought when I first saw you there was a brain under that golden mop and it was a pity to let it go to waste. If only there were something that mattered more to you than the idea of being made to do what you don't want to—''

It is queer to watch someone get a call on a built-in phone, some do a sort of twitch some shut their eyes, M'Clare just lets the focus of his slide out through the wall and I might not be there anymore, I wish I was not but I have to say something before I go away.

M'Clare has been using a throat mike but now he says out loud, ''Yes, come over right away.''

Now he is not tired anymore.

He says ''What happened to the reading machine, Miss Lee?''

I say ''It went crazy.'' Then I see this is kid's talk, but I have no time to put learned words to it, I say ''Look. You know how it starts? There is a sort of warmup and then a little click and it settles down to the right speed? Well it did not happen. What I think, the governor must have been off or something, but that is not all—it got quicker and quicker but it did something else—look I have not the right expression for it, but it felt like something opened my skull and was pasting things on the convolutions inside.''

He has a look of wild something, maybe surmise maybe just exasperation, then Doc Beschrievene comes in.

He says ''Miss Lee, if it was a joke, may we call it off? Readers are in short supply.''

I say if I wanted to make a joke I would make it a funny one.

M'Clare says ''Ask Miss Lee to tell you what happens when you start the reader.''

Beschrievene says ''I have started it! I connected it up and it worked quite normally.''

Now the thing has gone into hiding, it will jump out on someone else like it did on me, I have no time to say this; M'Clare says ''Tell Dr. Beschrievene about the reader.''

I say ''It started to go too fast and then—''

He says Start at the beginning and tell what I told before.

I say "When you sit in a reader there is normally an initial period during which the movement of the words becomes more rapid, then there is a short transitional period of confusion and then the thing clicks audibly and the movement of the words proceeds at a set rate, this time—"

Here Doc gives a yell just like me and jumps to his feet.

M'Clare says What was I reading in the machine?

I do not see what that has to do with it but I tell him, then he wants to know what I remember of it and where it stopped.

I would not have thought I remembered but I do, I know just where it had got to, he takes me backwards bit by bit—

Then I begin to catch on.

M'Clare says "What is your usual reading rate, Liz?"

I swallow hard, I say "Too low to show on the dial, I don't know."

He says "Is your father handicapped too?"

I lift my head again, I am going to say that is not his business, then I say Yes instead.

He says "And he feels badly about it? Yes, he would. And you never told anybody. Of course not!" I do not know if it is scorn or anger or what. Beschrievene is talking to himself in a language I do not know, M'Clare says Come along to the reading room.

The chair has its back off, M'Clare plugs in a little meter lying on the floor and says "Sit down, Liz."

There is nothing I want less than to sit in that chair, but I do.

M'Clare says "Whether or not you have a repetition of your previous experience is entirely up to you. Switch on."

I am annoyed at his tone, I think I will give that switch a good bang, I feel I have done it too.

But the light does not go on.

M'Clare says patiently "Turn on, please, Miss Lee."

I say "You do it."

Beschrievene says "Wait! There is no need to demonstrate, after all. We know what happened."

Then M'Clare's fingers brush over mine and turn the switch.

I jump all over, the thing warms up and then click! there is the little jump and the words moving steadily through.

And you know, I am disappointed.

Beschrievene says He will be the son of a bigamist, I jump out of the chair and demand to know what goes?

M'Clare is looking at a dial in the meter, he turns and looks at me with exactly the same expression and says, "Would you like to repeat your previous experience?"

Beschrievene says "No!"

I say "Yes. I would."

M'Clare bends and does something inside the machine, then he says again "Sit down, Lizzie Lee."

I do, I hit the switch myself too.

There it is again, words slide across slow and then quicker and quicker and there is something pressing on my brain, then there is a bang and it all goes off and Beschrievene is talking angry and foreign to M'Clare.

I climb out and say Will they kindly explain.

M'Clare tells me to come and look, it is the reading-rate dial of the machine it now says Seven thousand five hundred and three.

Beschrievene says How much do I know about the machine? seems to me the safest answer is Nothing at all.

He says "There is an attachment which regulates the speed of movement of the words according to the reaction of the user. It sets itself automatically and registers on this dial here. But there is also another part of the machine far more important although there is no dial for it, unless you fit a test-meter as we have done: this is called the concentration unit or Crammer."

I did know that, it is what makes people able to read faster than with an old-style book.

He says, "This unit is compulsive. When the machines were first made it was thought that they might be misused to insert hypnotic commands into the minds of readers. It would be very difficult, but perhaps possible. Therefore in the design was incorporated a safety device." He pats one individual piece of spaghetti for me to admire.

He says "This device automatically shuts off the machine when it encounters certain cortical wave-patterns which correspond to strong resistance, such as is called forth by hypnotically imposed orders; not merely the resistance of a wandering mind."

I say But—

He looks as though I suddenly started sprouting and says "M'Clare this is most strange, this very young girl to be so strong, and from childhood too! Looks are nothing, of course—"

M'Clare says "Exactly so. Do you understand, Miss Lee? One of your outstanding characteristics is a dislike of being what you call pushed around, in fact I believe if somebody tried to force you to carry out your dearest wish you would resist with all your might, you are not so set on free will as you are on free won't. The Crammer appeared to your subconscious as something that interfered with your personal freedom, so you resisted it. That isn't uncommon, at first, but not many people resist hard enough to turn the thing off.''

I say ''But it worked!''

Beschrievene says that the safety device only turns off the Crammer, the rest of the machine goes on working but only at the rate for unassisted reading about one-tenth normal rate.

M'Clare says ''You, my girl, have been trying to keep up with a course designed for people who could absorb information seven or eight times as fast. No wonder your knowledge seemed a bit sketchy.''

He sounds angry.

Well hells bells I am angry myself, if only I had told somebody it could all have been put right at the start, or if only the man who first tried to teach Dad the reader had known what was wrong with the way he used it, Dad would have had ordinary schooling and maybe not gone into prospecting but something else, and—

Then whoever got born it would not have been me, so where does that get you?

Beschrievene is saying ''What I do not understand, why did she suddenly stop resisting the machine?''

M'Clare says Well Liz?

It is a little time before I see the answer to that, then I say ''We cannot resist everything we can only choose the forces to which we will submit.''

They look blank, M'Clare says Is it a quotation?

I say ''Your speech on Opening Day, I did not listen. I heard it just now.''

This I never thought to see, his classical puss goes red all over and he does not know what to say.

Beschrievene wants to know more of what was said so I recite, at the end he says ''Words! Your students frighten me, M'Clare. So much power in words, at the right time, and you are training them to use such tools so young! To use them perhaps on a whole planet!''

M'Clare says ''Would you rather leave it to chance? Or to peo-

ple with good intentions and no training at all? Or to professional
ax-grinders and amateurs on the make?''

I say How do I stop doing it?

Beschrievene rubs his chin and says I will have to start slowly,
the machine produced so much effect because it was going fast,
normally children learn to read at five when their reading rate is
low even with the Crammer. He says he will take out the safety but
put in something to limit speed and I can have a short session tomorrow.

I say Exams in four weeks three days why not today?

He laughs and says Of course I will be excused the exam—

M'Clare says Certainly I will take the exam, there is no reason
why I should not pull up to pass standard; work is not heavy this
term.

Beschrievene looks under his eyebrows but says Very well.

After lunch I sit down in the doctored machine.

Five minutes later I am sick.

Beschrievene fusses and gives me antinauseant and makes me
lie down one half hour then I start again.

I last twenty minutes and come out head aching fit to grind a
hole, I say For all sakes run it full speed it is this push and drag
together turns me up, this morning it only scared me.

He does not want to do this, I try all out to persuade him, I am
getting set to weep tears when he says Very well, he is no longer
surprised my will was strong enough to turn off the machine.

This time it comes full on.

The words slide across my eyes slow, then quicker, then suddenly they are running like water pouring through my eyes to my
brain, something has hold of me keeping my mind open so that
they can get in, if I struggle if I stop one micro-second from absolute concentration they will jam and something will *break*.

I could not pull any of my mind away to think with but there is a
little corner of it free, watching my body, it makes my breath go
on, digs my nails in my hand, stops the muscles of my legs when
they try to jerk me out of the chair, sets others to push me back
again.

I can hear my breath panting and the bang of my heart, then I do
not hear it any longer, I am not separate any longer from the
knowledge coming into me from the machine.

and then it stops.

It is like waking with a light on the face, I gasp and leap in the seat and the blinkers pull my hair, I yell What did you do that for?

M'Clare is standing in front of me, he says Eighty-seven minutes is quite sufficient come out of that at once.

I try to stand and my knees won't unhinge, to hear M'Clare you would think it was his legs I got cramp in, I suppose I went to sleep in the middle of his remarks anyway I wake tomorrow in bed.

In the morning I tell it all to B because she is a friend of mine and it is instructive anyway.

B says Lizzie it must have been awful but it is rather wonderful too; I do not see this I say Well it is nice it is over.

Which it is not.

Four weeks look a long time from the front end but not when it is over and I have to take the exam.

I have made up my mind on one thing, if I do not pass I am not asking anyone to make allowances I am just straight off going home, I am too tired to think much about it but that is what I will do.

Exam, I look at all the busy interested faces and the stylers clicking along and at the end I am certain for sure I failed it by quite a way.

I do not join any postmortem groups I get to my room and lock the door and think for a bit.

I think That finishes it, no more strain and grind and Terrie voices and Please Tune in Daily For Routine Announcements and smells you get in some of this air, no more high-minded kids who don't know dead sure from however, no more essays and No More M'Clare, I wish they would hurry up and get the marks over so I can get organized to count my blessings properly.

However sixty four-hour papers take time to read even with a Crammer and M'Clare does them all himself, we shall get the marks day after tomorrow if then.

There is a buzz from the speaker in the study and B is not there, I have to go.

Of all people who should be too busy to call me just now it is Mr. M'Clare.

He says I have not notified him of my vacation plans yet.

I say Huh?

He says as my guardian he ought to know where I am to be found and he wants to be sure I have got return schedules fixed from wherever I am going to so as to make certain I get back in time for next term.

I say Hell what makes you think I am coming back next term anyway.

He says Certainly I am coming back next term, if I am referring to the exam he has just had a look at my paper it is adequate though not outstanding no doubt I will do better with time. Will I let his secretary have details of my plans, and he turns it off on me.

I sit down on the floor, no chair to hand.

Well for one thing the bit about the vacations was not even meant to deceive, he did it just to let me know I was Through.

So I have not finished here after all.

The more I think about studying Cultural Engineering the more doubtful I get, it is pushing people around however you like to put it more fancy than that.

The more I think about Terries the more I wonder they survive so long, some are all right such as B but even she would not be so safe in most places I know.

The more I think—

Well who am I fooling after all?

The plain fact is I am not leaving Russett and all the rest of it and I am so pleased with this, just now I do not care if the whole College calls me Lysistrata.

BROTHER ROBOT

Henry Slesar

It seems that no volume of science-fiction stories can be considered complete without a robot entry. If you think that all robots fit Isaac Asimov's mold, obeying the Three Laws of Robotics, be advised that they don't. Yet I think that the point made in this story would apply as well to a human child.

—PA

Slesar's remarkable career—as Edgar-winning mystery novelist, creator and chief scriptwriter of The Edge of Night, *and author of several hundred short stories which have appeared in all of the important magazines (he is still* Playboy's *most prolific contributor)—needs little explication here. There are those who feel (and I am amongst them) that despite Fred Brown's reputation, Slesar is the finest practitioner of the short-short story not only in science fiction but probably in American letters. (Jack Ritchie is a respectable place in the competition.) His very prolificity makes it possible for some stories to qualify, to our enormous luck, for this anthology.*

—bnm

I agree with Barry—Henry Slesar is a remarkable writer who had some thirty-five stories adapted by Alfred Hitchcock for his television shows. One story not adapted for any medium remains unforgettable to me—"The Jam," from Playboy, *November 1958, which must rank as one of the finest American short stories. Two now obscure mystery collections do exist—A Bouquet of Clean Crimes and Neat Murders (1960) and A Crime for Mothers and Others (1962), both Avon paperbacks. A science-fiction/fantasy collection is long overdue.*

—MHG

They found the old man in his study, slumped over the desk in what appeared to be sleep. But the quiet which had come upon him was deeper and gentler than sleep. Beside his opened hand stood an uncapped container of lethal tablets. Beneath his fine white hair, a pillow for his head, was a journal begun thirty years before. His name was on the first page: *Dr. Alfred Keeley*. And the date: *February 6, 1997.*

Feb. 6, 1997. This is a day twice-blessed for me. Today, at St. Luke's Hospital, our first child was born to my wife, Ila. The baby is a boy, seven pounds, two ounces, and according to Ila's sentimental appraisal, the image of his father. When I saw her this morning, I could not bring myself to mention the second birth which has taken place in my laboratory. The birth of Machine, my robot child.

Machine was conceived long before the infant Ila will bring home soon (we will call him Peter Fitzpatrick, after Ila's grandfather). Machine was conceived long before my marriage, when I first received my professorship in robotics. It is exhilarating to see my dream transformed into reality: a robot child that would be reared within the bosom of a human family, raised like a human child, a brother to a human child—growing, learning, becoming an adult. I can hardly contain my excitement at the possibilities I foresee.

It has taken me seven years to perfect the robot brain which will be the soul of my robot son, a brain whose learning capacities will equal (and in some regard, exceed) the capabilities of Peter Fitzpatrick himself. But I must keep the experiment perfectly controlled. My duties will consist primarily of careful observation, and of providing for the physical maturation of Machine. My robot child will not have the natural advantages of growth that Peter Fitzpatrick will possess; I must provide them for him. I will reconstruct his metal body periodically, so that he keeps pace with the growth of his human brother. Eventually, I hope that Machine will learn enough about the construction of his own form that he may make these changes for himself.

At the moment, Machine already has physical advantages over his brother. I did not wish to handicap my metal child; he will have serious shortcomings in a human world; the least I could do was to provide him with the advantages only a machine could boast. He will never know hunger or thirst, or the unpleasant necessities of human waste disposal. He will never know bitter cold or sweltering heat. The ills to which mankind are subject will never trouble his artificial body. The vulnerability of human flesh will never be his problem. He will live on, inviolate, as long as his robot brain pulses within the impenetrable housing of his beautiful head.

Have I said that Machine is beautiful? Yes, I have made him so. The world of humans will be critical enough of my experiment and my robot child; but they will not call him monster. I have made him beautiful with the beauty of perfect function. I have constructed him along human lines (nature was an excellent designer). I have given him a gleaming skin of silver, and flawless modeling. He shall inspire no loathing, my robot creation. Not even in Ila.

Ila! My heart constricts at the thought of my wife, who lies in happy slumber at St. Luke's this moment, unaware of the brother who awaits her infant son. How will she react? She has always been so helpful, so understanding. But an experiment like this, within her own domain, involving her own newborn son . . .

I must not worry myself needlessly. I must get ready. I must prepare for the arrival of Peter Fitzpatrick, brother of Machine.

June 11, 1997. I am outraged, outraged and deceived. Today I learned that the man who called upon me last month was not the scientific reporter he claimed to be. Now I know that he was a representative of a local newspaper, looking for a sensational Sunday feature with which to tickle the vulgar curiosity of its readers.

What a fool I was to grant him the interview! This morning, I found the article, illustrated by a terrible and inaccurate portrait of Mac and my son. ''ROBOTIC PROFESSOR RAISES ROBOT AND SON AS BROTHERS . . .''

I have hidden the scandalous article from Ila's eyes. She is still bedridden, and I am worried about her failure to gain strength. Can it be that my experiment is the real cause of her illness? I believed, after her first hysterical outburst of protest, that she had become accustomed to the idea. She seemed so willing to cooperate, so completely aware of what I was trying to do. And yet, the way she looks at Mac, the evident horror in her eyes when she sees him touch our son . . .

No, I am sure she understands. Ila was never strong; she had rheumatic fever as a child, perhaps this is the belated result. I am sure she will be better when warmer weather comes. Perhaps if we went away . . .

But I cannot go away, of course, not at this early stage of my experiment. So far, all has gone well. At four months, Fitz is developing along normal lines. His little body has gone from asymmetric postures to symmetric postures, his eyes now converge and fasten upon any dangling object held at midpoint. As for Mac, he is advancing even more rapidly. He is beginning to learn control of his limbs; it is apparent that he will walk before his human brother. Before long, he will learn to speak; already I hear rumbles within the cavity of the sound-box in his chest. Fitz can only gurgle and coo his delight at being alive.

I believe Ila was right; Fitz does look like me. I would have preferred him to have Ila's green eyes and fair skin, but he is dark like myself. I feel an unscientific pride in my boy.

Sept. 10, 1997. Must happiness and despair always live side by side? It would seem that is my fate. Today, I thought I would surprise Ila with the extraordinary progress of our robot child. I knew that Mac has been developing the power of coherent speech, and has already said some simple words. For the past week, I have been teaching him phrases, beginning with the one I thought would please Ila most. But I have been foolish. I believe Ila must resent Mac's rapid development. Fitz, at the age of seven months, is just now displaying coordination. He can reach and grasp things; vision and touch are correlating. He can transfer objects from hand to hand, and he makes sounds that might be taken, or mistaken, for words.

But Mac is far ahead of him. And this morning, at ten o'clock, I brought him into Ila's bedroom. She was still fast asleep; her illness seems to produce the need for sleep. She stirred when she heard our footsteps (Mac's metal feet are too noisy; I must muffle his lumbering stride). I said:

"Ila, I have a little surprise . . ."

She raised her head from the pillow and looked at me, avoiding contact with Mac's silvery face.

"What is it?" she said.

"It's Mac. He wants to say something to you."

"What are you talking about?"

I smiled.

"All right, Mac."

His metal face lifted towards her. From the featureless surface, a small, uncertain voice emerged.

"He . . . llo . . . mo . . . ther . . ."

I almost laughed aloud in satisfaction and delight, and turned to

Ila in search of her approval and pleasure. But her face bore an expression that amazed and frightened me, an expression of utter horror I had never seen before. Her lips moved soundlessly, and her eyes, always feverish, burned brighter than ever. And then she screamed. God help me, she screamed as if the devil were in the room, bringing up her hands to clutch at her hair. In the nursery next door, little Fitz set up a sympathetic wail, and I saw Mac's metal body shiver as if in reaction to the sound.

I tried to calm her, but she was lost in hysteria. Eventually her sobs stopped, but then she fell back upon the pillow with such exhaustion that I became concerned and telephoned for medical help. Dr. Foster arrived half an hour later and shut me out of the bedroom. When he finally emerged, he mumbled something about shock, and prescribed rest and tranquilizing drugs.

I went into Ila's room a few minutes ago. Her eyes were closed and her breathing was shallow. I spoke to her, but she merely lifted her hand and said nothing. My poor Ila! Why must she face so much misery, while I experience such joy and satisfaction in my work?

Jan. 1, 1998. It has been almost two months since I last touched this journal, but I must take strength in this New Year and continue. It has been hard for me to work at all; there has been too much bitterness in my mind and unhappiness in my heart since Ila's death.

As I write these words, little Fitz is sleeping peacefully in his crib, watched over by his new nursemaid, Annette. But Mac, who needs no sleep, is sitting in the study chair beside my desk, watching me through the expressionless eyes I have placed in his silver skull. Yet, blank as they are, somehow I sense emotion in those eyes as he watches me. Somehow, I feel my robot creation knows the torment I suffer, and knows the void in our home since Ila's death. Does he miss her, too? It is so difficult to tell. Even with Fitz, my human child, it is hard to recognize the signs of sorrow he must be feeling.

During these past weeks, I began to believe that my experiment was all a conceit. But now I realize it was only grief that brought such thoughts; I must continue. Already, I believe Mac thinks of Fitz as his brother, and I know that someday Fitz will reciprocate. There will be much to learn from both of them. I cannot fail my mission now. I will go on.

* * *

July 25, 2002. Today, my family and I begin life in new surroundings, and as difficult as the transplantation has been, I am glad now that we made the move. It had become too much of a burden to face the curiosity and gibes of the neighborhood; we have attracted too much attention. For this reason, I have purchased this small home in the exurbs of the city, just outside the town of Fremont.

Both my children seem happy in their new country residence. They are playing together now on the green grass that grows untamed behind the house; I will have to trim and weed it, like a truly domesticated homeowner. I think I shall enjoy the sensation.

Despite our problems, my joy is great as I watch the human and mechanical being outside my window, laughing and romping together as if the differences between them had no existence. In one respect, my experiment is already successful. In the eyes of Fitz, my human boy, and Mac, my inhuman invention, they are truly brothers. Fitz, at the age of five, is a sturdy, red-cheeked boy with dark eyes and a smile that easily becomes a laugh. There is a great deal of warmth in him; he is open and frank with people, and with his metallic brother.

As for Mac, of course, he is the same as ever; the same polished silvery body, encased in the simple tunic I have made to cover his metallic nakedness. They are almost the same height, but Fitz is a bit taller, and growing each day. Before long, it will be time to reconstruct my robot child's body again.

I have presented my first full-length paper on the experiment to the National Robotics Society. I must admit that I eagerly await their acceptance and publication.

Sept. 3, 2003. This morning, I opened my door upon a matronly woman whose pleasantries concealed an icy attitude towards myself and my family. She introduced herself as Mrs. Margotson, chairwoman of the local school board.

It was some time before Mrs. Margotson revealed the true purpose of her visit, which was to expose the board's reluctance to accept the enrollment of Mac, my robot child.

"You understand, of course," she told me, "that there is no question concerning your son. But the idea of this—machine entering our school is perfectly absurd."

I had written a lengthy letter which explained my experiment in detail, but it had made little impression upon the authorities. She kept referring to "that metal thing" and "that machine" and her lip curled in disgust. I wasn't too upset by her attitude; I rather expected it.

"I understand," I told her. "To be honest, I did not expect approval, but I felt it my duty to make the application. However, since the board refuses, I shall not enter either child. I will tutor them both at home."

Mrs. Margotson looked shocked. "Are you serious about this experiment, Dr. Keeley?"

"Certainly. They are brothers, you know."

"Really!"

Both Fitz and Mac were delighted with my plans for their education; it seemed that neither one was keen on the idea of entering the local school. I didn't find out exactly why until late that afternoon.

The reason became apparent when Mac and Fitz returned from some mysterious outing. There was a vacancy in Fitz's mouth where a tooth had been recently and forcibly removed. There was a faint bruise on his cheek, and a hole in the knee of his trousers. I was disturbed by this evidence of a brawl, but was even more shocked and surprised to see a large dent in Mac's silvery forehead. I knew he felt no physical pain, but it was startling.

"What happened?" I said.

Fitz, always the spokesman, shrugged his shoulders.

"Just a fight," he said glumly.

"What do you mean, just a fight? Who with? What about?"

"Some kids. Kids from the school."

"How many kids?"

"Five or six," Fitz said. "They threw things. Rocks."

I was appalled, and now I knew what had caused the dent. I don't know why I should have been surprised at the tale of violence. I had learned before, in our old city neighborhood, that my robot child was a natural target for the cruel taunts and unthinking violence of children.

I treated Fitz's wounds, and then drew Mac aside.

"What happened?" I asked gently.

"Fitz told you. We had a fight."

"I want to hear your version. Were they making fun of you, Mac? Is that it?"

"Yes."

"How did you feel about it?" I asked the question eagerly; it was important to me to learn the emotional responses of my creation.

Mac didn't answer for a while, his face a silver mask.

"Did you feel hurt, angry? Did you want to strike back? I've told you this often, Mac—you must never strike a human. They're soft, you know, not hard like you. Did you want to hurt them, Mac?" Instinctively, I reached for pencil and paper to record his reactions.

"Yes," he said.

My heart leaped. My robot child had felt anger!

"But you didn't?"

"No."

"Why, Mac? Because you realized you were strong and they were weak? Because they felt pain and you didn't?"

"No!" He was almost defiant.

"What, then?"

"Because I am little," he whispered.

The reply disturbed me. I hadn't yet gotten around to performing the mechanical surgery that would give Machine his new body. He was several inches shorter than his brother, shorter than most boys his age.

Patiently, I explained to him again the rules of conduct I expected of him, rules that could never be broken. There must be no harm to humans; it was the cardinal rule of our code.

"Do you understand that, Mac? Truly understand it?"

"Yes," he answered, his blank eyes on the floor.

I sighed.

"All right, then. I will make you bigger, Mac. I will build a new body."

April 23, 2008. It feels good to be recognized, I must admit it. The award conferred upon me by the National Robotics Society yesterday has meant a great deal to me. It has made a difference in the attitude of my neighbors; they no longer think of me as a half-mad creator of monsters, a new Frankenstein. And the monetary grant, while not enormous, will permit me to expand my laboratory facilities. It has come at an opportune time; I have been blueprinting a greatly improved physical housing for Mac, one which will permit his metal body greater flexibility and digital dexterity. I think, too, that I can create a superior sound system for him now, which will overcome the flat, metallic voice of my robot child.

Both Mac and Fitz are not overly impressed by my sudden fame. But I believe Mac is secretly excited by my promise to build him a better body. He has become acutely aware of his appearance; I have caught him gazing (with what emotion, I cannot say) into the mirrors of the house, standing before them with a stillness that only a robot can maintain. I have questioned him at length about his feelings, but have learned little. I must be sure to keep close to his emotional growth.

But if I have a real source of happiness now, it is my son Fitz. He has become a fine handsome boy, of such good humor and intelligence that he is extremely popular with all the residents of the town—and the power of his engaging personality has created an acceptance for Mac, his robot brother, that all my elaborate scientific titles couldn't have attained. He is still fiercely loyal to Mac, but I already detect signs of independence. These do not worry me; they would be natural even among human brothers. Fitz is discovering that he is an individual; it's a process of life.

But I wonder—will Mac feel the same way?

Jan. 4, 2012. There has been a quarrel, and it has taken me several days to learn the true details. I have never been disturbed about quarrels between Fitz and Mac; they have had surprisingly few for brothers. But for the first time, I sensed that the quarrel concerned the differences between them.

It began last week, when a boy of their age, Philip, a hostile surly youth, involved Fitz in a fight.

Philip is the son of a divorced woman in the town, named Mrs. Stanton. She is a strange, brooding woman, with a terrible resentment against her ex-husband. I am afraid some of the resentment has been passed on to her son, Philip, and that he is an unhappy youngster. For the last two months, Fitz has been a frequent visitor to their home, and Mrs. Stanton has displayed great fondness for him. Philip, of course, doesn't like this affection, this stolen love, and has developed a strong animosity towards Fitz. One day, it turned into violence.

Philip is big for his fifteen years, a tall boy, well over six feet, and well muscled. When he stopped Fitz and Mac on the street that morning, it was immediately apparent that he was seeking trouble. Fitz is not afraid of him, I know that; but Fitz tries to laugh trouble away. But the boy was in no mood to be put off with a smile. He lashed out and knocked Fitz down. When he got to his feet, Philip knocked him down again, and then leaped atop him.

I don't know what outcome the fight would have had if Fitz had been allowed to finish it. But he didn't have the chance. Mac, who was standing by, watching the altercation in his blank manner, suddenly threw himself upon his brother's assailant and pulled him away as easily as if Philip had been an infant. He lifted him into the air with his superhuman strength and merely held him there. He didn't hurt Philip, he traded no blows; he simply held him, helpless, in the air, while the boy kicked and screamed his frustration and anger. Fitz shouted at his brother to release him, and eventually Mac did. Philip didn't resume the attack; he was frightened by the easy, unconquerable strength in Mac's metal arms. He turned and ran, shouting threats and ugly names over his shoulder.

Of course, I know Mac's intent was good. He was protecting his brother, and wasn't violating the code of conduct. But I can also understand Fitz's emotion. He didn't feel grateful for Mac's help, only resentful. He turned upon the robot and reviled him, called him terrible names I never knew were in his vocabulary. He told Mac that he didn't want protection, that he could fight his own battles, that he didn't require Mac's metal strength to keep him from harm. He said a great deal more, and it is well that Mac is not more sensitive than he is.

There is a strain between them now. For the last few days, Fitz has been leaving the house without Mac's company. Mac, fortunately, doesn't seem injured by his behavior. He sits, blank-faced as ever, in his room. He reads or listens to his phonograph. Sometimes, he gets up and stares into the mirror, for interminable periods.

Oct. 15, 2016. It is extraordinary, the speed with which Mac has learned his lessons. For the past year, I have been teaching him the secrets of his own construction, and how he himself could repair or improve all or part of his artificial body. He has been spending five or six hours each day in my laboratory workshop, and now I believe he is as skilled as—or perhaps more skilled than—I am myself. It will not be long before he blueprints and builds his own new body. No, not blueprint. I cannot allow him to design the plans, not yet. The Face episode proved that.

It began last Friday evening, when Fitz left the house to take Karen to the movies. As usual, Mac seemed lost without his brother, and sat quietly in his room. About midnight, he must have heard the sound of my typewriter in the study, because he came to the doorway. I invited him in and we chatted. He was curious about certain things, and asking a great number of questions about

Karen. Not sex questions, particularly; Mac is as well read as any adult, and knows a good deal about human biology and human passions (I wonder sometimes what his opinion is of it all!) But he was interested in learning more about Fitz and Karen, about the nature of their relationship, the special kind of fondness Fitz seemed to display towards the girl.

I don't believe I was helpful in my answers. Half an hour later, the front door opened and Fitz entered, bearing Karen on his arm.

Karen is a lovely young girl, with an enchanting smile and delightful face. And, if I am not mistaken, very fond of Fitz. She greeted me warmly, but I think she was surprised to see Mac; ordinarily, he kept to his room on Fitz's date nights. Mac responded to her greeting with a muffled noise in his sound system, and retreated upstairs.

I didn't see Mac the next morning, or even the next afternoon. He seemed to have spent the entire day in the workshop. We were at dinner when Fitz and I saw him first, and when we did, we gasped in surprise.

Something had happened to Mac's face, and I knew it was the result of his efforts in the workshop. Instead of the smooth, sculptured mask I had created for him, there was a crudely shaped human face looking at us, a mockery of a human face, with a badly carved nose and cheeks and lips, tinged grotesquely with the colors of the human complexion.

Our first reaction was shock, and then, explosively, laughter. When we were calm again, Mac asked us for an explanation of our outburst, and I told him, as gently as possible, that his attempts to humanize himself were far from successful. He went to a mirror and stared for a long while; then he turned without a word and went back to the laboratory. When we saw him again the next morning, he was the old Mac again. I admit I was relieved.

Oct. 9, 2020. How lost Mac seems without Fitz! Since his brother's marriage last month, he stalks about the house, lumbering like the robot child of old, clanking as if he still possessed the clumsy metal body of his infancy and adolescence. I have been trying to keep him busy in the laboratory, but I think he knows I am indulging him rather than truly using his abilities. Not that I don't value his skill. At his young age, my robot son is as skilled a robotics engineer as any man in the country. If only the nation's robotics companies would recognize that, and overlook the fact that his ability stems from a nonhuman brain!

I have now written or personally contacted some seventeen major engineering concerns, and each of them, while polite, has turned down my suggestion. This morning, a letter arrived from the Alpha Robotics Corporation that typifies their answers.

> We are certain that your description of the applicant's engineering abilities is accurate. However, our company has certain personnel standards which must be met. We will keep the application on file. . . .

There is mockery in their answer, of course. The very idea of a robot employed in the science of robotics is laughable to them. They cannot really believe that I have raised Mac as a human child would be raised, and that he is anything more than an insensitive piece of mechanism. But if any proof were needed, Mac's present state would serve—the way he is pining for his absent brother, forlorn and lonely and unhappy. I wish I could help him, but I cannot find the key to his emotions.

But there is some joy in my life today. Fitz writes me from New York that he has been accepted into a large manufacturing concern that produces small and large electrical appliances. He will become, according to his letter, a "junior executive," and he is already certain that his rise to the presidency is merely a matter of time. I chuckled as I read his letter, but if I know Fitz, there is earnestness behind his humor. My son knows what he wants from this world, and the world is duty-bound to deliver it.

November 19, 2024. I am frantic with worry, even now that I know Mac is safe. His disappearance from the house three days ago caused me endless consternation, and I was afraid that his lonely life had led him into some tragedy. But yesterday, I received this letter from Fitz:

Dear Dad,

Don't worry about Mac, he's with me. He showed up at the apartment last night, in pretty bad shape. He must have been knocking around a bit; I'd guess he practically walked all the way into New York. He looked battered and bruised and rather frightening when I answered the door; Karen screamed and almost fainted at the sight of him. I guess she had almost forgotten about my robot brother in the past few years. I hope he wasn't too upset at her reaction; but you know how hard it is to know what Mac is thinking.

Anyway, I took him in and got him to tell me the story. It seems he was just plain lonely and wanted to see me; that was his reason for running off that way. I calmed him down as best I could and suggested he stay a day or two. I think he wanted more than that, but, Dad, you know how impossible that is. There isn't a soul here who even knows about Mac's existence, and he can be awfully hard to explain. This is a bad time for me to get mixed up in anything peculiar; as I've written you, the firm is considering me for branch manager of the Cleveland office, and any publicity that doesn't cast a rosy glow on dear old GC company can do me a lot of harm. It's not that I don't want to help Mac, the old rustpot. I still think of him as a brother. But I have to be sensible. . . .

I have just finished packing, and will take the copter into New York in the morning. I don't look forward to the trip; I have felt very fatigued lately. There is so much work to be done in my laboratory, and these personal crises are depriving me of time and energy. But I must bring Mac home, before he does any harm to my son's career.

March 10, 2026. Now at last it's been explained, the real reason for Mac's endless nights and days in the workshop. It is the Face episode all over again, but much, much worse. In the last year, Mac seems gripped by a strange passion (can there be something organically wrong with his robot's brain?), and the passion is the idea of creating a truly humanoid body for himself. But hard as he has worked, the effect he has gotten is so grotesque that it must be called horrible. Now he truly appears to be a monster, and when I expressed my distaste of what he had done, he fled from the house as if I had struck him.

This morning, I learned of his whereabouts, and learned the dreadful story of what had occurred after he left me. The local police discovered him in hiding in the deserted warehouse on Orangetree Road, and, luckily, they called headquarters before taking any drastic action. Captain Ormandy was able to prevent any harm from coming to Mac; the captain has become a friend of mine in the last two years. It was he who told me the story of Mac's escapades after he fled the house.

It will take me years to undo the harm. He has terrorized the local residents, and actually struck one man who tried to attack him with a coal shovel. This worries me; Mac had never broken this rule before. He went among the people of the town as if berserk, spreading fear and violence. I thank providence no great harm was done, and that he is safe with me again.

But now I must face the future, and it appears bleak. Captain Ormandy has just left me, and his words still buzz in my head. I cannot do what he asks; I cannot do away with this child of my own creation. But I am getting older, and very tired. My robot child has become a burden upon me, a burden I can barely sustain. What shall I do? What shall I do?

Dec. 8, 2027. It is good to have Fitz home, even if for so short a time, and even if it is my illness which brings him to my side. He looks so well! My heart swells with pride when I look at him. He is doing admirably, he has already earned a vice-presidency in the company that employs him, and he talks as if the future belongs to him. But more than anything, it is wonderful to be able to talk over my problem with him, to have him here to help me make the decision that must be made.

Last night, we sat in the study and discussed it for hours. I told him everything, about Mac's ever-increasing melancholy, about his untrustworthy behavior. I have told him about the proposition presented to me by the National Robotics Society, their offer to provide care for Mac. It is not the first time they have made this offer; but now the idea is far more appealing.

It was a strain for us both to discuss the matter. Fitz still feels brotherly towards Mac. But he is sensible about it, too; he recognizes the facts. He knows my health problem, he knows what a responsibility Mac is for me. And he, too, knows that Mac would be better off as a charge of the society. They would understand him. They would take good care of him.

My head is whirling. Fitz did not summarize his recommendation in so many words, and yet I know what he thinks I must do.

Feb. 5, 2027. I am locked out of my own laboratory. My robot child has taken possession, and works without ceasing. Around the clock he works; I hear the machinery grinding and roaring every minute of the day and night. He knows what will happen tomorrow, of course, that they will be coming for him from the society. What is he doing? What madness possesses him now?

Feb. 6, 2027. It is all over now, and the quiet, which fills the house lies heavily, as if entombed. In twenty-four hours, I have become the focal point of the world's horrified attention. For I am the father of the Thing which destroyed our town, the terrible metal monster that rampaged and pillaged and killed, in an orgy of insane destruction. . . .

But I must be factual, for this, the last page of my journal. Today, the thirtieth anniversary of his creation, Mac, my robot child, awaited the coming of his new captors with a body built for destruction. A monstrous, grotesque, sixty-foot body, engineered for violence and death. This had been his labor for the last two months. If the world would not accept him as human, then he would be truly a *robot*, the ancient robot of human nightmares, the destroying metal god who shows no mercy to human flesh.

I try to strike the pictures from my mind, but they are engraved there. I can see the terror on the faces of the scientists who came from the Robotics Society to claim their prize—I can hear their shrieks as he crushed the life from their bodies. I can see him stalking towards the town with his grim intent clear in every movement—to destroy all, everything, heedlessly. I can see him attacking, smashing, killing—

And then, I see the horror end. I see Captain Ormandy, moving swiftly with all the cunning of his strong young body, to fasten the cable about Mac's towering legs. I see him running headlong to the cave where the deadly black box had been planted. I see his hands on the plunger, and the mighty fire that springs from earth to sky, carrying Mac's destruction in its flames. . . .

Fitz was the last to leave me here tonight. We have talked a long time about Mac, and now that we have talked, I know the truth.

It was I who destroyed my robot child, and I who am responsible for the chaos his anger caused. I destroyed him; not today, but long ago, when he first came into being in my laboratory. For out of my science I created this life, this brother, this son, and I gave him everything. But how could I have forgotten the most important thing? I forgot to love him. . . .

THE RISK PROFESSION

Donald E. Westlake

Here is a straight murder mystery, set in space. You can do just about anything in science fiction: adventure, horror, mystery, humor, romance, or new wave. We'll get to the romance at another time; there is no new wave in this volume.

—PA

Donald E. Westlake has had a remarkable career in the mystery since 1959 and stands virtually at the top of the field (he has also written some straight novels, notably Adios, Scheherezade *and* Brothers Keepers, *which are superb), but what is almost unknown is that he started off in the world simultaneously as a science fiction writer, published variously in all of the magazines in the early 1960s, and then, in a famous letter published in Richard Lupoff's fan magazine, quit the field, which he accused of being a nest of chicanery, venery, simony, nepotism, self-delusion, and spite. (He later published a novel and a couple of short stories, but he had to create a pseudonym to do it and I won't reveal it here.) "Too hidebound, too conservative," Westlake called the field in a brief statement for the 1970 biographical compendium put together by Robert Reginald,* Stella Nova. *He was certainly right for the spirit of that deadly and poisonous time; one wonders what Westlake would have done in the field if he had come along exactly a decade later. Probably he would have pronounced it "uncontrollable, overexcited, and disgusting," Westlake tending to be in person if not in his fiction a man of some negativity.*

—bnm

Donald Westlake is the author of "The Winner," one of the least-known heavily anthologized stories in the history of science fiction (this statement makes considerable sense to me—my coeditors understand the multiple layers of meaning here). It appeared in Harry Harrison's late and to me lamented original anthology series Nova in 1970.

—MHG

Mister Henderson called me into his office my third day back in Tangiers. That was a day and a half later than I'd expected. Roving claims investigators for Tangiers Mutual Insurance Corporation don't usually get to spend more than thirty-six consecutive hours at home base.

Henderson was jovial but stern. That meant he was happy with the job I'd just completed, and that he was pretty sure I'd find some crooked shenanigans on this next assignment. That didn't please me. I'm basically a plain-living type, and I hate complications. I almost wished for a second there that I was back on Fire and Theft in Greater New York. But I knew better than that. As a roving claim investigator, I avoided the more stultifying paperwork inherent in this line of work and had the additional luxury of an expense account nobody ever questioned.

It made working for a living almost worthwhile.

When I was settled in the chair beside his desk, Henderson said, "That was good work you did on Luna, Ged. Saved the company a pretty pence."

I smiled modestly and said, "Thank you, sir." And reflected to myself for the thousandth time that the company could do worse than split that saving with the guy who'd made it possible. Me, in other words.

"Got a tricky one this time, Ged," said my boss. He had done his back-patting, now we got down to business. He peered keenly at me, or at least as keenly as a round-faced tiny-eyed fat man *can* peer. "What do you know about the Risk Profession Retirement Plan?" he asked me.

"I've heard of it," I said truthfully. "That's about all."

He nodded. "Most of the policies are sold off-planet, of course. It's a form of insurance for noninsurables. Spaceship crews, asteroid prospectors, people like that."

"I see," I said, unhappily. I knew right away this meant I was going to have to go off Earth again. I'm a one-g boy all the way.

Gravity changes get me in the solar plexus. I get g-sick at the drop of an elevator.

"Here's the way it works," he went on, either not noticing my sad face or choosing to ignore it. "The client pays a monthly premium. He can be as far ahead or as far behind in his payments as he wants—the policy has no lapse clause—just so he's all paid up by the Target Date. The Target Date is a retirement age, forty-five or above, chosen by the client himself. After the Target Date, he stops paying premiums, and we begin to pay him a monthly retirement check, the amount determined by the amount paid into the policy, his age at retiring, and so on. Clear?"

I nodded, looking for the gimmick that made this a paying proposition for good old Tangiers Mutual.

"The Double R-P—that's what we call it around the office here—assures the client that he won't be reduced to panhandling in his old age, should his other retirement plans fall through. For Belt prospectors, of course, this means the big strike, which maybe one in a hundred find. For the man who never does make that big strike, this is something to fall back on. He can come home to Earth and retire, with a guaranteed income for the rest of his life."

I nodded again, like a good company man.

"Of course," said Henderson, emphasizing this point with an upraised chubby finger, "these men are still uninsurables. This is a retirement plan only, not an insurance policy. There is no beneficiary other than the client himself."

And there was the gimmick. I knew a little something of the actuarial statistics concerning uninsurables, particularly Belt prospectors. Not many of them lived to be forty-five, and the few who would survive the Belt and come home to collect the retirement wouldn't last more than a year or two. A man who's spent the last twenty or thirty years on low-g asteroids just shrivels up after a while when he tries to live on Earth.

It needed a company like Tangiers Mutual to dream up a racket like that. The term "uninsurables" to most insurance companies means those people whose jobs or habitats make them too likely as prospects for obituaries. To Tangiers Mutual, uninsurables are people who have money the company can't get at.

"Now," said Henderson importantly, "we come to the problem at hand." He ruffled his up-to-now-neat In basket and finally found the folder he wanted. He studied the blank exterior of this folder for a few seconds, pursing his lips at it, and said, "One of

our clients under the Double R-P was a man named Jafe Mc-
Cann.''

"Was?" I echoed.

He squinted at me, then nodded at my sharpness. "That's right,
he's dead." He sighed heavily and tapped the folder with all those
pudgy fingers. "Normally," he said, "that would be the end of it.
File closed. However, this time there are complications.''

Naturally. Otherwise, he wouldn't be telling *me* about it. But
Henderson couldn't be rushed, and I knew it. I kept the alert look
on my face and thought of other things, while waiting for him to
get to the point.

"Two weeks after Jafe McCann's death," Henderson said,
"we received a cash-return form on his policy.''

"A cash-return form?" I'd never heard of such a thing. It didn't
sound like anything Tangiers Mutual would have anything to do
with. We *never* return cash.

"It's something special in this case," he explained. "You see,
this isn't an insurance policy, it's a retirement plan, and the client
can withdraw from the retirement plan at any time, and have
seventy-five percent of his paid-up premiums returned to him. It's,
uh, the law in plans such as this.''

"Oh," I said. That explained it. A law that had snuck through
the World Finance Code Commission while the insurance lobby
wasn't looking.

"But you see the point," said Henderson. "This cash-return
form arrived two weeks after the client's death.''

"You said there weren't any beneficiaries," I pointed out.

"Of course. But the form was sent in by the man's partner, one
Ab Karpin. McCann left a handwritten will bequeathing all his
possessions to Karpin. Since, according to Karpin, this was done
before McCann's death, the premium money cannot be considered
part of the policy, but as part of McCann's cash on hand. And Karpin wants it.''

"It can't be that much, can it?" I asked. I was trying my best to
point out to him that the company would spend more than it would
save if it sent me all the way out to the asteroids, a prospect I could
feel coming and one which I wasn't ready to cry hosannah over.

"McCann died," Henderson said ponderously, "at the age of
fifty-six. He had set his retirement age at sixty. He took out the
policy at the age of thirty-four, with monthly payments of fifty
credits. Figure it out for yourself.''

I did—in my head—and came up with a figure of thirteen thousand and two hundred credits. Seventy-five percent of that would be nine thousand and nine hundred credits. Call it ten thousand credits even.

I had to admit it. It was worth the trip.

"I see," I said sadly.

"Now," said Henderson, "the conditions—the circumstances—of McCann's death are somewhat suspicious. And so is the cash-return form itself."

"There's a chance it's a forgery?"

"One would think so," he said. "But our handwriting experts have worn themselves out with that form, comparing it with every other single scrap of McCann's writing they can find. And their conclusion is that not only is it genuinely McCann's handwriting, but it is McCann's handwriting at age fifty-six."

"So McCann must have written it," I said. "Under duress, do you think?"

"I have no idea," said Henderson complacently. "That's what you're supposed to find out. Oh, there's just one more thing."

I did my best to make my ears perk.

"I told you that McCann's death occurred under somewhat suspicious circumstances."

"Yes," I agreed, "you did."

"McCann and Karpin," he said, "have been partners—unincorporated, of course—for the last fifteen years. They had found small rare-metal deposits now and again, but they had never found that one big strike all the Belt prospectors waste their lives looking for. Not until the day before McCann died."

"Ah hah," I said. "*Then* they found the big strike."

"Exactly."

"And McCann's death?"

"Accidental."

"Sure," I said. "What proof have we got?"

"None. The body is lost in space. And law is few and far between that far out."

"So all we've got is this guy Karpin's word for how McCann died, is that it?"

"That's all we have. So far."

"Sure. And now you want me to go on out there and find out

what's cooking, and see if I can maybe save the company ten thousand credits.''

''Exactly,'' said Henderson.

The copter took me to the spaceport west of Cairo, and there I boarded the good ship *Demeter* for Luna City and points out. I loaded up on g-sickness pills and they worked fine. I was sick as a dog.

By the time we got to Atronics City, my insides had grown resigned to their fate. As long as I didn't try to eat, my stomach would leave me alone.

Atronics City was about as depressing as a Turkish bath with all the lights on. It stood on a chunk of rock a couple of miles thick, and it looked like nothing more in this world than a welders' practice range.

From the outside, Atronics City is just a derby-shaped dome of nickel-iron, black and kind of dirty-looking. I suppose a transparent dome would have been more fun, but the builders of the company cities in the asteroids were businessmen, and they weren't concerned with having fun. There's nothing to look at outside the dome but chunks of rock and the blackness of space anyway, and you've got all this cheap iron floating around in the vicinity, and all a dome's supposed to do is keep the air in. Besides, though the belt isn't as crowded as a lot of people think, there *is* quite a lot of debris rushing here and there, bumping into things, and a transparent dome would just get all scratched up, not to mention punctured.

From the inside, Atronics City is even jollier. There's the top level, directly under the dome, which is mainly parking area for scooters and tuggers of various kinds, plus the office shacks of the Assayer's Office, the Entry Authority, the Industry Troopers, and so on. The next three levels have all been burned into the bowels of the planetoid.

Level two is the Atronics plant, and a noisy plant it is. Level three is the shopping and entertainment area—grocery stores and clothing stores and movie theaters and bars—and level four is housing, two rooms and kitchen for the unmarried, four rooms and kitchen plus one room for each child for the married.

All of these levels have one thing in common. Square corners, painted olive-drab. The total effect of the place is suffocating. You feel like you're stuck in the middle of a stack of packing crates.

Most of the people living in Atronics City work, of course, for International Atronics, Incorporated. The rest of them work in the service occupations—running the bars and grocery stores and so on—that keep the company employees alive and relatively happy.

Wages come high in the places like Atronics City. Why not, the raw materials come practically for free. And as for working conditions, well, take a for instance. How do you make a vacuum tube? You fiddle with the innards and surround it all with glass. And how do you get the air out? No problem, boy, there wasn't any air in there to begin with.

At any rate, there I was at Atronics City. That was as far as *Demeter* would take me. Now, while the ship went on to Ludlum City and Chemisant City and the other asteroid business towns, my two suitcases and I dribbled down the elevator to my hostelry on level four.

Have you ever taken an elevator ride when the gravity is practically nonexistent? Well, don't. You see, the elevator manages to sink faster than you do. It isn't being *lowered* down to level four, it's being *pulled* down.

What this means is that the suitcases have to be lashed down with the straps provided, and you and the operator have to hold on tight to the handgrips placed here and there around the wall. Otherwise, you'd clonk your head on the ceiling.

But we got to level four at last, and off I went with my suitcases and the operator's directions. The suitcases weighed about half an ounce each out here, and I felt as though I weighed the same. Every time I raised a foot, I was sure I was about to go sailing into a wall. Local citizens eased by me, their feet occasionally touching the iron pavement as they soared along, and I gave them all dirty looks.

Level four was nothing but walls and windows. The iron floor went among these walls and windows in a straight straight line, bisecting other ''streets'' at perfect right angles, and the iron ceiling sixteen feet up was lined with a double row of fluorescent tubes. I was beginning to feel claustrophobic already.

The Chalmers Hotel—named for an Atronics vice-president— had received my advance registration, which was nice. I was shown to a second-floor room—nothing on level four had more than two stories—and was left to unpack my suitcases as best I may.

I had decided to spend a day or two at Atronics City before taking a scooter out to Ab Karpin's claim. Atronics City had been Karpin's and McCann's home base. All of McCann's premium payments had been mailed from here, and the normal mailing address for both of them was GPO Atronics City.

I wanted to know as much as possible about Ab Karpin before I went out to see him. And Atronics City seemed like the best place to get my information.

But not today. Today, my stomach was very unhappy, and my head was on sympathy strike. Today, I was going to spend my time exclusively in bed, trying not to float up to the ceiling.

The Mapping and Registry Office, it seemed to me the next day, was the best place to start. This was where prospectors filed their claims, but it was a lot more than that. The waiting room of M&R was the unofficial club of the asteroid prospectors. This is where they met with one another, talked together about the things that prospectors discuss, and made and dissolved their transient partnerships.

In this way, Karpin and McCann were unusual. They had maintained their partnership for fifteen years. That was about sixty times longer than most such arrangements lasted.

Searching the asteroid chunks for rare and valuable metals is basically pretty lonely work, and it's inevitable that the prospectors will every once in a while get hungry for human company and decide to try a team operation. But, at the same time, work like this attracts people who don't get along very well with human company. So the partnerships come and go, and the hatreds flare and are forgotten, and the normal prospecting team lasts an average of three months.

At any rate, it was to the Mapping and Registry Office that I went first. And, since that office was up on the first level, I went by elevator.

Riding *up* in that elevator was a heck of a lot more fun than riding down. The elevator whipped up like mad, the floor pressed against the soles of my feet, and it felt almost like good old Earth for a second or two there. But then the elevator stopped, and I held on tight to the handgrips to keep from shooting through the top of the blasted thing.

The operator—a phlegmatic sort—gave me directions to the M&R, and off I went, still trying to figure out how to sail along as gracefully as the locals.

The Mapping and Registry Office occupied a good-sized shack over near the dome wall, next to the entry lock. I pushed open the door and went on in.

The waiting room was cozy and surprisingly large, large enough to comfortably hold the six maroon leather sofas scattered here and there on the pale green carpet, flanked by bronze ashtray stands. There were only six prospectors here at the moment, chatting together in two groups of three, and they all looked alike. Grizzled, ageless, watery-eyed, their clothing clean but baggy. I passed them and went on to the desk at the far end, behind which sat a young man in official gray, slowly turning the crank of a microfilm reader.

He looked up at my approach. I flashed my company identification and asked to speak to the manager. He went away, came back, and ushered me into an office which managed to be Spartan and sumptuous at the same time. The walls had been plastic-painted in textured brown, the iron floor had been lushly carpeted in gray, and the desk had been covered with a simulated wood coating.

The manager—a man named Teaking—went well with the office. His face and hands were spare and lean, but his uniform was immaculate, covered with every curlicue the regulations allowed. He welcomed me politely, but curiously, and I said, "I wonder if you know a prospector named Ab Karpin?"

"Karpin? Of course. He and old Jafe McCann—pity about McCann. I hear he got killed."

"Yes, he did."

"And that's what you're here for, eh?" He nodded sagely. "I didn't know the Belt boys could get insurance," he said.

"It isn't exactly that," I said. "This concerns a retirement plan, and—well, the details don't matter." Which, I hoped, would end his curiosity in that line. "I was hoping you could give me some background on Karpin. And on McCann, too, for that matter."

He grinned a bit. "You saw the men sitting outside?"

I nodded.

"Then you've seen Karpin and McCann. Exactly the same. It doesn't matter if a man's thirty or sixty or what. It doesn't matter what he was like before he came out here. If he's been here a few years, he looks exactly like the bunch you saw outside there."

"That's appearance," I said. "What I was looking for was personality."

"Same thing," he said. "All of them. Closemouthed, antisocial, fiercely independent, incurably romantic, always convinced that the big strike is just a piece of rock away. McCann, now, he was a bit more realistic than most. He'd be the one I'd expect to take out a retirement policy. A real pence-pincher, that one, though I shouldn't say it as he's dead. But that's the way he was. Brighter than most Belt boys when it came to money matters. I've seen him haggle over a new piece of equipment for their scooter, or some repair work, or some such thing, and he was a wonder to watch.''

"And Karpin?'' I asked him.

"A prospector,'' he said, as though that answered my question. "Same as everybody else. Not as sharp as McCann when it came to money. That's why all the money stuff in the partnership was handled by McCann. But Karpin was one of the sharpest boys in the business when it came to mineralogy. He knew rocks you and I never heard of, and most times he knew them by sight. Almost all of the Belt boys are college grads—you've got to know what you're looking for out here and what it looks like when you've found it—but Karpin has practically all of them beat. He's *sharp*.''

"Sounds like a good team,'' I said.

"I guess that's why they stayed together so long,'' he said. "They complemented each other.'' He leaned forward, the inevitable prelude to a confidential remark. "I'll tell you something off the record, mister,'' he said. "Those two were smarter than they knew. Their partnership was never legalized, it was never anything more than a piece of paper. And there's a bunch of fellas around here mighty unhappy about that today. Jafe McCann is the one who handled all the money matters, like I said. He's got IOUs all over town.''

"And they can't collect from Karpin?''

He nodded. "Jeff McCann died just a bit too soon. He was sharp and cheap, but he was honest. If he'd lived, he would have repaid all his debts, I'm sure of it. And if this strike they made is as good as I hear, he would have been able to repay them with no trouble at all.''

I nodded, somewhat impatiently. I had the feeling by now that I was talking to a man who was one of those who had a Jeff McCann IOU in his pocket. "How long has it been since you've seen Karpin?'' I asked him, wondering what Karpin's attitude and expression was now that his partner was dead.

"Oh, Lord, not for a couple of months," he said. "Not since they went out together the last time and made that strike."

"Didn't Karpin come in to make his claim?"

"Not here. Over to Chemisant City. That was the nearest M and R to the strike."

"Oh." That was a pity. I would have liked to have known if there had been a change of any kind in Karpin since his partner's death. "I'll tell you what the situation is," I said, with a false air of truthfulness. "We have some misgivings about McCann's death. Not suspicious, exactly, just misgivings. The timing is what bothers us."

"You mean, because it happened just after the strike?"

"That's it," I answered frankly.

He shook his head. "I wouldn't get too excited about that, if I were you," he said. "It wouldn't be the first time it's happened. A man makes the big strike after all, and he gets so excited he forgets himself for a minute and gets careless. And you only have to be careless once out here."

"That may be it," I said. I got to my feet, knowing I'd picked up all there was from this man. "Thanks a lot for your cooperation," I said.

"Anytime," he said. He stood and shook hands with me.

I went back out through the chatting prospectors and crossed the echoing cavern that was level one, aiming to rent myself a scooter.

I don't like rockets. They're noisy as the dickens, they steer hard and drive erratically, and you can never carry what *I* would consider a safe emergency excess of fuel. Nothing like the big steady-g interplanetary liners. On those I feel almost human.

The appearance of the scooter I was shown at the rental agency didn't do much to raise my opinion of this mode of transportation. The thing was a good ten years old, the paint scraped and scratched all over its egg-shaped, originally green-colored body, and the windshield—a silly term, really, for the front window of a craft that spends most of its time out where there isn't any wind—was scratched and pockmarked to the point of translucency by years of exposure to the asteroidal dust.

The rental agent was a sharp-nosed thin-faced type who displayed this refugee from a melting vat without a blush, and still didn't blush when he told me the charges. Twenty credits a day, plus fuel.

I paid without a murmur—it was the company's money, not mine—and paid an additional ten credits for the rental of a suit to go with it. I worked my way awkwardly into the suit, and clambered into the driver's seat of the relic. I attached the suit to the ship in all the necessary places, and the agent closed and spun the door.

Most of the black paint had worn off the handles of the controls, and insulation peeked through rips in the plastic siding here and there. I wondered if the thing had any slow leaks and supposed fatalistically that it had. The agent waved at me, stony-faced, the conveyor belt trundled me outside the dome, and I kicked the weary rocket into life.

The scooter had a tendency to roll to the right. If I hadn't kept fighting it back, it would have soon worked up a dandy little spin. I was spending so much time juggling with the controls that I practically missed a couple of my beacon rocks, and that would have been just too bad. If I'd gotten off the course I had carefully outlined for myself, I'd never have found my bearings again, and I would have just floated around amid the scenery until some passerby took pity and towed me back home.

But I managed to avoid getting lost, which surprised me, and after four nerve-racking hours I finally spotted the yellow-painted X of a registered claim on a half-mile-thick chunk of rock dead ahead. As I got closer, I spied a scooter parked near the X, and beside it an inflated portable dome. The scooter was somewhat larger than mine, but no newer and probably even less safe. The dome was varicolored, from repeated patching.

This would be the claim, and this is where I would find Karpin, sitting on his property while waiting for the sale to go through. Prospectors like Karpin are free-lance men, working for no particular company. They register their claims in their own names, and then sell the rights to whichever company shows up first with the most attractive offer. There's a lot of paperwork to such a sale, and it's all handled by the company. While waiting, the smart prospector sits on his claim and makes sure nobody chips off a part of it for himself, a stunt that still happens now and again. It doesn't take too much concentrated explosive to make two rocks out of one rock, and a man's claim is only the rock with his X on it.

I set the scooter down next to the other one, and flicked the toggle for the air pumps, then put on the fishbowl and went about unattaching the suit from the ship. When the red light flashed on and off, I spun the door, opened it, and stepped out onto the rock, moving very cautiously. It isn't that I don't believe the magnets in the bootsoles will work, it's just that I know for a fact that they won't work if I happen to raise both feet at the same time.

I clumped across the crude X to Karpin's dome. The dome had no viewports at all, so I wasn't sure Karpin was aware of my presence. I rapped my metal glove on the metal outer door of the lock, and then I was sure.

But it took him long enough to open up. I had just about decided he'd joined his partner in the long sleep when the door cracked open an inch. I pushed it open and stepped into the lock, ducking my head. The door was only five feet high, and just as wide as the lock itself, three feet. The other dimensions of the lock were: height, six feet six; width, one foot. Not exactly room to dance in.

When the red light high on the left-hand wall clicked off, I rapped on the inner door. It promptly opened, I stepped through and removed the fishbowl.

Karpin stood in the middle of the room, a small revolver in his hand. "Shut the door," he said.

I obeyed, moving slowly. I didn't want that gun to go off by mistake.

"Who are you?" Karpin demanded. The M and R man had been right. Ab Karpin was a dead ringer for all those other prospectors I'd seen back at Atronics City. Short and skinny and grizzled and ageless. He could have been forty, and he could have been ninety, but he was probably somewhere the other side of fifty. His hair was black and limp and thinning, ruffled in little wisps across his wrinkled pate. His forehead and cheeks were lined like a plowed field, and were much the same color. His eyes were wide apart and small, so deep-set beneath shaggy brows that they seemed black. His mouth was thin, almost lipless. The hand holding the revolver was nothing but bones and blue veins covered with taut skin.

He was wearing a dirty undershirt and an old pair of trousers that had been cut off raggedly just above his knobby knees. Faded slippers were on his feet. He had good reason for dressing that way; the temperature inside the dome must have been nearly ninety degrees. The dome wasn't reflecting away the sun's heat as well as it had when it was young.

I looked at Karpin, and despite the revolver and the tense expression on his face, he was the least dangerous-looking man I'd ever run across. All at once, the idea that this antisocial old geezer had the drive or the imagination to murder his partner seemed ridiculous.

Apparently, I spent too much time looking him over, because he said again, "Who are you?" And this time he motioned impatiently with the revolver.

"Stanton," I told him. "Ged Stanton, Tangiers Mutual Insurance. I have identification, but it's in my pants pocket, down inside this suit."

"Get it," he said. "And move slow."

"Right you are."

I moved slow, as per directions, and peeled out of the suit, then reached into my trouser pocket and took out my ID clip. I flipped it open and showed him the card bearing my signature and picture and right thumbprint and the name of the company I represented, and he nodded, satisfied, and tossed the revolver over onto his bed. "I got to be careful," he said. "I got a big claim here."

"I know that," I told him. "Congratulations for it."

"Thanks," he said, but he still looked peevish. "You're here about Jafe's insurance, right?"

"That I am."

"Don't want to pay up, I suppose. That doesn't surprise me." Blunt old men irritate me. "Well," I said, "we do have to investigate."

"Sure," he said. "You want some coffee?"

"Thank you."

"You can sit in that chair there. That was Jafe's."

I settled gingerly in the cloth-and-plastic foldaway chair he'd pointed at, and he went over to the kitchen area of the dome to start coffee. I took the opportunity to look the dome over. It was the first portable dome I'd ever been inside.

It was all one room, roughly circular, with a diameter of about fifteen feet. The sides went straight up for the first seven feet, then curved gradually inward to form the roof. At the center of the dome, the ceiling was about twelve feet high.

The floor of the room was simply the asteroidal rock surface, not completely level and smooth. There were two chairs and a table to the right of the entry lock, two foldaway cots around the wall beyond them, the kitchen area next, and a cluttered storage area around on the other side. There was a heater standing alone in the center of the room, but it certainly wasn't needed now. Sweat was already trickling down the back of my neck and down my forehead into my eyebrows. I peeled off my shirt and used it to wipe sweat from my face. "Warm in here," I said.

"You get used to it," he muttered, which I found hard to believe.

He brought over the coffee, and I tasted it. It was rotten, as bitter as this old hermit's soul, but I said, "Good coffee. Thanks a lot."

"I like it strong," he said.

I looked around at the room again. "All the comforts of home, eh? Pretty ingenious arrangement."

"Sure," he said sourly. "How about getting to the point, mister?"

There's only one way to handle a blunt old man. Be blunt right back. "I'll tell you how it is," I said. "The company isn't accusing you of anything, but it has to be sure everything's on the up-and-up before it pays out any ten thousand credits. And your partner just happening to fill out that cash-return form just before he died—well, you've got to admit it is a funny kind of coincidence."

"How so?" He slurped coffee, and glowered at me over the cup. "We made this strike here," he said. "We knew it was the big one. Jafe had that insurance policy of his in case he never did make the big strike. As soon as we knew this was the big one, he said, 'I guess I don't need that retirement now,' and sat right down and wrote out the cash-return. Then we opened a bottle of liquor and celebrated, and he got himself killed."

The way Karpin said it, it sounded smooth and natural. *Too* smooth and natural. "How did this accident happen anyway?" I asked him.

"I'm not one hundred percent sure of that myself," he said. "I was pretty well drunk myself by that time. But he put on his suit and said he was going out to paint the X. He was falling all over himself, and I tried to tell him it could wait till we'd had some sleep, but he wouldn't pay any attention to me."

"So he went out," I said.

He nodded. "He went out first. After a couple minutes, I got lonesome in here, so I suited up and went out after him. It happened just as I was going out the lock, and I just barely got a glimpse of what happened."

He attacked the coffee again, noisily, and I prompted him, saying, "What did happen, Mr. Karpin?"

"Well, he was capering around out there, waving the paint tube and such. There's a lot of sharp rock sticking out around here. Just as I got outside, he lost his balance and kicked out, and scraped right into some of that rock, and punctured his suit."

"I thought the body was lost," I said.

He nodded. "It was. The last thing in life Jafe ever did was try to shove himself away from those rocks. That, and the force of air coming out of that puncture for the first second or two, was enough to throw him up off the surface. It threw him up too high, and he never got back down."

My doubt must have showed in my face, because he added, "Mister, there isn't enough gravity on this place to shoot craps with."

He was right. As we talked, I kept finding myself holding unnecessarily tight to the arms of the chair. I kept having the feeling I was going to float out of the chair and hover around up at the top of the dome if I were to let go. It was silly, of course—there was *some* gravity on that planetoid, after all—but I just don't seem to get used to low-g.

Nevertheless, I still had some more questions. "Didn't you try to get his body back? Couldn't you have reached him?"

"I tried to, mister," he said. "Old Jafe McCann was my partner for fifteen years. But I was drunk, and that's a fact. And I was afraid to go jumping up in the air, for fear *I'd* go floating away, too."

"Frankly," I said, "I'm no expert on low gravity and asteroids. But wouldn't McCann's body just go into orbit around this rock? I mean, it wouldn't simply go floating off into space, would it?"

"It sure would," he said. "There's a lot of other rocks out here, too, mister, and a lot of them are bigger than this one and have a lot more gravity pull. I don't suppose there's a navigator in the business who could have computed Jafe's course in advance. He floated up, and then he floated back over the dome here and seemed to hover for a couple minutes, and then he just floated out and away. His isn't the only body circling around the sun with all these rocks, you know."

I chewed a lip and thought it all over. I didn't know enough about asteroid gravity or the conditions out here to be able to say for sure whether Karpin's story was true or not. Up to this point, I couldn't attack the problem on a fact basis. I had to depend on *feel-*

ing now, the hunches and instincts of eight years in this job, hearing some people tell lies and other people tell the truth.

And my instinct said Ab Karpin was lying in his teeth. That dramatic little touch about McCann's body hovering over the dome before disappearing into the void, that sounded more like the embellishment of fiction than the circumstance of truth. And the string of coincidences was just too much. McCann just coincidentally happens to die right after he and his partner make their big strike. He happens to write out the cash-return form just before dying. And his body just happens to float away, so nobody can look at it and check Karpin's story.

But no matter what my instinct said, the story was smooth. It was smooth as glass, and there was no place for me to get a grip on it.

What now? There wasn't any hole in Karpin's story, at least none that I could see. I had to break his story somehow, and in order to do that I had to do some nosing around on this planetoid. I couldn't know in advance what I was looking for, I could only look. I'd know it when I found it. It would be something that conflicted with Karpin's story.

And for that, I had to be sure the story was complete. "You said McCann had gone out to paint the X," I said. "Did he paint it?"

Karpin shook his head. "He never got a chance. He spent all his time dancing, up till he went and killed himself."

"So you painted it yourself."

He nodded.

"And then you went on into Atronics City and registered your claim, is that the story?"

"No. Chemisant City was closer than Atronics City right then, so I went there. Just after Jafe's death, and everything—I didn't feel like being alone any more than I had to."

"You said Chemisant City was closer to you *then*," I said. "Isn't it now?"

"Things move around a lot out here, mister," he said. "Right now, Chemisant City's almost twice as far from here as Atronics City. In about three days, it'll start swinging in closer again. Things keep shifting around out here."

"So I've noticed," I said. "When you took off to go to Chemisant City, didn't you make a try for your partner's body then?"

He shook his head. "He was long out of sight by then," he said. "That was ten, eleven hours later, when I took off."

"Why's that? All you had to do was paint the X and take off."

"Mister, I told you. I was drunk. I was falling-down drunk, and when I saw I couldn't get at Jafe, and he was dead anyway, I came back in here and slept it off. Maybe if I'd been sober I would have taken the scooter and gone after him, but I was *drunk.*"

"I see." And there just weren't any more questions I could think of to ask, not right now. So I said, "I've just had a shaky four-hour ride coming out here. Mind if I stick around awhile before going back?"

"Help yourself," he said, in a pretty poor attempt at genial hospitality. "You can sleep over, if you want."

"Fine," I said. "I think I'd like that."

"You wouldn't happen to play cribbage, would you?" he asked, with the first real sign of animation I'd seen in him yet.

"I learn fast," I told him.

"O.K.," he said. "I'll teach you." And he produced a filthy deck of cards and taught me.

After losing nine straight games of cribbage, I quit, and got to my feet. I was at my most casual as I stretched and said, "O.K. if I wander around outside for a while? I've never been on an asteroid like this before. I mean, a little one like this. I've just been to the company cities up to now."

"Go right ahead," he said. "I've got some polishing and patching to do, anyway." He made his voice sound easy and innocent, but I noticed his eyes were alert and wary, watching me as I struggled back into my suit.

I didn't bother to put my shirt back on first, and that was a mistake. The temperature inside an atmosphere suit is a steady sixty-eight degrees. That had never seemed particularly chilly before, but after the heat of that dome, it seemed cold as a blizzard inside the suit.

I went on out through the airlock, and moved as briskly as possible in the cumbersome suit, while the sweat chilled on my back and face, and I accepted the glum conviction that one thing I was going to get out of this trip for sure was a nasty head cold.

I went over to the X first, and stood looking at it. It was just an X, that's all, shakily scrawled in yellow paint, with the initials J-A scrawled much smaller beside it.

I left the X and clumped away. The horizon was practically at arm's length, so it didn't take long for the dome to be out of sight. And then I clumped more slowly, studying the surface of the asteroid.

What I was looking for was a grave. I believed that Karpin was lying, that he had murdered his partner. And I didn't believe that Jafe McCann's body had floated off into space. I was convinced that his body was still somewhere on this asteroid. Karpin had been forced to concoct a story about the body being lost because the appearance of the body would prove somehow that it had been murder and not accident. I was convinced of that, and now all I had to do was prove it.

But that asteroid was a pretty unlikely place for a grave. That wasn't dirt I was walking on, it was rock, solid metallic rock. You don't dig a grave in solid rock, not with a shovel. You maybe can do it with dynamite, but that won't work too well if your object is to keep anybody from seeing that the hole has been made. Dirt can be patted down. Blown-up rock looks like blown-up rock, and that's all there is to it.

I considered crevices and fissures in the surface, some cranny large enough for Karpin to have stuffed the body into. But I didn't find any of these either as I plodded along, being sure to keep one magneted boot always in contact with the ground.

Karpin and McCann had set their dome up at just about the only really level spot on that entire planetoid. The rest of it was nothing but jagged rock, and it wasn't easy traveling at all, maneuvering around with magnets on my boots and a bulky atmosphere suit cramping my movements.

And then I stopped and looked out at space and cursed myself for a ring-tailed baboon. McCann's body might be anywhere in the Solar System, anywhere at all, but there was one place I could be sure it wasn't, and that place was this asteroid. No, Karpin had not blown a grave or stuffed the body into a fissure in the ground. Why not? Because this chunk of rock was valuable, that's why not. Because Karpin was in the process of selling it to one of the major companies, and that company would come along and chop this chunk of rock to pieces, getting the valuable metal out, and McCann's body would turn up in the first week of operations if Karpin were stupid enough to bury it here.

Ten hours between McCann's death and Karpin's departure for Chemisant City. He'd admitted that already. And I was willing to bet he'd spent at least part of that time carrying McCann's body to some other asteroid, one he was sure was nothing but worthless rock. If that were true, it meant the mortal remains of Jafe McCann were now somewhere—*anywhere*—in the Asteroid Belt. Even if I assumed that the body had been hidden on an asteroid somewhere between here and Chemisant City—which wasn't necessarily so— that wouldn't help at all. The relative positions of planetoids in the Belt just keep on shifting. A small chunk of rock that was between here and Chemisant City a few weeks ago—it could be almost anywhere in the Belt right now.

The body, that was the main item. I'd more or less counted on finding it somehow. At the moment, I couldn't think of any other angle for attacking Karpin's story.

As I clopped morosely back to the dome, I nibbled at Karpin's story in my mind. For instance, why go to Chemisant City? It was closer, he said, but it couldn't have been closer by more than a couple of hours. The way I understood it, Karpin was well known back on Atronics City—it was the normal base of operations for him and his partner—and he didn't know a soul at Chemisant City. Did it make sense for him to go somewhere he wasn't known after his partner's death, even if it *was* an hour closer? No, it made a lot more sense for a man in that situation to go where he's known, go someplace where he has friends who'll sympathize with him and help him over the shock of losing a partner of fifteen years' standing, even if going there does mean traveling an hour longer.

And there was always the cash-return form. That was what I was here about in the first place. It just didn't make sense for McCann to have held up his celebration while he filled out a form that he wouldn't be able to mail until he got back to Atronics City. And yet the company's handwriting experts were convinced that it wasn't a forgery, and I could pretty well take their word for it.

Mulling these things over as I tramped back toward the dome, I suddenly heard a distant bell ringing way back in my head. The glimmering of an idea, not an idea yet but just the hint of one. I wasn't sure where it led, or even if it led anywhere at all, but I was going to find out.

Karpin opened the doors for me. By the time I'd stripped off the suit he was back to work. He was cleaning the single unit which was his combination stove and refrigerator and sink and garbage disposal.

I looked around the dome again, and I had to admit that a lot of ingenuity had gone into the manufacture and design of this dome and its contents. The dome itself, when deflated, folded down into an oblong box three feet by one foot by one foot. The lock itself, of course, folded separately, into another box somewhat smaller than that.

As for the gear inside the dome, it was functional and collapsible, and there wasn't a single item there that wasn't needed. There were the two chairs and the two cots and the table, all of them foldaway. There was that fantastic combination job Karpin was cleaning right now, and that had dimensions of four feet by three feet by three feet. The clutter of gear over to the left wasn't as much of a clutter as it looked. There was a Geiger counter, an automatic spectrograph, two atmosphere suits, a torsion densiometer, a core-cutting drill, a few small hammers and picks, two spare air tanks, boxes of food concentrate, a paint tube, a doorless jimmy-john, and two small metal boxes about eight inches cube. These last were undoubtedly Karpin's and McCann's pouches, where they kept whatever letters, money, address books, or other small bits of possessions they owned. Back of this mound of gear, against the wall, stood the air reconditioner, humming quietly to itself.

In this small enclosed space there was everything a man needed to keep himself alive. Everything except human company. And if you didn't need human company, then you had everything. Just on the other side of that dome, there was a million miles of death, in a million possible ways. On this side of the dome, life was cozy, if somewhat Spartan and very hot.

I knew for sure I was going to get a head cold. My body had adjusted to the sixty-eight degrees inside the suit, finally, and now was very annoyed to find the temperature shooting up to ninety again.

Since Karpan didn't seem inclined to talk, and I would rather spend my time thinking than talking anyway, I took a hint from him and did some cleaning. I'd noticed a smeared spot about nose level on the faceplate of my fishbowl, and now was as good a time as any to get rid of it. It had a tendency to make my eyes cross.

My shirt was sodden and wrinkled by this time anyway, having first been used to wipe sweat from my face and later been rolled into a ball and left on the chair when I went outside, so I used it for a cleaning rag, buffing like mad the silvered surface of the faceplate. Faceplates are silvered, not so the man inside can look out and no one else can look in, but in order to keep some of the more violent rays of the sun from getting through to the face.

I buffed for a while, and then I put the fishbowl on my head and looked through it. The spot was gone, so I went over and reattached it to the rest of the suit, and then settled back in my chair again and lit a cigarette.

Karpin spoke up. "Wish you wouldn't smoke. Makes it tough on the conditioner."

"Oh," I said. "Sorry." So I just sat, thinking morosely about nonforged cash-return forms, and coincidences, and likely spots to hide a body in the Asteroid Belt.

Where would one dispose of a body in the asteroids? I went back through my thinking on that topic, and I found holes big enough to drive Karpin's claim through. This idea of leaving the body on some worthless chunk of rock, for instance. If Karpin had killed his partner—and I was dead sure he had—he'd planned it carefully and he wouldn't be leaving anything to chance. Now, an asteroid isn't worthless to a prospector until that prospector has landed on it and tested it. *Karpin* might know that such-and-such an asteroid was nothing but worthless stone, but the guy who stops there and finds McCann's body might *not* know it.

No, Karpin wouldn't leave that to chance. He would get rid of that body, and he would do it in such a way that nobody would *ever* find it.

How? Not by leaving it on a worthless asteroid, and not by just pushing it off into space. The distance between asteroids is large, but so's the travel. McCann's body, floating around in the blackness, might just be found by somebody.

And that, so far as I could see, eliminated the possibilities. McCann's body was in the Belt. I'd eliminated both the asteroids themselves and the space around the asteroids as hiding places. What was left?

The sun, of course.

I thought that over for a while, rather surprised at myself for having noticed the possibility. Now, let's say Karpin attaches a small rocket to McCann's body, stuffed into its atmosphere suit. He sets the rocket going, and off goes McCann. Not that he aims it toward the sun, that wouldn't work well at all. Instead of falling into the sun, the body would simply take up a long elliptical orbit *around* the sun, and would come back to the asteroids every few hundred years. No, he would aim McCann *back,* in the direction opposite to the direction or rotation of the asteroids. He would, in essence, slow McCann's body down, make it practically stop in relation to the motion of the asteroids. And then it would simply *fall* into the sun.

None of my ideas, it seemed, were happy ones. If McCann's body were even at this moment falling toward the sun, it was just as useful to me as if it were on some other asteroid.

But wait a second. Karpin and McCann had worked with the minimum of equipment. I'd already noticed that. They didn't have extras of anything, and they certainly wouldn't have extra rockets. Except for one fast trip to Chemisant City—when he had neither the time nor the excuse to buy a jato rocket—Karpin had spent all of his time since McCann's death right here on this planetoid.

So that killed that idea.

While I was hunting around for some other idea, Karpin spoke up again, for the first time in maybe twenty minutes. "You think I killed him, don't you?" he said, not looking around from his cleaning job.

I considered my answer. There was no reason at all to be overly polite to this sour old buzzard, but at the same time I am naturally the soft-spoken type. "We aren't sure," I said. "We just think there are some odd items to be explained."

"Such as what?" he demanded.

"Such as the timing of McCann's cash-return form."

"I already explained that," he said.

"I know. You've explained everything."

"He wrote it out himself," the old man insisted. He put down his cleaning cloth, and turned to face me. "I suppose your company checked the handwriting already, and Jafe McCann is the one who wrote that form."

He was so blasted sure of himself. "It would seem that way," I said.

"What other odd items you worried about?" he asked me, in a rusty attempt at sarcasm.

"Well," I said, "there's this business of going to Chemisant City. It would have made more sense for you to go to Atronics City, where you were known."

"Chemisant was closer," he said. He shook a finger at me. "That company of yours thinks it can cheat me out of my money," he said. "Well, it can't. I know my rights. That money belongs to me."

"I guess you're doing pretty well without McCann," I said.

His angry expression was replaced by one of bewilderment. "What do you mean?"

"They told me back at Atronics City," I explained, "that McCann was the money expert and you were the metals expert, and that's why McCann handled all your buying on credit and stuff like that. Looks as though you've got a pretty keen eye for money yourself."

"I know what's mine," he mumbled, and turned away. He went back to scrubbing the stove coils again.

I stared at his back. Something had happened just then, and I wasn't sure what. He'd just been starting to warm up to a tirade against the dirty insurance company, and all of a sudden he'd folded up and shut up like a clam.

And then I saw it. Or at least I saw part of it. I saw how that cash-return form fit in, and how it made perfect sense.

Now all I needed was proof of murder. Preferably a body. I had the rest of it. Then I could pack the old geezer back to Atronics City and get proof for the part I'd already figured out.

I'd like that. I'd like getting back to Atronics City, and having this all straightened out, and then taking the very next liner straight back to Earth. More immediately, I'd like getting out of this heat and back into the cool sixty-eight degrees of—

And then it hit me. The whole thing hit me, and I just sat there and stared. They did not carry extras, Karpin and McCann, they did not carry one item of equipment more than they needed.

I sat there and looked at the place where the dead body was hidden, and I said, "Well, I'll be a son of a gun!"

He turned and looked at me, and then he followed the direction of my gaze, and he saw what I was staring at, and he made a jump across the room at the revolver lying on the cot.

That's what saved me. He moved too fast, jerked his muscles too hard, and went sailing up and over the cot and ricocheted off the dome wall. And that gave me plenty of time to get up from the chair, moving more cautiously than he had, and get my hands on the revolver before he could get himself squared away again.

I straightened with the gun in my hand and looked into a face white with frustration and rage. "Okay, Mr. McCann," I said. "It's all over."

He knew I had him, but he tried not to show it. "What are you talking about? McCann's dead."

"Sure he is," I said. "Jafe McCann was the money-minded part of the team. He was the one who signed for all the loans and all the equipment bought on credit. With this big strike in, Jafe McCann was the one who'd have to pay all that money."

"You're babbling," he snapped, but the words were hollow.

"You weren't satisfied with half a loaf," I said. "You should have been. Half a loaf is better than none. But you wanted every penny you could get your hands on, and you wanted to pay out just as little money as you possibly could. So when you killed Ab Karpin, you saw a way to kill your debts as well. You'd *become* Ab Karpin, and it would be Jafe McCann who was dead, and the debts dead with him."

"That's a lie," he said, his voice getting shrill. *"I'm* Ab Karpin, and I've got papers to prove it."

"Sure. Papers you stole from a dead man. And you might have gotten away with it, too. But you just couldn't leave well enough alone, could you? Not satisfied with having the whole claim to yourself, you switched identities with your victim to avoid your debts. And not satisfied with *that*, you filled out a cash-return form and tried to collect your money as your own heir. *That's* why you had to go to Chemisant City, where nobody would recognize Ab Karpin or Jafe McCann, rather than to Atronics City where you were well known."

"You don't want to make too many wild accusations," he shouted, his voice shaking. "You don't want to go around accusing people of things you can't prove."

"I can prove it," I told him. "I can prove everything I've said. As to who you are, there's no problem. All I have to do is bring you back to Atronics City. There'll be plenty of people there to identify you. And as to proving you murdered Ab Karpin, I think his body will be proof enough, don't you?"

McCann watched me as I backed slowly around the room to the mound of gear. The partners had had no extra equipment, no extra equipment at all. I looked down at the two atmosphere suits lying side by side on the metallic rock floor.

Two atmosphere suits. The dead man was supposed to be in one of those, floating out in space somewhere. He was in the suit, right enough, I was sure of that, but he wasn't floating anywhere.

A space suit is a perfect place to hide a body, for as long as it has to be hid. The silvered faceplate keeps you from seeing inside, and the suit is, naturally, a sealed atmosphere. A body can rot away to ashes inside a space suit, and you'll never notice a thing on the outside.

I'd had the right idea after all. McCann had planned to get rid of Karpin's body by attaching a rocket to it, slowing it down, and letting it fall into the sun. But he hadn't had an opportunity yet to go buy a rocket. He couldn't go to Atronics City, where he could have bought the rocket on credit, and he couldn't go to Chemisant City until the claim sale went through and he had some money to spend. And in the meantime, Karpin's body was perfectly safe, sealed away inside his atmosphere suit.

And it would have been safe, too, if McCann hadn't been just a little bit too greedy. He could kill his partner and get away with it; policemen on the Belt are even farther apart than the asteroids. He could swindle his creditors and get away with it; they had no way of checking up and no reason to suspect a switch in identities. But when he tried to get his own money back from Tangiers Mutual Insurance, *that's* when he made his mistake.

I studied the two atmosphere suits, at the same time managing to keep a wary eye on Jafe McCann, standing rigid and silent across the room. Which one of those suits contained the body of Ab Karpin?

The one with the new patch on the chest, of course. As I'd guessed, McCann had shot him, and that's why he had the problem of disposing of the body in the first place.

I prodded that suit with my toe. "He's in there, isn't he?"

"You're crazy."

"Think I should open it up and check? It's been almost a month, you know. I imagine he's pretty ripe by now."

I reached down to the neck fastenings on the fishbowl, and McCann finally moved. His arms jerked up, and he cried, "Don't! He's in there, he's in there! For God's sake, don't open it up!"

I relaxed. Mission accomplished. "Crawl into your suit, little man," I said. "We've got ourselves a trip to make, the three of us."

Henderson, as usual, was jovial but stern. "You did a fine job up there, Ged," he said, with false familiarity. "Really brilliant work."

"Thank you very much," I said. I was holding the last piece of news for a minute or two, relishing it.

"But you brought McCann in over a week ago. I don't see why you had to stay up at Atronics City at all after that, much less ten days."

I sat back in the chair and negligently crossed my legs. "I just thought I'd take a little vacation," I said carelessly, and lit a cigarette. I flicked ashes in the general direction of the ashtray on Henderson's desk. Some of them made it.

"A vacation?" he echoed, eyes widening. Henderson was a company man, a *real* company man. A vacation for him was purgatory, it was separation from a loved one. "I don't believe you have a vacation coming," he said frostily, "For at least six months."

"That's what you think, Henny," I said.

All he could do at that was blink.

I went on, enjoying myself hugely. "I don't like this company," I said. "And I don't like this job. And I don't like you. And from now on, I've decided, it's going to be vacation all the time."

"Ged," he said, his voice faint, "what's the matter with you? Don't you feel well?"

"I feel well," I told him. "I feel fine. Now, I'll tell you why I spent an extra ten days at Atronics City. McCann made and registered the big strike, right?"

Henderson nodded blankly, apparently not trusting himself to speak.

"Wrong," I said cheerfully. "McCann went to Chemisant City and filled out all the forms required for registering a claim. But every place he was supposed to sign his name he wrote *Ab Karpin* instead. Jafe McCann *never did make a legal registration of his claim.*"

Henderson just looked fish-eyed.

"So," I went on, "as soon as I turned McCann over to the law at Atronics City, I went and registered that claim myself. And then I waited around for ten days until the company finished the paperwork involved in buying that claim from me. And then I came straight back here, just to say good-bye to you. Wasn't that nice?"

He didn't move.

"Good-bye," I said.

THE STUFF

Henry Slesar

Here is Slesar again, and no, there isn't any law against having a given writer twice in the same volume. He poses the stark question: If you know you are going to die soon, how would you like to go? Death is not a minor concern to me, and I think I would settle for this way.

—PA

"No more lies," Paula said. "For God's sake, Doctor, no more lies. I've been living with lies for the past year and I'm tired of them."

Bernstein closed the white door before answering, mercifully obscuring the sheeted, motionless mound on the hospital bed. He took the young woman's elbow and walked with her down the tiled corridor.

"He's dying, of course," he said conversationally. "We've never lied to you about that, Mrs. Hills; you know what we've told you all along. I hoped that by now you'd feel more resigned."

"I was," she said bitterly. They had stopped in front of Bernstein's small office and she drew her arm away. "But then you called me. About this drug of yours—"

"We had to call you. Senopoline can't be administered without permission of the patient, and since your husband has been in coma for the last four days—"

He opened the door and nodded her inside. She hesitated, then walked in. He took his place behind the cluttered desk, his grave face distracted, and waited until she sat down in the facing chair. He picked up his telephone receiver, replaced it, shuffled papers, and then locked his hands on the desk blotter.

"Senopoline is a curious drug," he said. "I've had little experi-

205

ence with it myself. You may have heard about the controversy surrounding it.''

''No,'' she whispered. ''I don't know about it. I haven't cared about anything since Andy's illness.''

''At any rate, you're the only person in the world that can decide whether your husband receives it. It's strange stuff, as I said, but in the light of your husband's present condition, I can tell you this—it can do him absolutely no harm.''

''But it will do him good?''

''There,'' Bernstein sighed, ''is the crux of the controversy, Mrs. Hills.''

Row, row, row your boat, he sang in his mind, feeling the lapping tongues of the cool lake water against his fingers, drifting, drifting, under obeisant willows. Paula's hands were resting gently on his eyes and he lifted them away. Then he kissed the soft palms and pressed them on his cheek. When he opened his eyes, he was surprised to find that the boat was a bed, the water only pelting rain against the window, and the willow trees long shadows on the walls. Only Paula's hands were real, solid and real and comforting against his face.

He grinned at her. ''Funniest damn thing,'' he said. ''For a minute there, I thought we were back at Finger Lake. Remember that night we sprang a leak? I'll never forget the way you looked when you saw the hem of your dress.''

''Andy,'' she said quietly. ''Andy, do you know what's happened?''

He scratched his head. ''Seems to me Doc Bernstein was in here a while ago. Or was he? Didn't they jab me again or something?''

''It was a drug, Andy. Don't you remember? They have this new miracle drug, senopoline. Dr. Bernstein told you about it, said it was worth the try . . .''

''Oh, sure, I remember.''

He sat up in bed, casually, as if sitting up in bed were an everyday occurrence. He took a cigarette from the table beside him and lit it. He smoked reflectively for a moment, and then recalled that he hadn't been anything but horizontal for almost eight months. Swiftly, he put his hand on his rib cage and touched the firm flesh.

''The girdle,'' he said wonderingly. ''Where the hell's the girdle?''

''They took it off,'' Paula said tearfully. ''Oh, Andy, they took it off. You don't need it anymore. You're healed, completely healed. It's a miracle!''

''A miracle . . .''

She threw her arms about him; they hadn't held each other since the accident a year ago, the accident that had snapped his spine in several places. He had been twenty-two when it happened.

They released him from the hospital three days later; after half a year in the hushed white world, the city outside seemed wildly clamorous and riotously colorful, like a town at the height of carnival. He had never felt so well in his life; he was eager to put the strong springs of his muscles back into play. Bernstein had made the usual speech about rest, but a week after his discharge Andy and Paula were at the courts in tennis clothes.

Andy had always been a dedicated player, but his stiff-armed forehand and poor net game had always prevented him from being anything more than a passable amateur. Now he was a demon on the court, no ball escaping his swift-moving racket. He astounded himself with the accuracy of his crashing serves, his incredible play at the net.

Paula, a junior champion during her college years, couldn't begin to cope with him; laughingly, she gave up and watched him battle the club professional. He took the first set 6–0, 6–0, 6–0, and Andy knew that something more magical than medicinal had happened to him.

They talked it over, excited as schoolchildren, all the way home. Andy, who had taken a job in a stockbrokerage house after college, and who had been bored silly with the whole business until the accident, began wondering if he could make a career on the tennis court.

To make sure his superb playing wasn't a fluke, they returned to the club the next day. This time, Andy found a former Davis Cup challenger to compete with. At the end of the afternoon, his heart pounding to the beat of victory, he knew it was true.

That night, with Paula in his lap, he stroked her long auburn hair and said: ''No, Paula, it's all wrong. I'd like to keep it up, maybe enter the Nationals, but that's no life for me. It's only a game, after all.''

''Only a game?'' she said mockingly. ''That's a fine thing for the next top-seeded man to say.''

''No, I'm serious. Oh, I don't mean I intend to stay in Wall

Street; that's not my ambition either. As a matter of fact, I was thinking of painting again.''

"Painting? You haven't painted since your freshman year. You think you can make a living at it?''

"I was always pretty good, you know that. I'd like to try doing some commercial illustration; that's for the bread and potatoes. Then, when we don't have to worry about creditors, I'd like to do some things on my own.''

"Don't pull a Gauguin on me, friend.'' She kissed his cheek lightly. "Don't desert your wife and family for some Tahitian idyll. . . .''

"What family?''

She pulled away from him and got up to stir the ashes in the fireplace. When she returned, her face was glowing with the heat of the fire and warmth of her news.

Andrew Hills, Junior, was born in September. Two years later, little Denise took over the hand-me-down cradle. By that time, Andy Hills was signing his name to the magazine covers of America's top-circulation weeklies, and they were happy to feature it. His added fame as America's top-ranked amateur tennis champion made the signature all the more desirable.

When Andrew Junior was three, Andrew Senior made his most important advance in the field of art—not on the cover of the *Saturday Evening Post,* but in the halls of the Modern Museum of Art. His first exhibit evoked such a torrent of superlatives that the *New York Times* found the reaction newsworthy enough for a box on the front page. There was a celebration in the Hills household that night, attended by their closest friends: copies of slick magazines were ceremoniously burned and the ashes placed in a dime-store urn that Paula had bought for the occasion.

A month later, they were signing the documents that entitled them to a sprawling hilltop house in Westchester, with a north-light glassed-in studio the size of their former apartment.

He was thirty-five when the urge struck him to rectify a sordid political situation in their town. His fame as an artist and tennis champion (even at thirty-five, he was top-seeded in the Nationals) gave him an easy entrée into the political melee. At first, the idea of vote-seeking appalled him; but he couldn't retreat once the movement started. He won easily and was elected to the town council. The office was a minor one, but he was enough of a celebrity to attract countrywide attention. During the following year, he began to receive visits from important men in party circles; in the next state election, his name was on the ballot. By the time he was forty, Andrew Hills was a U.S. senator.

That spring, he and Paula spent a month in Acapulco, in an enchanting home they had erected in the cool shadows of the steep mountains that faced the bay. It was there that Andy talked about his future.

"I know what the party's planning," he told his wife, "but I know they're wrong. I'm not presidential timber, Paula."

But the decision wasn't necessary; by summer, the Asiatic Alliance had tired of the incessant talks with the peacemakers and had launched their attack on the Alaskan frontier. Andy was commissioned at once as a major.

His gallantry in action, his brilliant recapture of Shaktolik, White Mountain, and eventual triumphant march into Nome guaranteed him a place in the High Command of the Allied Armies.

By the end of the first year of fighting, there were two silver stars on his shoulder and he was given the most critical assignment of all—to represent the Allies in the negotiations that were taking place in Fox Island in the Aleutians. Later, he denied that he was solely responsible for the successful culmination of the peace talks, but the American populace thought him hero enough to sweep him into the White House the following year in a landslide victory unparalleled in political history.

He was fifty by the time he left Washington, but his greatest triumphs were yet to come. In his second term, his interest in the World Organization had given him a major role in world politics. As First Secretary of the World Council, his ability to effect a working compromise between the ideological factions was directly responsible for the establishment of the World Government.

When he was sixty-four, Andrew Hills was elected World President, and he held the office until his voluntary retirement at seventy-five. Still active and vigorous, still capable of a commanding tennis game, of a painting that set art circles gasping, he and Paula moved permanently into the house in Acapulco.

He was ninety-six when the fatigue of living overtook him. Andrew Junior, with his four grandchildren, and Denise, with her charming twins, paid him one last visit before he took to his bed.

"But what *is* the stuff?" Paula said. "Does it cure or what? I have a right to know!"

Dr. Bernstein frowned. "It's rather hard to describe. It has no curative powers. It's more in the nature of a hypnotic drug, but it has a rather peculiar effect. It provokes a dream."

"A dream?"

"Yes. An incredibly long and detailed dream, in which the patient lives an entire lifetime, and lives it just the way he would like it to be. You might say it's an opiate, but the most humane one ever developed."

Paula looked down at the still figure on the bed. His hand was moving slowly across the bedsheet, the fingers groping toward her.

"Andy," she breathed. "Andy darling . . ."

His hand fell across hers, the touch feeble and aged.

"Paula," he whispered, "say good-bye to the children for me."

ARCTURUS TIMES THREE

Jack Sharkey

One of the great things about science fiction is its sense of wonder, but this can be difficult to capture. When a person first enters the genre, the wonder is manifest in every word, but as time passes his taste becomes jaded, and he assumes that the stories aren't as good as they used to be. He has changed, not the stories, but he doesn't understand this. Perhaps this is what is wrong with critics: they project their own disenchantment onto the genre, condemning everything, so that their comment has no relevance for the newer readers. I've seen this sort of burnout in editors, too, and even in writers. But once in a while a story of the old type shows up again, brimming with new discoveries and insights and wonder, and perhaps even significance. How such stories make it past the editorial gantlet I don't know, and obviously they don't get anthologized much. Here is an example; this is very much my kind of fiction.

—PA

Jack Sharkey, a former midwestern advertising copywriter, wrote some very good stories, mostly for Galaxy, in the 1960s and then, perhaps due to promotions, perhaps due to various discouragements, perhaps simply because he wanted to, drifted away from the field. No novel, no critical attention of any sort, but an excellent, near-forgotten writer now who deserved better. Most of us do. Except for those of us who aren't deserving at all. (There is no one in the prosefic business who has gotten precisely equitable treatment. Oh, maybe Hilma Wolitzer or Cynthia Ozick.)

—bnm

I

Lieutenant Jerry Norcriss stood at the edge of the wide green clearing, sniffing contentedly of the not-unpleasant air of Arcturus Beta. Three hundred yards behind him, crewmen and officers alike labored to unload the equipment necessary for setting up camp for this, their first night on the planet.

No one had asked him to lend his strong back to the proceedings. Space Zoologists were never required to do anything which might sap, even slightly, any of their physical energies. Moreover, they were under oath *not* to take any orders to the contrary.

Now and then, a hotshot pilot would feel resentment at the Zoologist's standoffish position, and take out his feelings with a remark like, "Would you pass the sugar, if you don't think it would sprain your wrist, sir?" Such incidents, if reported back to Earth, inevitably resulted in the breaking of the pilot, and his immediate removal from command. It was seldom the Zoologist himself who made the report. Any crew member who overheard such statements would make the report as soon as possible, no matter what feelings of loyalty they might otherwise have for the pilot or person who had spoken.

From the moment of landing, the lives of every man aboard a ship were in the hands of the Space Zoologist.

From Captain Daniel Peters, the pilot, down to Ollie Gibbs, the mess boy, there was nothing but respect for Jerry Norcriss, and no envy whatsoever for the job he would soon be doing. That is not to say they were on friendly terms with him, either.

It was the next thing to impossible to call a Space Zoologist "friend." Even amongst themselves, the Zoologists were distracted, bemused, withdrawn from their surroundings. After their first Contact, they never were able to join in amiable camaraderie with other men. Such social contact was not forbidden them. It was merely no longer a part of their inclination. In their eyes a cool, silvery light shimmered, an inner light that marked them for the ultimate adventurers they were. No person would ever suffice them. They lived only for the job they did. Without it, few lived longer than a terrestrial year. Even with it, there was often sudden death.

Jerry was barely thirty, but his thick shock of hair was almost totally white and his mouth a firm line which never curled in a smile nor twisted in a frown. At the edge of the clearing, his bronzed flesh glowing ruddily in the failing sunset light of Arcturus, he stood and waited. Off in the distance behind him, Daniel Peters started across the clearing from the sunset-red gleaming of the sleek metal spaceship.

He drew abreast of the solitary figure, and said respectfully, "All in readiness, sir."

The words reached Jerry as from across a void. He turned slowly to face the other man, focusing his will with the effort it always took just to use his voice.

"Thank you, Captain," he said.

That was all he said, but as he followed Peters across the clearing toward the scorched circle where the great ship had descended on its column of fire, the pilot could not suppress a shudder. Jerry's voice was oddly disconcerting to the nervous system of the listener. It seemed like the "ghost-voice" of a medium at a séance. The mind that was Jerry Norcriss was only utilizing a body for the purpose of speaking. It did not actually belong there.

And that was true enough. Jerry and the others of his kind no longer lived in their bodies. They merely existed there, waiting painfully for the next occasion of Contact.

Beside the ship's ladder, hooked to an external power outlet beneath a metal flap on one towering tailfin, was the couch and the helmet Jerry Norcriss would use.

Jerry lay back with the ease of long habit and adjusted the helmet strap beneath his chin, as Peters read to him mechanically. The data came from the translated résumé of the roborocket that had gathered data on Arcturus Beta for the six months prior to the landing of the spaceship.

". . . three uncatalogued species," his voice droned on. "An underground life-pulse in the swamplands near the equator; the creature could not be spotted from the air. . . . A basically feline creature, also near the equator, but in a desert region, metabolism unknown. . . . And pulses of intelligent life, and of some unfamiliar lower animal life, on the northern seas. . . . All other lifeforms on the planet conform to previously discovered patterns, and can be dealt with in the prescribed manners."

A small section of Jerry Norcriss's mind found itself mildly amused, as always, by this bit of formality. The outlining of the planetary reconnaissance to a Space Zoologist was mere protocol, a holdover from the ancient custom of briefing a man who was about to undergo a mission of importance. Vainly did the Zoologists try to convince authority that this briefing was futile. A man in Contact was no longer a man. He *was* the creature whose mind he inhabited, save for a minuscule remnant of personal identity. His job was to Learn the creature from the inside out. As his mind, off in the alien body, Learned, the information was relayed via the Contact helmet to an electronic brain on the ship, to be later translated into code cards for the roborockets.

Man's expansion throughout the universe was progressing faster than his mind could memorize or categorize.

The roborockets obviated his need to learn. For every known kind of alien-species problem, there was a solution. The scanner-beams of the rocket would sense each life-form over which they passed, in the rocket's six-month orbit about the planet. If all species conformed to already known types, then a signal would fly by ultrawave across the void to Earth, declaring the planet fit for immediate colonization. But if new species were encountered, the beam to Earth carried a hurried call to the Naval Space Corps, with a request for the next available Zoologist.

Zoologists spent their Earthside time at Corps Headquarters, in the Comprehension Chamber. There, with the millions of index cards at fingertip control, they lay back upon their couches and learned, through dreamlike vicarious playbacks, about the species Contacted by their confreres. Any Space Zoologist with even five years' service had more accumulated knowledge in his brain than any dozen ordinary zoologists. And more intimate knowledge, too. A man who has *been* an animal has infinitely more knowledge of that animal than a man who has merely dissected one.

So Jerry lay there, letting his ears record the voice of the pilot but closing his conscious mind to the import of the words. It never did any good to know that the creature you were about to be was unknown. And no comment on what sort of animal it *might* be could be half so informative as actually *being* what it was.

Jerry repressed an urge to fidget. This was almost the worst part of Contact: the wait, while the senseless briefing took place. Soon enough he would know more of the species under observation than could be held on ten reams of briefing sheets. Soon enough he would be sent, for an irreducible forty minutes, into the mind of each of the creatures to be Learned.

The irreducible time-extent of Contact was its primary hazard. When the Contact helmet had been developed, it had been found that approximately forty minutes—forty-point-oh-three minutes, to be exact—had to be spent in the creature's mind. No amount of redesigning, fiddling, or tinkering could change that time. The Zoologist could spend neither more nor less than that amount in a creature's mind.

Since all creatures have natural enemies, Contact called for more than simply curling up and relaxing inside the alien mind. The Zoologist's host-alien might have a metabolism which called for it to drink a pint of water every fifteen minutes or shrivel. In which case the Zoologist would shrivel with it, his punishment for not sufficiently Learning his host.

This, then, was the reason those irreducible forty minutes were a hazard. Should the creature being Contacted die, the Zoologist died with it. There was no avoiding death if it came to the inhabited creature. A good Zoologist Learned fast, or perished. Which is why there is no such thing as a bad Space Zoologist. You're either a good one or a dead one.

Peters's voice came to a halt and he closed the plastic folder over the briefing sheet.

"That's about the size of it, sir," he said. "We've focused the Contact-beams toward the indicated areas and made a final check of all the wiring, tubes, and power sources."

Jerry sighed contentedly and shut his eyes.

"Whenever you're ready, then, Captain," he whispered, and relaxed his body in preparation for his first Contact. His mind and imagination toyed a moment with brief fancies about his forthcoming existences in swamp, desert, and sea, then he pushed the thoughts away and let his mind go empty.

Faintly, he heard Peters calling an order to the technician within the spaceship—

The silent lightning flashed across his consciousness.

II

He opened his eyes. Six eyes. In two rows of three eyes each.

He did not, however, see six images. The widespread belief in the multitudinous images seen by the faceted eyes of a housefly had been debunked the first time a helmeted biochemist had intruded upon that insect's puny brain. As with human eyes, the images were fused into a whole when they reached the mind. Save for the disconcerting sensation of possessing a horizontal and vertical peripheral vision of approximately three hundred degrees sight was comfortably normal.

Jerry looked over his surroundings and noted one slightly annoying side effect of his hexafocal outlook. As a human will see—as when looking at the tip of a pencil pointed at the face—two images at the far end of any object looked upon, so Jerry, while able to zero in anywhere he chose, could see six ghost-images corresponding in their angle of perspective to the positions of his six eyes. Had he a pencil tip to stare at, it would have appeared, beyond the tip, to be vaguely like a badminton bird seen head on, with images of the pencil body comprising the "feathers."

A few moments of glancing about soon took care of the primary irritation of this unfamiliar sensation, and Jerry began to study his surroundings carefully.

He was inside a circular cavity of some sort, facing toward brightness at the opening ahead of him. The walls of the cavity were dark, sandy-smooth, and slightly moist, so he reasoned he was in some sort of burrow in the soil. Beyond the opening, there was light and warmth and a hint of greenery which his host's eyes could not bring into sharp focus.

"I wish I knew my size," he thought. "Am I some small insect awaiting a victim, or a rabbit-souled mammal hiding from a predator, or a lion-sized carnivore sleeping off a heavy meal?"

Attempts to turn his head for a look at his host's body availed him nothing. Jerry relaxed for a moment, and tried to sense his body by *feel*. He had, he knew in a moment, no neck. Head and torso were a one-piece unit, or at least inflexibly joined.

Carefully, Jerry moved his right "hand" out before his face for a look. He saw a thin, flesh-covered bony limb, with a double "elbow," terminating in a semicircular pad which seemed suited for nothing but support. No claw, talon, or digit on the pad; just a tessellated rubbery bottom, the tessellations apparently acting as treads do on a tire.

"Whatever I am," Jerry sighed, "I'm nonskid." He considered a moment, then added, "I can't be an insect, then. Insects can't rely on weight to keep them right-side up, and need gripping mechanisms. Okay, insect-size is out."

Jerry extended the pad before him and cautiously leaned his weight on it, then removed it back beneath his torso and studied the earth where it had rested. There was a concavity there, corresponding to the pad. It was not especially deep.

"Well, that lets out elephant-size," he reasoned, "and most oversize forms. I must be somewhere between a mouse and a middle-sized wolf. But *what* am I?"

Jerry tried breathing. Nothing happened; there was no sense of dilation anywhere in his body. "Odd," he thought. "Unless I get oxygen—or whatever gases this creature breathes—through my food. . . . Or maybe I have air tubes like an insect's. . . . No, I'd have to shift my body now and then for air circulation, and I feel no discomfort remaining still. Besides, I have flesh, and that tube arrangement only functions well in a body with an endoskeleton. Must be dependent on food intake, then. Stores its oxygen or whatever."

He extended the tessellated pad, and rubbed it cautiously against the soil. There was a dim sensation of touch in the pad. But it was subordinate to a somacentric sense of location. His pad "knew" where it was in relation to his body, but had no great tactile capacity for his surroundings. "Well," Jerry thought, "that lets out *feeling* my body to determine shape or function."

As it sometimes did when he was enhosted, his mind went back to old Peters, his instructor, who had taught "Project C" to the eager young Zoologists. Project Contact had been mostly devoted to giving the student an open mind on metabolism and adaptability to environment. A Learner had to be able to reason out—and quickly—the metabolism of his host. It was little use knowing a Terran life-ecology; man lives on combustibles and oxygen, the oxygen combining with combustibles to provide heat, and plants live on carbon dioxide and water and sunlight, renewing the atmospheric oxygen. So old Peters had always stressed the student's learning their Basic Combinations.

Basic Combinations prepared the student—or so the school board hoped—for a wide variety of chemical relationships between a host and its environment. The students had to know what to do to survive should the host, for instance, live in a chlorine atmosphere, and need large amounts of antimony in its diet for proper combustion and survival. There were a good many chemical elements in the universe; the student had to know how to deal with any combination of them in a host's metabolism.

For the most part, the instincts of the host would carry a Learner through the Contact period. A species tended to keep its physical needs not only in its mind, but in its body as well. Mr. Peters had a saying he'd been fond of emphasizing to the students: "When in doubt, black out.'' The saying became a cliché to the student body, but they had the sense not to disregard it. A cliché is, after all, only a truth which has become trite because it is vitally necessary to use it often.

"When in doubt, black out" meant simply that if a situation arose which seemed impossible to handle rationally, the enhosted Learner's last resort was reliance upon the instinctive behavior of the host. The only thing to be done was to pull the mind into a tiny knot bobbing in the host's own brain, and let the host itself, once more in control, take the Learner instinctively to environmental victory. Or defeat.

There were dangers, of course. A Learner enhosted in a chicken, for instance, would be a fool to trust the chicken's instincts regarding, say, a snake. A chicken confronted by a snake tends to become hypnotized by its deadly adversary, and to stand stupidly in place until it is killed. In cases of that sort, the Learner would be safer taking control and going clucking off to the nearest high ground.

On the other hand, a Learner inhabiting something with the hair-trigger instincts of a bat would be much better off letting the animal's instincts take over in moments of grave risk, such as flying through the blades of a revolving fan. A bat could get through without a second thought about those whirling metal scythes, but a man's mind could not think fast enough to avoid a grim death by all-over amputation.

"Maybe," Jerry thought hopefully, "I've got an *easy* one." It was possible, of course. His host might be in the midst of an afternoon siesta, and Jerry could relax and "sit out" his forty minutes of Contact. But such cases were few. At any moment a predator might come down into that orifice in the soil, and Jerry would have to fight for his host's life to preserve his own. Relaxed Learning was seldom feasible.

"I'd better see what sort of fighting equipment I have," he decided, wishing vainly that he could just turn his head and look his body over. This proceeding by *feel* was a slow, tortuous, and sometimes deceptive process. Hollow fangs that seemed capable of injecting venom into an enemy might—as in the case of the Venusian Sea Vampires—turn out to be an organ for drinking water, the sacs above the fangs being for digesting liquids and not for storing poisons.

Jerry stimulated what should be his tongue into action, checking for the presence of fangs. Within the mouth of the creature, which felt large in relation to its head, he sensed a rasping movement, a kind of dull dry rustling, but could feel nothing with the tongue itself. "Best have a look at it," he decided suddenly, and, opening his jaws, extended the tongue.

Jerry was distinctly shocked by the thing that skewed and writhed forward from beneath his eyes. His sensation was not unlike that of a man who opens his mouth and finds a snake in it. And Jerry further realized that he was now seeing with another sextet of eyes, at the end of the tongue.

He was not one alien—he was two!

His primary six eyes took in the pink-and-gray horror extending ahead of him. The tongue was almost like another animal, serpentine in construction, and had two horny—what?—arms?—pincerjaws?—at either side of the "head." They were tubular, like a cow's horns, and lay at either side of a wide slit-mouth in the tongue itself.

On impulse, Jerry swiveled the tip of the tongue back upon itself, and gazed through the six eyes around the tongue-slit-and-jaws/arms at the main body of his host. Then, suddenly feeling ill, he snapped the tongue back into his mouth and shut his jaws.

It had been a horrible sight. Where he'd expected to see the abdominal region of his host, just behind the thoracic section, there lay a wet, red concavity, in the midst of gaping jaws, Jerry himself was enhosted in a "tongue" of some still larger creature within that soft earthen burrow! And some remaining fragment of his host's awareness told him that the creature of whom he was the tongue was itself the tongue of yet another creature. He was a segment of some gigantic segmented worm-creature whose origin lay who-knows-how-far beneath the earth.

Carefully, stilling a mental feeling akin to *mal de mer,* he reprotruded his tongue and looked more carefully at it. Sure enough, just behind the "head" of the thing were two stubby growths, not yet mature. In time, Jerry realized, those growths would develop into a pair of double-elbowed front "arms" with semitactile tessellated pads at the base, and the curving jaws/arms would drop off or be reabsorbed, while that "tongue" extended a "tongue" of its own.

"And then what happens to *my* segment?" he wondered. "Do I simply lie here forever with jaws agape?"

As he pondered this, there came a movement in the greenery

just beyond the burrow orifice. A squiggly thing with an ill-assorted tangle of underappendages came prancing with almost laughable ill-balance into view. Jerry, intent on observing this creature—very like a landbound jellyfish walking clumsily upon its dangling arms—relaxed his vigil as regards control of the host.

Before he realized it, his jaws were flung wide, and that self-determined tongue was leaping for its prey. The horny jaws/arms clamped into the viscous body of the passing creature, and the slit-mouth extended upper and lower lips like pseudopods to cover the writhing, squealing victim. Then a huge lump appeared in the tongue, just behind its "head." Jerry waited with a distinct lack of relish for the still-squirming "meal" to make its alimentary way back into his own esophagus.

However, it did not. Just short of his lips, it halted. And after a few moments, it ceased to struggle.

Annoyed, but uncertain just why he was, Jerry attempted to remouth his tongue. It did not come back. His jaws lay open wide, and his tongue remained where it had shot forward to grasp the ten-tacled creature.

Something clicked in Jerry's mind, and he once more tried "seeing" out of the tongue's six eyes. He found that he still could, but dimly.

It took him about three seconds to figure out his peril.

The segment behind his own would never reswallow *his* segment, which had been its tongue. It couldn't. It was dead. For the time period in which his own segment had existed as the third segment's tongue, it had some control over it. It could extend the tongue, and could see through the eyes in the tongue. But then Jerry's segment had fed, had grown, and the parent-segment had died, as had its parent-segments before it. The thing, whatever it was, grew fast, too.

That was the frightening part.

Even while he thought this, he saw that the lump was gone from his tongue. But his tongue was twice the size it had been!

Repeated efforts on his part to withdraw it back within his jaws met with failure. Again he tried looking through its eyes, and found his tongue-vision even dimmer. Then, with a tremor of shock, he realized that his own vision was dimmer, too.

His host was dying. It was no longer needed to house the tongue.

Up ahead of him, the tongue-part was digging busily with those pincers, erecting for itself an extension of the burrow. Like a mole in reverse, it did not make a mound by tunneling through the soil, but by lying atop the soil and erecting itself a circular tunnel in which to await victims.

Jerry's mind brought to him a vision of what this section of this unknown morass must look like, with miles and miles of curving tunnels, each housing a hideous worm-creature, of whom all segments were dead except the front one, which would in turn be dead as soon as its tongue had fed a bit and grown to mature size.

Shivering within his mind, Jerry wondered how much of the forty-minute period had gone by.

He had no way of estimating. His personal time-sense was overpowered by that of his host. A man within a gnat, with the life span of a day, would feel subjectively that he had lived a lifetime within it, although only those same forty minutes would pass by until his return to his own body, helmeted upon the couch.

Each new segment might take a day to grow, or it might take a few minutes. Jerry could not tell. He could only wait until he was sent to his next Contact. There was no method of self-release from Contact. That was why survival was imperative.

A flicker of movement caught his dimming vision, and he realized that his tongue had snared yet another of the jellyfish-things. The second lump was quickly absorbed as he watched, and he found he could no longer make contact at all with the six eyes of the tongue tip. His own six were blurring, with a rapidity he was able to observe, and he knew that the life of the host could not last very long.

Vaguely, he was aware that the stubby growths of his tongue had now sprouted into appendages such as his own. The tongue could no longer be called that, because it was nearly a full-grown segment. Within it, he imagined, it was growing a new tongue of its own, the faster to hasten its own eventual demise.

"I've got to stop it," he thought. "But how can I? It won't withdraw, no matter how hard I try. And if it would, it's grown too large to fit inside my jaws anymore, even if I tried cramming it in with these stupid pads of mine. . . ."

He stopped the pointless line of reasoning and lifted his pair of double-elbowed "arms" before his failing sextet of eyes.

"They look strong enough, but are they?"

He could feel his control slipping. His life would hang upon the success or failure of his experiment, but there was no time to try and reason out a better attempt at survival.

Swiftly, ignoring the wriggling protests of the segment before his own, he encircled it tightly with those two-jointed "arms" and held it tight and painfully taut. It was still soft, still relatively raw from its rapid growth, and was not equipped to fend off attack from the rear. Jerry, straining terribly, ignoring the searing pain that licked his consciousness, cruelly and methodically tore out what had been his tongue.

The dripping end of the thing flopped once, then lay still. And Jerry's vision, after swimming in gray haze for a moment, coalesced once more into sharp focus and he knew his host was alive again.

"Whew!" he gasped, grateful to shut the great jaws once more. "It'll be tough, but I know how to survive, now. My segment's low enough on the evolutionary scale to regenerate lost parts; it will grow itself a new tongue. If I don't get lifted to a new Contact in the meantime, I'll simply tear *that* one out, too, and hang on until I get *out* of this damned thing!"

Then the segment ahead of him moved, and Jerry knew cold fear.

At the mouth of the burrow, one of the squiggly jellyfish-things had inserted a tentacle into the burrow and was busily ingesting the torn-out segment into a gaping hole in its underside amongst the shiny, wiggling arms. Even as he watched, it had completed its meal, and with a shiver of gustatory pleasure, readjusted its relative dimensions until it was three times its former size.

"This," said Jerry, bitterly, "is one hell of an ecology. Each creature is the other's chief natural enemy!"

Then his fright grew as he saw that the jellyfish—he could no longer think of it as anything else—was methodically ripping down the walls of the burrow, and coming for *him*.

Frantically, Jerry tried getting at the thing with his tongue, but the raw stump within his jaws was still in the process of generating a new head-and-eyes part. A mere stub shot forward to wag futilely at the approaching enemy.

Jerry shot his tessellated pads forward, trying to push and pummel the thing away, but the few blows that landed rebounded from that shiny body like pith-balls bouncing from an electrostatic plate.

Then the jellyfish grappled with, and held on to, one of Jerry's arms, and began calmly to tuck it into its digestive cavity. If the pad had been only lightly tactile before, it became supersensitive now, as the creature's digestive juices began to erode it into its component chemicals.

Jerry felt as if he'd rammed his hand into an open wood fire. He tried to scream; nothing emerged between his jaws except that futile tongue-stump. The jellyfish, climbing in a leisurely fashion down the limb it was ingesting, flicked out a tentacle and began doing something horrible to Jerry's upper right eye. It sent waves of pain into his mind, and almost blotted out all thought, except for a maniac notion that urged Jerry to laugh at the creature's ambition. For its highly maneuverable tentacle tip was diligently attempting to *unscrew* the eye.

Jerry's right arm was gone. Tentacles flipped and floundered all about his head-section. The digestive cavity of the jellyfish was widening, trying to take in Jerry's head at a single swallow. He saw, with the five usable eyes remaining, a crystally concavity, the sides glinting with digestive fluid tinted beautiful emerald by the foliage out beyond its semi-transparent body. Then the thing closed over his head, and the last of the eyes began to sear and sting.

Jerry's mind cried out in anguish . . . and lightning flashed across his consciousness. White, silent lightning.

Pain ceased.

The time of Contact had passed.

III

Captain Daniel Peters paced agitatedly back and forth before the couch holding that still figure in its bulky helmet. The last glow of the sunset had vanished behind the trees around the clearing minutes before. Peters took three puffs from a just-ignited cigarette, then crushed the white cylinder under his heel.

"Sir?" said a man at the airlock of the ship.

Peters looked up swiftly, and identified the speaker as the technician for the Contact mechanism.

"How's it going?" he asked, trying to keep his voice matter-of-fact.

"First report's just come in," said the man, with a brief smile. "Information's being coded onto a new card for the roborocket index. I guess Norcriss came through the Contact all right. His life-pulse still shows on the panel. It was flickering badly for a few minutes, though. Think I should terminate?''

Peters hesitated, then shook his head. ''No, I guess not. They tell me there are no aftereffects to even a hazardous Contact. Norcriss'll be wanting to get on with it . . . poor devil,'' he added, with a wry smile that touched only his lips, didn't reach his eyes. ''Proceed, seaman.''

The other man nodded, and vanished within the ship. . . .

IV

Vast flat fields of sun-bronzed stone stretched in all directions to the horizon, pockmarked with rimless craters, seething with red liquid which flickered with dusty blue fingers of fire here and there on its surface. Every so often a pale plume of steamy white rose toward the coppery overturned bowl that was the sky.

Cautiously Jerry sniffed the air. Sulfur. That was the red liquid burning in those many pits: yellow sulfur melted into gluey scarlet pools amid the nearly invisible shimmer of its consuming fires.

''Sulfur doesn't steam,'' Jerry thought idly, still sniffing at the fumes. ''So the white plumes mean there is water, or some volatile liquid, mingled with the deposits in those pits.''

After a moment, he realized that he was no longer taking random sniffs of the fumes, but was actually indulging himself in a regular orgy of breathing. The smell of the sulfur was as strong and piercing as he'd ever known it, but absent was the almost simultaneous effect of raw throat, streaming eyes, and hacking cough.

''The desert air must be nearly *all* sulfur gases,'' he realized. That would explain the hue of the sky, and the not-unpleasant silvery haziness of the atmosphere.

''And I, if I don't keel over in a few more moments, must be a sulfur-breathing creature.''

Sunlight, from nearly directly overhead, was warm and comfortable upon his head, back, and hindquarters. An unusually flexible feeling in the caudal region of his spine told him that he had a tail, even before he swung his huge head about for a glance at it. The body, as bronzed as the rock on which it stood, was something like a lion's, although the taloned feet, from heel to the first leg-joint, were horny and rough in appearance. They were not unlike those of a barnyard fowl, if considerably thicker and decidedly more lethal.

That, save for a hard-to-see fringe of darker fur that ran up his neck toward where he felt his ears to be, was all of his body that he could view.

"I wonder," he mused, "what my head looks like."

A brief turning of the problem in his mind gave him the solution to it. It wasn't the best possible way of getting an idea of his latest cranial conformations, but—unless there was a looking glass lying about—it was the only way at hand.

Jerry tilted his head until his eyes fell upon his shadow on the brown rock beneath him. By tilting it from one side to the other, and joining the various silhouettes in his mind by a simple application of basic gestalt, he knew what his head looked like.

Very like a lion's, except that it seemed to have no external ear. A single slender silhouette that fell from the forehead region, stiletto-pointed, must be a sort of horn, unless it deciduated periodically, like a deer's antlers.

Further speculation on his appearance was interrupted by the appearance of another creature, trotting like a terrier between the fuming sulfur pits, coming his way.

It could be a twin to what he now knew he looked like, but it seemed just a bit smaller, somehow. And it was carrying something carefully in its teeth.

"Should I run, fight, or just ignore it?" Jerry wondered. "It doesn't seem menacing. But neither does a Pekinese till you try to pet it."

He allowed his mind to retreat a fractional bit from control of his host, and watched its reactions to the newcomer. Jerry felt a surge of emotion, a sort of fond, proud, doting feeling, and knew that this approaching creature was his cub. "That's a help," he thought, relieved, and resumed control of the animal.

The cub halted a short distance away, and gently set its burden upon the rock, placing a forefootful of talons upon the thing before letting go with its jaws. Under the talons, the thing moved. Jerry saw that it was a sort of squirrel, except that it had well-developed forepaws, the pads of which hinted that it undoubtedly ran quadripedally instead of climbing trees. Then the memory of the sort of terrain he was in recrossed his mind, and Jerry felt foolish.

Naturally it didn't climb trees in a region that was devoid of any vegetation whatsoever.

Jerry noticed that the cub seemed to be waiting for something. He wished he could speak. He had the goofy feeling that he was supposed to say, like a man confronted by a bottle of Château-Neuf in the hopeful hands of a wine steward, "That'll do nicely, thank you."

A nod was almost universally a sign of acquiescence, so he tried that instead. The cub seemed pleased, and immediately, by lowering that forehead-horn between a pair of the talons enfolding the struggling land-squirrel, snuffed out its life with a thrust through its neck. Then it removed the talons from its prey, and took a backward step.

Apparently, as the sire, Jerry was to get first bite.

"Now don't go all picayune," he cautioned his digestive tract. "Come on, Jerry boy. You eat oysters while they're alive. You should be able to eat a squirrel when it's dead. Besides, if you like the smell of this lion-creature's atmosphere, you'll probably like the taste of its food. Eat hearty."

With that, Jerry lowered his head and let his sharp teeth snap off a haunch of the squirrel-thing. He went to chew it, then realized that—unlike his prior Contact's overequipage—he had no tongue. This was strictly a bolt-your-food host. So he tossed his head back, and managed, with a spasmodic effort of his thick muscular throat, to get the morsel into his stomach.

The cub stepped forward then, bit off a chunk for itself, and got it down with less apparent effort.

"Well, he's had more practice at tongueless eating," Jerry consoled himself. Then, noting that the cub was standing patiently awaiting something, he swayed his head from side to side, trying to convey, "No, thanks, it's all yours, kid."

But the cub, its head tipped perplexedly to one side, was still watching him, waiting for something, a sort of puzzled anxiety in its gaze. Jerry reasoned that if he simply backed off, the cub would take that as a gesture of refusal to eat any more, so he took a few steps away from the squirrel-thing.

And the cub, an almost human look of bafflement on its face, gurgled a whine from its throat. It began to bounce about on its legs like a housebroken dog that very urgently wants out.

Jerry thought hard. The frantic desire of the cub for him to do something was more than mere pettishness on its part. There was real panic in its eyes, now. Jerry felt the first thrill of danger. What was he doing wrong? Or what wasn't he doing *right?*

Mere after-you-Pop protocol could not explain the glint of fright in his cub's eyes. Or could it?

Jerry tried to remain calm and think reasonably. The sire-and-cub relationship was throwing him. Most animals—in the narrow group that remained linked by relationship and affection even after the cubs matured—ran along opposite lines. The parent went out and got food for the kids, and not vice versa. On this planet, apparently, having a cub was the nearest thing to Social Security.

"Remember, you idiot," Jerry snapped at himself, "this is a species. It is no beast rational mind you are dealing with, but an animal mind. That means that the cub's apparent protocol is instinctive, and not a matter of etiquette. And an instinct has a reason behind it, doesn't it? Only man can skip over protocol. You have to do something before the cub feels that it can do it—and whatever it is you're not doing, it's driving the cub to distraction. You'd better go for a second helping of squirrel, and fast, or you're going to have your kid in a mental institution!"

Not exactly relishing completing the meal, Jerry stepped back to the furry little corpse on the rock, and only as he came near enough to bite into it was he suddenly aware of another odor mingling with that of the sulfur fumes. Unbelieving, he stared at the spreading pool of putrescence that ringed the remains of his cub's prey. He stared, silent and amazed, as flesh and bone crumbled and dissolved there on the ground, until there was nothing there but the noisome liquid and a few tiny teeth.

"Incredible!" thought Jerry. "To decompose so damned fast! But it certainly explains why Junior brought me that thing still alive and kicking. It didn't last more than a few minutes after it died— *Ugh!*"

The sickly retch boiled out from his stomach with a painful expansion, and he scented the same foul odor on his breath as arose from the liquid that now lay drying in the burning sunlight.

"The damn thing's going rotten *inside* me!" he said to himself, feeling the first wave of illness shake him from horn to tail tip.

His flesh, beneath its bronze-colored fur, felt suddenly cold and greasy. Jerry knew that feeling well, from one summer when he'd eaten a sandwich with mayonnaise that had lain too long outside the refrigerator. It was the onset of ptomaine. He and the cub could be dead, in a very ugly manner, within less time than he had to await his next Contact. Or was it less time? It was subjective, wasn't it? Maybe this period would be over more quickly than the last one. Or maybe more slowly. . . .

Jerry turned to look at the cub. Its eyes were glazing. It was breathing in gasps through its open mouth, staggering as it tried to remain on its feet.

"We're poisoned," Jerry groaned. "And it's not on purpose. That cub didn't trot here with that squirrel just to knock off its old man! There's something else has to be done, something I've overlooked. And my stupidity is killing us."

Weakly, almost automatically, Jerry's conscious mind did the only thing possible under the circumstances. Cliché of old Peters or not, "When in doubt, black out" was the only solution. Jerry swiftly relinquished his grip on the controls, and let the lion-thing take over its own destiny.

The first thing it did was rush toward the scarlet surface of the boiling sulfur pit near the cub. The muscles relaxed and showed no sign of relaxing in that flame-bound gallop, and Jerry grabbed at its mind and got back in control just as its forefeet stood on the brink of that blue-flaming red pool.

"Oh, damn!" he groaned, agonized by both his fear of fire and the growing discomfort within his stomach. "Of all the creatures in the universe, I have to hit one with the lemming instinct. This damn thing's bent on boiling itself alive if I let go. And if I stay in control, I die of ptomaine!"

Jerry Norcriss wasted nearly thirty seconds feeling sorry for himself. And then he remembered something about lemmings. And also something about cubs.

Lemmings, those strange little rodents that take it periodically in their heads to all go rushing into the ocean and drown, are not suicide-bent. Their ancestry is older than the continent on which they live. At one time the spot wherein they plunge into the ocean was linked with the next continent over. The migration—for that's what it is with lemmings—had at one time been perfectly safe. So safe that the migration of the lemmings became instinctive. And, after the continents separated, or the band of land joining them sank beneath the sea, the lemmings blithely continued their trek, and perished. Lemmings might die, but the ages-old instinct of the species wouldn't.

No animal, Jerry realized, is deliberately self-destructive. No animal but man—who is more than animal, and can decide upon his own destiny despite what his instincts buck for.

And cubs, Jerry recalled with chagrin, are not always born knowing survival tactics. Some cubs have to be taught how to survive. And this one is still in the process of learning, and only senses that—since it is becoming deathly ill—something is horribly wrong. It wants its sire to show it survival, and its sire is in the hands of a nincompoop like me. . . .

Fortunately for Jerry and the cub, his thoughts on cubs and lemmings lasted only a fractional second, so all-inclusive is the mind's apprehension of a situation.

And then, Jerry, feeling greatly relieved, let go of the controls once more and let the lion-thing bend and drink from the blazing sulfur pool at its feet.

Of what the host was constructed, Jerry had no idea. Its cell structure might be high in silicates, or possibly be akin to asbestos. Whatever it was, the blazing red sulfur went down its gullet like sweet warm wine, and the decaying squirrel-thing was transformed into chemicals that were comfortably digestible.

Jerry was glad to see that the cub, standing on shaky legs, was drinking, too. It seemed likely to survive its brush with death.

Not a bad life, he thought. Catch a meal, take a swig of wine, and then just loaf around in the sun. Nice planet . . . if you like sulfur, and have a bright-eyed young kid who won't make a move without your approval and example—

Jerry's ruminations were cut short by a sound of leathery wings, high in the coppery sky. Abruptly alert, he lifted his shaggy head and saw an ominous formation of Vs in the sky. They grew in size, and became the forms of gigantic airborne things, a cross between the ancient Terran pterodactyl and a sort of saber-toothed ape.

Something told him these approaching things were not friendly.

He turned his head to the cub, but this, apparently, was a lesson already learned, because all he saw of his scion was a disappearing blur of buttocks and tail as the cub scurried in a clumsy gallop across the plains of sunburnt rock. In another instant, Jerry was scurrying right after him, for reasons above and beyond Togetherness.

The paws wouldn't manage right, so he finally dropped back a bit and let the lion-thing's brain take over the job of escape, his own mind merely going along for the ride.

"But where can we *hide?*" he wondered, fascinated despite his fear. "Can we pull the hollow-reed routine under the surface of a sulfur pit? Or are there caves someplace in the vicinity? Or do we just run until either our legs or those simianipters' wings give out?"

Then his mind got entangled with the purely empirical cogitation about the validity of coining a word like *simianipters* (which seemed to mean "ape-winged" when the coinage he desired was "winged apes"), and his mind was bouncing so busily between this knotty problem and the chances of escape from those creatures and the puzzle of just what constituted safety from the flying things that he barely noticed the white flash of silent lightning that heralded cessation of Contact.

V

"Contact completed," said the technician to Peters, in the purple twilight slowly deepening to black starry night. "Slight dimming of Norcriss's life-pulse this time, not so bad as last time."

Peters nodded as he ripped open a fresh packet of cigarettes. "Machine functioning properly?"

"Yes, sir." The technician nodded. "Norcriss could go on at least three more Contacts with the power we have left. Shall I activate him again, sir?"

"Go ahead," murmured Peters, his eyes fastened on the pallid face of the young man on the couch. . . .

VI

Noise. Footsteps on metal. Metal meant refined ores, and that in turn meant intelligence. Yet he *couldn't* inhabit an intelligent mind!

Jerry opened his eyes and took in the scene before him. His vista was oddly diverted into vertical panels, and then, as his mind settled into full control, he knew that the panels were spaces between bars.

The thought crossed his mind that bars must be vertical everywhere in the universe. Horizontal ones would hold a prisoner as well, but the origin of bars lay in primitive stockades, stakes plunged into the ground about a prisoner. Primordial tribal habits were not easily broken, even after attainment of civilization.

Through the bars he saw—well—men. They were at least bipedal, and walked upright, and had two upper limbs with facile digits at the ends, all in keeping with the nearly universal rule of bilateral identity.

Beyond that, the resemblance to man ceased.

The creatures he saw were clothed in satiny uniforms, yet something about the material told him it would hold up under heavy stress. Wherever their actual bodies showed—head and hands, mostly, through a man of apparently lesser rank was bared to the waist, working on a machine set against one wall—they were covered with short (or cropped) white down. Jerry could detect on the heads no sign of ears or nose, but in the midst of the furry expanse of face, tiny green-glinting beads of jet were eyes, and a thin, wide blue-gray slit further down was the mouth.

The hands, he noted with interest, were furred even within the palms. Or so he thought until one of the creatures, idly flexing a hand, showed Jerry that the fingers bent on double joints in either direction. There were no nails as such, but each digit on those deceptively soft-looking hands terminated in a tapering cone of some hard black material, as shiny as the eyes in those coconut-frosted faces.

Jerry once more had cause to regret the impossibility of Contact within a mind of an intelligent creature. Intelligence equated with impenetrability, so far as Contact went. You could learn of an intelligent race only so much as their words and gestures and behavior cared to let you know.

Jerry knew he was in a sea region, but whether over it, on it, or under it—no. The room, so far as he could see, was windowless. It could mean that the vehicle was carrying its own atmosphere, in order to keep the riders alive, whether the outside surface of the ship were within inimical gases or liquids, or the deadly nothingness between planets.

Then again, he might simply be within a fortress, or below sea level in a ship. Jerry gave it up, and concentrated on himself, and his barred container.

The cage was as high as one-fourth the height of any of the men before it, so Jerry reckoned his own size as about one-sixth. If they were all six-footers, then he must be about rabbit-sized. He glanced down his body and saw hard gray scales over a curving belly, with a pair of hind feet that seemed to be all phalanges and no metatarsals. From "heel" to foot tip, Jerry had three long, hard-looking black spikes. "Something like a swan's foot with the webbing removed," he mused.

A look at his forepaws before his face showed him three similar phalanges, though only two-thirds the length of the hind ones, and having in addition a sort of stubby rudimentary thumb. His forearms were scaly, too, and possessed a wicked spur of the same black material jutting downward from the elbow.

Happily, three sides of his cage were polished metal walls, so he was able to get an inkling of his facial characteristics in the warped uncertain mirror of the surfaces. He saw startled-looking eyes, round as quarters, with red irises that dilated greatly with each tilt of his head toward the shadowy rear of the cage, and narrowed the orifice about the pupil to a pinprick when he turned near the front. He seemed to be noseless, also. When he tried to sniff, nothing happened. The attempt made his head feel stuffed up, but he knew that the feeling was only inside his mind, and not an actual sensation.

Jerry looked at his mouth. It was just a wide slit in his round, earless head—no, not earless; there were auricular holes under a flange of gray scale—just a wide slit with a glint of sharp-pointed bright orange teeth.

"Well," he thought, "I'm at least a carnivore, possibly an omnivore, with teeth like that. The light in this room is apparently not intolerable to those fur-faces out there. So—if the slight shooting pains in my head plus the shutting of the irises when I face into the room are any criteria—I must be a nocturnal beast of some kind. Eyes like this would be blinded by sunlight."

He decided he was, in the ecology of the fur-faces, something along the lines of a raccoon, even if his flesh were scaly as a pangolin's. "Maybe I'm a pet," he hoped. "But there's something about the atmosphere of this room—"

Something rustled and clacked against the wall of his cage.

Jerry withdrew his control a fraction to let the host's mind tell him what it might be. The mind of his host was atingle with antagonism. Yet, as Jerry heard a similar movement somewhere off to the far side, the mind of his host grew suddenly tender and excited.

Jerry reassumed control, having the information he needed. His cage was one of at least three, possibly many more, housing animals like the one enhosting him. The nearby cage contained an animal of his own sex, the other contained an animal of the opposite sex, possibly a mate. Whether male or female, Jerry had no idea. He had in any Contact—barring a procreative arrangement beyond the simple bisexual—a fifty–fifty chance of being male. The worm had been self-generating, the unicornate lion-thing had been male. What Jerry's present sex was, he had no idea. Even on Earth, scaly creatures tended to baffle all but the experts as to sex. Jerry inspected the mind of his host for a few moments, but could find out only that it yearned for that other one in the other cage. The intensity of the yearning gave no clue if the urge were man-for-woman, woman-for-man, mother-for-child, child-for-parent, or—it was barely possible—friend-for-friend.

Jerry decided to ignore the yearning by taking full control of the host once more. He took stock of his circumstances. Here he was, a nocturnal carnivore, caged with many of his own kind in a vehicle moving through space or water.

He was not just there for the ride, that was certain.

Being delivered somewhere? No, the room beyond the bars looked little like a storage hold. Of course, these fur-faces might have alien ideas about the way a storage hold should look. Still, they seemed to be bosses of some kind. There was no mistaking the dressy look of their uniforms. A high-ranking officer might go into a storage hold, but it would be for an inspection only, and these creatures were busily doing something in the center of the room.

There were three of them, discounting the bare-to-the-waist man working on that odd-looking machine. They stood by some waist-high object—two with their backs to Jerry, one in profile—very intently absorbed in something on that surface.

Jerry twisted his head about, but could make out no relevant details on that surface. "They could be studying a map laid out on a table," he pondered, curiously. "Or maybe they are shooting dice at a crap table, or—"

Further conjecture was suddenly, and horribly, obviated.

The man at the wall straightened up from his labors and announced something, unintelligible to Jerry (the voice was an unbroken hum that rose and fell in pitch, unarticulated into consonants or vowels), which undoubtedly meant, "She's all fixed." The fur-face in profile turned with quick attention and stepped to the machine. He pulled from its slot a thing like the cable-supported arm of a small crane terminating in a cone-shaped flexible surface, and arranged it over the thing on the table which his movement to the machine had exposed to Jerry's gaze.

The thing on the table was the face of another of the white-furred men, and Jerry suddenly knew that this was an operating room. These men were doctors, involved in surgery.

The machine, so hastily repaired, was some sort of anesthetizing gadget. They'd had to wait for it before proceeding. All this information Jerry worked out with only a small part of his mind; the majority of his concentration was focused upon the other thing he'd seen upon the table, strapped wide-eyed into position beside the patient.

It had scales, sharp orange teeth, and might have been a rabbit-sized cross between a raccoon and a pangolin, and the wide eyes were tightly irised into disks of coppery red, with no visible pupils, under the light that overhung the operating table.

"What the hell is going on here?" Jerry thought, with dismay. "Surgery? In the same room with cages full of animals? What about sanitation? What about infection? The doctors are maskless. The room is only passably clean—certainly not scoured with green soap, alcohol, or live steam. And that repairman is standing beside the table scratching his stomach!"

Bewildered, yet drawn to watch with morbid fascination, Jerry ignored the pain that staring into the room brought to his eyes, and gave full attention to the proceedings.

They were—from a raccoon/pangolin's viewpoint—pretty ghastly. The men, muttering to each other as medics the universe over must while engaged in surgery, started snipping and plucking and sawing and clamping with lackadaisical facility upon the two bodies strapped to the table. One medic concentrated upon the man, the other upon the animal, while the anesthetist merely held the cone lightly upon the patient's face, and glanced now and then at dials upon the machine proper, as if for reassurance, or possibly to show that they were efficient and well trained.

They did not trouble to anesthetize the animal.

As they shifted about in their work, Jerry got a better look at the patient. All along his chest and belly, the white fur was gone. From the edges of the empty region, Jerry could see that the fur had been scorched away. The surviving fur in the periphery was stunted and slightly carbonized. The "flesh" beneath that exposed region was smooth, excepting a few blistered spots near the center. It resembled thin, flexible green plastic, of the sort that seems to be translucent, but is actually transparent, the darkness of the color tending to make it seem opaque unless light could be placed directly behind it. Into this surface went the scalpels and clamps and pins of the medics, until they had a triangular flap lying back to expose the organs within.

Jerry, well versed in all the metabolisms available to the scientists of Earth, was completely baffled by this one. None of the internal organs was fastened to anything.

The abdominal hollow of the creature was filled with a clear lemon-colored liquid. The organs just floated within the liquid. They were, Jerry noticed with amazement, not even juxtaposed with any sort of permanence. Even as the medic reached for them, they bobbed and moved about each other in the yellow fluid, as impermanent of locale as apples in a rain barrel.

Then Jerry had it.

"They're colloidal!" he gasped within his mind. "A tough, flexible outer shell! The whole thing hollow from cranium to fingertip to toe, containing a liquid that acts as reagent, catalyst, suspensor, and electrolyte for the mineral crystals, cell globules, and chemical coagulates. These fur-faced creatures are nothing more than ambulant, intelligent hunks of protein! The whole set-up's there. The lemon-colored fluid is the dispersion medium, and those 'organs' they're lifting out are the disperse-phase. But . . . what do they need the raccoon/pangolin for?"

His fellow creature, hissing in agony, was already a glittering, almost formless thing under the grisly tools of the medic standing over it.

It was, Jerry realized, being laid belly-open with no more regard than is given a lobster's tail muscle by the gourmet with his tiny three-pronged fork.

Jerry could only watch and wonder and wait to see the use to which the animal would be put. He had not long to wait.

Once laid open, the animal's internal fluid, a pale gray solution, was sucked out into a bulb-headed tube, much as a housewife gets the turkey drippings from under the bird for basting. The fluid was dribbled into a row of transparent jars with calibrated sides, some getting more, some getting less. Then a drop of liquid—a brown liquid for this one, a red for that one, and so on—was added to each. While Jerry gazed at the scene, fighting the headache that began to grow with the brightness of the lights over the operating table, the medic captured each jar and gave it a sharp, practiced shake.

And then the whole picture was clear to Jerry.

"Crystal-clear," he said, with bitter humor.

For that was the answer. The fur-faces were colloidal, the raccoon/pangolins were crystalloid. Whatever fluid lay within the bellies of the animals, it was a supersaturate, needing but the right chemical additive before coming out of its liquid state to form the right crystals.

In each jar, almost instantly after shaking, bright crystals had begun to form within the liquid. Within but a few moments, the jars were being uncapped and the medics, with neat little tongs, were lifting the crystals from the solutions and placing them within the abdominal cavity of their anesthetized patient. The flap was fastened down into place with a gadget that seemed to work on the principle of a soldering iron. As it slid along the angled edges of the incision the sides met and fused, leaving only a tiny ridge to attest to the fact of the operation.

One of the medics nodded to the bare-to-the-waist creature still standing by. The man shoved over a wheeled cart, slipped the patient onto it, and wheeled him out of the room through an archway barely within Jerry's field of vision.

Jerry's main concern, however, was for the fate of the crystalloid creature, lying so still upon the table. One of the medics undid the straps across the body, lifted it by a hind leg, and shoved it through a hinged metal flap against the wall, then stabbed a button. . . .

A red flare went off beyond the still-oscillating metal flap, and Jerry had all the information he needed. A nice little incinerator, for hollowed-out corpses.

"I wonder," Jerry thought dismally, "how long my forty minutes will take in *this* Contact!" His headache was growing worse, and it wasn't just from the lights.

At that moment, a sudden lurch sent him crashing against the wall of the cage. A clamor of alarm bells began throughout the vessel.

One of the medics yelled something, and threw a switch against the wall opposite that housing the anesthetizing machine. A panel slid away, revealing a large mosaic of close-packed little spheroids. As the medic twisted a dial at the base of this arrangement, some of the spheroids began to flicker whitely, while others remained dark.

Then Jerry recognized it for what it was. A form of television screen, composed of individual lights instead of phosphorescing dots activated by magnetically guided electrons from a cathode. The effect was the same.

A picture, sharply etched by the alternation and varying intensities of the bulbs, appeared on the mosaic-screen. Across the dreamlike surging of the black-gray-and-white heavy seas in the foreground, Jerry made out an armada of strange-looking vessels coming across the ocean toward wherever the pickup camera lay. Unlike Earth vessels, they tapered *inward* as the sides of the vessels rose from the waters, then were abruptly truncated near what would have been a peak by a railinged area that was the deck.

"Unless I'm much mistaken," thought Jerry, grimly, "I am on a ship which—be it alone or one of many in a convoy—is about to be attacked by those vessels out there."

A second later he knew he was right.

From the approaching fleet there had come no sign of armament, no flash or flame or belch of smoke or blaze of ray, but the room he was in jolted violently, then canted crazily for a sick moment before righting itself. The alarm bells grew louder in their metallic clangor.

Footsteps pounded down the corridor. The bare-to-the-waist man or another like him—Jerry could not distinguish between the creatures—came into the room shouting something. The surgeons shouted back and then the man raced out again.

Another jolt made the room tremble, but this time it felt different, as though the room were built to take that sort of stress. Jerry recognized that his ship was in the process of firing back, with whatever strange weapons these fur-faces employed. Even as he reasoned this out, one of the enemy vessels on the screen shuddered, split into almost-matching halves, and plunged beneath the waves amid much flame and confusion.

The medics were not watching. One of them had moved out of Jerry's view and now stepped back into it, carrying the wriggling form of one of the animals from the cages. As Jerry watched, the animal, its orange teeth snapping vainly at those hard black fingertips on the medic's white-furred hands, was lashed to the table in the gray-smeared spot where its predecessor had perished. Then the bare-chested man was coming back into the room, wheeling a man on a cart. This one was missing fur from an arm and part of the chest area. Jerry was able to confirm his earlier theory that the hollowness of the creatures was extended throughout the flexible green body-sheaths.

"Sonics," thought Jerry, all at once. "They're using sonic rays on each other. A good dose of heavy infravibration could *ruin* a collodial creature! The loss of the fur through subsonic friction is only a side effect. The main damage is the breakdown of those colloid organs when the beam focuses on a man.''

That would explain the way the other ship had simply sundered. Artificially induced metal fatigue, by the application of controlled vibration.

"Damn," thought Jerry, "this is *dangerous!*"

Other alien vessels were visible now on that granulated "screen," heading *away* from the camera. At least Jerry's ship was not alone in the face of that armada. His ship was one of at least a dozen—with more, possibly, outside the pickup range of the camera—involved on his side of the battle. Some of them shattered silently apart and boiled into the churning waters with a violence so great that Jerry could "feel" the sound with his eyes.

Apparently the medics, while anxious about the course of the fray, did not want their surgical endeavors bothered with the actual noise of the battle. Or perhaps the technology which had evolved this type of TV screen had never stumbled upon the familiar-to-Earth methods of transmitting sound by electromagnetic radiation.

"How long can forty minutes *last?*" Jerry wondered in growing concern. By his own time sense, warped by the life span of his host, he felt he'd been present in that room well over an hour. And still he was captive to the environment of the scaly crystalloid raccoon/pangolin creature, and doubly imperiled of survival. Even if "his" side took the lead in the struggle, many fur-faces would need this treatment—which destroyed one of his species with each operation.

Jerry did not know whether or not the animals were chosen in any special order. But his mind told him that even were his host the last so chosen, his odds for survival were dwindling fast.

Assuming the wall against which his cage was stacked with the others were the same size as the wall opposite his cage—and symmetrical construction of rooms seemed a strong likelihood—then, judging by his cage-size, the maximum number of cages that could be so stacked was six high and four across, or twenty-four cages. Figuring one animal per cage, that left some twenty-one animals ahead of him.

Possibly—barely possibly—this tier of cages might not be against a wall. It might be the forefront of hundreds of rows of similar stacked cages. But no medic hurrying to save a life would walk to Row #2 when Row #1 was still undepleted.

"So if I just sit here," he thought, gloomily, "I'm bound to end up alongside a fur-face on that table. My life gone so that his may survive. 'It is a far, far better thing I do' and so on, but I don't know as I'm ready to lay down my life for a fur-face without even being given the *choice,* damn it! Let's figure a way *out* of this mess!''

The ship went *whooomp,* suddenly. The room gave a crazy tilt again before—rather sluggishly, Jerry noted with alarm—righting itself. At the same moment the TV screen blanked out.

''Well, there goes the camera,'' he thought, his insides feeling oddly cold and upset. ''That may mean that if I don't die on the operating table, I may well be forced to succumb to a watery grave. Damn! *When* will those forty minutes be *up*?''

He was jerked from his thoughts by the appearance of a huge white-furred hand fumbling with the catch on his cage.

Hard, pointed black fingertips reached in through the opened door for him. Jerry snapped and clacked his teeth upon them in vain, as he was carried toward the strap-sided concavity beside a new fur-scorched patient on the operating table.

''Use your head!'' he screamed at himself. ''These fur-faces aren't expecting an *intelligent* attack from a lab animal! The other crystalloid creatures have the paltry instinctive self-preservation mechanism to bite at the objects gripping them, those impervious black fingertips. But you know better, right?''

And with that thought, Jerry tilted his head just a bit further forward, and let his orange fangs crackle through the thin chitinous green ''flesh'' beneath the stiff white fur on the alien's wrist. . . .

Yellow dispersion-medium spurted with a satisfactory gush from the scalloped gap in the alien's forearm.

Jerry landed nimbly on his hind feet on the metal floor as the shrieking medic dashed to a confrere for whatever first aid is given when a colloidal creature's liquid contents are spilling out.

While a minor part of his mind wondered idly if they'd employ a tourniquet or just a cork, the rest of his mind concentrated on directing those forepaw-and-foot phalanges to carry him swiftly up the face of the stacked cages. There were twenty-four of them, all right, against the wall. He perched precariously on the top, in the cage-roof-to-ceiling space that was too small for another layer of the same.

As the fur-face medic fiddled around with the wrist of the man Jerry had bitten (it was the raccoon/pangolin medic, of course), the anesthetist dragged a small stool over to the base of the stacked cages and began climbing up after him.

"Oh, hell," thought Jerry, cowering weakly against the wall. "If I had a piece of chalk or a charcoal stick I could write something. Or draw a picture, maybe, on the ceiling. Then they'd know I was intelligent, and— They'd probably use me anyhow. The middle of a battle is no time for writing learned scientific papers about new zoological 'finds.' "

Those black fingertips were coming for him, too carefully for a repeat wrist-crunching performance. If he were taken this time the bearer would handle with care.

Jerry skittered and scrabbled for the corner near the wall, hoping to engage the anesthetist in a game of you-climb-up-at-*this*-point-and-I-run-back-to-*that*-point. But the fur-face had too long a reach to make it practical. As Jerry cowered helplessly, those black fingertips gripped him about the throat with strangling force. It apparently made no difference if he died on the top of the cages or under the scalpel. He could only fend feebly with his paws at the creature as he was lifted down to the table and set into the concavity, dizzy and sick.

"White lightning?" he begged. "Come on, white lightning! Please, test, be over. How long can forty minutes *last?*"

Then the room gave a horrible shudder and all the lights went out.

Jerry, not yet strapped in place, heard the cries of the medics, and then the terrifying sound of rushing seas in the invisible corridor as the room canted swiftly onto its side. This time it did not right itself. A thick, falling-elevator feeling bunched up inside Jerry. He knew that the warship was plunging beneath the heaving surge outside.

He scrambled about on the floor—no, it was the wall now—almost brained by the crashing bulk of the operating table. He kept jumping futilely upward, hoping somehow to escape to the corridor and get outside the ship before all that water got inside this room.

Then icy tons of fluid crashed down upon him, flattening him against the wall beneath his feet. The cries of the medics were suddenly gurgles, then a brief, faintly heard sound of bubbling.

Jerry, trying to swim against the swirling pressures of the flood that now lifted him from against the wall and spun him end over end, could hold his breath no longer.

In despair, he felt his jaws widen and take in the chill liquid in which he was whirled.

It went in without gagging him, and did not come out. Not through his mouth, at any rate. It came out through long slots just in front of those auricular vents in his head.

Gills! Jerry was an amphibian.

Webbing, hitherto folded away, appeared on his feet. "I'll be damned," he sighed, with weary relief.

Then he paddled determinedly about in the utter blackness until he found a cage lying on its side, the door sprung open. Jerry got inside, closed the door until it caught as well as its broken catch would allow, and settled himself for a nice wait.

"At least I won't have to worry about getting gobbled by a natural underwater enemy," he figured.

He had to wait another subjective hour before the silent flash of white lightning lifted him out of his third, and last, Contact on Arcturus Beta.

VII

"All right, sir?" asked Peters, removing the bulky helmet with care.

Jerry sat up and nodded, blinking his eyes as he adjusted to his body once more. He was hard-pressed not to start testing his own joints and lungs and limbs for knowledge, and had to forcibly remind himself that this frail shell was his "normal" body.

Now to await the technician's analysis of the data.

Jerry, waving off Peters's hand, outstretched in automatic offer of assistance, sat up wearily on the edge of the couch. After a deep breath he got to his feet. Within the ship, the data-analyzer clattered busily.

"Some hot coffee, sir?" asked Peters, helpfully.

Jerry was annoyed at the effort it cost him just to talk. "That will go nicely, Captain," he managed.

The technician leaned out the airlock door, his homely face split in a grin. "No problem with the aliens, sir," he said to Peters. "Amiability indeterminate, but their basic weapon is infrasonics. They're built like hard bubbles, sure suckers for bayonets or bullets. I don't think, with sonic-shields, we'll have much trouble with them."

Peters, in the process of pouring Jerry's coffee, shrugged.

"Well, we're not here to *make* trouble, either. The roborocket reported that the aliens live either at sea or at least always in coastal regions. They shouldn't object to our starting a settlement this far inland."

"And," said Jerry, suddenly, as he took the coffee and sipped at the hot brown liquid, "I suppose those worm-creatures and the horned lions are to be eliminated?"

The technician dropped his eyes. "We can't have new colonists getting pulled into those burrows, or impaled on those horns, sir." He handed the report, translated by the machine into readable English, to Peters. The pilot scanned the sheets, and nodded.

"Seems easy enough," he said agreeably. "Those jellyfish-things and the flying apes are similar to species encountered before. They'll respond to simple gunfire. Removal of the worm-things will be automatic, once their source of sustenance is destroyed."

Jerry continued to sip his coffee and made no comment.

"As for the lion-things," Peters continued, "I doubt we'll have to attack them directly, since their digestive mechanism calls for sulfur from those pits. When we cap off the pits, or dry them up, to clear the air for the incoming colonial wave, that should starve them out within a week."

"Less than that," Jerry remarked emotionlessly. "Being hungry they'll eat, regardless. Then, unable to go on to the next step in the process—the ingestion of the sulfur—they'll die of food poisoning. Simple, neat, and efficient."

Peters smiled and gripped Jerry's hand with his own.

"We have you to thank for the information, sir," he said, in obvious admiration. "At least we know we won't have to fight the intelligent aliens. We'll have the central regions; they'll have the coasts and seas."

"And"—Jerry pointedly withdrew his strong fingers from the pilot's hand—"what happens when mankind decides to spread out? When the colony grows awhile, it's bound to want some of the coastal regions. Then what?"

Peters looked uncomfortable, then said, "I don't think that's likely to happen, sir. Not for some time, at any rate."

"But it *will* happen," said Jerry, somberly. "It always happens. Earthmen meet new races, arbitrate a bit, sign pacts, and move in. Then, when they're settled pretty well, they ask the other race to move out. It's almost a truism, Captain, that Earth can't comprehend anyone but an Earthman having any rights to survival.''

The tight-lipped technician exchanged a look with Peters, then ducked back inside the ship. Adverse commentary about a Space Zoologist was dangerous. But no one had yet been broken in rank or discharged for a facial expression.

''Well, sir, you're entitled to your opinion, of course,'' said Peters, wishing he had the moral courage to duck inside after the technician and avoid conversing with Norcriss. The job was done; why not forget it?

Jerry, sensing the other man's discomfort, dropped the topic, and contented himself with sitting there in the increasing darkness, sipping his coffee. After a minute or two, Peters gratefully mumbled his excuses and went into the ship.

Jerry sighed, finished his coffee, then began to walk toward the edge of the clearing, to watch the stars glow more brightly than they could in the interference of the ship's lights illuminating the camp.

When he reached the rim of the wooded area, he stopped, then lay on his back in the cool grass and watched the night sky, his thoughts rueful ones and his inner amusement ironic.

People always were puzzled about how a Space Zoologist could stand being a creature other than a human being. And Space Zoologists always were puzzled about how a human being could stand being part of that conquering race called man.

The twinkling stars distracted Jerry. Lying there watching them, he wondered to which of their planets he would be sent next, and to what dangers he might—in his new bodies—be subjected.

Neither he nor any of his fellow Zoologists had any real apprehensions about death in an alien body. Fear of death, yes. That was normal enough, and inescapable in any creature. But he had no fear of perishing as a crawling thing, or multilegged thing, or soaring winged thing.

To Jerry Norcriss—indeed, to any Space Zoologist—to die like a man was a dubious honor at best.

THEY ARE NOT ROBBED

Richard McKenna

*As with Shaara, I have known people who knew McKenna, but
I never met him myself. It makes no matter; he was one of the
finest writers I have read. He wrote one of my favorite light
stories, "The Fishdollar Affair," and one of my favorite adventure novelettes, "The Night of Hoggy Darn." If I could have
run both of those here—sigh. The irony is that it seems that
McKenna was only practicing, in science fiction. Once he got
his writing in shape, he moved on to mainstream, wrote the
award-winning The Sand Pebbles, and died. (I may have con-
tracted his career somewhat, here.) He was one of those who,
like Theodore Sturgeon and Walter M. Miller, had magic in
their pens, so that even his lesser pieces have wonder and
power. Here is one of these, dated now, but still intriguing.*

—PA

*No, Piers, you're not contracting McKenna's career; The Sand
Pebbles was serialized in the old, the original Saturday Evening
Post and published to enormous acclaim in 1962, and in 1965
he was dead, suddenly and permanently, only in his mid-
fifties. A posthumous story, "The Secret Place," published in
Orbit, won the second Nebula for short story in 1966; a posthumous novella, "Fiddler's Green," published in Orbit 2, is
even finer, and had it not been for the ground rules of this
anthology—nothing that had ever before appeared in book
form was eligible—it would have been here. McKenna is ru-
mored to have been a man of saintly disposition and quietude.*

—bnm

Black-market gasoline cost ten dollars a gallon at the energy-crisis
peak in 1980. The Carson Treaty, negotiated between the United

Nations and the UFO entities in that year, seemed a godsend to men and gadgets despairingly uncritical. A few old people muttered about long spoons.

The Aliens agreed to sell electricity for two mills per kwh and to expend the monies paid them within the domestic economy from which it came. They set up gray boxes with massive protruding bus bars in power plants everywhere. Power output was unlimited. Hydrocarbon reserves went back into motor fuels and wheels rolled again across the exultant nations.

No cultural exchanges, the Aliens stipulated, and no wonder, for they were strange past description. Most people could not see them at all. Others saw them as light aberrations on the edge of vision and swore their own eye muscles refused to fix and focus. Photos showed only a distortion of background. Mostly from children's reports, a composite image emerged: tall, pliant, gray-white, a hint of feathers and a long beak. The people called them Star Birds.

The Star Birds spoke and acted through human Agents, and a few old men thought the greatest mystery about these was the public incuriosity. They were personable young single women who had been living unnoticed all along as white-collar girls in the world's large cities. They insisted they were of Earthly origin, but none could remember just where. The life data in their papers was fraudulent. They gave each other as next of kin, but they were of all races and obviously not all sisters.

Amnesia cases, the public explained to itself, kidnaped and conditioned by Star Birds. But the Agents seemed healthy and happy, the treaty kept them under law and taxes, and wheels rolled. So what, then?

So the Star Birds opened Purchasing Offices in city after city.

Always the same pattern: An Agent bought up leases along a hundred-foot small-business frontage. Instantaneously in some predawn a shimmering, fifty-foot gray wall replaced the shabby fronts. Tangent to the sidewalk, in the center, a ten-foot circular area served as door. Tiny lightnings played over its opalescent surface. Along the wall, two on each side of the door, silver ellipses one by two feet were inset horizontally at shoulder height.

Force-field structures, the public explained to itself, because the impassable walls gave no tactile sensation except at the silver test plates. Those who wished to sell were told to place forehead and palms against the test plates. If they qualified, a self-luminous golden ovoid would materialize under one hand, and it would pass them through the circular door area. It was dangerous for any person other than the recipient to touch the ovoid. Scores failed to activate the test plates, for each one who succeeded. Those who did go inside the Office did not come out again.

They always reappeared, vague about how and where and about what they had experienced. But where needed their bones were straightened, muscles made strong, teeth restored, skins firmed and cleared, and blurred senses sharpened. Within a few days each received from the local Star Bird business office a check for any sum from one to fifty thousand dollars.

This caught the public interest. Time stasis and biofields, it explained to itself. The Star Birds bought raw neural energy or else recorded dynamic patterns of neural energy. But what *use* did they make of it? What *good* was it?

No one could say. Aldous Huxley came out of retirement to try his luck. When reporters found him again, he said it was like a long dream during which he wrote the novel that had struggled in vain all his life to shape itself within him. He could not remember what it was about. That same day an Italian janitor in Chicago tried to speak plainly. He said it was all glorious music in which he was himself a theme endlessly, variously repeated. He tried to hum it, but could not.

The Star Birds sent Huxley seventy thousand dollars. The janitor received four hundred thousand.

Occult and pseudoscientific pamphlets explained the Star Birds in a hundred ways. Training courses for those unable to activate the test plates mushroomed in a cloud of worthless guarantees and testimonials. Like a lottery, unfair, the people cried.

The UN asked the Star Birds to sell health. Not possible, the spokesman Agent said; those who can, heal themselves incidental to the sale. Buy raw materials and manufactured articles, the UN urged. We do, said the spokesman Agent, such as we can use. Duress was not practicable while the power need lasted. Legislative bodies placated the people with confiscatory surtaxes on Star Bird windfalls, and it was not enough.

Unfair, unfair, the people cried.

Red-haired young Christopher Lane whistled as he worked alone in his bay of the cavernous assembly wing. It was Acme Furniture Company's day to picket the Eagle City Purchasing Office, and Lane had paid a fellow workman ten dollars to take his place in the picket line. He liked working best when half the force was off picketing.

Lane cast wary hazel eyes each way, then scribbled "The secret smile of a cat. It pounces." on a cedar lining slab. He lay the pine top over it, power-drove home the long corner screws, and slid the completed dresser shell into the next bay where Gault would veneer it. Last one today.

Writing those things pleased Lane. It gave each dresser something they couldn't get their fingers on, not knowing.

In the crowd waiting to punch out through the time clocks, Lane heard tall Dan Gault up ahead arguing hotly about Star Birds.

"So what if they do grow new teeth or new eyes in some lucky ape? I don't *lose* nothing, do I?"

"It ain't *fair*, God damn it!" insisted Reilly, the fat, frog-voiced little shop steward. "They should do it for everybody or nobody."

"It's what they get, bothers me," said the man with his chin on Lane's left shoulder.

"Must be worth a thousand times what they pay us," said the man on Lane's right foot.

"If we only knew what it *was*," said the man with the elbow.

"Or even just how to *use* it," said the man with the foul breath.

"Yeah," Lane said. He broke free through the chrome turnstile.

Ten minutes of rapid walking brought him to Mrs. Calthorp's white-painted, two-story boardinghouse with its wide veranda and smooth lawn. Lane had forty minutes left to bathe and dress for his routine Thursday night date with Alma Butelle. Old Mrs. Greene, all chins and hair wisps, halted him on the veranda for a rambling chat. He agreed Mrs. Calthorp was stingy about food because she was losing her figure and promised to help Mrs. Greene repot her geraniums, come Sunday.

After dressing in his neat, gray-papered room he looked regretfully at the book on his desk, Graves's *White Goddess,* and tiptoed out along the upstairs hall. Miss Weber, the skinny, pinch-faced schoolteacher, popped out of her room by the stairwell. Simpering, she showed Lane where she wanted the little shelf put, he was so handy with tools and all.

"No trouble, Miss Weber. Be glad to, come Sunday."

Lane excused himself several times and at last ran downstairs into the lower hall. St. Martin Buckley stopped him with a hail from the red plastic TV parlor to right.

"Hey, Chris boy, howsabout wheels and beers and babes tonight, out on the road?"

"It's Thursday, Buck. My date with Alma, I'm late now—"

"Bring her along, boy! Nothing like wheels to shake 'em loose from that stuff!"

Lane made his self-depreciatory gesture and his thin face flushed under its freckles.

"I'm sorry, Buck, got a table reserved at the Golden Pheasant and all. . . ."

"O.K., Chris, skip it. How's to take twenty till payday?"

"Sure, Buck."

Walking the ten blocks to Alma's apartment, Lane thought about Buckley. His lean, dark vigor, his coarse features, his way of standing too close and looking down at Lane, talking too loud and fast. The borrowings never repaid. Lane knew obscurely that the gift-loans absolved him of his sin of not needing all he earned. They bought him permission to go on being Lane.

Both Alma and Buckley worked in Sales at Acme. Once she had been Buckley's girl, now she was somehow Lane's, at least on Thursdays. Tall as Lane, plump, dark-haired, full-lipped, driven by ancient hungers, she might have been Buckley's sister. She too was a ransom he paid for the right to be Christopher Lane. But paid to whom, in the end?

To his knock Alma called through the door come in, she was in her bath. He entered, knowing the rest.

"Make us a drink, Chris lamb, while you wait." Splashing.

Red sofa and rug, bamboo coffee table, maple TV, movie and fashion magazines, white enamel in the alcove. He mixed two highballs, one weak.

"Chris lamb, please bring my robe from the bedroom. You know how I run around just wearing me when I'm alone."

Scented bedroom. Filmy stockings on the pink chenille. Black lace bra and panties lying apart in *just* the positions—that much was new.

The perfumed bare arm took the robe around the door edge.

"We're all naked just inches in behind here," it undulated at him.

"No fair peeking!" Alma giggled.

It bothered him, all right. He would have to go to South Bend

Sunday afternoon, to that hotel and the placid Polish girl. The Graves book was almost overdue—oh well.

Long pink legs flashed through the robe clutched under the dark smile as Alma scuttled across to the bedroom. She came out again in rhinestones and red wool and gulped the strong highball.

"I just *love* the way you mix 'em," she said. "Oh, Chris, Ruth tried to paint her apartment and she's made *such* a mess. I told her Saturday and Sunday."

"Oh . . . all right."

Alma giggled. "We'll both wear our new playsuits just for you, Chris. You'll *love* that!"

Alma loved the movie, she said. She clutched Lane's arm in the tense parts, leaned on his shoulder through the tender ones, and munched popcorn steadily. She chewed steak tirelessly through the floor show at the Golden Pheasant and drank martinis afterward, waiting for the midnight show. She chattered of food and movies and told Lane he really *must* learn to dance, he'd *love* it.

When he took her home, Alma insisted that he pay off the cab and come up for coffee. He sat glumly on the red sofa while she worked in the alcove.

"I hear talk in the front office," she said, coffee water splashing. "You turned down being assembly foreman again."

"Well . . . yes." He clasped and unclasped thin, nervous hands.

"Chris, you're *hopeless!* You drift and people take advantage of you and your talent and all—look when you invented the thingajig for dresser frames."

"I got a bonus," he said defensively.

"Yes, and they were able to take away your helper and make it back in a month. Now you have to do the same job alone."

That was the bonus, he thought, but how tell her? She plopped beside him on the red sofa.

"If you were foreman, you could buy a car. You could anyway."

"Being foreman eats up living time," he said slowly. "So does a car."

"Something's *wrong* with you, Chris! You don't want to live. There's just nothing like a car for killing time."

He moved away slightly.

"I wonder if I shouldn't go try my luck at the Purchasing Office," he said.

"No!" she said. "You could only keep a few hundred dollars and the Star Birds would *change* you."

"Well, don't I need to change?"

"No, no! Don't think about Star Birds!"

The silex boiled over, hissing, and she ran to take it off the gas flame.

What *changes* in Star Bird victims? the people demanded. Health and wholeness, yes yes, but the catch? the gimmick?

In England, Grey Walter, Nobelman and world dean of electroencephalography, found a clue. The evanescent Tau component, isolated and named by Walter in the sixties, was always present abnormally in the EEGs of persons examined who later were able to activate the silver plates. Tested after the Purchase experience, their Tau was better developed and no longer subject to experimental interference. All Agents tested had strong Tau. But all Walter could say about Tau was that it gave queer subjective time distortions under resonant energy input with flicker. Factor analysts around the world correlated Tau with all measurable trait complexes.

Ministers who denounced Tau as unholy could usually be brought to say they felt it so because it was new in human experience. Some critics and psychologists wondered whether the Star Birds might not be siphoning off a store of mankind's unused creativity. Nonsense, said others, pointing to galleries dripping with new paintings and editorial offices bulging with manuscripts. Radio and TV were never silent. And wheels rolled.

In Terre Haute, psychiatrist Joseph Weinstein found Tau in many patients. He took them a few at a time to the local Purchasing Office and emptied two back wards. Then Federal Judge Frederick Welborn enjoined the practice—Tau therapy, Weinstein called it—to protect the certified. Better lobotomy than Tau, the people agreed. We don't *know* yet what Tau does to you.

People began to display their personal, certified Tau-free, EEG charts. Radio and TV comics made Tau jokes. Liability insurance companies began requesting EEG charts of applicants and increased rates sharply for Tau people.

Neighbor watched neighbor and wondered.

Lane, dressed for work, came down to the white-enamel and green-tile kitchen at 4:00 A.M., as was his habit. Mrs. Calthorp al-

ways left dry cereal and bread for him on the worktable and milk
and butter in the refrigerator. It was Lane's best time of day. As he
poured milk on his cereal, Mrs. Greene, bulging and frowzy of an
unaired bedroom, shuffled in wearing her faded pink wrapper.

"Old bones sleep light," she said. "Why do you always get up
so early, Mr. Lane, and not eat breakfast with the rest of us?"

"I like to go to work early," Lane said apologetically. "Then I
can go roundabout and stop places."

"Well, it's a shame you have to eat alone. I said to myself,
'Sally, the least you can do . . .' "

Lane half listened, eating rapidly. New girl coming to take old
Mr. Pelham's room. Her name was Martha Bettony and she
worked in the business office for those Star Birds. Pretty, but so
young and probably flighty. Had he read about the Agent accused
of murder over in Des Moines?. . .

Lane put his bowl in the sink and went out, taking a slice of
bread with him. He half turned and half bowed placatingly back toward Mrs. Greene, who kept raising her voice as he moved away
from her. Once outside he ran lightly across vacant lots and fields
until he came to Folwell dump.

It was a glacial marsh remnant of the Folwell Steel and Wire
property. Lane stood by a shoulder-high gray boulder while dawn
expanded the sky and washed him with first-light. Birds twittered
in the straggling bushes, small feet rustled in the grass and weeds.
The marsh emerged, patches of oily water, clumps of rush and
reed, the high, crumbling edge of the rubbish-and-cinder landfill.
It had nearly stopped moving forward, now that Folwell no longer
burned coal but used cheap Star Bird power. Old auto bodies, half
submerged, looked like beetle skeletons. Lane stood a long time.

As always on leaving, he laid the slice of bread on the boulder
and patted its rounded side. Old, gray, mysterious, glacial, erratic,
sturdy under the poised rubbish-wave of Folwell's landfill, it had
no more business in Folwell's backyard than Lane himself. He
loved the boulder. He thought it cleaned the air around itself.

Something always took the bread. Brown bird, white-foot
mouse, bare-tail rat from the dump, Lane never knew.

At work he wrote on a cedar slab, "The quiet of unbreathed air.
A bird sings."

Reilly could have caught him at it but didn't notice.

"Chris," said the frog voice, "how's to help me put a new roof
on my double garage? Can you start tonight?"

"I suppose so," Lane said. "Nothing in the way but a book I was going to read."

"Books," Reilly croaked. "The old woman's cooking cabbage and ham hocks. Beer in the icebox. The kids'll swarm all over you. You'll love it, Chris."

Lane came home to Mrs. Calthorp's tired and quite late. He caught a glimpse of the new girl going upstairs. He saw short blond hair and a crisp yellow dress, white, rounded arms, trim waist and ankles. St. Martin Buckley sat glowering alone in the TV parlor.

"Just brought her back from riding," he told Lane. "Lay off her, Chris. Won't drink, someway takes the starch right out of a man. She ain't for the likes of us, boy."

"Not drinking's not so bad," Lane said.

"I'm telling you, Chris, you won't make out in a month of Sundays," Buckley said angrily. "I got ways to know them things."

Lane went up to bed. He heard soft music from the new girl's room, across the hall from his own. Then a hand slapped on a wall and Miss Weber's scrannel voice, from the room by the stairwell, cried, "Stop that noise! People have to sleep!"

The music stopped and Lane slept.

It took a week, counting Alma's Thursday, before Lane finished Reilly's roof and ate dinner again at Mrs. Calthorp's. Martha Bettony sat to his right at the table. Lane introduced himself and made a few remarks during the meal. The girl was not shy, speaking readily in a clear, low voice, but drawn into herself in some strange way so that unless he looked at her he was hardly aware of her presence.

He kept looking at her. She had wide-set blue eyes under thick eyebrows and her round face glowed with health. She wore no makeup or jewelry and she seemed as cool as the crisp, blue-and-white-patterned cotton dress she wore. *She cleans the air around her,* Lane thought involuntarily.

Miss Weber watched Lane and at the meal's end asked across the cluttered table, "Miss Bettony, are you just an employee at your office or are you an Agent?"

The girl smiled. "I'm an Agent," she said.

"Well! I don't know *why* I didn't think of that before!" Miss Weber said.

"No wonder I couldn't make you talk about your home and

your folks,'' Mrs. Greene said. "You don't have any, do you, dear?''

"With what those Star Birds must pay you, I wonder you live in this miserable sty," Miss Weber said. "You could afford the Blackhawk-Sheraton."

"I take what I need," the girl said. "I don't need to live at the Blackhawk-Sheraton."

"Well, I do!"

Miss Weber rose and ran upstairs, suddenly crying. Chairs scraped and a general indignant exodus followed, leaving Lane alone with the girl.

"Not needing is a kind of payment, isn't it?" he asked her.

"Not the kind they can tax." She looked at him curiously.

"They have ways," he said, flushing. "Is it all right if I call you Martha?"

"Of course. It's my name."

"I want to be your friend, Martha. You're going to need a friend, in this house."

"Then let's be friends." She smiled again.

He stood up.

"Come and go walking with me, there'll be moonlight," he invited. "There's a place I want to show you."

Four hours later they were still talking, she seated and leaning against the gray boulder, arms clasping knees. Lane stood looking down at her in the moonlight.

"I don't know *where* I came from, Chris," she said. "I dream about a place—my world, I call it—but it is only a dream. All I remember is working in Chicago offices and no first day . . . it . . . it fades out."

"Can't you ask the Star Birds?"

"No. They only talk *through* us. We don't hear ourselves or even know, until afterward."

"You said you couldn't see them, except as a twinkle. But what do you think about them? *Are* they devils, like people say?"

She rubbed her blond curls against the rock, looking up at him.

"How does one know a devil? Here's all I do know, Chris, from talking to other Agents. The Star Birds have been around for a long, long time. They have some special reason now for showing themselves. None of us knows the reason."

"It's a little scary, when you think about it," he said. "People are jumpy, too. They say bad things about Agents. I'm worried about you coming and going in Eagle City."

"I'm not afraid," she said. "It's still like it was in Chicago, something keeps them from really seeing me. They just see a girl bent over a desk or hurrying along a street, not ever *me*. It's as if they were all sleepwalking and only I am awake."

"Would the Star Birds protect you if . . . if . . . ?"

"I don't think they *could,* not directly. And sometimes in the crowd an eye, just one eye, comes open for a second. Then I do feel afraid."

"I'm not much," Lane said wistfully, "but when you need me, I'll be there. I'll be there, Martha."

She stood up beside him.

"I think I do need you, Chris. *Your* eyes are open. I like it here, by this old rock."

"Nobody tries to crowd in here with me, looking for the best place," he said. "Martha, let's make this a regular Friday night date. We can go to movies, too."

"And concerts," she said. "Yes, I'd enjoy it."

"Monday nights too?"

"All right, Monday nights too."

When Lane said good night to Martha in the hall, he noticed Miss Weber's door ajar. He closed his own door audibly behind him. Martha did the same.

Crothers, working under Grey Walter in England, learned more about Tau. He explored the bizarre, subjective space-time distortions caused by Tau-synchronic flicker and came up with the objective case of the silver unicorn.

His subject, a middle-aged Pole named Hurwitz, experienced a kind of hyperstereognosis under Tau stimulation. Blindfolded one day, Hurwitz was trying to describe the shape of the whole statuette while touching only the hinder part of it with a pencil. His Tau amplitude surged unexpectedly to a record height, and the five experimenters saw two metal unicorns on the table. They had time to confer and verify, even to touch and photograph the pair of statuettes. Then the twin objects leaped together in a flash of darkness and the scientists felt a moment of vertigo. The single unicorn remained.

Next day the experimenters discovered that they were all color-blind for red-green. It was not possible to know about the effect on Hurwitz because he had gone that same evening to the Lambeth

Purchasing Office. Next day his vision was, of course, perfect and his Tau no longer subject to flicker resonance. Good Tau subjects became increasingly hard to find.

Rumors about Tau people spread around the world. They were bad luck. Damage suits snowballed and juries almost always found for non-Tau plaintiffs. Liability insurance rates went up and up for Tau people and some companies refused them altogether. In Des Moines a jury found Agent Jane Fereday guilty of murder and she was hanged.

By God, they can die all right, I guess you know! people told each other.

A reporter for the *Register* learned that nine thousand feet of the hangman's rope sold at once wholesale at a dollar an inch. It was to be made into charms against Tau malignancy.

Lane found the inch-long rope segment, whipped at each end with three turns of silver wire, hidden under his clean underwear. He mentioned it at the table, unthinking, and got no response. Later Miss Weber came privately.

"It's a Tau charm, Mr. Lane. I paid five dollars for it," she whispered. "Please, *please* always carry it in your pocket."

Buckley was more forthright.

"Christ sake, the gal's a freak! She'll dry the juice in your backbone! Her kind never comes across!"

Mrs. Greene, at her now-unfailing breakfasts with Lane in the Calthorp kitchen, was more persistent.

"I'm old enough to be your mother, Mr. Lane, and it's my Christian duty . . . she has no parents, no relatives . . . she might *turn into something* after dark . . . her babies might have *scales*—"

Lane dropped his spoon.

"My God, Mrs. Greene, I don't dream of *marrying* her—"

"It's not you has the say of that, young man! You're for that nice Miss Butelle!"

Mrs. Greene's spittle sprayed his face and his cereal.

Alma never spoke of Martha Bettony, but she took his Tuesdays and Saturdays in the same irresistible way, never quite clear to Lane, that she had taken his Thursday to begin with. She made him learn to dance and pace her in alcohol and food intake. She flailed his spirit.

Lane claimed Martha for Wednesdays, to balance and preserve himself. Concerts, long walks, long talks and healing silences by the rock in Folwell dump, he found her whole-making. Somehow her mere presence, the clean, sun-on-fresh-linen look and smell of her, drew off the aching charge.

One Wednesday Lane came home from work to see Martha struggling with a dozen teenage boys on the Calthorp lawn. They had torn off her dress and were rough-handling her around their circle, plucking at her underwear. Mrs. Greene and Miss Weber watched from the veranda and neighbors watched placidly from porches across the street.

Lane flashed in like lightning and went down under the pack. He bit, gouged at eyes, bent fingers, butted and jabbed with knees and elbows. Twice he struggled to his knees and smashed solid blows into loose, pimpled faces only to go down again. Then a car halted squealing and he had help.

"Come on, you punks, try gangin' up on *two* men!"

St. Martin Buckley, grinning savagely, yelling with each blow he landed. Lane got to his feet and knocked down two of the dungaree-clad youths before they fled, leaving four stretched on the grass.

"Why didn't you *yell*, Chris?" Buckley asked. "Punks go weak in the knees when they got to fight a man, only you got to *tell* 'em. It ain't enough just to fight like a man, you got to *yell.*"

Lane felt his eye and left cheek. One of the prone boys sat up and the others were stirring. Buckley nudged Lane.

"Go give that one hell," he whispered. "You got to learn."

"Damn it, he's whipped already," Lane muttered. He went over to the boy. "If you do something like this again, I'll beat your face in," he said.

The boy looked at Lane sullenly. Buckley strode over and kicked him in the ribs. The boy cried out and pressed his hands to his side.

"Listen, punk, if I see you on this street again, I'll kick your tail up between your shoulders," Buckley told him. "You lay a finger on another girl, I'll choke you with your own teeth, and that goes for all your cute little playmates!"

The boy looked at Buckley wide-eyed and slack-jawed. Buckley kicked him again.

"Take a hint, God damn you!" he roared. "Clear out and stay gone!"

The boy got up and ran, still holding his side. The three others crept off silently.

"Chris boy, you just got to learn to yell," Buckley said. "You got too much respect for people, is your trouble."

Lane went in to wash his bruised face. For his date with Martha that night he listened to music in her room, keeping the door open. Mrs. Greene passed it at sentrylike intervals, coming and going from her corner room.

"The eye came open for me today, Chris," Martha said. "I'm not protected anymore."

"I'll walk to work with you. Isn't there a police guard at your office?"

"Yes, but I won't go back there. I have instructions to go into the Purchasing Office in the morning."

"To work in there? But you'll still live here—"

She shook her head and smiled faintly.

"No. When an Agent goes into a Purchasing Office, she doesn't come back. We don't know what happens, but our office has lost four girls that way this month."

"Well, don't go, Martha. . . ."

"The Star Birds say I must. I'm afraid not to, after tonight. I *have* to trust them, Chris."

"Well . . . well, then. . . ."

"We'll have to say good-bye tonight," she said. "You tell our old boulder good-bye for me, in the morning."

"I will," he said. "But, Martha, there's so much I never got to say. . . ."

"I've some special music I want to play tonight, too," she said. "Chris, you take my records after tomorrow. But now we'll talk and listen to music."

Mrs. Greene shuffled up the hall and stopped in the door.

"My, that's sweet music," she said.

She came inside.

"Wasn't that sauce flat on the spareribs tonight? I *do* say it, Mrs. Calthorp gets stingier every day."

She sat down.

"Now, when I was a girl my mother used to say, 'Sally,' she'd say . . ."

Lane said good night to Martha and Mrs. Greene at 1:00 A.M. When he got up again at 4:00 A.M., he opened Martha's door very gently. She was gone. Mrs. Greene joined him as usual for breakfast.

Lane's vision blurred slightly as he neared the Folwell boulder in the darkness. For one hideous moment he thought he saw Mrs. Greene sitting on top of it.

Alma, that night, made no comment on his closed eye and swollen cheek. She seemed to know about Martha, because she had plans for Lane on Friday. When he came up with her for coffee, after steak and martinis at the Golden Pheasant, she switched on a small radio.

"Oh, *news*," she said vexedly from the sink. "Change the program, Chris."

"Wait," he said.

Purchasing Offices were disappearing as the dawn swept round the world, the announcer said breathlessly. Starting an hour ago in India and Siberia, they flickered out of existence, revealing the same old buildings that had been there before. In the old buildings perishable food that had been left was still fresh, in one case kittens still ungrown. But not all the Offices were going, not even half, stand by for further announcements. . . .

Then Lane noticed that Alma's TV was gone. She sat down beside him on the red sofa.

"I'm so ashamed, Chris," she said. She put her head on his shoulder and began to cry. "It was the TV or else my coat, I couldn't keep up the payments."

"I could help," he offered.

"Not only money," she sobbed. "It's not enough, not enough."

"I'm sorry, I wish I could help," he said, becoming unaccountably frightened.

"Oh, Chris, you're so strong and good!" Alma clung to him convulsively.

"Tomorrow I'm going to the Purchasing Office," Lane's voice said without his willing it.

She jerked erect. "No! I won't let you!"

He rose. "If it's still there, I'm going."

"No!" she cried, dry-eyed now. Her voice was ugly.

"I'm going," he insisted. He pulled away from her toward the door. The coffee boiled over, unheeded.

"We'll go from the plant, then," she gave in. "Wait for me after work by the bus stop."

Alma in russet wool sat beside Buckley when he drove up to the bus stop.

"Hop in, boy," Buckley said to Lane. "We'll all take a flying gander at them star geese."

Lane got in and Buckley drove off. Wrong direction, Lane protested. Eat first, Buckley said, speeding up. Alma's hungry. A few snorts too, hey, boy?

Eating, they reasoned with Lane. No money in it, to speak of. You're healthy already. Why get in wrong with the whole damned world? We like you the way you are, Chris boy, Chris lamb.

In the men's room Buckley told Lane, "She's ripe, boy. I got the eye to know it. Stay with us drinking and she'll lose something where you can find it."

"I'm sorry, Buck, I just *have* to go."

"*Chris* boy, I tell you she's ripe to let you in. Them knockers, that curly black nest, boy, they're a-*calling* to you!"

"You take her, then. I'll call a cab."

Buckley drove downtown in silence.

Arms linked, Alma central, they merged into the crowd before the Office. Picket banners swayed above the heads in the street. Police tended short queues before each test panel and guarded the tax-control booth by the opalescent door. A woman walked through the opalescence, her hand extending a golden twinkle, and the mob growled deep in its throat. People left the mob to join the queues and left the test panels to come back to it.

"Let's tail on, kid," Buckley whispered to Alma.

"No, Buck, remember how we felt—"

"Never know, kid. Gotta try again."

Buckley first, then Alma, then Lane. The line moved fast.

"No use hanging on, bud," the policeman told Buckley. "It happens right off or never."

He tugged at Buckley's arm, then jerked him away bodily.

"Right away or never, lady," the policeman told Alma in her turn. He pulled her away, gruffly gentle. Lane stepped forward.

Metal cool on forehead and palms. Something pressed and his left hand closed over it. The policeman smiled cryptically and waved him on. Lane put the object in his pocket and looked around. Buck was nowhere, but Alma stood crying in the street. She stretched out her arms to him. He led her off, hailed a cab, and took her home.

Seated beside Lane on her red sofa, she demanded, "You've got it. Show me."

He held up the radiant golden ovoid. She reached and he jerked it away, spilling his drink.

"It'll hurt you, Alma. You've heard the warnings and the stories."

"It won't, it won't. Give it to me, Chris."

"You can't use it, Alma. It's *dangerous—*"

"I can so use it! All I need to do is get inside, one little inch *inside*, I'll know what to do!"

He closed his hand and light streamed softly between his fingers. She pursued his hand, face hectic, pleading, "Just let me *touch* it!"

She did touch it, jabbing a red-nailed forefinger past Lane's thumb web. The light dimmed and a silent force hurled man and woman apart in crumpled heaps on the floor. Lane recovered first. He got up shakily and went to her, pocketing the ovoid.

Kneeling, he rubbed her temples until she came around. Then he made her another drink and sat beside her again on the sofa. He rubbed her arm until power and feeling came back into it while she cried steadily.

She gulped the drink, glugging her throat, and calmed. Finally she spoke.

"Get rid of it, Chris. Flush it down the john."

"I wouldn't dare."

She stood up, face dark, eyes swollen, her voice ugly.

"I tell you, flush it down the john! Do as I say!"

"No." Lane stood up and walked firmly to the door. He turned to look back.

Her face was wild. She tore open her bodice, baring provocative, dark-areoled breasts that matched her burning eyes, and advanced on him with red-nailed fingers held like talons.

"Spit on it, snot on it, flush it away, come to bed and damn you to hell forever!" she shrieked.

Lane opened the door and she sank to the rug, legs doubled under, propped on arms that seemed oddly long. Eyes burned through tossed black hair and she *growled*.

"I'll never let you go! Do you hear me? Never never never!"

Lane's neck hair bristled as he ran downstairs. Folwell dump was sanctuary, the rock his altar. After a long while there, sure of himself again, he went to Mrs. Calthorp's.

Late as it was, Buckley waylaid Lane in the lower hall.

"Got a proposition, boy. That thing—I'll buy it. I'll hock my car and stuff, raise a thousand for you." Whiskey breath.

"No, Buck. I have to use it myself. Tomorrow."

"Thousand's a lot of cat manure, boy."

"You *know* it's dangerous to anybody but me, Buck. I'm sorry."

Buckley gripped Lane's shoulders and shook him gently.

"Okay, Chris. You go put salt on them Star Birds. Bring me back a tail feather."

Lane went upstairs and turned in. He woke feeling a hand under his pillow and came up swinging. The fight raged through the dark room, breaking glass and splintering furniture, yet Lane heard nothing but hoarse breathing that smelled of whiskey. He drove the thief through the door and closed it. Outside the hoarse breathing became a kind of sobbing that sounded like Mrs. Greene. Lane slept again.

He came fully awake at his usual time, sore all over, but found his room intact. Mrs. Greene failed to join him at his breakfast. For all its otherwise familiar pattern, his morning seemed excitingly unroutine. When he reached Acme just before time to punch in, he boarded a downtown bus at the curb instead. He got off the bus two blocks from the Purchasing Office.

Lane showed the ovoid at the tax-control booth, registered, and walked toward the opalescence. The low, sustained mob growl behind him bristled his neck hairs. The door flowed along his outstretched arm in a sparkling mist that pulled him through itself into abrupt silence.

Before him a desert of white sand and gray rock stretched away under a brassy sun. He whirled, and it stretched behind him too, as far as he could see. He stood irresolute. He said, "I'm here," and waited. Then he laughed, placed his wristwatch on a rock for a marker, and strode off.

Thirst and fatigue and the sun's enwrapping blaze, foot over foot, endlessly. He crossed thin sand sifted over an iridescent basketwork pavement of serpent bodies and walked softly, that their sleepy stirring be not aggravated. He came to a red-haired skeleton, prone, right arm outstretched. Beyond it, wedged in rocks like a flung spear, he saw a wooden staff and plucked it out as he passed.

Rising ground, coolness, stunted shrubs and the tiny sound of his own name inside his head. Alpine scenery, bracken and thorn, fresh, scented wind blowing from pines blue on the heights, and it was a tiny voice calling him from above. A mountain meadow in a steep-walled, shaggy glen and the voice was a girl's voice, desperate with fear.

Ahead a majestic, draped woman-figure who raised her arms slowly in menace and benediction. As if evoked by the gesture, in two lines like arm shadows along the meadow, black shapes rose from the earth and closed around him.

Dwarfish men, gross-featured, red-eyed, hairy, ithyphallic, grimacing with obscene menace. Lane swung his staff, silenced their thin chattering, beat them back into the earth. Victorious, he saw the woman-figure smiling, swelling and attenuating, merging into rocks and trees and tumbling water that still smiled at him. Where she had stood, atop a rock in midstream, lay a white-clad body that cried his name.

It was Martha Bettony. She sat up with blank eyes and tumbled blond hair.

"I had a terrible dream," she whimpered. "I'm still dreaming. Please don't hurt me."

"Don't you know me, Martha? I'm Chris."

"I was calling you, wasn't I? I always call you and you never come. The dream never ends. . . ."

Lane kissed her and she clung to him. Her eyes regained their light.

"Why, this is my world, Chris, my dream world. This is the first time I've ever been awake in it."

"It's a beautiful world," he said. "It fits you, Martha."

"Come see it," she cried, jumping down from the rock.

They went hand in hand down the glen. The land gentled and the stream wound into a wide valley in tree-lined meanders. Lone oaks and rock outcrops dotted smooth grassy slopes starred with red and blue flowers under a smiling sun.

She led him through groves musical with bright birds, along streams of cascading crystal, around still pools overhung with cypress. They ate wild red strawberries and lay together in the sun by a gray rock outcrop. He opened her white dress.

They burst free to become the wind that caught up emmer-grass pollen and dusted it on stigmata across the hillside. They were the living wind that cooled the bodies locked and laboring below there.

Afterward, the shadow of the memory of a guilt.

"Martha, I'm supposed to undergo something here. Where are the Star Birds?"

"They've just come," she said. "There and there."

Where she pointed, above them, he saw something like two moving refractive flaws in a sheet of invisible glass. He looked at Martha and her eyes were fixed, pupils greatly dilated.

"What must I do?" he asked her.

"Return to your own world and break phase," she said.

"Break phase? Can't I stay here? May I come back?"

"You must break phase in your own world. You cannot stay here until your broken phase angle comes full circle. To cause that to be you must return here, often, to see Martha."

"Phase angle? Please explain—" Lane noticed the girl's eyes move again and the pupils contract.

"The Star Birds are gone," she said. "Did I talk? What did I say?"

He told her. "I thought they'd take this," he added, pulling the ovoid from his pocket. "What do they mean by *phase angle?*"

"I don't know," she said. "But the glain, that will bring you back to me. Leave it here in this rock."

She touched his eyes with her fingertips. Suddenly he saw into the gray rock beside him, saw a geode in the secret heart of it, in-pointing hexagonal crystals guarding a cavity. He reached into the rock and placed the ovoid in the cavity. Its soft light refracted through the crystals.

He pulled out his hand and it was early morning by the Folwell swamp remnant. Lane watched the dawn and stood thinking until he felt hungry and ate the slice of bread that lay on top of the boulder. Then he put on his wristwatch and walked to work.

Just as he came to Acme's gate a bus pulled up at the curb. Lane turned in at the gate and instantly a nausea flooded through him, a great shudder and a soundless rending. He leaned against the gate-post for a moment. Dan Gault passed him going in, grinned, and said "Morning, Chris." Lane answered "Hi, Dan," and looked around, feeling better. Then he saw himself boarding the down-town bus. He went on through the gate. About ten o'clock Gault came into Lane's work bay.

"Chris, did you hear?" he asked. "The Purchasing Office downtown disappeared half an hour ago."

Lane punched out at noon because it was Saturday, Alma's day now. He took her swimming in the afternoon and dancing in the evening. She seemed to have forgotten the ovoid episode and made gay plans for their Sunday's food, drink, and entertainment. Early on Monday morning, after a smelly, garrulous breakfast with Mrs. Greene, Lane stood again by the gray boulder in Folwell dump.

He reached his hand hesitantly toward the rock surface. His knuckles tingled and a prickling crept up his arm. Then his hand moved through the solid rock and his sight followed it to the glain radiant in the jeweled cavity. He pulled it out and stood again on the hillside in Martha's world.

She ran to him and cried, "Chris! Oh, welcome back!"

He kissed her and kneaded her shoulder. "Can you call up the Star Birds, Martha?" he asked. "I'm scared. I want to ask them things."

"No, but let's hope they just come. Let's walk."

As they walked along the gentle hillside, Lane told Martha how he felt.

"It's like I woke up in my world, just like you here," he said. "It's like all my life I had a pain and couldn't know it because its beginning was before my beginning. Now it's gone and I feel like a giant."

She smiled up at him. "I know music that says that too. Sometimes I hear it, dropping out of the air."

"My world is a big machine," he said. "Now I can see the wheels. Once I thought Buck and Alma had a strange power over me. Now I know it was really the machine's power. They're only parts. But I won't let them know—"

"That's right, never despise them," she said. "From their machine you draw the energy, more than your share, that frees you into this world. They can't use it, although they try to take it back into themselves through you, but sometimes they *almost* know it and are sad. Be gentle with them."

Lane looked at her eyes, fixed and dilated. He saw an erratic air flaw above her head.

"Star Bird," he pleaded, "what do I do next? I saw myself apart from me. What does it mean?"

"You have broken phase. You must do so repeatedly until your doublegangers in the time eddies summate to circularity. Then, with proper management, this world will become your own."

"What must I *do*, then?"

"You must never let your doubleganger touch you. It is fatal."

Lane shook the girl.

"How will I know the *time?* How do I escape him, if he comes?"

"The Star Bird is gone," she said. "Tell me what I said, Chris."

She couldn't explain her words. "We just have to *trust* them, Chris," she said. He nodded gravely.

Sometime later, Lane could not estimate time intervals in Martha's world, he heard footsteps and the skin crawled on his arms and back. Martha heard nothing.

Lane looked around wildly and saw himself coming with blank eyes and outstretched arms. He pointed and caught his breath.

"It's only an air wiggle, a Star Bird," Martha said beside him.

Lane jumped up and ran toward the rock outcrop, Martha running after him. "Good-bye, Martha," he called back, and thrust the glain into the cavity.

It seemed like a vivid guide dream when he woke at his usual time in his bed at Mrs. Calthorp's. He shaved, ate breakfast with Mrs. Greene, went on to Folwell dump, and stood again by the gray boulder. He removed the glain and stood again in Martha's world. She ran to him . . . and it seemed like a vivid guide dream when he woke . . . and . . . and . . . he never knew how many times he went around in the eddy. But a strong *déjà vu* grew in him and at its height, outside the bathroom door, he turned abruptly back and entered the broom closet.

He felt again the nausea and inner rending that had racked him outside the gate at Acme, but this time milder. He heard himself making shaving noises in the bathroom and realized he had broken phase again, out of the time eddy. Grimly he thought it through.

He felt his beard stubble and knew that the eddy would go on forever. It back-lapped on his world-line. In a few minutes, while Lane-2 ate breakfast downstairs with Mrs. Green, he, Lane-1, would shave for the second time that morning. All the events in the eddies and back-laps repeated to eternity and he himself multiplied to infinity. All Aleph-null of him would shave twice that morning until time ended.

Lane-2 went downstairs. Shortly afterward Mrs. Greene shuffled by the broom closet. Lane-1 crept out and shaved hurriedly, knowing how much time he had. The shaving brush was wet. He hid in the closet again until Mrs. Greene shuffled back to her room. Then he crept out of the house and ran, but not to Folwell dump.

For his own safety after that experience, Lane always made the phase break in the lonely darkness just before entering Folwell dump. It reduced the amount of doubled world-line in the back-lap, and his times with Martha would have to seem like a vivid

dream to him in any case. Each time the break was less disturbing.
When he dared to look he could see a shadowy Lane-2 walking toward the boulder.

Lane-2 never looked back. When Lane-1 walked toward the
boulder, he was often tempted almost irresistibly to look back, to
make *sure* there was no phase-phantasm of himself on the alternate
path. He ached for reassurance that he was really the first term in
the infinite regress. But he knew if he did so, Lane-2 would look back
in his turn and see Lane-1 and in that was dreadful danger. A compel-
ling inner wisdom told Lane-1 that all the Lanes to Aleph-null must
each believe he was the first term. The price of their ignorance was
Lane-1's own uncertainty, and he found it hard to pay.

Each day swept away Purchasing Offices. The chief spokesman
Agent, the day before she disappeared with the Staten Island Office, assured the UN that the power boxes would continue to fur-
nish power indefinitely. Then all Agents and Offices were gone,
but the Tau people remained as an acute social problem.

It was nothing they could be shown to be or do; they seemed un-
changed. But rumors and strange beliefs grew monstrously. They
could make themselves invisible. They could be in two places at
once, people whispered. They could see through walls, even walk
through them. Our wives, our daughters, Fort Knox, men cried in
fear and hatred. Tau people resigned or were driven from all posts
in public life. Lynchings fed a market avid for rope and cinders to
be carried as Tau charms.

Lane felt his inconspicuous life pattern and placatory usableness
protected him. No one taunted him with his Tau status. Tax control sent him a check for eight hundred dollars, and he bought
Alma a stereo-TV. She took his Wednesdays for dancing.

He learned to dance quite well, with enough whiskey. Alma
liked to close her eyes and squeeze his left arm as she danced.
Sometimes Lane closed his eyes too, and then only the squeeze on
his biceps kept him from feeling that he was not there at all. But in
the early mornings, outside of time, he walked with Martha Bettony. Until the footsteps. . . .

Martha's world had night and day, but the season remained early
summer. Fruits and berries abounded in defiance of botanic law. It
was a small world, the valley and a few glens. Beyond them, as Lane
and Martha explored, reality tone faded. They could see and hear, but

not feel or smell or taste. Here animals thronged, larger than life and with a strangeness of shape and color about even the familiar ones. The animals seemed not to perceive the two humans.

Here also they could walk through trees, on or under water, and even under the earth. Underground they saw shadowy white roots groping and further down the texture and joints and bedding planes of the living rock itself. They feared to venture far in any way they went.

"Out here it's like my own world was before you woke me up," Martha said. "Only then, I couldn't come here at all."

In the strange world Lane could not count back days or even hours to arrange memory in linear sequence. But once as he and Martha watched a clumsy, shaggy elephant-thing eat spruce boughs, a voice spoke behind them.

"Hello! I didn't know anyone lived near this part of the Pleistocene."

Lane turned to see a slender, dark man in a business suit.

"I didn't know anybody lived anywhere here," he said. "Or where here is, even. Pleistocene, you say?"

The man nodded. He had a quick, nervous manner. "Let me introduce myself," he said. "Stepan Hlanka, professor of geology in Belgrade." He bowed.

They exchanged names and handshakes. Lane was pleased to find that Hlanka's hand felt as real as Martha's.

"You speak good English," he told Hlanka.

"I am speaking the purest Croatian," Hlanka said, smiling, "and that is what I hear from you. It's that way with everyone you meet, here in the time-lands."

"Well, that's good," Lane said. "How many people are here?"

"I've met dozens myself. There must be many thousands, but most are afraid to leave their islands."

"Islands?" Martha asked.

"Like your world, I think he means," Lane said. He described the little valley-world to Hlanka.

"Yes," Hlanka said. "They are all small, and it seems that only the women can stabilize them. But one would quickly tire of this impalpable life in the time-lands if he had not his woman and her island."

"We're afraid to go very far," Lane said. "You see. . . ."

"I know." Hlanka nodded. "The footsteps. But you can get back to your island almost at once, from wherever you happen to be in the time-lands, by simply walking in the air. I'm on my way now to my sweetheart's island in the Upper Cretaceous. Why not come along and meet her?''

"We will, and thanks," Lane said.

Hlanka led them over ice fields and seething lava flows, across game-crowded Pliocene steppes, and through Oligocene forests with their browsing giants. He pointed out index life-forms as he went.

"I can't resist showing off," he said. "No geology professor ever had such a laboratory. I could rewrite all the books now and I don't dare."

Crossing an Upper Cretaceous plain spotted with duck-billed and three-horned dinosaurs browsing along swampy watercourses, they met another man. He was stocky, black-bearded, and had grave, oxlike eyes. Hlanka knew him and introduced him as Lev Hurwitz, of London. He walked along with them.

"You're the unicorn man," Lane said. "I remember reading."

"Have you found an island for yourself yet, Lev?" Hlanka asked.

"No," Hurwitz said. "I carry my island in my head. I may never need one here, always supposing I will get across when the time comes."

"I want to talk about that," Lane said.

He felt reality tone flood back as they crossed a swell of ground. The earth pressed up against his feet, a warm breeze fragrant of spices caressed his face, and the plants around were suddenly great green ferns and fronded cycads.

"It's your island," he said to Hlanka.

"O Yuki's island," Hlanka corrected. "She shares it with me."

O Yuki was small and neat and shy in her bamboo spray kimono. She was from Nagoya, Lane and Martha learned, and had found her island as her experience in the Purchasing Office. Hlanka, wide wandering with a geologist's curiosity, had met her in the time-lands. She was interested to learn that Martha was an Agent and did not have to go back to the machine world. The two women went aside to talk.

The men talked too, sprawling on a moss bank under a great fern. Lane repeated what the Star Birds had told him through Martha. Hurwitz nodded.

"Each to his own language," he said. "The time eddies coalesce in the Pleroma. Enough of them and our doublegangers come alive. They will combine forces and break through into the machine world on a given day, no longer bound by the time tracks we lay for them. They will pursue us."

"I half understand," Hlanka said. "What do *we* do, on that day? What happens?"

"By then there will be a tremendous potential of time-energy between each of us and his doubleganger," Hurwitz said. "It will suffice to translate us here permanently and fasten the burden of our world-lines on the doublegangers."

He smiled and stroked his beard while Lane and Hlanka frowned.

"But just *how* we bring this about, I have no idea," he went on. "I know, from the lore of ancient times, that we must not let them *touch* us. Beyond that, the old writings are silent."

"Perhaps there is no one thing to do," Hlanka said. "Perhaps the circumstances will suggest the action. I only hope we all, every last one of us, will get across."

"Amen. And I hope it comes soon," Hurwitz said. "Tau people are in great danger in London these days."

"So are we in America," Lane said. "And still, when I think of leaving them forever, I feel a little cowardly and ungrateful."

"You need not," Hurwitz said gravely. "You will leave them your simulacrum, and it will be just what they have wished you to be. They lose only what they hate. They are not robbed."

Lane nodded soberly. Hurwitz got to his feet.

"I must go," he said, pointing. "There I come after me."

Lane squinted and saw only a bobbing air flaw. Hurwitz trotted hastily over the land swell, turning to wave from the top. Lane felt a premonitory prickling.

"I haven't got much longer," he said, rising too. "Come on, Martha, let's start for home."

"Just walk a straight line through the air and think about your island," Hlanka said. "When your weight comes back, you'll know you're on the border. It takes only a few minutes. I brought you here the long way round just to show off."

"Well, good-bye, O Yuki, Stepan," Lane said. "We're glad to have you for friends here. We'll see you again."

With Martha beside him, Lane walked back into the time-lands. Walking through the air was as easy as walking under water. But even in the air, he heard the footsteps when the time came.

Tau tension passed a breaking point. Experiments on condemned Tau people developed a dozen refinements of lobotomy and cortical cautery that would extirpate the Tau component. All nations set up Tau rehabilitation centers. But the humanists won a partial victory in the UN, and instead of initiating mass extirpation, the world's legislative bodies enacted variants of the modal Ward Law.

The courts assigned Tau people to wardens, preferably normals of their own families. The Tau person was required to report to his warden as frequently and for as long periods as the warden thought advisable to safeguard society. Wardens were granted fees, to be paid by the Tau person. Wardenships might be sold or leased, with court permission.

Any warden-reported delinquency, including nonpayment of warden fees, was punishable by automatic rehabilitation of the Tau person. Those who objected to their status were permitted to request voluntary rehabilitation.

Lane, sniffing the varnish and floor-oil smell of the dark old courtroom, felt real fear. Judge Fonteiner, a potbellied old skeleton, august in black robes, looked down from the bench at Lane and Alma Butelle. Alma wore a white jersey, pearls, and a small hat.

"Christopher Lane," the judge intoned, "your wardenship is hereby awarded to Miss Alma Butelle. This court has already instructed you in your duties and responsibilities and the single penalty attached hereto. Miss Butelle is your protectress in a society enraged, justly or unjustly, against the quality that sets you apart from it. You owe her, in a sense, your very life itself. I adjure you to conduct yourself accordingly. You should be very happy now."

He rapped his gavel. The disappointed applicants, Reilly, Miss Weber, and Mrs. Greene, left their seats to congratulate Alma.

"I hope you'll still let me have him for breakfast, Miss Butelle," Mrs. Greene said.

Outside in the warm sunlight Alma was jubilant.

"Isn't it just *wonderful*, Chris?" she bubbled. "I don't know what to *do*, I'm so happy! Let's go somewhere for a drink."

Over the drinks she planned a party that night in the Golden Pheasant.

"It's got to be *special*, Chris. I'll ask Buck and Ruth and Emily. . . . We'll have . . . oh . . . we'll have *steak* and . . . and *champagne!*"

In Martha's world next morning Lane was still afraid.

"Let's go find Stepan and O Yuki," he told Martha. "I need moral support."

"I wish I could share the danger with you, Chris, as O Yuki does with Stepan," Martha said.

"No, Martha. That would make it all the harder for me."

They found Hurwitz with Hlanka and O Yuki among the great ferns. All of their faces were grave.

"I am summoned to court today," Hurwitz said. "My landlady will get me. For years she has hated my freedom and wished to destroy me."

"It's fortunate that both O Yuki and I are already married to parts of the machine," Hlanka said. "It hasn't made much difference to us."

"When I first broke phase, I felt free of the machine, I felt like a giant," Lane said. "Now it's got me again, out in the open where I can see and know all its workings. It's almost more than I can stand."

"We will have a deliverance," Hlanka said. "It should be soon now."

"I hope it is," Hurwitz said. "I do not have long, after today. Oh, she will have mouse sport with me—my flesh crawls on my bones."

"Thousands of us get dragged to the rehab centers every day," Lane said. "Will any of us be left, when the time comes?"

"Still more will be lost in the crossing over," Martha said. "It is needed that many fail so the field may be reseeded."

Lane looked at her eyes. "Lev, Stepan, the Star Birds—" he began.

"I know," Hurwitz said. "Star Birds, how long? *How long?*"

"Within three months after the last phase break," Martha said. She shook her head. "They're gone. Oh, your *faces!* What did I say?"

"Something that makes us think we may soon no longer be able to come here," Hlanka said.

"That will be a long, dark night in the machine world," Hurwitz said. "Let us say a solemn good-bye hereafter, each time we part."

Back in her island Lane kissed Martha a particularly tender good-bye. The next time he reached into the gray boulder by Folwell dump he skinned his knuckles on unyielding rock. On the following mornings it remained unyielding.

Lane took a second job, unloading produce in the early mornings. Alma took his Sundays and Mondays. She took a larger apartment and bought a new car. Lane took her drinking, dancing, and eating, often with Buckley along, sometimes in Buckley's car, sometimes in Alma's. Buckley was exuberant.

"Now you're living, Chris boy! Got it made and waiting for you!"

"Have another snort," Lane said.

Alcohol was a Tau depressant. Lane drank heavily and never needed rest.

" 'Nother snort it is! Yea, boy, on wheels and snapping at you. You lucky, lucky dog!"

Alma came back from the powder room.

"Chris lamb, you have to get up at four. Let's go and tuck you in now."

At work, Lane wrote one Wednesday on a cedar slab, "Cold stone in the guts. Something breaks." All the dressers looked sad and glowering now.

The Day was Thursday. Lane stood in the door of his room at Mrs. Calthorp's and watched his simulacrum fumble in eager blindness at the still-warm bed. He ran foodless to work. He knew that the tracks were fusing, that the phase angle had come full circle.

At the produce market he dodged the thing again, interposing crates of lettuce and celery. Refractive flaws moved through the air all around him—Star Birds or other men's fetches, Lane could not tell. The laborers' voices sounded jerky and overloud in the tension-charged air.

Lane lost his own pursuer running to Acme and had a free hour. "A last day brings a first day. No robbery." he wrote on a cedar panel. He wondered what he would do at that last second. Then the eerie game of blindman's bluff began once more. The thing moved in short, blind rushes, stopping to ape Lane's motions of a few minutes earlier, as if it were sniffing on a trail.

Dan Gault in the next bay was behaving strangely. He and Lane exchanged glances.

"Let's swap jobs back and forth," Gault proposed, grinning slightly.

For a while that made it easier. Normals in the plant picked up a nameless fear, laughed, talked, whirled to look behind themselves. The air crackled with tension.

The workday ended. For Lane that night, dinner and dancing:

Alma, wearing zircons and black wool, picked him up at the curb before Mrs. Calthorp's just as the thing came out on the veranda.

Wheels rolled. Fast motion shook it off the trail.

Early as they came, the roadhouse was crowded. Frantic music jangled, voices rang out, the crowd drank heavily. Lane wolfed his steak as greedily as Alma, watching all around. Other men and women at nearby tables did the same.

Then Lane saw the thing—*his* thing—among the tables near the door across the small dance floor. It was making short, swooping casts to right and left. Flaws winked through the smoky air, and Lane knew that he was not alone in his trouble.

"Let's dance," he said.

"Why, *Chris!*"

Dancing, she gripped his left arm and talked dreamily about the dinner, eyes closed. Lane dared not let his feet carry him unthinking through the dance pattern, as he had learned to do when drunk enough. He made the dance an agony of conscious effort.

He crossed glances with a woman whose eyes pleaded "Help me!" He watched a man in gray swing his partner as if he were fending off an invisible beast of prey.

Lane's fetch was on the floor now, no longer groping but peering. Lane kept Alma between them when he could. The thing came nearer, and he had no eyes for the other Tau people in their trouble. Abruptly, the music sounded far away.

"My steak was not rare enough, Chris," Alma repeated. "You should have sent it back."

The thing strode directly toward Lane, raising its arms. Their glances met. An electric shock ran down Lane's spine and along his limbs. Convulsively, he flung Alma at the thing.

And they two were dancing, she gripping its arm. It struggled and looked toward Lane, but the music entangled its feet and its eyes were filming over.

"They charge enough for steak, they ought to give you what you order," Alma said to it crossly.

"Wheel her away, Chris lamb, you lucky, lucky dog," Lane whispered in his heart. He felt titanically unloaded.

He let himself down through the shadowy floor and walked in starlight through a stunted spruce forest of the time-lands. People were all around him. He came on the woman whose eyes had pleaded for help.

"I was worried for you," he told her.

"My husband *almost* knew," she said. "Did you see the poor man in gray? It was pitiful."

"I'm glad I didn't see. Do you have someone here?"

"No, but I have a beautiful place to go, if I can only find it now."

"I'm all alone and lost too, but I like it a million times better than back there," said a tall young man.

"Both of you come with me," Lane said. "I know a little and I have friends who know more. We'll all team up for a while."

A miracle, the people said. Minds cleansed of Tau taint mercifully overnight. Everyone normal. Wardenships dissolved or ritualized. Star Birds gone forever. Art flourished, wheels rolled, life was wonderful.

The Hlankas called on the Lanes in Martha's island.

"We met Lev in the time-lands but he wouldn't come with us," O Yuki said.

"He is following the indices I taught him through the Pleistocene," Hlanka said. "He thinks now the barrier will be lifted and he can find his way to early man."

"I'd like to go too, even clear to our own old time," Lane said. "If Lev finds a way, I'll ask him to take me."

"The time-lands' beasts can't perceive us," Hlanka said, "but I *wonder* about man. Perhaps that is why there is a barrier."

"There is no more barrier," Martha said. "Men will not see you, but the poets among them will know you are there."

Lane looked at her eyes.

"Listen to the wise woman," he said.

Hlanka sat up straight.

"Star Bird, what is the law? What may we or must we do among men?"

"You tend the crop. In time you will harvest it."

"As we were harvested?" Hlanka asked.

"As you will harvest yourselves," Martha said.

Hlanka looked wonderingly at Lane. Lane looked at Martha and saw no air flaw above her head. He looked back at Hlanka in exploding surmise.

"Then *we* are the Star Birds!"

"Chris, what did I say? Tell me what I said," Martha asked teasingly.

THE CREATURES OF MAN

Verge Foray

*I am a vegetarian because I am sensitive to the rights and feel-
ings of animals as well as those of human beings (critics ex-
cepted). Suppose animals could be enhanced, so as to possess
powers unknown today? I love this type of story.*

—PA

*Verge Foray was an early pen name (he later published un-
der his own name) for the very good writer Howard L. Myers
(1930–1971), a North Carolinian and violist who in the
years between 1966 and his death was just beginning to
build a remarkable body of work until he was so cruelly and
untimely cut off. He was one of John Campbell's mainstays
in Campbell's final, Late Blue period and only a few stories,
evidently passed by JWC, appeared outside of that market.
Author of a posthumously published novel (Cloud Chamber, Popular Library, 1976), Myers is probably to remain in
an obscurity which would not have been his if he had been
granted another decade. He was one of the only two violists
(the other is the fan and critic Joanne Burger) in science fiction and for that alone would generate for me a real sense of
loss.*

—bnm

*I'm not so sure that Myers would have avoided obscurity if he
had lived. This book is in part testimony to the fact that even
long careers don't guarantee recognition, but I would like to
believe that Barry is right.*

—MHG

I

The butterfly with a wounded wing glided clumsily down to settle
on a leaf by the spider's web. The spider knew he was there, but
she was drowsy and ignored him for a time. The butterfly waited
patiently, knowing that a hastily aroused spider tends to be bad-
tempered. Patience was often desirable in mingling with the lesser
creatures of Man, and the butterfly was, after all, in no hurry.

At last she turned to regard him with her principal eyes. Her
dark mind spoke: "Was that your caterpillar that fell in my web
near dusk yesterday?"

"Yes, I was its sire," he replied.

"Delicious," she commented lazily.

"I'm glad you enjoyed it," he said.

She moved across her web to study him more closely. "Your
left hind wing has a fracture in it," she said. "How did that happen?"

"I was watching the metal-secreters being attacked by the bees.
One of them ejected at me and hit the wing."

"Hold it out," she directed. He lowered his wings, and she examined the broken area with her feet and mandibles. "I can taste
the metal," she remarked. "This won't be hard to fix so it will
mend straight. Who won the fight?"

"The metal-secreters retreated into their flying hive, but then
they destroyed many flowers, along with some of the bees and
other insects, by ejecting flaming poison from their hive." He
could feel and observe the spider's repair work on his injured wing
while he conversed with her. The pain was a minor annoyance.

"Are the metal-secreters creatures of Man?" she asked.

He hesitated—unusually—before answering: "That is beyond
my knowing. Whatever they are, they are outside my knowing of
the now-moment. I'm trying to learn more about them."

"So am I," she replied snappishly, "but hardly anybody bothers to tell me anything. They seem to think I can sit here all day
and have as big a knowing as any creature that flies. All I get is bits
and snatches when somebody thinks past me. Man himself could
return, and I wouldn't know it unless he lit in my web!"

"I'll tell you about the metal-secreters, then, while you fix my
wing," said the butterfly. In a way he felt sorry for the spider, because her complaints were largely justified. Man had favored her
with some intelligence, but far too little for her to achieve a real

knowing of the now-moment. In fact, she had only a vague notion of what the phrase really meant.

Butterflies, the most favored of the creatures of Man, had the fullest knowing, thanks in part to their varied and highly developed sensing abilities and to the routine thought-sharing which took place between all members of the order of Lepidoptera. Too, the central nervous system of butterflies was organized for extreme efficiency in the use of stored knowledge—not for remembering, which any of the favored creatures, including the spider, could do very well, but for defining the now-moment. The butterfly had a clear conception of what was taking place, from instant to instant, at all points in the populated portion of the world. It knew the now-moment.

Perhaps the prime contributor to the butterfly's knowing was its long period of development as a caterpillar.

This period lasted most of the seventy-four days—each day five hundred hours in length—of the warm season of the world's year. During that period the caterpillar was a passive receiver of all the traffic of thought taking place around it. It read and stored the knowing not only of butterflies and moths but of bees and even ants. The caterpillar could not act upon any of this knowledge. Indeed the central nervous system contained within the larva was actually two separate systems—one listening detachedly while waiting to serve the adult butterfly, and the other a primitive system guiding the caterpillar through its mindless life of eating and growing. This latter system vanished completely later, during the world's long winter of utter cold, to serve as one more morsel of warming fuel while the encapsulated insect was in the pupa stage. When warmth returned and the world sprang alive with soaring flowers, the adult butterfly emerged from its wrappings, fully grown and educated.

Only the moth shared so favorable a life cycle, and the moth's need for special sensory perception for night flying apparently left less room for intellectual development. In any event, the moth's knowing was less full than the butterfly's. Third in knowing were the bees, and fourth the ants. The spiders ran a poor fifth, but were certainly far superior to the many unfavored creatures needed to complete the world's ecology—the aphids, beetles, termites, and various others. And since knowing the now-moment was beyond the spiders' abilities, they used their knowledge for the lesser function of remembering. They took considerable pride in their memories, which they claimed were superior to those of more favored creatures, but the truth was that the higher insects seldom bothered with remembering. The now-moment, to a butterfly, was sufficient.

But, to please the curiosity of the spider, who was repairing his wing, the wounded butterfly exercised his memory of the day's now-moments sufficiently to recount the story of the metal-secreters.

"Their hive flies, you know," he told her, "and is made of a hard metal. I have no knowing of how it is organized inside, or of how it flies without wings. It came down shortly after sunrise today and settled on top of the Rock Hill."

"How far from here is that?" she asked.

"About half a mile west," he said. "It's a small mountain of solid rock in my hunting ground." He was trying to keep the story simple for her, not going into detail about the kind of metal used in the flying hive or the geological nature of the Rock Hill. "The ants saw it land. When the creatures in it unplugged its door, the ants tried to go in and know what was there. But the creatures ejected metal at the ants and killed several, so the ants retreated. When they did, some of the creatures came out of the hive, still ejecting metal at the particular ants who were carrying the bodies of those already killed. Well, you know how ants are when somebody tries to take food away from them . . ."

"I'm the same way," she interrupted.

"They swarmed back, and the creatures retreated into their hive and plugged the door. The ants were then able to carry away their meat."

"What are those creatures like? Would they be good meat?" the spider asked with considerable interest.

"They are hard to describe to you, since I can't make you see pictures. They are big. Their bodies are almost six times as long as an ant's—twice as long as mine. They move about in a very peculiar manner. They have no wings, so of course they crawl on their legs, which they have too few of . . ."

"So do you, for that matter," sniffed the spider.

"They crawl somewhat like a mantis, or at least more like a mantis than like us. Their bodies are thicker than the mantis, though. And I suppose they would be good meat, unless they contain poison metal salts."

"I'd like to try one," she murmured half to herself. "If I wasn't in such a good location right here, I would go hang a new web close to their hive and try my luck.''

''They may be intelligent,'' the butterfly reminded her.

''If they are they wouldn't get caught in the web,'' she answered; and added rather gloatingly, ''And for all your *knowing* you don't know if they are even creatures of Man.''

''That's true,'' he conceded.

''What happened after the ants left?''

''The bees came. They are more disturbed than the ants were, because it is a hive as well as an emptiness in their knowing. It could mean competition for the bees. They swarmed around the hive for a while, until it began ejecting metal at them. They flew some distance away and concealed themselves among the flowers. Nothing more happened for perhaps twenty hours, and the sun was well above the horizon when some ants who were keeping watch saw the hole in the hive unplugged again.

''This time the ants and the bees stayed off the Rock Hill and kept their bodies hidden when five of the creatures came out.''

''What good did they think hiding their bodies could do?'' asked the spider. ''Didn't they think the creatures have good senses?''

''That's what they did think,'' the butterfly answered, ''and seemingly they are right. The metal-secreters never seem to eject at anything that cannot be sensed by vision. The bees and ants stayed hidden among the flowers while the creatures crawled down from the hill and began exploring the edge of the foliage. That was when I decided to fly over there and observe the creatures directly.

''When I arrived, the creatures had moved a short distance away from the hill, using some sharp metal extrusion from their upper legs to cut a path through the flowers. If they are knowing creatures, then our world is as concealed from them as the inside of their hive is from me, because they obviously did not know the bees were concealed all along one side of the trail, waiting for the creatures to get deep enough in the flowers for their retreat to be cut off. Some ants were waiting, too, hoping to get some meat for themselves.

''I approached from the side of the trail opposite from where the bees were hiding and arrived just as the bees moved in to attack. The creatures saw me first and kept looking up at me until the bees almost had them. Then they turned and started ejecting at the bees. I saw several bees go down, but only one of the creatures got stung. Evidently the creatures have very tough exoskeletons, made mostly of metal, and the bees could not find weak spots into which the sting could be inserted. Nevertheless, the creatures started back to their hive, dragging the stung one with them, and they finally made it—with bees and ants snapping and punching at them all the way back to the Rock Hill. I was still flying about observing, and as soon as the creatures were out of the flowers one of them ejected at me and hit my wing. I came here, and the creatures are all in their hive now. As soon as they were in, the hive ejected a flaming mass of poisonous substance onto the area where they had cut the trail. Luckily, the bees had scattered by then, and the ants were most of the way back to their nests loaded with ant and bee meat, so the fire did not kill very many.''

The spider was almost through repairing his wing as the butterfly ended his account. With a delicate touch, she smoothed the surface of the hard-setting modification of web-stuff with which she had encased the major vein-fracture.

''What are you going to do now?'' she asked.

''Now?'' he asked. ''In the next now-moments? As soon as you say my wing is ready to be used, I'll take nourishment.''

''That's not what I mean,'' she snapped impatiently. ''I mean what about the metal-secreters.''

A strange question, thought the butterfly. He queried the other butterflies, and they too agreed it was a strange thing to ask. So did the moths who, living on the night half of the world, were awake at the moment. One moth remarked that it was just the kind of question one might expect from a spider, whose life was one long introspection with insufficient introspecting equipment.

''Nothing,'' he answered at last. ''Of course, I will continue trying to fit them into my knowing of the now-moment.''

''If you could ever fit them in,'' she asked, ''don't you think you could have done so by now?''

That ''ever'' was a meaningless, spiderish term. What personal significance could ''ever'' have to the butterfly, who had awakened and climbed from his pupa enclosure seventeen days before and who knew he would die fifty-five days from this particular now-moment, when the winter cold returned? ''Ever'' to a butterfly is one summer season; it is the same to a spider, but perhaps engrossed in her legends of memory she would not agree with that.

He answered her question: ''Perhaps.''

"In case of emergency," she recited, "a butterfly may call Man."

"That is true," he said.

"Then why don't you?" she urged. "This is an emergency, and you're a butterfly."

"Why is this an emergency?" he countered. "A few bees and ants have died before their normal time, and a few flowers have been destroyed in one tiny area. For the world as a whole, life continues as always for the creatures of Man."

The truth was that the butterfly—all butterflies—regarded Man as a rather mythic being. Man had doubtless once existed, but an accurate definition of his attributes was no longer available to his creatures. The clear picture of Man had been lost with the passage of thousands of years and thousands of generations. The act of calling Man, the butterfly felt, could not be integrated into his knowing of the now-moment.

"This is an emergency," the spider told him, "because you admit those metal-secreters are a blank spot in your knowing. When a butterfly admits something like that, it's an emergency!"

"If I called Man and he came," said the butterfly, "he would be another such blank spot. How do you know these two blanks would be mutually eliminating?"

"All I know is that we are creatures of Man," she huffed rather piously, "and we are supposed to call him in need. He brought us to this world and remade us and the flowers so that we could live here alone from him, because this world is not suited for Man's needs, and Man does not remake himself. The gravity of this world was too slight, and the air much too thick, for Man to dwell here in comfort, nor were the seasons suited to beings such as he, who may endure for a hundred years." (She was reciting again, the butterfly noted.) "He fitted us for this world, and gave it to us, but kept us for himself, as his creatures, to live for Man as well as for ourselves. We have a responsibility to Man. You should call him."

"The old knowledge says we 'may' call him," retorted the butterfly.

"Yes, and we 'may' disappoint him, if he returns someday to find his creatures gone and the world filled with metal-secreting monsters!"

"The creatures in that hive won't find much metal to secrete if they try to live here," the butterfly responded. "Our stones contain mere traces of the heavy elements."

Though he was arguing with the spider, the butterfly was not at all sure he was right. The calling of Man was an event that had never occurred; thus it was difficult to fit into his knowing of the now-moment. But perhaps it was the appropriate action to take under the present circumstances. As the spider had reminded him, it was a recourse suggested by Man himself.

"I will go feed while I think about it," the butterfly agreed at last.

"Will you let me know what you decide?" she asked.

"Yes."

II

He took to the air and found his mended wing was as sturdy as ever—as he had known it would be. Flying to a group of flowers he had not yet visited, he lit on a tall, deep-cupped blossom and unrolled his proboscis. As he sipped the sweet nectar from the bottom of the cup he realized that he had made his decision.

There was no question about it being his decision to make. Butterflies do not vote. The others were, certainly, interested in what his decision would be, but he was the individual directly involved in the matter of the metal-secreters.

The strange hive was on his hunting ground. He had seen it himself and had been attacked by one of the creatures. He had discussed the situation with the spider. In short, this was his affair, and his ability to decide how to conduct it was as good as any other butterfly's.

He would call Man. The other favored creatures would assist him if he requested their help.

Having decided, he continued to feed for two hours. Man could not be called from his hunting ground—that had to be done at a special place hundreds of miles away. It was best to be well nourished before beginning such a journey. When his feeding took him close to the spider's web, he kept his promise to tell her what he was going to do. She haughtily approved.

The day was still younger than midmorning when he took a last sip, climbed higher in the air than usual, and began the long flight westward. He had never come this way before—in fact, he had never traveled far from his hunting ground in any direction. But he found nothing strange in the countryside below him, no wonderful new sights to see. He knew the now-moment, and what he saw was what he had known was there to see.

When he grew hungry after several hours of flight, another butterfly, a Swallowtail like himself, called invitingly: "Come down and feast and rest. My flowers are suitable, sweet, and plentiful." He accepted the offer and lighted in the other's hunting ground where he fed, napped, and fed again until midmorning. Then he resumed his journey.

He made five more such stops before the terrain began to change from the lush, slightly undulating plain into a more rugged and elevated landscape where the flowers grew in less abundance. He was approaching a towering range of mountains. As he climbed with the land, the atmosphere grew noticeably thinner; breathing and flying required increased vigor, and his periods of rest became longer and more frequent. But he was nearing his goal.

He reached a spot near the upper end of a high valley, with only one more tremendous barren ridge to fly over. He had left the area in which butterflies lived and hunted far behind; at this elevation the flowers were too small and sparse to support the likes of himself in comfort.

He fluttered down to light on a rock near a beehive. Several bees came out and examined him with wonder. To their limited knowing he was a sight at which to marvel, gigantic in size and with wings the colors of many flowers. And he was a butterfly, which meant he was wise.

"You are welcome here, butterfly-who-is-going-to-call-Man," they told him, "though you will eat so much, doubtless, that you will set our population-expansion program back at least a year. Never has a butterfly visited our hive before. It will please us to serve you well."

"I am grateful," he responded, "especially since you do not have plenty."

"What we have you will find good," they replied.

And he did. The bees fed him honey, and his knowing was shocked most pleasantly by its heavy richness and almost overwhelming sweetness. Never before, he realized, had a butterfly been so hungry and fed so deliciously. It was a wonderful and novel now-moment to know.

After he had been fed and had drunk from a shaded, icy spring, he napped by the water for several hours. Then the bees fed him more honey and, thoroughly invigorated, he began the last segment of his journey.

He needed all the strength the honey gave him. As he made his way up the steep final slope, the thinning air became hardly sufficient to sustain him, no matter how hard he worked his wings, and it seemed all but impossible to pump his abdomen fast enough to bring as much oxygen as he needed into his body. Long before he reached the summit he was reduced to making short, hopping flights of only a few yards at a time, from one ledge to the next, interspersed with rests for breathing.

The last fifty yards of the ascent he did not fly at all, but crawled. When he came in sight of the Nest That Man Left he was tempted to stop where he stood and sleep, but the chill in the air told his knowing that this would be unwise. He made his way clumsily over the leveled ground of the mountaintop toward the entrance of the rambling metal structure.

As he did so he realized that the Nest That Man Left was another emptiness in his knowing. That was not surprising, though, since it was at an unpopulated, unvisited location. His knowing told him only what the outer appearance of the Nest would be, and where it was to be entered. The inside was as blank as that of the metal-secreters' hive. With a sense of uneasiness in the face of the unknown, intensified by the strained condition of his body, the butterfly crawled to the entrance.

The Nest sensed his presence and opened the door as he approached. He went inside without a pause, and the door slid closed behind him.

III

The interior was dark at first but brightened immediately as overhead panels shifted to let in sunlight through a wide expanse of glass. The walls hissed as an oxygen-rich flood of air pressed in to bring the thickness up to a level the butterfly found comfortable. A trough in the floor gurgled and filled with water, and he drank gratefully. These events were all unexpected, of course, but there was a definite rightness about them. This was the way a butterfly should be received in the Nest That Man Left, and it was not difficult to place in his knowing.

The Nest addressed him: ''You are a butterfly, and you are here

to call Man.'' The mind of the Nest was shrouded, somewhat like
that of the spider except for an absence of personality.

"Yes," the butterfly responded.

"I am the voice of the Nest, a contrivance that does not live but
that can converse with you to a limited extent. Do you have injuries or unmet needs that are an immediate danger to you?''

"No." The butterfly's senses searched his surroundings while
the voice addressed him, and he gained a partial knowing of the
nature of the voice contrivance. Man had to be wise, indeed, to
construct such a complex dead device and to shelter it so perfectly
that, after untold thousands of years, it could still awaken and engage in a conversation of minds.

"Do butterflies continue to know the now-moment?" the Nest
asked.

"Yes."

"That is an ability Man did not give me, and one that he lacks
himself," the Nest told him. "Thus I do not know the nature of the
emergency that brings you here. Nor do I know where Man is, nor
what he may have become during the centuries since he made me,
mutated your ancestors, and departed.''

"Man does not change himself, according to my knowing,"
commented the butterfly.

"Not intentionally, perhaps, but he changes nevertheless. He is
a discontented being who, not knowing the now-moment, wanders
and searches for new things to know. What he finds changes him,
not in the orderly manner in which he fitted you for conditions on
this world, but in ways that are unplanned and sometimes undesir-
able. Occasionally he finds something very damaging to him,
something that darkens his intelligence and causes him to forget
much of his learning from previous findings.''

The butterfly struggled with this information. His difficulty was
not that what the Nest told him was new. On the contrary, it was
ancient; so ancient that it had been all but forgotten—dismissed as
having no meaning to current knowing. It occurred to the butterfly
that perhaps the creatures of Man had *wanted* to forget that Man
could not know the now-moment, which implied that Man was inferior to themselves. But then, he quickly reassured himself, Man
must have completely different abilities that made him superior—
abilities so far beyond a butterfly's comprehension that the Nest
would not attempt to describe them.

At last he addressed the Nest: "Then if I call Man, the being who responds may be unlike the beings who established the creatures of Man on this world. He may even have forgotten that he has such creatures as us."

"That is correct," the Nest responded. "Man instructed me to be sure you understood that before he was called. If he comes, the results will be unpredictable. You are to reconsider the nature of your emergency with this in mind and decide if your need for Man is sufficient for you to accept the uncertainties of his present nature."

This was a difficult decision indeed. The butterfly thought about it for several minutes before saying, "In essence, the emergency is an intellectual one. An area of blankness has entered our knowing. Since Man does not know the now-moment, it is possible that we could not explain to him the nature of the emergency."

"That is possible," agreed the Nest. "In any event, unless Man has changed greatly, you will be unable to communicate with him directly. Man does not speak mind to mind, the way you and I are conversing, but through the use of special sounds he can emit, each sound being a symbol of a fragment of thought."

"Then how could we have ever communicated?" asked the astonished butterfly.

"Through intermediary devices such as myself," said the Nest. "You can talk to me and I can put your thoughts into the words of Man, like this." The Nest emitted, from a wall cavity, a complex series of noises.

The butterfly listened in stunned recognition. He had never heard such sounds before today, but as he had hovered over the metal-secreters earlier that morning just such noises, though dim and muffled, had struck his sensors. But Man was supposed to be ten-fingered—more manipulatory members than even the spider! And the metal-secreters had clearly been deficient in this respect, having only two pairs of legs.

The Nest was continuing: "Communication is rendered more complex by the use of differing sets of sound-symbols, called languages, and by the fact that a given set of symbols tends to change with the passage of years to become an entirely new language. I probably would not know the sounds man uses today, but would have to communicate your thoughts, with some explanation, to a device similar to myself that Man brought with him, and that device in turn would speak to Man."

"Man uses metal extensively, does he not?" asked the butterfly.

"Yes. Metals were abundant on his, and your, original planet. He built his nests of them and other dead materials, and also his flying shelters in which he journeyed here and to many other worlds."

"What are fingers?"

"They are relatively small, slender extensions of Man's arms, his upper legs. They are useful for gripping and manipulating. He has ten of them, normally."

"I wish to call him," said the butterfly.

"Very well. . . . The call is now being emitted. I do not know when he will arrive. He may have to come far, a journey of more than a day for his fastest shelter. Certainly, he cannot be expected to arrive within a hundred hours at best. As there is no food stored for you here, I suggest you return to your hunting ground to await him."

"My knowing is unsure," replied the butterfly, "but I believe Man to be quite close. I will wait outside, at least for a while. It is certain he will respond to the call?"

"If he does not," the Nest said, "he will have changed too greatly to be of any assistance to you. I am preparing to open the door."

The air thinned; the door opened, and the butterfly went out onto the mountaintop. This was the kind of air Man could breathe without the protection of an artificial exoskeleton, the butterfly reasoned. Thus this mountaintop was the place where Man should be met by his creatures.

IV

He was hardly outside when the knowing came that the flying hive of the "metal-secreters" had lifted from the Rock Hill back in his hunting ground. It was hurtling toward him almost with the speed of a meteorite, but when it arrived it landed as gently as the butterfly could have descended onto a flower.

The Nest commented: "So your emergency was Man himself. . . . They have a device with them to permit communication." Nearly an hour passed before the butterfly was addressed again: "A Man is coming out now. I have told him about this world."

The butterfly watched with a touch of awe as the Man came out of the unplugged hole in the flying hive. Without his artificial exoskeleton, but with most of his body covered with brightly colored woven material, he still looked very odd—but not like some freakish creature who could secrete metal. The butterfly's senses informed him that, without his woven coverings, Man would appear rather drab: pink all over except for a scattering of dark hair and for the eyes which were small and one-faceted.

Still, there was an austere attractiveness in the Man's appearance and a startling grace in the way he crawled, precariously balanced on his rear legs. The Men had looked less graceful earlier in the morning, using all four legs to push their way through the flowers and the attacking bees, or to climb the steep side of the Rock Hill. Apparently Man was designed to crawl best over level, unobstructed ground.

The Man advanced to stand before the butterfly, his small eyes studying the insect as the insect studied the Man. The wings seemed to fascinate the Man. When held in a resting, vertical position their tips were approximately a third as high off the ground as the top of the Man's head.

A series of sounds came from the Man's mouth.

"He is asking your name," explained the Nest. "That is an abstract symbol you would use to identify yourself, as an individual, from the other butterflies. I have explained that, while butterflies have individuality, you have no use for names because of the way you communicate."

"You (Man) may give me a name if you wish," said the butterfly.

"No," said the Man. "If you need no name, you should not have one. How can I serve you in a manner that suits your need?"

"I do not know. I came to the Nest to call you because the flying hive was a blank in my knowing of the now-moment. Perhaps I expected you to destroy the hive, or cause it to go elsewhere. But the hive is your contrivance, and this is your world. Thus I have nothing to ask."

"This is *your* world, butterfly," contradicted the Man. "Long ago, men gave it to you and left. I'm beginning to realize why they went away, even though there must be many mountains such as this on which men could live in comfort. We too must depart soon, for the same reason. And we will take our flying hive with us."

"The seasons of this world are not suited," the butterfly quoted, "for beings who live a hundred years."

"That is a minor problem," the man said. "Men are not as long-lived as you believe. Our hundred years, or season cycles, are very brief years compared to your own. This planet turns much more slowly on its axis and takes much longer to circle its sun than the planet that gave birth to both our species. Also, this planet's orbit is far more eccentric than that of our birth-planet, giving you brief, warm summers and very long, cold winters. Men restructured you genetically to fit in this environment as intelligent life. The ancient geneticists must have chosen you for this world because you metamorphose. You can survive the winter as a pupa or, in the case of spiders and some of the other insects, as an egg. That was long ago, according to the way man experiences time. We have lost all records of having populated this planet. Before our flying hive leaves, there is much about your life cycles we would like to relearn."

"It will please us to tell you," said the butterfly. "There is a spider at my hunting ground who, I am certain, will delight in talking to you for a whole day." The butterfly was somewhat puzzled by the workings of the Man's mind. Evidently the Man had started to tell him the reason why the Men who had shaped the creatures had not stayed, and why now these Men would have to depart quickly. However, the Man had strayed from the subject. But perhaps the butterfly knew the reason without being told.

"Now that we know what the flying hive is," he said, "its blankness is far less disturbing. It is quite tolerable, in fact. You need not go quickly on that account."

"That is not why we must leave," said the Man. "If it were, we could solve our problem quite easily by allowing you to enter the flying hive and investigate its contents until it ceased to be a blank. You may do that, anyway, for that matter."

"Then why must you go?" the butterfly asked.

The Man replied hesitantly. "Because it may not be good for men to associate too much with you. Not bad for you, but bad for men. Tell me, butterfly, do you know that on the birth-planet men regarded you as the most beautiful creature in existence?"

"No."

"Neither did I—since I had never seen a butterfly until today. Nor even a picture of one. That is the reason for the incidents earlier this morning. I wish to apologize for not recognizing you and the ants and bees."

"That's all right," replied the butterfly. "We didn't recognize you either."

"Anyway, you are the most beautiful creature that I've ever seen on any world, excepting of course certain females of my own kind," the Man went on. "And in your mutated form, which has increased your size and given you a unique intelligence, you impress us as being—totally admirable. Man sees no other creature that way. And what men admire, they try to imitate in themselves."

He hesitated, then finished hurriedly and almost angrily: "If men stayed here, they would wind up being fake butterflies, trying to look and think like you when they can do neither. It's best for us to stay away from your world and continue being men, whatever that may be."

The butterfly found this speech astonishing to the point of incomprehensibility, the final words no less than what came before. "But you made us as we are," he protested. "Surely you know your superiority to us."

"No."

"You do not know the now-moment," the butterfly persisted, "but isn't that for a reason similar to my not remembering in the manner of the spider? The thought comes to me that perhaps you combine remembering and knowing in a way I cannot comprehend, to know all moments that have been or will be."

The man made a sound signifying amusement. "That is a flattering thought. It attributes to us the supreme knowledge we sometimes imagine in our own gods—the hypothetical beings who created all life. No, we don't have that kind of knowing. And the fact that you have part of it is a reason why men must avoid you. They would tend to consider you half-gods."

This, to the butterfly, was monstrous. "But surely you must have some form of knowing . . ." he began.

The Man was shaking his head. "Men have seen much and learned much. And we know much. But not as you know."

Suddenly the butterfly understood and gazed at the Man with awe. To know the now-moment, he realized dimly, was a complete thing, and what was complete was limited to its totality. Man's knowing had no completeness—no limits—because Man did not even know himself.

Breathing hard in the thin mountain air, the butterfly marveled at the boundless wonder of Man.

ONLY YESTERDAY

Ted White

Ted White and I go way back. He grew up as an ornery fan, doing many fine fan articles and engaging in fannish fracases, and broke into pro print about the time I did, in early 1963. Later he took over the editing of Amazing Stories and Fantastic Stories, when Barry Malzberg departed, and had the great good sense to serialize my novels Hasan and Orn there. But those who engage in the melee of fractious fandom are not universally liked, especially when they are good at it (and he was one of the very best infighters), and so his personality and his writing have at times been denigrated. (I know; I've done some of it myself.) He has been considered by some to be the epitome of insensitivity, but I, having dealt with him on both personal and professional levels, have a fairly solid respect for his talents. He fights hard, and he makes some mistakes, but he has done some very good work. He had an almost impossible situation at Amazing, as I suspect Barry Malzberg will agree, yet did a quite creditable job there. As a writer, too, he has been underrated. I read one of his juveniles (and these are not all that easy to do well)—my memory may betray me, but I think it was The Secret of the Marauder Satellite—and found it to be an excellent novel of the type, that I think should have had more recognition than it got. Insensitive? No—Ted White is sensitive, and this story shows it.

—PA

Ted White did a magnificent job at Amazing. I was his predecessor. Trust me.

—bnm

He was waiting for her when she stepped down from the trolley. The grass was dry and dead under his feet, and the crisp air

291

made his nose run. He pulled a tissue from the packet in his overcoat pocket, blew into it, wadded it, looked around at the straight lines of the tracks, the receding trolley, the brown fields, the little half-open waiting shed in which he stood—then self-consciously shoved the used tissue back in his pocket.

The overhead wire was still singing. The girl's step on the cinders as she started across the tracks was loud and crisp. She was the only one to get off. She gave him a quizzical glance, then turned diagonally to his left to the well-worn path that cut across the fields. In the distance wooded hills rose darkly; closer—less than a quarter of a mile away—were a cluster of white-painted frame houses. The path headed in their direction.

Snuffling, he started after her.

"Ah, miss?" he called.

She stopped and turned, facing him. She was carrying a leather bag, a briefcase really, with a shoulder strap. It bulged and it looked heavy. He fought down the giddy impulse to ask her if he could carry her books.

"Yes?"

"You're—ah, Donna Albright?"

She started to nod, then shook her head. "You're half right. I'm Donna Smith."

He felt like doing something violent, like smacking his head with the palm of his hand. God, he felt tense about this. Instead he mumbled something incomprehensible and then said, "Umm, yes. That's what I meant. Donna Smith, I mean. My mistake."

He looked young; younger than he was. He'd shaved off his beard and he looked eighteen. He felt nervous and ill at ease. His stomach was knotted and he could still taste breakfast. He wondered why in hell he was doing this. God, she was pretty.

"Okay, so I'm Donna Smith. Were you waiting for me?"

Her brown hair was long, and hung in tight curls from under her cloche hat. The hat looked stupid, he thought; they always had. Her eyes were dark, and an impish smile lurked behind her lips. She was a lot prettier than the old photographs. He tried to think of something to say. He'd planned lots of things: clever, witty things. They were all evaporated by the reality of the scene.

"Uh, I wonder if I might, uh, walk with you . . . ?" He felt himself flush. God, there it was: the schoolbooks gambit!

She laughed. "Okay. But I warn you—I have a pair of husky brothers at home." Her tone implied she didn't think they'd be necessary, though. He fell into step beside her; the path was a wide one. "But who are you, though?" she asked.

His fingers fidgeted with the tissues in his overcoat pocket. He'd worn that coat—the one he'd gotten from the Salvation Army—because it had seemed appropriate for the time. If he didn't take it off or open it, the clothes he had under it wouldn't matter. But now . . . well, what was he going to tell her? What *could* he tell her?

"Uh, I'm Bob," he said. The name felt clumsy on his lips, but he'd agreed not to use his real name. He remembered one of the lines he'd rehearsed. "I'm a friend of a friend, sorta . . ."

"Oh! Are you one of the guys Griff knows, down in Richmond?"

He started to deny it, then agreed.

"Have you been in the city? I mean, did you come out from Washington?"

"I was on an earlier trolley," he replied truthfully. The eight-mile trip had been quite an experience. The wooden-bodied car had swayed alarmingly from side to side as it took the long downstretch onto private right-of-way outside Rosslyn, across the bridge from Georgetown. The grade-schoolers, laughing and shouting back and forth up and down the aisle, had just whooped a little louder when the car hit the bend and then the upgrade again, and he'd clawed the worn seatback in front of him like the guard bar on a roller coaster. "I wanted to see the countryside," he added.

"This part of Virginia is very pretty in the fall," Donna said, "but you missed the best part. I mean, when the trees turn colors. That was a couple of weeks ago; it's been a short fall. It's getting cold so fast. I expect we'll have snow soon. You can kind of smell it, you know?"

He snuffled again. "My sinuses," he offered in explanation. He dug another tissue from his pocket. It was half shredded; he'd been working it with his fingers. He pulled the cellophane packet and found a whole one. He blew on it. He glanced up to see Donna's large eyes staring at him, and he felt his face get hot again. Packets of pastel tissues—anachronistic? He hadn't thought.

The path dipped into a hollow, then crossed a stream gully on a wooden bridge. He felt very uncomfortable. The cold had started in his feet and worked well up his legs while he'd waited for her there at the trolley stop. Now he was chilled all over, and walking hadn't warmed his feet; it had only deadened them.

"You certainly are the strange one," Donna said.

He laughed nervously. He sure was.

"Uh, tell me: what year are you in college? You go to American U, don't you?"

She laughed. "Sophomore. I had a room with a girl in town last year, but I couldn't keep it up. It's almost as easy to come home nights. Good old AU. . . ." Her voice trailed off almost dreamily. He realized he'd given her nothing, really, to say.

"Yeah, Griff told me about that," he said, trying to keep it going.

They reached the road. It was graveled clay, tufts of frost-killed weeds growing here and there down the center. They skirted an ice-filmed puddle. He glanced to the west. The sun was a weak, washed-out red blob half hidden in the tree line. Getting dark.

She noticed his glance. "Be home soon. You'll come in? Hot chocolate, tea, coffee?"

He agreed, grateful at the thought of something warm to drink. Then panic hit him: face her parents, her brothers? *Could* he?

The houses were to the left, grouped along the road about two hundred yards from where the path came out. Mott's Corners. Old Man Mott had put them up for each of his children. He followed Donna to the right, following the road down a gentle slope. Donna kicked a rock that skittered along the worn track of the road and splashed into another puddle.

The sound of the car saved him from a final desperate attempt at conversation. He heard it before he saw it: a wheezing, rattling, four-banger with a muffler that had to be about shot. Then it appeared over the hill to their left, heading down a side road on a collision course with theirs. At first only its high square roof was visible over the tall tangled weeds of the field. The field was fenced off with two strands of rusty barbed wire, but he couldn't see that they served much of a purpose.

"Hey, there's Jimmy!" Donna said. "It's my brother Jimmy!" She jumped up and down and waved her arm at the approaching car.

The car answered with a raucous honk and then, with a clatter of gravel, made the turn at the foot of the hill onto their road. It was bearing down on them so fast that he made a hasty jump into the weeds at the side of the road.

"Hey!" Donna shouted, and the car jolted to a stop in front of them. It was a Model T, black. The top was frayed and the side curtains flapped loosely. The driver was a freckled kid with a wide grin. He had to be at least three years underage for a license.

"Hiya, Donna! How'dya like it? I got her running again! Thought I'd come over and pick ya up. You're late. Who's this?"

Jimmy. James Smith. It was hard to believe.

"This is Bob. He's a friend of Griff's. He's come out for the evening. He's half frozen, I think. I'm glad you came along." Donna introduced them, and Jimmy gave him a salute and waved them aboard.

The car had a nominal backseat, but all that was left was an old orange crate. He squatted on it and peered over the cracked leather back of the front seat as Donna settled next to her brother and Jimmy ground the gears to begin a lurching crawl backwards.

They backed to the intersection, then turned up the short hill. The color had faded from the sky. The farmland had the brown tinge of sepia-tone photographs. The world seemed very thin then: two-dimensional, attic-dry and musty. But at the same time every pothole the car struck was another jolt to his cold-deadened body, the car had an overpowering gasoline smell that cut through even his clogged sinuses, and Donna's head was so close to his face as he leaned forward that he could feel the heat of her skin. Getting schizy?

The car topped the rise, then raced wildly down the slope and up a more gradual grade. Ahead, two windows warm glows in the blackness of its tar-paper exterior, stood the Smith house.

Jimmy swerved the car across the hard ruts, over the rough ground, and halted it with a screech from its mechanical brakes within inches of the footings for the new wing.

Tall oaks hung like black skeletons over the narrow two-story house, a few tattered leaves still clinging to their branches. The house itself was only half finished; he recognized that without Donna's quick remark, "Dad and the boys've been building the house in their spare time; it's still got some to go." There was a note of pride in her voice, but the porch was only a rude platform without a roof, the north wing was just a line of trenches, and the siding wasn't on yet—thin strips of furring that followed the interior studs were all that held the tar paper over the subframe walls. There was no yard in front. Behind and to one side was the chicken house and chicken yard. But the garage hadn't been built next to it yet, and a truck garden showed its empty furrows on the other side of the house. It was a rude place. When he climbed awkwardly down from the car, he almost tripped over an engine block. Jimmy apologized. "Chevy engine," he said. "Next spring, boy . . ."

Dad Smith was a big man; he looked more like a lantern-jawed Swede than a mathematician whose parents were from Liverpool. He had a full head of bushy brown hair, and his high forehead was still clear of liver spots. He stuck out his bony hand and it was engulfing. "Friend of Griff's, huh?" Smith said, nodding. "How they treating Griff down there?"

"As well as you'd expect," he replied with a nervous laugh.

"I expect as long's you're here, you'll want to go up to the Ballards' for a chat?"

He shook his head, then improvised. "Actually, I don't know Griff that well . . . I mean, when I said I'd be out in this neck of the woods, he said to say hi to Donna, and . . . Well, I didn't expect to do more than, uh, just that. Just a 'Hi,' and . . . well, I'm pushing my schedule a bit already, sir." Damn that Griff Ballard story, anyway! And damn Donna for going around so much with him, too. Of course, the Ballards and the Smiths were neighbors, and when she'd suggested it, he'd picked up on Griff as a likely introduction, so . . .

"This is my mother, Bob."

Mrs. Smith was tiny standing next to her husband. She had come from the doorway that led to the kitchen, wiping her hands slowly and carefully on her apron. When she spoke, it was with a touch of the Midwest—Iowa, he remembered—as she welcomed him and asked what he'd like to drink.

Soon he was settled in a comfortable chair, a mug of hot chocolate in his hand. A potbellied iron stove in the corner radiated a warm glow into the cozy room, and the smell of woodsmoke and occasional crackling of the burning logs was strangely nostalgia-evoking. He felt a warming tingle return to his toes.

"Where's Paul?" Donna asked, once she had him out of his coat and settled with the chocolate.

"Upstairs," Mr. Smith said, eyes twinkling. "Pitching pennies."

"Oh, Dad! Not again! Don't you have enough statistics by now?"

"I'll run up and get him," Jimmy volunteered.

So far no one had said anything about his clothes. "Pitching pennies?" he asked.

"Dad's a statistician—he's with the Bureau of Standards, in Washington," Donna said. She let the smile quirk up the corners of her mouth. It seemed to include him in their private joke; it made her delicately impish. "He's always got us doing things like that."

A clumping on the stairs heralded Paul, Jimmy right behind him.

"How goes it?" Mr. Smith asked.

"Cold," replied Paul, laconically. You could see he took after his father—the same big frame, bushy hair, lumberjack look, only thinner, younger. *He hasn't changed much.* "The longest run was thirteen heads."

"You have the register open?" his father asked. There was an opening in the ceiling over the stove for hot air to move into the upstairs rooms.

"I lose too many pennies that way." Paul's expression didn't change.

"Paul, this is Bob. He's a—a friend of Griff's," Donna said.

He pulled himself up out of the chair and offered his hand to Paul. Paul gave it a negligent shake, and him a vague nod. He seemed not at all interested in the boyfriends of his young sister.

"You make chocolate?" Paul asked. "I could use some; keep my hands warm, anyway."

Donna frowned, but went out to the kitchen.

He felt awkward, standing like that, so he returned to his seat with a strange guilty little knot tight in his stomach. *He had no business here.*

When Donna returned with another steaming mug, a calico cat followed her out. The cat stalked immediately over to him and sniffed at his shoes. He smiled, leaned over, and held out his hand. The cat gave one brief sniff, then turned tail and retreated to the kitchen.

"Don't mind Paul," Jimmy said, inclining his head toward the stairs. Above, a door shut. "He's that way with everybody. He's going for his doctorate next spring."

"Mathematics?" he asked, surprised.

"English," Jimmy replied.

"Jimmy," Mr. Smith said, rising from his rocker. "Time for the chores." He led the way to the door, lifting down a tent of an old coat from the peg to the right of the door. A moment later, the front door slammed shut and the stove chucked to itself in the fresh onslaught of cold air.

They were alone then, the two of them, by themselves in the sudden silence of the room. From the kitchen came the clang of a cast-iron skillet on the heavy metal top of the old wood-burning kitchen stove. Above them, floorboards creaked at odd moments.

She was staring at him. Again he asked himself, *What am I doing in this place?* But he made no move to get up.

Nervously fingering his narrow lapel, he broke the silence, saying, "I'd like to tell you some things . . . Totally outrageous things. You have to promise me just one thing first."

"What's that?" Her voice was soft. Their voices would not carry beyond the room.

"That you won't believe a word of it." That was weaseling, and he knew it. He wasn't supposed to be doing this. *This was forbidden*.

She giggled, and in that moment he was starkly aware of her youth. "Okay," she said. "Shoot."

What was he supposed to be? Could he just enter her life like this and leave it again, without telling her *any* of the truth? "I'm going to try to tell your fortune," he said, lying. It wouldn't be hers.

"You want to see my palm?"

He laughed. "Not that sort of fortune. I am going to close my eyes and see your aura, your fourth-dimensional aura. I am going to follow it into the future and tell you what I see for you there. . . ." He squeezed shut his eyes; they felt dry and stinging. He paused. He felt as though his voice might break.

"Well?" She leaned forward eagerly. "What do you see?"

"I see you meeting a tall man with black hair," he said. "You're going to marry him."

She laughed. "I thought you knew Griff," she said. "He's short and blond."

He nodded. "That's true. . . . I—I see great metal airliners with wings as big as this house, airplanes that can carry hundreds of people, scores of cars or trucks. They're flying so high overhead that the sound they make follows across the sky far behind them, they're so fast and far away. I see, I see great rockets, tall as high buildings, poised like bullets to shoot out into space and to the moon. . . .

"I see sleek, low automobiles built of plastic and shimmering with iridescent colors, streaking along vast highways at speeds over a hundred miles an hour. I see . . . radios the size of cigarette packages . . . Phono—uh, gramophones that play hour-long records . . . Television sets that receive wireless broadcasts of color pictures on their own screens . . ."

She laughed again. "Oh, I've seen all those! The *Times-Herald* Sunday supplements are full of that sort of stuff."

She shouldn't have laughed.

"I see war," he said. His voice tore from his throat, and his expression was tight and twisted. "War, beyond any war you've dreamed. Bombs—so many bombs exploding over cities that the very air itself catches fire. And the airplanes that carry the bombs—so many hundreds of them that they blacken the sky. I see whole countries—continents, even—devastated, laid waste.

"A war to end all wars," he went on bitterly. "But more wars follow, more boys die, and the bombs get bigger, until a single bomb can wipe out a city the size of New York.

"I see populations growing unchecked, squalid slums and mass poverty and starvation, creeping over the world. I see death, and destruction—hatreds that tear this country apart by its roots. I see our cities collapsing in riots, mobs thronging the streets looting and killing, and the soldiers coming out in tanks and firing their guns at their countrymen.

"I see napalm washing liquid fire over a mother who sits in a gutter holding her dead baby—"

"Stop!"

He opened his eyes. She was staring at him, shocked, wide-eyed. Her cheeks glistened.

"Why? Why are you saying all these things?"

"I—I'm sorry," he said. "I shouldn't have." His voice shook. "I told you, you weren't to believe me."

"I don't. Maybe we're in a Great Depression, like they say, but that's no reason to talk like *that.*"

"You're right," he said. She was right. He'd been warned. "It was a bum idea. Forget it."

"You made it all up." It wasn't quite a statement.

He nodded. "Yes," he said, "yes, I made it all up. I guess I get depressed sometimes. Things—like the Hoovervilles, you know." His mug was empty and cold. He got up. "I better go now."

She looked up at him. "You're very strange," she said.

You should only know.

"Thanks for the hospitality," he said. "Thank your mother for the hot chocolate, please." He pulled on his overcoat. "Say goodbye for me to Jimmy, Paul . . ."

"Bob—" She put her hands on his and looked up at him. He couldn't keep his eyes from hers. "I . . . You *were* making it all up?"

He felt disoriented and distant. He seemed to be staring down a long tunnel into her eyes, while somewhere else, in another place, her hands were warm and soft and alive on his.

"I'll close my eyes once more," he said. "Ahh . . . I see you, married, happy, in a sunlit yard beside a red-brick house. It's close by here; your father will give you the land to build on." Only her hands held him from swaying in the darkness that engulfed him. "I see no wars, only sunshine, for you," he said. It was the truth—as far as it went. He owed her at least that much.

"I believe you," she said.

The stars were cold and hard and bright, and the frosty air cut his throat. Underfoot, frozen grass crunched. Woodenly, his whole body feeling at once adrenalated and drained, Donald Albright followed the almost-familiar rutted road back down the hill. He did not see where he was walking. He could still smell her hair, still feel her soft handclasp. Wherever he looked, her dark eyes seemed to stare back at him. She was so young, so pretty, so . . . innocent. He began to shake with hard dry sobs.

Mother, he thought. *Why did you have to die? Before I could even know you—?*

AN AGENT IN PLACE

Laurence M. Janifer

*The author is a year or so older than I am, and started ap-
pearing in print a decade or so earlier, but I suspect I have
picked up a bit of ground since then. I can't say for certain that
I have read any of his fiction other than this present piece,
though probably I have. I am aware of him for two discon-
nected reasons. First, there is something about the way his
name starts that appeals to me, though it bears about the same
relation to his mundane one as does mine; had I not gone to a
literary pseudonym, I would have been jammed next to him in
the JA's, instead of finding myself squeezed between Anderson
and Asimov. It took me a good decade to elbow those two far
enough apart to give me shelf room at the bookstore. I suspect
Janifer would have been kinder. Second, he once wrote, in a
fanzine (amateur genre magazine), one of the most bitter and
significant statements to appear in print. He said that those
who fight to get better contract terms may be deceiving themselves, because (here I set up as a direct quote what I remember only approximately, may the author of the original forgive
me) "the publisher will not honor the contract." This is the
dirty little secret that all hopeful writers should have graven on
their keyboards. You won't see it in how-to-write books, you
won't hear it in writing seminars, but it is a truth that got me
blacklisted for a number of years at several outfits, because I insisted that publishers honor their contracts. Janifer is the only
one I know of who had the guts to say it in print, and I don't
know what price he paid for that, but I have respected him for
it ever since. I regard him as a kindred soul—which is to say an
ornery cuss. More recently, writers' organizations have tried—
largely in vain, I suspect—to get publishers to honor their
agreements, but back when Janifer said it, he was alone.*

—PA

* * *

Laurence M. Janifer, born on St. Patrick's Day in the month of FDR's inauguration, is the author of several science-fiction novels both alone and in collaboration (three about telepathic spies, teleporting juvenile delinquents, and omnipotent directors of the FBI were written with Randall Garrett and, as published serially in the 1959–1961 Astounding *were probably the only good longer work which JWC was printing in that period). He is also the author of close to a hundred science-fiction short stories, of which the following, published in a 1973* Analog, *was both remarkably of its time and modestly prognosticative in its circumstance, inducing that frisson which close-in science fiction, competently done, can give.*

—bnm

It will be very interesting to find out whether I can write this one down and get it published. I'm asking a science-fiction writer to polish it for me, and it will go out under his byline if only because a habit of anonymity is hard to break; but none of that should make any difference. Whatever else they have their eye on, and I know they're spread thin, they have their eye on me. There is no doubt of that.

Which sounds paranoid until you know the facts. Such as my profession, which is Special Agent, and who *they* are. They're Central Intelligence—not the CIA, though around Washington we've mostly given up trying to make the distinction; Congress can think what it likes, and our appropriation comes out of the "Miscellaneous" barrel anyhow. CIA is mostly an international net specializing in data recovery, though like everybody else they take on other jobs now and then. Central Intelligence is "specifically nonspecialist," as the Director put it once to a House Committee: we do a little of everything from spy-eye work to protective guarding, and sometimes we make a connection that somebody looking at only one area might miss. We don't get into the news much but we earn our pay. Until recently I didn't know just how thoroughly we earned our pay. But, as I said, they're spread thin. This report may have a chance of getting through. And you might like to know where our small piece of your tax dollar is going.

The Director was telling me that he had access to files "not quite as extensive as Hollywood's Central Casting, but adequate for our purposes," and I was wondering just what sort of impersonation deal I was up for, since to my knowledge I didn't look much like anybody in the news. It had to be that: why mention Central Casting otherwise?

So I slumped a little in the chair next to his desk, and took one long, sad drag on my cigarette, and said: "All right, sir. Who am I supposed to be?"

He didn't congratulate me on the deduction. He wastes very little time. "You don't like impersonation work, I take it?"

"Frankly, sir: no," I said. "You're loaded with makeup and memorization, and you have nothing to do but wait until somebody tries to pot you. It may be useful; it may even be necessary now and then; but it's depressing."

"This isn't quite the usual thing," he said. He frowned at my cigarette. He'd given me a lecture about the Surgeon General once—but only once. "There isn't much makeup, and there isn't much memory. You're going to be triggered for one phrase—we can do that under depth hypnosis, but I'll tell you what the phrase is and what your action will be; beyond that, we won't tamper with you at all."

The Director is very big on keeping things as open as he can with the rest of us. I've heard him say that we were "valued professional aides, and not chess pieces"—in that same Committee hearing. It irritates me to think about that, now.

"And nobody will try to pot me?" I said. "It *sounds* unusual."

"Well . . . ." He pushed an ashtray across the desk to me and I stubbed out the cigarette. "I wouldn't quite go that far," he said. Which made matters clear, if not comforting.

"All right," I said. "So . . . who's in danger? Who am I supposed to be?"

"A man named Welkin—Beer Barrel Dave Welkin," he said. "And, as for who's in danger—"

He went on with quite a speech about the election year, and everybody being in danger, the spate of assassinations in this country since 1963, the job the FBI and the Treasury men were trying to do, and the fact that we were spread so thin we couldn't cover every danger spot or even every possible target: "We have to confine ourselves to what we can see and know, which isn't much," he said, but I was trying to get Beer Barrel reduced to a nickname instead of an insult. It isn't the beer anyhow, and never has been; it's the way I'm built.

By the time he was through I was calmed down enough on Beer

Barrel to realize that I had never heard of anybody named Dave Welkin, with or without the descriptive pendant.

"Welkin," I said. "All right, sir. If you say so. Who is he?"

"Oh," the Director said, "he's a bum. A Bowery bum."

I didn't ask, "Why?" because I don't like wasted time either. If he'd wanted me to know why he'd have told me; he really does like to be as open as he can with us. Of course he has to decide how open that is.

All the same, as I was picking up what background there was on Beer Barrel Dave Welkin, letting my beard grow, allowing Cosmetics to skin-tone me an unattractive and very dirty gray, and getting used to the clothing, both for wear and for smell, I was trying to get the answer for myself.

All I had to go on was that the job wouldn't last over thirty days, and that the hypnotic-trigger business was the phrase *Czechoslovakian boundary disputes*, which, when I heard it, was going to make me move rapidly toward whoever had said it. It was a good trigger; wandering around the Bowery I wasn't likely to hear it by accident.

I learned that Beer Barrel Dave Welkin would be held under hypnotics in a New York cubbyhole of ours, returnable after I reported in, and I learned that he had a great fondness for beer, had been on the Bowery "over five years" and was about my age, though he looked fifteen or twenty years older, and that his preferred method of panhandling was heading for crowds and bumping his way through them. He sounded as if he might have wanted to be a pickpocket if he'd been a little less bleary; as it was, he probably thought that crowds gave him more handout chances per square panhandling foot.

The trigger sounded as if I were in for a political impersonation job, but nothing else did; Beer Barrel Dave (after the first few days I got so I could hear the phrase without wincing, even inside) was hardly the type. And as far as I knew—and I think I'd know—there were no Czechoslovakian boundary disputes going on anywhere in the world, unless you count a perennial tendency toward revolt against Moscow as a boundary dispute.

I came up with quite an assortment of theories. The first notion was that I was being sent in as an agent in place—an inconspicuous type who does nothing at all until the word comes through, and then pops up from within an organization and starts wrecking it. But agents in place have tours of duty that tend to start at twenty years and go straight on up; and moving toward a person who spoke a single phrase didn't look much like helping to wreck anything. Not to mention the fact that nobody could call the collection of Bowery bums among whom Beer Barrel spent his time an organization, and even if it was it didn't look like one anybody was very anxious to overthrow.

The big question was: Who would want to pot a Bowery bum? And for that I developed a variety of ingenious answers. Here are a few:

1. The bum had managed to drift by and hear part of a supersecret conversation, maybe involving some brand-new scientific breakthrough, and couldn't be left alive to repeat it to anybody else. Objection: Supersecret conversations are seldom carried on around the Bowery, and it was doubtful that, if he'd heard anything, Beer Barrel would retain much of it for any longer than ten minutes—recoverable under hypnosis, maybe, but that implies that you know exactly who and what to look for. Improbable.

2. The bum had picked up a bit of some supersecret scientific paper, and had to be rubbed out before he could pass it on. Objection: The same as 1. To begin with, there is really very little supersecrecy going on near the Bowery. And one other question hard to answer: Why would Beer Barrel hang on to the paper? If he did happen to stuff it into the one pocket of his clothing that didn't have a large hole in it, what was so tough about simply getting the paper back, and letting Beer Barrel drift on down the street? Of course, if he'd read the paper, and it was known that he'd read it, the contents might be recoverable hypnotically . . . but that chain of reasoning gets even more improbable than the previous one. No.

3. The bum was really an agent in place for somebody else. That made a certain amount of superficial sense until I wondered about the thirty-day limit, and about returning Beer Barrel to the Bowery after the job was over. The usual procedure with agents in place, if discovered, is either (a) watch carefully, and try to dig up the communications link and from there the rest of the apparatus, or (b) dispose of immediately. This didn't fit either procedure, and I couldn't come up with any reasons why not.

4. The bum was really a being from outer space, and . . .

Well, that will give you an idea. What I'd be doing impersonating a being from outer space who was impersonating a

Bowery bum, for thirty days or less, I was completely unable to imagine.

And what any of these ideas, or any one of several others I dreamed up, had to do with my hypnotic trigger and response, I couldn't see at all. The thing was, as far as I could get into it, absolutely senseless; the only trouble was that we're not much given to senseless assignments.

Though that gave me a brand-new idea: suppose the whole thing were a loyalty test, designed to see how far I'd follow orders even if I didn't and couldn't understand the reasons for them. . . .

I've been with Central Intelligence since 1947. It was a very strange time to pull a loyalty test on me, after twenty-five years.

That was my last theory. By the time I had tossed it out I was on Third Avenue near Canal Street, and I was Beer Barrel Dave Welkin.

Three weeks went by as quickly as if they'd been decades.

You have no idea how slowly time passes for a Bowery bum who doesn't drink very much. I spent all of the time I wasn't sleeping in a scratch room or an alley, or panhandling for small change in the cheap bars that straggle all the way up to Fourteenth Street, but I did a lot less beer drinking than I seemed to be doing. I couldn't afford to be too hazy when the trigger came, or I'd miss hearing it, or be unable to move quickly, or something. And there are a lot of simple techniques for getting rid of a drink without making it obvious you're doing so—especially around the Bowery, where getting rid of a drink is just not what people are looking to see happen.

I found a lot of crowds, mostly at the uptown end of my run: the Bowery meets both NYU and the East Village up there, and Stuyvesant Town is only two blocks away from Fourteenth and Third, so I made my way through a variety of student rallies, young-politics meetings, just plain political rallies, and an assortment of rush hours, mostly evening: Beer Barrel didn't usually get up too early.

There was, of course, one candidate most of the students and youngsters favored; you know all about that. Normally, maybe he'd have left the whole area off his speech route, but he needed some big youth-appeal and student-appeal footage for the evening TV shows, so he scheduled an appearance at Union Square—the uptown western edge of my daily travels—for a Friday evening.

Naturally, there was a crowd, a nice big one.

Naturally, Beer Barrel Dave was on hand.

And just as naturally, that speech went on for fifteen minutes and hit the sentence I was, by then, half expecting:

"It is not in our interest—in the interest of the people of this country—to charge out to settle every possible disagreement in the world, from possible arguments over Japanese fishing rights to putative Czechoslovakian boundary disputes—"

And I was triggered. I started for the candidate a good deal faster than Beer Barrel Dave was used to moving.

Of course I never reached him. Somebody potted me instead.

I woke up in our New York cubbyhole, hospital section—where the original Beer Barrel had been stacked away while I worked his tour. I had a large ragged hole in one shoulder, and a variety of bruises and abrasions from hitting the pavement and being slightly trampled in the rush to collect the character who'd tried to shoot the candidate. He was collected, naturally, before he could get off another shot, and a small bag of psychiatrists is still going around and around about whether or not he's sane, or legally insane, or what. The one sure thing—and it *is* sure: our section checked it out, and we don't report what we don't know for certain—is that he was an individual, acting entirely on his own, with a specific grudge against this one candidate.

So I found out what my assignment had been. Bodyguard for the candidate, against an assassination attempt.

For a little while, this made no sense at all to me. You've probably ironed out all the wrinkles, but it took me a little longer, being under medication while the shoulder put itself back together.

Obviously, we can see into the future.

We can't see very far, and we can't see anything but the specific matter we try to see (or, first, there'd have been no attempt at all, and, second, there would *never* be a successful attempt—I hope; but wait around). But we can look through time and see a tiny piece of the near future.

Which is changeable.

Somebody saw that the shot was going to be fired right after that *boundary dispute,* and that it would hit the candidate unless deflected. Now, guards are one thing: people are used to guards, what with the President and his Secret Service and all. But a bullet-proof shield, completely surrounding the candidate, is something else again. A lot of people would feel it made the candidate look like a coward, or somehow made a personal appearance no better than a TV spot, or . . . anyhow, politicians and their managers feel that way even about the breast-height combination shield-and-podium gimmick that's now being used here and there. I've heard them. A whole bulletproof shield? Ridiculous, they'd say. Lose the election right then and there.

(Which may or may not be logical, or reasonable. But politicians and political managers aren't logical or reasonable except in spots—thereby making them fair copies of the rest of us.)

No, the only acceptable deflection for a bullet is a special agent, I suppose. Somebody, maybe, took a look and saw that, in one possible future, I would be just where I was in the crowd, and I started moving toward the candidate at just the right time. Then matters were carefully gimmicked so that I was set up in the crowd (apparently just that much gave them a future which put me in the right spot inside that crowd) and started moving on cue, at speed.

Sure. Somebody juggled alternatives. Let the bullet hit its mark; let it hit me instead; bulletproof the candidate (out, unacceptable, ridiculous); get the assassin out of the way beforehand; arrest him on the spot with his weapon—and, out of that bag and one or two more minor possibilities (maybe in one future the bullet hit some *really* innocent bystander), somebody settled for me. Beer Barrel Dave Welkin, the human target. The fat and tattered X marking the safest spot.

I think I know why.

Let's say that the future involved a successful assassination. If it's going to be changed, two things have to be considered, and the first of these, simply, is: What's the least possible change required? Clearly, you don't want to add in any more factors than you have to, because every new factor has new results of its own, and so forth . . . so you find a real Bowery bum, someone who would legitimately be in that crowd anyhow. And you replace him (keeping the bum in cold storage, so to speak, and putting him back on the street in a slightly damaged condition, with a hole in his memory due to a month under hypnotics—but a hole in a bum's memory is just not all that unusual, especially after he's been, theoretically, shot at and trampled some); that way the bum's life goes on with minimal interruption and no stir anywhere, and the replacement is a setup to intercept the bullet. Given a shut mouth and a career of other odd actions for the replacement type, anyhow, you get the least possible amount of change.

The second thing to be considered, I'm afraid, is that you want to keep your time viewing top secret. (Which is why you don't even *mention* a bulletproof wraparound to the candidate's people—not even if one of them, in a fit of political insanity, might agree.) Hauling in the assassin beforehand needs explanation—in these days of maximum courtroom civil liberty, it needs a *lot* of explanation. Grabbing him with his gun, on the spot, needs explaining, too: it's hard to say that he got careless and made it visible too soon, when he did his shooting, with that short-barreled .38, through the pocket of his jacket, and never showed the gun at all. (And maybe, in the future or futures that carried that alternative, the guy managed to get off a shot or two while being grabbed . . . and hit somebody more consequential than old Beer Barrel.)

No: being able to see the future, and wanting to keep the ability secret, is the only explanation that fits the facts.

When I got out of my hospital bed I asked the Director about it. "Our job is doing our job," he said, "not wondering about it."

Which may be true. But . . . whoever can see into the future, right now, in the United States, is also involved in changing it. For the better? That depends . . . what do you mean by *better?* In this country, it's supposed to be the people who do the deciding; but if somebody is rigging the dice by choosing his own favorites among possible futures . . . (See what I mean? Are you sure that this Somebody would *never* allow a successful assassination?) . . . then Somebody is doing enough deciding, all by himself, to deserve that capital letter. And that is an idea I don't like at all.

The Director knows how I think about public knowledge and public decision making: my dossier's on file, and has been for twenty-five years. And he knows I know about time viewing, too. So, no matter how thin observers are spread, I know that whoever, or Whoever, does the viewing, in Central Intelligence or further up the line, has an eye on me.

But maybe not all the time—and not very far into the future.

And just maybe, when I come to think of it, the viewers, too, want the rest of us to know that such a thing exists and is being used—and picked me for the impersonation job at least partly because they knew I *would* do something like this. Letting the news out this way looks to me like doing it with a minimal amount of change. . . .

I hope that's it, I really do; it would show that, up there in the higher echelons, there is as much faith in the people as I hope there is, and think there had better be. But we'll find out. . . .

I'm writing this four months after the event. It will be very interesting, as I've said, to see if it gets through.

AFTERWORD

Barry N. Malzberg

Science fiction—I am borrowing from an introduction to another
anthology Martin Greenberg and I put together seven years ago,
but what the heck, self-plagiarism is not an indictable offense—
science fiction, as I was saying, has done a better job than most
other genres of literature in preserving and recycling its finer work,
but nothing is perfect, and a surprising amount has slipped through
the cracks. There are writers as good as many of our household
names who have virtually fallen out of print and are unknown to
most contemporary readers. And there are stories of quality which
were *never* reprinted after their initial magazine appearances. That
is the premise of this anthology.

Despite the fact that "Nightfall," "By His Bootstraps," and
"The Cold Equations" have been reprinted 5,271,009 times
(apiece), there are stories of the most remarkable achievement
which fell into oblivion, were never preserved. In some cases the
reasons are fairly obvious . . . the stories were by unknown
writers, one-shot appearances, or were (like Fred Brown's "Martians Go Home!" *Astounding*, 1954) dry runs for novels which,
expanding upon them, made preservation of the shorter version
seen as redundant. (Even if the short stories were better than the
eventual novels, as I take to be the case with "Martians Go
Home!") In other instances, the exclusion seems absolutely anom-
alous . . . the wondrous "Unwillingly to School" was cited by
Damon Knight as the best first story in the genre in years and years
and made Judith Merrill's annual year's best honor roll, and yet
this is, to our astonishment, the first appearance of the story since
original publication almost three decades ago. And in other instances yet, there is an explanation of a weak sort . . . Kuttner's
"Time Enough" is by a very prolific writer whose stories of that
period were being recycled from anthology to anthology, but the
first nets cast missed this story and future anthologists, perhaps be-

cause of the miserable illustrator (may he rot), missed it. In fact, there are probably as many explanations as there are uncollected stars; science fiction is a branch of literature festooned by example, which is why we all love it so.

In any case, due to the generosity of Piers Anthony, who graciously lent his time, expertise, editorial skills, and honor to a project which has been on our minds for a long time, *Uncollected Stars* has seen print. Of Piers's kind remarks on my career or noncareer I can, obviously, say nothing; of the authors herein I have tried to say something in headnotes. Of the premise of this anthology, however, I would say this:

An overweight critic of science fiction, author of the single most vicious review I have ever received (my palpable cries of pain must have made the critic feast; he is ever heavier now when I occasionally see him), expanded upon that review and its motives after the fact. "You look for exemplary failures," the O.C. said, "you go out of your way to search for examples that will confirm your perceptions of defeat. First the verdict, then the trial." O.C. was talking of my book of critical and reminiscent essays on science fiction, *Engines of the Night,* but he might as well, I suppose, have been discussing the theme of this anthology, the impulse which gave it birth. It is true—oh, Fast Eddie Felsen, how true it is!—that I have a certain sympathy for losers.

Losing, however (as Fitzgerald might have commented), can teach you things that winning never can. It also has put in your hands, *ad hoc propter hoc,* an anthology of very fine stories which would otherwise never have been brought back, at least all together, at least in this form. Losing can be its own reward. Or so this aging, out-of-print writer hopes in another January, a later winter; snow in the air, snow all around the grounds, snow falling from on high to cover the living and the dead alike down here, down here in the Dream Quarter.

24 January 1985: New Jersey